PRAISE FOR CAROLYN HAINES AND THE SARAH BOOTH DELANEY MYSTERIES

BOOTY BONES

"Delightful…[a] satisfying beignet of a mystery."
—*Publishers Weekly*

"[Haines] delivers a riveting love story alongside the mystery, leaving her readers in hot anticipation of her next novel."
—*Mississippi Magazine*

"Entertaining." —*Booklist*

SMARTY BONES

"Raucously entertaining. This entire series is filled with mystery, humor, and more than a touch of the romantic South . . . not to be missed." —*Criminal Element*

"If you enjoy mysteries with rich Southern settings, fascinating history, and quirky characters, you'll devour this one quicker than a plate full of buttermilk biscuits."
—*Mystery Scene* magazine

"The South's answer to a feminine Sherlock Holmes, the marvelous and smart Sarah Booth Delaney is on the trail of another fun and fascinating mystery." —*Fresh Fiction*

"A satisfying mystery framed by a well-drawn small-town Southern setting." —*Booklist*

BONEFIRE OF THE VANITIES

"Delightfully fun." —*New York Post*

"Wildly entertaining." —*Criminal Element*

"This is the twelfth entry in the series featuring the spunky Sarah Booth Delaney. For loyal followers or new fans, *Bonefire* is a happy romp filled with colorful characters."
—*Houston Press*

"We have to admit being hooked by the title, but even urbane Tom Wolfe would get a kick out of this delightfully fun twelfth installment of Haines's Southern mystery series."
—*New York Post*

"An entertaining romp with enough twists to hold interest to the end."
—*Booklist*

BONES OF A FEATHER

"A lesson in lying, Mississippi style . . . Haines diverts the reader . . . with great dollops of charm."
—*Kirkus Reviews*

"Entertaining . . . Sarah and Tinkie must strive to thwart a plot of brilliantly diabolical proportions."
—*Publishers Weekly*

"Sarah Booth Delaney has a funny way of ending up in extremely strange situations . . . a perfectly written mystery with a cast that is humorous, charming and deadly. Haines certainly is one of the best mystery writers working today."
—*RT Book Reviews*

BONE APPÉTIT

"Distinctive characters and a clever cooking background make Haines's tenth Sarah Booth Delaney mystery the best yet in this Southern cozy series."
—*Publishers Weekly* (starred review)

"A whole lot of Southern sass . . . Haines's novel is definitely a page-turner."
—*Jackson Free Press*

GREEDY BONES

"The cast is in fine form (including the helpful ghost, Jitty), and it's good to be back in Mississippi . . . One of the more entertaining episodes in the series."   —*Booklist*

"Captivating—readers will enjoy *Greedy Bones* from cranium to phalanges."   —Don Noble, Alabama Public Radio

"Jitty, Dahlia House's wonderfully wise 'haint,' [is] one of the best features of this light paranormal mystery series infused with Southern charm."   —*Publishers Weekly*

"Never undone by a ghostly spirit, a handsome movie star, or even the oddball small town Southern folks most of us will easily recognize, Delaney is at her best when unraveling multiple puzzles. Ramp up the excitement and tension, add the often chuckle-out-loud humor, and they add up to one of the best of the Sarah Booth Delaney mysteries."   —*Delta* magazine

"As usual in Haines' 'Bones' series, the latest entry is charming light entertainment; a few serious notes about biological terror and family ties add interesting depth."
        —New Orleans *Times-Picayune*

"An excellent 5-star read."   —Armchair Reviews

WISHBONES

"Funny, ingenious . . .and delightful."   —*Dallas Morning News*

"*Wishbones* is reminiscent in many ways of Janet Evanovich's Stephanie Plum novels, only fresher with a bit more of an edge . . . Light, breezy, and just plain fun. Call Haines the queen of cozies."   —*Providence Journal-Bulletin*

"Stephanie Plum meets the Ya-Ya Sisterhood! Non-Southerners will find the madcap adventure an informative peek into an alien culture."   —*Kirkus Reviews*

Bone to Be Wild

CAROLYN HAINES

St. Martin's Paperbacks

This is a work of fiction. All of the characters, organizations, and events portrayed in this novel are either products of the author's imagination or are used fictitiously.

BONE TO BE WILD

Copyright © 2015 by Carolyn Haines.
Excerpt from *Rock-a-Bye Bones* copyright © 2016 by Carolyn Haines.

For information address St. Martin's Press, 175 Fifth Avenue, New York, N.Y. 10010.

ISBN: 978-1-250-04616-1

Our books may be purchased in bulk for promotional, educational, or business use. Please contact your local bookseller or the Macmillan Corporate and Premium Sales Department at 1-800-221-7945, ext. 5442, or by e-mail at MacmillanSpecialMarkets@macmillan .com.

Printed in the United States of America

Minotaur hardcover edition / May 2015
St. Martin's Paperbacks edition / May 2016

St. Martin's Paperbacks are published by St. Martin's Press, 175 Fifth Avenue, New York, NY 10010.

10 9 8 7 6 5 4 3 2 1

For Hope Harrington Oakes—

a true Delta Belle and a good friend

Acknowledgments

A book is a lot of work. Many thanks to Suzann Ledbetter Ellingsworth for her edits, comments, and support.

As always, thanks to the great staff of editors and artists at St. Martin's Minotaur. You always make my books better.

And thanks to my agent, Marian Young. It takes a village to raise a writer. I have a great village.

And this cover rocks!

1

From my observation point two floors above the central ballroom, I watch the dancers in their elegant ball gowns shimmying to the throb of Scott Hampton's lead guitar. It's a kaleidoscopic scene filled with the decadence of the French court, updated by two and a half centuries. Cece Dee Falcon, journalist, ball director, and friend has done herself proud with this year's Black and Orange Ball. She's raised thousands of dollars for charity, and proven once again that a Mississippi Delta girl knows how to host a party!

Wealthy people from across the Southeast have gathered in the City that Care Forgot for Halloween night to party and donate to a worthy cause. Women Growing Strong (WGS) is the beneficiary of this year's ball. Cece always picks something dear to her heart. This educational program to help battered women find jobs and gain independence from abusers is a good one.

New Orleans is a city that celebrates the past and present with equal graciousness. The Marble Ballroom of the elegant Treillage Hotel is a wonder of floating staircases and columns sculpted with vines. Cece has used every inch of the place to showcase her patrons, the donors who contributed large sums to WGS. The sumptuousness of the event rivals Oscar night in Hollywood. Designer gowns and jewelry worth millions adorn the women who are here to see and be seen. There is nothing like a no-holds-barred fashion competition to draw out the wealthy socialites for a night of rivalry and frivolity.

The ballroom fairly crackles with energy. Floral arrangements of lehuas and wallpeles, flown in from Hawaii late last night, festoon tables, their unique orange blossoms mixed with black tulips, black roses, and black hyacinths. Pots of the newly created Black Velvet petunias are at the center of every table. The petunias also serve as boutonnieres for the men. And Scott Hampton's band is the perfect blend of dance music and wailing blues that makes people want to rub belly buttons and forget that intimacy and attraction often come at a heavy price. The sexual charge of the music touches even me, and I'm half dead from emotional trauma.

The wee hours of All Saints' Day, the time when the veil between the living and dead is thinnest, has slipped over us. I feel like Cinderella as the bell tolls midnight. My magic has run out, and my carriage will revert to a pumpkin. It's time to go home. I want nothing more than my bed and the blessed forgetfulness of sleep.

Unfortunately, I can't leave. My friends are relying on

me to be here. And what would I go home to? My fiancé—
well, ex-fiancé—is in the air heading for Los Angeles.
Flying away from me to begin a new life with the daughter he never knew he had, until last week. I approve of
his decision, though I can't stop my heart from breaking.

I don't even have the company of Jitty, my resident
haint. Since my return to Mississippi and my ancestral
home of Dahlia House, she's been my constant—and constantly annoying—companion. Right now I would give a
lot to hear her tormenting advice, her know-it-all tone of
voice. Too bad Jitty has her own ball of string to rewind.

I'm alone at *the* ball of the year in an incredible gown
from Armani on Rodeo Drive that Graf Milieu, the afore-
mentioned former fiancé, bought for me. I need a cigarette, which is why I've slipped upstairs to a balcony over
the street. My high heels tap like a sophisticate as I make
my way to the French doors. They open onto a narrow
ledge and a starry night. Spread out before me is a city
that has charmed visitors for centuries. The French Quarter hugs the curve of the Mississippi River, a place soaked
with history, romance, war, voodoo, jazz, and sadness,
as well as joy. Just a few blocks down from the ball, Bourbon Street churns with life and laughter.

Music wafts up to me and I observe the tourists as I
enjoy my smoke and drink. The best band is here at the
ball, but I catch snatches of Dixieland, metal, rock, Irish,
and country. New Orleans is a mishmash of music and
culture, and it's one of the most fascinating cities in the
world, at least to me.

I inhale the musty, sweet, spicy fragrance of the city,
and my breath catches on a sob. At last I can grieve. I've
held in so much that I feel like Scarlett when Mammy
laces her into her corset. Now, while I am alone and no

one is here to watch, I can yield a little to my grief. Not hysterics, just a release.

The ornate balustrade is too inviting to ignore, and I perch on it and dash away the tears with the heel of my hand. Tomorrow I'll go home. I'll rebuild the rhythm and routine of my life as a single woman. I've done it before, and I can do it again. My friends will be there. My work will keep me busy. Jitty will ride roughshod over my periods of depression and force me to action. The weeks will pass and I will wake up next spring or sometime in the future and realize that my heart is on the mend.

The tempo of the music coming from the ballroom changes, and the scent of gardenias comes to me so strong that I look around. A figure in a red sequined ball gown steps out of the shadows.

"I've got a bad case of the blues," she sings in a gritty, clear voice. "And, baby girl, you've got a heartache you don't deserve." She says the last as she sways toward me, the ebony hair upswept in a fashion from an era long gone.

I recognized the voice, but it took me a minute to place her. Dinah Washington. I'd been a fan of hers for years, though she'd died before I was born. My parents had all of her records in the music room, the big 78s and later the 33s, and I loved listening to them and remembering my folks dancing together like teenagers. "What are you doing here, Dinah?" New Orleans had plenty of ghosts and a melancholy singer was a perfect fit.

"The blues come to those who suffer, honey. I feel your pain, Sarah Booth Delaney."

"Well, you're in the right place." I realized that after all the time spent with Jitty, I wasn't a bit surprised that a dead vocalist would show up. "Sing away. I feel lower than a snake's belly. Sing about a good woman who lost her man."

She laughed, and I detected a more familiar sound. "Jitty!"

Before my eyes, Dinah transformed into Jitty the ghost, who'd lived during the Civil War with my great-great-great grandmother Alice. "I thought I'd left you back at Dauphin Island," I told her. My latest PI case had been as traumatic for Jitty as it had been for me, in a different way. She had a lot of reasons for hanging around the barrier island for a few days, at least.

"I learned what I needed. I thought you might enjoy some familiar company. Watching your dreams turn into dust brings on the need for a good friend."

She was that and so much more. She was dead and demanding and sometimes demented, but she was my friend. "So what's shaking in the Great Beyond?" I couldn't talk about Graf or the broken engagement. I didn't want to talk about how she'd come to be a slave at Dahlia House. Our stories were both too sad.

"Folks are worried about you," Jitty said.

Jitty sometimes carried messages—always cryptic and never straightforward—from the Great Beyond. "Yeah, I'm trying as hard as I can. I don't want to be a downer at Cece's big ball, but I can't hold up for much longer. I want to go in my room, soak in a tub, and drink Jack Daniels in copious amounts."

"You know I love the blues more than anything, but you got to shake this fugue settlin' over you. Dinah's got some great numbers, but maybe a little Stephen Stills is what you need. You know, 'Love the One You're With.' "

I studied Jitty, all elegance in her 1940s gown. She represented the generation of World War II women who waited for their men to come home from work and war. And she was advocating love the one I was with? "Bad advice." I made the sign of the cross with my index fingers.

"You had feelings for Scott Hampton not so very long ago."

She stated the truth. I'd had a hot and thrilling affair with Scott not so long after I returned to Zinnia. Touring as the main squeeze of a blues musician wasn't a life I could buy into, though it had been hard to let Scott go. But that was the past. "And I'm *in love* with Graf." I shook a finger at her. "What is wrong with you? I need to grieve. It's part of the healing process. Why are you trying to push me into the sack with another man?"

"Fertile eggs that soon won't be good for nothin'. Tick-tock! And Scott Hampton is here to stay. He's putting down roots. And a fine specimen of manhood."

"Jitty, this is no time for that foolishness. I don't want to raise a child by myself. I have a lot of good years left. Stop haranguing me about viable eggs and ticking clocks and—" She was laughing at me. "What?"

"Feel better?"

Amazingly, I did. The burst of anger had brought with it a tide of adrenaline. My body had shucked off the sob sister mode. "Dirty trick, though."

"All is fair in love and war, and I love you, Sarah Booth. Your mama would kick my butt if I didn't pull you out of the dumps."

I thought of Graf and felt myself slipping back to the bottom of a deep pit. "I can't help it. I had a ring." I held out my bare finger. "I was engaged. We were to marry and have children. We had careers and dreams and a future. All of that was taken from me. Just with the snap of his fingers."

Jitty came to sit beside me, her perfume sweet and thick like the New Orleans air. "It wasn't deliberate."

"I know."

"It ain't over 'til the fat lady sings."

"It's over, Jitty. I know it here." I put my palm over my heart. "Graf and I were standing at a crossroads. He went right and I went left. That's a good-bye. We're traveling in different directions."

"Sarah Booth, there is no certainty in life except uncertainty. It's my fault for pushin' at you so soon. It just seems such a waste of . . . talent not to jump that Scott Hampton standing right there on the stage. Your friend, Cece, is makin' eyes at the harmonica player. Lord, those two are about to catch on fire."

I wanted to punch her arm, but I feared I'd pass right through her, lose my balance, and fall into the street below. "Scott isn't some hot body to be used and cast aside."

Jitty's chuckle was rich and smooth. "I don't think he'd mind being used a little. Not judging from the way he was lookin' at you. That boy's still carryin' a torch."

It wasn't what I wanted to hear. Not now. "I need a new case."

"You need some viable sperm."

"If you can't stop pestering me about sex, go home to Dahlia House. Maybe spruce the place up, cook something comforting. In other words, be useful, not annoying."

"To what end? Useful was my past. Annoying is my present. You'll just have to put up with me, Sarah Booth. You're powerless to control me."

I wanted to say something clever, but she was gone. She'd lifted me from my depression, but I still had a ways to go to reach feeling good.

The balcony doors opened and Scott walked toward me. "I saw you leave the dance floor. You okay?"

"I am." I held up the cigarette pack. "Indulging in a very bad vice."

He carried two drinks, and he gave one to me. He'd remembered my fondness for Jack Daniels. "There are times for rigid discipline, and then there are times to cut yourself some slack. This would be a time to indulge."

"The music is terrific, Scott. Even better than I remembered." A truthful statement. He'd been the Blues Blizzard when I first met him, the icy-eyed, blond-haired, guitar wonder who came out of a non-blues tradition and took serious music aficionados by storm. A year in Europe had added a level of sophistication to his music that made it truly unique and totally his. The confidence he'd gained was also attractive.

"We've had to cover a lot of other people's material tonight. Folks like to dance to songs they know. When we get back to Zinnia, I want you to hear us at the club. The band and I have written some songs. I'm so excited about this, Sarah Booth. My very own club right in the heart of the place where the blues were born."

"I'm glad for you, Scott. And it's the perfect location. That crossroads at Sawmill and Pentecost roads is said to be the location where the devil made more than one bargain for a musician's soul." He'd taken every penny he could scrap together and put a down payment on Playin' the Bones, a wonderful blues venue in Sunflower County. The former owner had run it successfully for several years, but decided to sell when he got an offer in Chicago.

Some locals said the club had a special magic for a guitarist lucky enough to play there. At any rate, the location had a solid, loyal following and the hint of supernatural intervention only made it more exciting. Scott and his band, Bad to the Bone, would take the club to megavenue status, if his gamble paid off.

"I don't want to crowd you, Sarah Booth. You're going through a hard time. I want to be a friend right now, nothing more."

I forced a smile and put my hand on his arm. "Thank you. I'm so confused, I don't know what I really feel, except hurt."

"Who would? You took a blow. I'm sorry."

Scott had never been anything other than sincere. While his words threatened to open my wound, I knew they were meant to comfort. "It's done. I just have to adjust to the new reality."

"On another topic, Sarah Booth, I need your help."

"Did Tinkie put you up to this?" Tinkie Bellcase Richmond was my partner in the detective agency and the daughter of the man who owned Zinnia's only bank. She wasn't above sending a hot guitar player, who also happened to be an ex-lover of mine, to ask for help with a made-up problem.

"I haven't talked to Tinkie, but Cece thought it was a good idea for me to seek your counsel."

I snorted. "Cece has been panting after your harmonica player all night long. I'm not so sure she's capable of determining whether an idea is a good one or not. Her brain isn't working."

"I noticed she was getting cozy with Jaytee." Scott took my arm and led me back inside where the warmth was welcome. I hadn't realized how cold I was.

"Take a look," Scott said.

Cece's black-and-orange gown flowed around her tall, lean body like it was bewitched. Her upswept hair, elegant carriage, and the dress turned heads. She stood near the stage and watched the harmonica player with undisguised lust. Cece was due for some fun, and Jaytee looked like he could deliver.

"Cece's on the hunt." And was not holding back.

"And Jaytee is a man who likes to get caught." Scott finished his drink. "So will you help me with my problem?"

"Depends on what it is. I can't do math and I'm not all that great at investment advice."

He laughed, and I could clearly see the relief in his eyes. Everyone was afraid I'd spin into a bad depression and . . . do what? Leave town? Drink myself silly? If either one would help, I'd do it, but a heartache wasn't something I could run away from or drown. Grief always found its target.

"I don't want to push this out of proportion, but I've gotten some threatening calls at the bar."

"What kind of threatening?"

"The caller said death was stalking each of us and would strike when we least expected."

That got my attention. Some folks didn't like the blues for what they labeled religious reasons, and others because white boys were playing what was once considered traditionally black music. And some people resented what they viewed as Yankee musicians coming to town to own businesses and put local musicians out of work. But to threaten bodily harm or death was a bit over the top, even for the ignorant/backward contingent.

"Male or female caller?"

"Male."

"Death was stalking" was a peculiar way to phrase the threat. "Did the caller specifically refer to the band members?"

He shook his head. "No he didn't. I assumed it was aimed at the band."

"When did the calls start?" I wished I had my little PI notebook. I liked to write it all down.

"I bought the club the first of October and—"

"You've been in Sunflower County the whole month and I never knew?"

He shook his head. "I closed the deal the first of October, but we just got into town last week. We've been unpacking and working on the sound system, finding a cook, deciding on hours and music and how this is going to operate. I want Playin' the Bones to be the premier blues club in the Southeast. Memphis won't have anything on us."

I was only a little hurt that Scott hadn't bothered to let me know he was in Zinnia. I had been engaged, true enough, and everyone in town knew it. Just as they would now know I'd been dumped.

"Okay, so you bought the club."

"The first call came in last week. I'd bought some new tables and chairs and was paying for them at the furniture store when my cell phone rang."

"Your cell? How did the caller get your number?"

"I don't know."

"Do you think it's someone you know?"

He looked miserable. "I don't want to think that. I had a business partner, and he's a little upset with me. He would have my number, and he could have disguised his voice."

I had a good place to start. "I'll need his name and contact information."

"I don't want to accuse anyone who may not be guilty."

"I won't accuse anyone of anything. Tinkie is very adept at this kind of situation."

His gaze sparked with humor. "Yes, she's a woman with multiple talents. I can clearly see she'd finesse this situation."

"Thanks." I rolled my eyes. "I'm just the bull in the china shop stomping around."

"I didn't mean it as an insult." He caught a waiter's attention and signaled for two more drinks.

"I know." And I did. I knew exactly what he meant. Tinkie could charm a man into telling her most anything. I had to rely on trickery, bribes, or ultimatums. "So how many threatening calls?"

"Three, so far."

"All the same message?"

"More or less that someone associated with the club is going to die."

The waiter brought the drinks and Scott gave him our empties. As he took a sip, his phone rang. Pulling it out of his pocket he checked the caller ID and frowned. "Private number, same as the other threatening calls."

"Put it on speaker," I whispered.

"Scott Hampton?" a male asked.

"Who is this?" Scott demanded.

"You've been warned. Abandon the club or someone will die." The caller disconnected.

Two things were clear. The caller was male, and he had no fear of being traced. "I'll track down Coleman Peters. He needs to know about this."

"Do you think it's a serious threat?" Scott was torn between worry and feeling a little foolish. "It's a juke joint. It's not like it's a casino or brothel. We play music."

"That's a good point, Scott. Why would anyone care so much about a venue in Zinnia, Mississippi?"

The obvious motives were financial, racial, monetary, jealousy—pretty much the same for most crimes. I just didn't see where any of them came into play. Sunflower County had hosted blues festivals and clubs in the past. The memory of the musicians who cultivated the unique sound and shared it on early recordings was viewed with great pride by most Mississippians. Maybe the reasoning behind the calls was more personal and directed at Scott. Someone who had a bone to pick with him. "Tinkie and I will stay alert. When we get home, you and I need to have a serious talk."

Scott nodded. "Do you think the caller would really hurt one of my band members?"

"The majority of the time, calls are as far as the person will take it. But there aren't any guarantees."

"Can you find out who's behind the threats?"

"I can try."

"Thank you, Sarah Booth. Now I have to get back to the stage. Our break is over. Just promise you'll dance with me when we play a slow one. Jaytee's a great ballad singer."

"You got it."

We hurried down the stairs and into the swirl of the party. Tables laden with food flanked the stage and ran down each side of the ballroom. In the back of the room five bartenders worked nonstop. Folks were eating, drinking, and laughing, but when the band picked up their

instruments, all attention focused on them. I drifted to
the outer edges of the crowd where I'd last seen my partner.

Instead of Tinkie, I found Coleman Peters, sheriff of
Sunflower County, and the man I'd once thought would
be my life partner. Unfortunately, Coleman had already
had a wife—a disturbed one, but Connie was his legal
spouse. Coleman had done his best to honor his vows,
even when Connie lost her tenuous hold on sanity. By the
time he divorced, the moment between us had passed. I'd
begun dating Graf, and Coleman had squired several
Delta belles to various social functions, but had avoided
serious entanglement.

"How're you holding up?" he asked.

My train wreck of a relationship was on everyone's
mind. "I'm okay."

"I could mouth a bunch of platitudes, but you know
them all."

"I do." I appreciated his restraint. "Someone has been
making phone threats against Scott and his band. He just
got one. The male caller said if Scott opened the club,
someone would die."

Coleman indicated a quiet corner outside the ballroom. When we were out of the party's din, he said, "I
don't like this, Sarah Booth. There's a real meanness
afoot these days. It doesn't take much to push some of
these people into rash action. Is Scott taking the threats
seriously?"

I hesitated. "He asked me to look into them. You don't
think my friends are colluding on a plot to keep me from
getting depressed, do you?"

Coleman's laughter was warm and deep. "You do have

good friends, but that's extreme even for them. When we get back to Zinnia, tell Scott to stop by the office. If it turns out this is a setup, I want a front-row seat for the ass kicking."

"Thanks, Coleman."

"I'm heading out early tomorrow morning. DeWayne is holding down the fort, and everything is quiet, but I need to get back."

"What's going on?" I could tell by his lack of eye contact that something was troubling him. Good thing for Coleman that his only deputy, DeWayne Dattilo, worked as hard as Coleman did.

"We had an arson last week. Ned Gaston's house was burned to the ground. Luckily he and his family were visiting relatives in Memphis."

I knew Ned. He'd been a friend of my parents. "Who would set fire to a man's home?" Ned was a quiet man who owned a shoe repair shop in Zinnia. He and his wife were chronic do-gooders. They'd taken in numerous abandoned children and tutored classes for the migrant workers who passed through the county when the row crops came in.

"I'll have the fire marshal's report Monday morning."

I read a lot more into the situation than he was saying. Coleman was worried, but he wasn't ready to talk about it. "I'll help Cece finish up here and then I'll be home, too. Tinkie wants me to drive her Cadillac. She's riding with Oscar."

"Be safe, Sarah Booth. I know it's easy to be distracted. If someone really means harm to Scott or the band, they might not wait for them to get back to Sunflower County."

"Constant vigilance," I promised and gave him a kiss on the cheek. Even in a tuxedo he still carried the scent of a starched shirt and sunshine. In my mind he would forever be associated with summer and the flap of sun-drenched shirts on a clothesline.

2

Sweetie Pie, my red tick hound, was sound asleep in my bed when I got back to my hotel room. The big dog was curled around a rotund mound of black fur—Pluto the cat. They both snored lightly.

The ball was over. Cece and Jaytee and other band members had gone to Bourbon Street for an after-gig celebratory drink. Tinkie and her husband, Oscar, chose bed. I, too, opted for the solitude of my room.

As I stepped out of the beautiful gown, I couldn't help but wonder what Graf was doing. If I called or texted, he would answer. But what was the point? He needed, and deserved, time to put his life in order. And I had to do the same. Calling Graf would be moving in the wrong direction.

Tinkie had left her computer in my room, and because I was too tired to sleep, I booted it up and indulged in a little Internet research.

Engrossing and delightful photos of Scott Hampton popped up when I searched his name. I tracked his career since he'd left Zinnia. He'd stormed across Germany, but really found his niche in the club scene in Paris. He was the best thing since sliced baguettes in France. There were magazine covers, television interviews, and YouTube clips of the band performing. I had never doubted his talent, but the accumulation of material let me know exactly how the world viewed him. He was an icon.

And he had moved to Zinnia. Playin' the Bones, his club, would highlight the Blues Trail through Mississippi and honor musicians like Robert Johnson, Arthur "Big Boy" Crudup, Skip James, Son House, Howlin' Wolf, and Mississippi John Hurt. They'd influenced the great rock 'n' rollers from Mick Jagger to Eric Clapton and even the Beatles.

I hadn't really had a chance to meet the band members, but I did a quick check on Jaytee, for Cece's sake. If he was married or had "issues," I wanted to know. My friend was head over heels in lust, which was fine. She was long overdue for a fling. I just didn't want to see her hurt.

The information I found on Jaytee showed he was single, never married, no children, and ripe for the picking.

The only controversy I could find about Scott and the band involved a dispute with a former manager. When Scott fired Wilton Frasbaum, it made headlines in the music world. After an angry interview in a tabloid where Frasbaum called Scott a cheat and embezzler, he disappeared from the public eye. If there was a lawsuit or a settlement, it had been handled discreetly. Frasbaum dropped off the radar and the band went on to bigger and better venues and more lucrative recording contracts. I made a note, though, just to be on the safe side. I'd ask Scott tomorrow.

When the last amplifier and mic stand were loaded on the bus, Scott gave the band a wave and jumped in Tinkie's Cadillac with me. It was early Sunday morning, November 1. My Celtic ancestors had once built fires to celebrate Samhain, the holiday marking the beginning of the descent into winter, the subconscious, and the darker half of the year. I was certainly entering my own gloomy time, but I was determined to be perky and a good conversationalist on the drive back to Zinnia. I was glad to see Scott, and glad he felt no need to ask questions of a personal nature. Of all the men I knew, Scott understood the blues.

We had a long drive home, but the weather was perfect and we were as full as ticks. We'd breakfasted on beignets and delicious café au lait with the band, Cece, and Tinkie at Café du Monde. Now it was home to Zinnia and my horses.

I was waiting to pull into traffic when Harold Erkwell came out of the hotel. Harold was Oscar's right-hand man at the Bank of Zinnia, and one of the most eligible bachelors in the Delta. I'd seen him during the ball talking to Coleman, a very handsome and distinguished older man Cece identified as Yancy Bellow, and Bijou La-Roche, a wealthy Delta woman who had a reputation for getting what she wanted. *Everything* she wanted. This morning Harold, who was never less than dapper, appeared absolutely furtive. He was slinking! "Check that out." I pointed.

"What gives with Harold?" Scott asked.

"I'm not sure." The car idled as we watched the handsome banker call for his car to be brought from the parking garage. In less than a minute, Bijou appeared. Even after dancing all night, she was as put together as a Parisian model. Long and lean with a mane of red hair and a figure impossibly slender, she sashayed up to Harold and put a possessive hand on his arm. He was in her crosshairs, and she never missed.

"Harold! Harold Erkwell!" She looked up at him and simpered. "Are you leaving so early? I thought we'd have breakfast and maybe go to Jackson Square. I have a yen to get my fortune told. I think there's a new man in my future, and I want some psychic help in learning to please him. I do take pleasing a man very seriously."

Harold glanced left and right as if he expected help to arrive. I turned off the car to better take in the entertainment. Harold was high on the headhunter list for a number of Delta women who valued his good looks, charm, social graces, and money. Harold, though, didn't enjoy the role of prey. No matter how beautiful the huntress might be.

"I woke up early and decided to leave." He tried for dignity, but it was clear he knew he'd been caught sneaking away.

"Harold, darling, let's enjoy this gorgeous day in New Orleans."

"Another time, Bijou. I need to get back to Zinnia. It's my dog!" His face brightened when he hit on an excuse.

"Roscoe is a very bad dog and the house sitter called. He's in big trouble. I have to go sort through this, before he's put on doggy death row."

"How horrid! I really don't care much for the canine species, always sniffing each other's derrieres and fighting. Can't you stay long enough for breakfast?"

"Roscoe is my responsibility," Harold said in a weary voice. "He's my cross to bear."

I almost blew Harold's falsehood by laughing out loud. Roscoe was a devil and a torment, and Harold adored every one of his dirty, sneaky little tricks.

Bijou pouted. "Well, if you must you must."

"I must." Harold peered into the maw of the darkened garage. No doubt he was praying for the valet to bring his car.

"Then I'll go with you. I can support you in this. I'd hoped for a frolic in the French Quarter, but I can make the Delta as exotic as anything here. I have my own pasties and g-string, should the occasion arise. Now, we need to rescue the dog, and then we can have dinner at The Club. Afterward, I can promise you some entertainment."

Scott poked me in the ribs lightly. "Are you just going to sit here? He's your friend."

"I know." I mentally debated what action to take. "He gets himself into these scrapes with desperate women. What am I supposed to do?"

"Go help him. He doesn't want to be unkind. And trust me, it's highly possible he didn't do a thing to egg this on. Women like her, they think everything in life is theirs for the asking or at least at a price they can afford to pay."

Scott didn't have to tell me he'd had his share of avid

fans. With his looks, the sexual element of the blues, his charm and charisma, women had surely thrown themselves at him. Such a thing might be fun for an hour or two, but it would wear thin. There was a line—and when people crossed it, life became difficult. As far as I could tell from my research last night, Scott hadn't fallen victim to any serious relationships since he'd left Zinnia.

"Okay. I'll back Harold's play." I jumped out of the Caddy and charged up to Harold. "I just got a call from Coleman. DeWayne has been trying to reach you. That evil Mrs. Hedgepeth is pressing charges against Roscoe. She's claiming he committed a licentious and lewd act in her front lawn."

"Damn Roscoe!" Harold feigned shock and horror like a Shakespearean actor. Or maybe an escapee from a George Romero film.

"DeWayne is holding him in a cell at the courthouse, but he said he would have to call the dogcatcher if you didn't come get him right away."

"Bijou, so sorry, but I have to handle this. I'll call you soon." Lucky for him, his car arrived and he was able to jump into it and drive away. I was left standing on the sidewalk with one huffy socialite.

"What man puts his dog above a good time in New Orleans?" she asked me.

I gave her the wide left eye—an expression Tinkie said made me look very disturbed. "Why, any sane man," I answered. "Have fun at Jackson Square."

"Sarah Booth Delaney, you're not nearly as amusing as you think you are. There are some folks in Sunflower County who are sick of you poking your nose in their business. Remember my words when you get it cut off."

She pivoted and marched back into the hotel.

I returned to the car, an amused Scott, a sleeping hound, and a cranky cat. "Now you finessed the situation. Bijou is mad at you and not Harold. He really owes you."

"Oh, yes he does." I checked to be sure the critters were safe in the backseat. "Now let's start this road trip. I'm eager to get home to my horses."

Dahlia House loomed like an old familiar friend as I turned down the driveway. I'd dropped Scott at the house Jaytee had rented on the edge of town. The bus with the band and equipment was behind us. Scott assured me they would pick him up on the way to the club. Returning home to a Dahlia House empty of Graf was something I needed to do alone. The first time would be the hardest—I just had to get it behind me.

I slowed for a minute to drink in the vista of my fields and home. The pounding of horses came to me as my herd topped a small rise.

I continued toward the house and Reveler, Miss Scrapiron, and Lucifer raced along with the car. It was the perfect fall morning, from a horse's point of view. Brisk, with the sun shining and just the faintest breeze. My equine friends were in fine fettle, and Sweetie Pie serenaded them with a series of bays and hollers. Pluto, who'd taken the front seat after I let Scott out, practiced feline disdain. He was not going to be sucked into the frolics of dog and horse.

As glad as I was to see Dahlia House, I entered with reluctance. I was reminded of my return to the Delta after my failed attempt at acting on Broadway. My heart was broken then, too, and by the same man. Neither breakup derived from malice or bad behavior. One was career and the second was his daughter. The word *star-crossed* came to mind.

I unloaded the car, listening for Jitty. She liked to pop up and scare the bejesus out of me. While I didn't want an adrenaline jolt, I sought her company. I'd learned much about Jitty in the past week. Born into slavery, orphaned at a young age, she'd built a life for herself. She was my connection to the loved ones I'd lost, to my past, to the indomitable spirit and will that marked her and my Delaney ancestors.

The house was empty. My footsteps echoed, and I was sad when Sweetie Pie and Pluto disappeared out the back doggie door. They were eager to explore their turf and re-mark their boundaries. I didn't begrudge them. After I'd unloaded the car, I made a drink and went to the front porch.

The land spread out in waves of white cotton. I leased my fields to a farmer, and that crop was his survival. Soon the mechanical cotton pickers would be crawling across the rows. I knew the intensive labor of picking by hand. My father had taken me picking one time, and we worked together to fill the sack that extended far behind us. I was exhausted before it was half-full. My father never said a word, but I think the whole exercise was for me to appreciate the hard work that was the backbone of Dahlia House. The Delaney wealth had been built on cotton, and that cotton had been picked by slaves. It was a hard and ugly past, and one I was never to forget.

My journey to the past was interrupted when a black sedan headed down the driveway. The car progressed through the lane of bare sycamore trees until it stopped at the front door and Harold exited the driver's seat. A little dog with a strange goatee and wiry, untamable hair hopped out behind him.

"God is going to get you for lying to Bijou." I kept a straight face.

"Seems I had a little help in the fabrication department. And you're the one who slandered Mrs. Hedgepeth."

"That old bat deserves all the slander I can muster." She hated dogs and children and had ever since I could remember.

"You served up a lie well within the probability of reality. Had I not come home, Roscoe would surely have been in hot water by tonight. He doesn't do well when I leave him alone. And by alone I mean with a professional dog sitter who he manages to evade and torment."

Roscoe could find trouble when Harold was sitting beside him. I shook my head. "Bijou is a handsome woman. She's got it bad for you."

"I'm the last man in Sunflower County she hasn't sucked the juices out of," Harold said wryly as he came up the porch. "If she got her hooks into me, I'd be nothing but a dried husk. Like a cicada. She'd probably nail me to the pasture fence." He picked up my glass, sniffed, and took a long sip. "Perfect."

I rose to refresh my drink and make one for him. "To what do I owe the pleasure of your company?" I ushered him into the house and led the way to the parlor where the bar was. When I'd first returned to Sunflower County, Harold had expressed an interest in more than friendship, but we'd never pursued the possibility. This evening, I needed a friend, and Harold knew the importance of that role.

"Primarily I came to check on you. I didn't see a lot of you at the ball. I know this is a hard time. I wanted you to know I'm sorry. I really liked Graf, and I can't help but feel he's pinched up pretty good himself."

I poured the Jack over ice, added water, and handed it to him. "I'm not mad at Graf." It would be so much easier if I were.

"He didn't know about his daughter. Let me just clarify that point. Because if he lied to you, I'll—"

"No, he didn't. He was as shocked as I was."

"It wasn't like he deceived you."

I'd made all of the same arguments to myself. "Harold, I'm not upset with him. I understand exactly what he's doing. And why. His life has been upended. He's a father, responsible for another life. His acting career took a hit when he was shot. Everything he believed to be the future isn't any longer."

Harold studied me and picked up my hand. My thumb gave the weakest tingle. I wasn't dead yet, but my reactions were dulled by grief. "Then why are you acting like everything is over? Life intervenes, Sarah Booth. Past decisions, good and bad, come back to haunt everyone. I'm sure you have your buried secrets that could derail a situation if they ever rose from the crypt."

"It's not even that." I'd tried to untangle the knot of my emotions. Without success. "I can only tell you that I'm numb, which is a good thing right now. When my nerve endings wake up, I'll be able to tell you more."

He took a seat and patted the uncomfortable old horsehair sofa beside him. I slipped down and leaned against him. For a long moment we simply sipped our drinks and relaxed.

"You need time, and there's nothing for it but to wait it out and determine what you feel on the other end."

"That's sort of the conclusion I came to." I hadn't felt as at ease since Graf dropped his bombshell.

"There is something else." He propped me up so I faced him. "It's about Scott and the bar."

"What?"

"I heard about the threats against the band."

"What? How did—"

"Tinkie told me. The bank holds the mortgage on the bar. I believe the caller might have been attempting to intimidate the bank into pulling out the financing. If Scott can't open the bar, he'll default on the loan for sure. Oscar gave very lenient terms, and the board of directors may have second thoughts."

"How would the directors know anything about this?" Gossip was the lifeblood of a small town, but the only people who knew about the threatening calls were Scott's friends.

Harold brushed a tiny piece of lint from his jacket, a delaying tactic to give him time to think. "I got a call on my private cell phone this morning as I was driving home. Unidentified male voice. He threatened to burn down Playin' the Bones unless Scott and the band leave town."

"That is outrageous." The only reason to include Harold in such threats would be to make the bank think the club was a risk. "Did you let Coleman know? He told me about Ned Gaston's arson. Someone isn't playing around."

"I did talk to Coleman. DeWayne tried everything to trace the call, but no luck."

"What did Scott say?"

"He's concerned. He told me he'd hired you because of death threats to the band members."

I nodded. "I'd hoped this wasn't serious. I did a little research into the band's history, and it's remarkably clean. At least there weren't any paternity suits or breach of contract. No legal action. Nothing easy to put my finger on."

"Then who would be making death threats?"

"I'm not sure. Pissed-off ex-manager, undoubtedly some girls are angry over being left behind, competitors who'd like Scott to fail." I had a pretty vague list of suspects.

"I didn't recognize the voice, Sarah Booth, but the man sounded . . . peculiar."

"Foreign or northern?"

"Antique. Or archaic may be a better word choice. He said the blues club would 'perish in a conflagration.' "

"That helps." But it didn't. Who would threaten a blues club in such a formal manner?

"I know." Harold polished off his drink and stood. "Now I have to take Bijou to The Club for dinner. Care to join us?"

"I'd rather have a colonoscopy."

He shuddered. "She showed up at my front door about twenty minutes after I got home. Sometimes it's just easier to give in than to fight. I'll let her think she's reeled me right up to the boat, and then I'll turn into Jaws and break free."

"Be careful you don't get caught for real."

"I'll see you at Playin' the Bones tomorrow night. Grand opening. Curtis Hebert is barbecuing."

"I wouldn't miss it for anything."

Harold blew me a kiss as he left. Roscoe zoomed out of the bushes and jumped into the front seat when Harold opened the car door. I waved them down the driveway. At least tomorrow night I had something fun to do.

3

Dark dreams niggled at me throughout the night, but I couldn't remember anything except vague impressions of rushing water and smoky blue lights when I woke. I made coffee and indulged in shooting whipped cream from the can straight into my mouth for breakfast.

"Sarah Booth, whipped cream will go right to your hips."

I nearly choked on a huge gob of Reddi-wip as I whirled around to confront Tinkie. She'd entered without alerting me or my critters. Chablis, her lionhearted Yorkie, was right at her feet, looking at me like I was the social equivalent of a Snopes.

"I'm hungry and there's nothing to eat." Why did I

feel the need to explain my actions? I was a grown woman. I could eat like a savage if I wanted.

Tinkie tapped her high-fashion boot. She was stunningly turned out in stiletto lace-up boots, skinny jeans, and a plush teal top that made her blue eyes pop. "Let's go to Millie's," she said. "Oscar dropped me off to pick up the Caddy, and I'm free for the morning. I have a massage at one. Since we haven't officially begun Scott's case, I thought I'd pamper myself."

I licked a stray swirl of whipped cream from the back of my hand. "Oh, but we have begun." I filled her in on the threatening phone calls to Scott and to Harold.

She gave her musical laugh that always made me think of Miss Woody and music classes in grammar school. Tinkie's laughter would make a silver bell jealous. "That blues boy will do anything to get in your panties."

"Tinkie!"

She only laughed harder. "He still has feelings for you, but he has too much sense to let you see it. He's biding his time, waiting for you to feel better."

Her chatter made me suddenly sad. "I don't feel anything at all."

She was instantly contrite. "Honey, you're just numb." She enveloped me in a big hug. "Squirt some more of that whipped cream. It'll make you feel better."

And it did.

"Now, let's go to Millie's and you can tell me all about Scott's case. He was such a huge hit at the ball. Everyone is still talking about him. I've gotten at least three dozen calls. Oscar hinted that one person asked about investing in the club. *And* I heard a New Orleans promoter is trying to book a twenty-city tour for the band."

I wondered if Scott would go on the road since he'd just bought a nightclub. To my surprise, I didn't have an opinion one way or the other. My emotions could be zoned arctic.

Tinkie continued recapping the ball, the gowns, the catfights, the acts of generosity, the men who could dance and those who couldn't as we rode to town and parked at Millie's Café. The place was bustling, and I realized that while my life had effectively stopped, everyone else was having a normal day.

Millie greeted us with a hug and never gave me a chance to order. She brought coffee and plates heaped high with her special portobello and cheese omelet, biscuits, buttered grits, and homemade scuppernong jelly she served to honored customers.

"Eat up, Sarah Booth. Broken hearts dissipate in the flames of carbohydrates."

"It's supposed to be alcohol," I told her. The old adage was not one of Aunt Loulane's, but something every Ole Miss student knew by heart.

Millie was undeterred. "Hangover, cracked heart, not a lot of difference in my opinion. Now eat until you're ready to go home and sleep again. That's the best. Food, sleep, friends. And time. Time does heal many things."

"You and Aunt Loulane." My father's sister had moved into Dahlia House to care for me after my parents were killed in an auto accident. Aunt Loulane was a proper lady, and she had a saying for every occasion. She insisted they were true—which was how they became popular sayings. I couldn't argue with her logic.

"The older generation knew some things, Sarah Booth."

"I know."

Tinkie and I worked hard to belong to the clean plate

club, but there was too much food. We did the damage
we could, and Millie waved us away when we tried to pay.
"Don't be foolish. This one's on me. My horoscope in *The
Enquirer* said I should be generous today and it would
come back tenfold."

"You're always generous," I reminded her.

We'd risen in preparation to leave when the front door
opened and a distinguished gentleman came in. I recognized him instantly as Yancy Bellow. He'd been at the ball
in New Orleans.

Several men greeted him, but he came directly to our
table. "Sarah Booth Delaney," he said, extending his hand,
"I regret I didn't have a dance with you. You are the
spitting image of your mother, Libby."

"Thank you, Mr. Bellow." I shook his hand.

"Please, call me Yancy."

Tinkie smoothly stepped in to help me out. "Mr. Bellow is a financial advisor and a sponsor of the Youth for
America campaign. He organizes volunteer groups of
young people to go across America and help the elderly
with lawn work or home repairs. He offers the young
people a college scholarship or pay. It's an inspiring program."

"Mrs. Bellcase, so good to see you. I had a wonderful
chat with Oscar in New Orleans. The man is a genius
with business plans."

"Are you the person interested in the blues club?" Tinkie softened the question by looking up at him through
her eyelashes.

"News does fly around Sunflower County. I think a
place with live music and a dance floor would add a lot
to the nightlife here, don't you?"

"I do," Tinkie said. "Is that a yes?"

"I never kiss and tell, Tinkie. But I am on my way to the bank. I needed some sustenance before wrangling with Oscar over interest rates on my investments." He laughed. "We are so lucky to have a hometown bank run by one of us."

"I'll be sure and pass the compliment to Oscar. I know he'll appreciate it."

Yancy leaned down and lowered his voice. "You know Gertrude Strom will have a bail hearing today? She's asking for a reduction in the half-million bond the judge set. Highest on record, I do believe. I anticipated you and your fiancé would be at the courthouse, Sarah Booth."

I must have blanched because Tinkie stepped between us. "I think they'll call Sarah Booth when they need her. Gertrude is the unpleasant past, as far as we're concerned. We have a new client to attend to."

"Anything interesting?" Yancy asked. "I've watched with fascination the way you two dispatch cases. Bravo! If I ever need any investigative work done, I know exactly who to call."

"We'd appreciate your business," Tinkie said, taking my elbow and leading me out of the café.

"Get in the car," she directed. "Just get in and sit down."

"Why didn't someone tell me about Gertrude?" I asked. I wasn't angry, just flattened. This was the woman who'd shot my fiancé and sent my relationship spiraling. She'd targeted Graf because she thought my mother had betrayed her. In an attempt to poison a meddling college professor, Gertrude killed a harmless graduate student. Gertrude was a hot mess, and if she got loose on bail, I had no doubt she'd do whatever was in her power to harm me and those I cared about.

"This is just a bail-reduction hearing. No testimony. The judge won't lower it and she'll never come up with the cash. We decided to spare you."

"Should Graf be here?"

"Unnecessary." Tinkie pushed me into the car seat and slammed the door. She walked around and got behind the steering wheel. In a moment we were cruising out of town.

"She won't get a lower bail, will she?" I'd never considered that Gertrude might get out. She was nuts. And extremely dangerous. And she had a hard-on for me.

"The judge won't let her bamboozle him. They have psychiatric evaluations that show she's a danger to society. Don't worry." Even as she tried to calm me, I could see she was upset.

"What's wrong?"

She sighed. "I just wish we could have avoided telling you about the bail hearing. Mr. Bellow meant no harm, but he sure stepped in it."

"Do you know Yancy Bellow well?" He was a handsome man, very charming, tailored suit, obviously successful at his business. He'd spoken of my mother with warm affection.

"Buford, Oscar's cousin, managed some of his accounts before Buford went off the deep end. Buford said Yancy is gifted in the financial market. He never had children of his own, but he's been very active in helping the county youth and the elderly."

"He lives in Sunflower County, but I don't know anything about him."

Tinkie shrugged one shoulder. "There are those rare birds who've escaped your eagle eye. He spends part of the year in New York and part in Geneva."

"Family?"

"Never married. I heard he played the field when he was in his twenties. He was well-known for taking young women on private jets to 'the Continent' for breakfast and a shopping spree. He's led a very exciting life, by all accounts. We were in college when he was in his heyday. I haven't seen him for the last two or three years. He may have been in Europe or New York."

Out of sight, out of mind, as Aunt Loulane would say. "He's very good looking. I'm surprised one of the Delta belles hasn't snapped him up. He was talking to Bijou at the ball."

"He's a sly fox." Tinkie laughed. "He's led some ladies on a very merry chase, but he has yet to be caught. Are you interested?"

"Not in the least. Nothing about that lifestyle appeals to me. And he's a little old for me, don't you think?"

"Oh, I don't know, Sarah Booth. Maybe a more mature man is the ticket for you."

"No, thanks. I have no interest in a man, young or old."

She didn't press it and I was glad. She'd meant to tease me and lighten the mood, and she had. Tinkie had the soul of an angel. She knew when to prod and when to simply be a friend to lean on.

We drove to the club and walked into major event preparation. Scott and the band tweaked and checked equipment, hung lighting for the grand opening, and discussed the menu Curtis Hebert had prepared. Laughter and bustle ruled the afternoon, and it was balm for my wounded spirit. I put red-checked tablecloths on the tables and arranged chairs. Everyone chipped in to make the evening a success.

I also kept a close watch on the band members and bar staff, wondering if someone working with Scott was behind the threats. It wasn't that I distrusted any of the people—heck, I didn't know them—but trouble as often came from the inside as the out. Jealousy between brothers dated back to Cain and Abel.

Tinkie went over the playlist with Scott. "Who is this secret performer?" she asked, showing me the names. "She's going to sing 'I'd Rather Go Blind.'"

"Taking on a cover of Etta James is pretty darn bold." I smoothed the last tablecloth into place. "Who is she, Scott?"

"I promised I wouldn't tell."

"Dah-link!" Cece sidled up to us. "You act like the Spanish Inquisition. What's a night without a little mystery?"

Right behind Cece was Jaytee. He was tall and slender, with wonderful olive skin. His black eyes followed Cece's every move. He was smitten. I had no doubt Cece had been scrupulously honest with him about her past. He didn't care that she'd once been Cecil. He saw the woman we all loved, a person of tremendous courage. While the bond between Jaytee and Cece had quickly strengthened, I understood how long it had been since Cece had risked her heart. Jaytee's loving acceptance was everything Cece had ever wanted. It did my heart good to see her so happy.

"Can we have a hint?" I asked.

Jaytee put an arm around Cece's shoulders and kissed her cheek. "If we told, it wouldn't be a surprise."

"We'll be right here. We don't need to be surprised." Tinkie couldn't stand being in the dark. It was one reason she was such a good PI.

"You'll have to wait it out with the rest of the crowd," Scott said. "I promise, you'll be glad you didn't know."

"Now I'm simply dying to figure this out," Tinkie huffed. "Talk about a tease."

I was about to excuse myself and call the circuit court clerk to check on Gertrude Strom's hearing when Joel Buckhalter, who was with the local radio station, interrupted. He was working a live spot from the club and needed crowd participation. The band jumped onstage to perform a preview for his radio show. The energy of everyone in the club lifted me up, and I was standing and clapping with Tinkie, Cece, and the bar staff when the number finished.

"Play 'When a Man Loves a Woman,'" Cece suggested. She moved closer to the stage, a moth to the flames.

"I'd better get a hose," Tinkie said under her breath. "When Jaytee starts to play the harp on that song, Cece is going to burst into flames."

I tried to strangle the laughter, but to no avail. Jaytee was sexy, and when he leaned into the harmonica and really began to blow, it sent a chill down me. But as much as Jaytee commanded the spotlight, I couldn't stop watching Scott. He was purely professional as he sang the ballad Percy Sledge made the number one dance song for all juke joint lovers. When his gaze strayed to me, I felt as if my soul had been touched.

"He is one fine-looking man," Tinkie said. She hadn't just fallen off a turnip truck. She could feel the electricity.

"He is," I agreed. "And I'm glad he's back in Sunflower County."

"He couldn't have come at a better time." Tinkie slipped her arm through mine. "I know you're not ready to move on with your life, but it sure never hurts to have a compelling man for company."

She was right about that.

The band finished the number, and Joel continued with his broadcast. When he'd closed out the spot and turned off the microphone, Scott signaled everyone to the bar for a celebratory drink. "To the blues," he said when everyone had a glass.

I downed the drink and headed toward the back door, phone in hand. I never made it outside. The front door opened and the silhouette of a tall, slender man entered. "Can I reserve two tables for tonight?" Yancy Bellow asked. "I want to bring some friends from Memphis."

Scott walked forward and extended his hand. "Scott Hampton. I'm sure we can help you out. Where would you like to sit?"

"Right here." Yancy pointed to the two tables closest to the stage. "My friends are in the music business and I thought they might be interested in hearing the new band."

"We'll hold them for you."

"Miss Delaney," Yancy said as he walked over to me. "And Mrs. Bellcase. What brings you two to a blues club in the middle of a Monday afternoon? I thought you'd be out tracking felons."

"We're helping a friend," Tinkie said. "Scott and I go way back. Have you been a blues aficionado for a long time?"

"I'm an investor. Think what this club could do for the economy. Sunflower County could become a star on the Blues Trail, bringing thousands of tourists to Zinnia. The whole area." He waved his arm indicating the entire Delta. "Mr. Hampton and his band have such a following in the European market that Zinnia could become the home to a very big international music scene."

I had to hand it to Yancy, he'd done his homework on Bad to the Bone. The band was super-hot in Europe. If they could bring their mojo to Zinnia, it would be a major economic boon to everyone from Millie's Café to the town's growing B&B business. In only the past year, three homes the size of Dahlia House had been converted from private residences to B&Bs. Such repurposing was one way for a home owner to keep his house and property in a down economy. And it would give me immense pleasure to see competition for Gertrude Strom, who ran the premier B&B in the region.

"You dream big, Mr. Bellow." Tinkie batted her long eyelashes at him. On another woman, the move would be cartoonish, but Tinkie could pull it off. Like Scarlett O'Hara, she could stamp her foot, fashion a dress from drapes, and out-business the most successful businessman, all while keeping the man ignorant of her abilities.

"What's the point of small dreams, Tinkie, and please, call me Yancy."

Tinkie had teased me about dating Yancy Bellow, but it looked like she was more up his alley, even though he was aware she was married to Oscar. Or perhaps it was a bit of friendly repartee with a hint of sex thrown in just to spice it up.

"In fact, if Mr. Hampton is looking for financial support, I'm here to make an offer." Yancy arched his eyebrows at Scott.

"I certainly appreciate your interest, Mr. Bellow, but we have sufficient investors. All we have to do is open the doors and put some musicians on the stage. If the folks like us, we'll do fine. If they don't, then all the investors in the world won't help."

"A true philosophy," Yancy said. "From the talk in town, everyone has great expectations."

Cece put a program in his hand. "The barbecue plates go on sale at six o'clock. The music starts at eight. Now if you'll excuse us, we need to put the finishing touches on the place."

"A gracious lady with an agenda." Yancy gave a stiff, courtly little bow to all of us. "I'll move along so you can finish your work."

"You do have the most elegant manners," Tinkie said, preening.

"To match a lady with grace," Yancy said.

I thought for a minute he would kiss her hand, but he took his leave.

As Yancy exited the club, Jaytee signaled Scott over. They consulted for a moment over Jaytee's phone and then Scott waved me toward them. "It's another threat," he said. "Tell her, Jaytee."

"It was a guy. Strange way of talking, but he was clear about what he said—that someone would pay if the club opened tonight."

"Pay how?" I asked.

"He wasn't specific. 'Wrath will rain down on the sinners if the club opens.' Those were the exact words." Jaytee looked miserable. "Maybe we should postpone, Scott. Get some serious security."

"I'll hire private security," Scott said, "but we're opening. We can't let an anonymous call, which may be nothing more than a prank, keep us from opening."

I agreed with him. "Call Coleman, just to be sure all

bases are covered. And if you hurry, you can get a security team from Memphis down here."

"I'm on it." Scott went to the office and I touched Jaytee's shoulder. "They called your personal cell phone?"

Jaytee handed the phone to me. "The number didn't come up and there's no way to call it back."

I could call the phone company but I knew only a warrant could motivate them to give up such information—if they had any information. Even in Zinnia people knew about burner phones. But Coleman had the power to obtain phone records, and I had no doubt he'd use it. I had a few questions.

"How would someone have your personal cell number?" There were a lot of possibilities, but I wanted to hear what Jaytee would say.

"The number isn't a big secret. I've given it out all over the place. It's on the club business cards." He motioned me to the bar. From behind the napkins he found a stack of business cards that showed the club phone number and his cell phone. "I told Scott I wouldn't mind fielding some calls." He looked sheepish. "It's a good way to meet girls, you know."

Oh, boy, did I. My hackles rose instantly. He couldn't treat Cece like an old shoe.

My face must have given me away. He held up both hands. "I've been single a long time, and I've enjoyed playing the field. But now that I've met Cece, I was going to ask Scott to get me a new phone. You know, trade. He could keep my old number for the club and get me a new one. I'm not interested in other girls. Cece and I are getting to know each other, but I have to tell you, I think my looking days are over. She's the one."

"Is Scott replacing your phone?"

"I haven't asked him yet. I just met Cece Saturday. Give a man a chance."

He had a point. The spark between Jaytee and Cece was only a few days old, and it took time to unwind lifestyles.

The bartender, a big, handsome mountain of a man, came up behind the bar. "What's going on?" he asked.

"Sarah Booth Delaney, Koby Shaver, the best bartender in the Southeast. You name it, he can mix it."

"Pleased to meet you, Ms. Delaney. Let me guess. Bourbon. Something with a little bite. You drink Jack."

"I do. How did you know?"

"I know my liquor and I know the ladies. I also know you're one lady I'd like to know better. What are you doing after the club closes?"

"Sarah Booth is Scott's friend." Jaytee's voice was low, but clear.

"Message received." He grinned at me. "Scott has excellent taste, but I withdraw my invite."

It was impossible to be offended. He was like a big, frisky puppy.

"How are we on ice and drink garnishes?" Jaytee asked.

"Full up on everything." Koby waved at the chilled containers of lemon and lime wedges, cherries, olives—all the fixings for drinks.

"I need to check the lights," Jaytee said. "Koby, make Sarah Booth a drink she won't forget."

I laughed but shook my head. "Later. It's too early to have another drink. I need a clear head tonight. Have you been in Sunflower County long?" I asked Koby.

"I met the band in Austin, Texas, and they invited me to be part of the club here. I like it a lot so far. Small towns are the way to go for me. Love the city for the excitement. Love the country for the living."

Tinkie hustled to my side. "Scott hired Nightshade Security out of Memphis. They're sending a team to work the opening."

I nodded. "A security force might seem a bit like overkill, but better safe than sorry." I almost slapped my own forehead. I was spouting adages just like my dead aunt Loulane.

Tinkie nudged my side and tipped her head toward Cece and Jaytee, who were huddled together like co-conspirators in a high-stakes game show. Cece was far too polished to giggle, but she did laugh at something Jaytee said. He put his arm around her and hugged her.

"Hey, what's wrong?" Tinkie demanded. "You look upset."

"You know me, I worry. I don't want Cece to ever be hurt again. She's had enough."

"I know what you mean," Tinkie said. "Suffice it to say, if he's messing with her, we'll repay him tenfold and in a way he'll never forget."

Tinkie kept her word when it came to protecting her friends. "Yep," I agreed. "We'll really hurt him."

"Sarah Booth!" Coleman's voice boomed across the bar and I faced him with a smile. The bomber jacket he wore suited his rugged build, and his cheeks were red from the cold and wind outside. He had something to share.

Before he could start, I blurted out my own question. "Gertrude?"

His hesitation told me everything.

"She's out?"

"Not yet, but she will be. The judge lowered her bail. He said she wasn't a flight risk."

"Hell no, she won't flee. She's too crazy to run. She'll hurt someone else. Likely me or Tinkie."

Coleman was calm, but he wasn't happy. "Keep your fingers crossed she won't be able to come up with the cash. Let's not borrow trouble."

"She hates me."

"I know that and I'm taking this seriously. I promise." His blue gaze held me long and steady. "I won't let her hurt you."

"Don't make promises you can't keep," I told him.

"That's not my style and you know it."

In fact, I did.

4

I returned to Dahlia House late in the afternoon to change clothes and get ready for the grand opening of the club. I'd managed to work through most of the day without thinking about Graf, but walking across the front porch of Dahlia House, the emptiness struck me. Graf and I had enjoyed sitting in the rockers this time of day, sipping a Jack and water, or sometimes Graf would whip up a frou-frou drink, just to make me laugh.

A gust of dead sycamore leaves skittered across the porch and hung in the runners of the white wicker rockers, scratching to get away as if they were alive. Nothing said abandoned and alone quite like brown and crinkled leaves blowing on a cold November day.

I entered the front door and stopped cold. The tinkling sound of a piano came from the music room, but no one was home. Stupid as it was, my heart leaped to the thought that Graf had returned. Even though I knew he didn't play the piano. Even though I knew it wasn't time. Even though I knew the only person it could be was . . . Jitty. My heart cracked a little more.

I went in search of my musical haint. The song was both sad and sexy, and I followed the sound until I locked in on Jitty in the middle of the music room. Sweetie Pie snoozed on the rug and Pluto sat on the piano bench where no one played but the keys moved of their own volition. Neat trick.

Jitty wore a floor-length white sequined gown and a hat that defied description. Something from the flapper era. She swung around to face me and sang, "Baby, won't you please come home."

I recognized the song and her persona, Bessie Smith, the tragic Mississippi singer who bled to death after a car accident not so far from Zinnia. The legend went that the local hospital refused to treat a black person.

"Stop it, Jitty! I get it. I have the blues." I tried to sound stern, but it was hard to do when the song spoke to my feelings.

She continued with the classic, which only made me sadder. I finally gave up and listened to the clarity of her voice. When she assumed the persona of someone, she gave it her all, and Jitty had a feel for the song. I closed my eyes and listened to the woman who, in the 1920s, was known as the Empress of the Blues. At a time when many black people weren't allowed to vote and segregation was the rule of the nation, Bessie had owned her own railroad car and traveled with Ma Rainey, selling merchandise and performing to crowds that made her a wealthy woman.

When the song was over Bessie morphed back into the haint I recognized and loved. And sometimes wanted to throttle. "What's the truth about Bessie's death?" I asked Jitty.

She turned sideways. "She was hurt bad. Her arm was almost severed. She died. I don't think anything would have changed that."

It wasn't an answer to the question that blues lovers had asked for seventy years, but it was all I was going to get out of Jitty right now. Instead of begging for answers, I decided to share a little music history with my haint. "Did you know Janis Joplin had a headstone made for Bessie and placed at her grave?"

"Lots of the early rockers recognized the black talent that inspired them. Doesn't surprise me a bit Janis would do the honors for a woman she admired." Jitty hated it when I knew something she didn't.

"Well, did you know that vehicular and plane accidents and murder are leading causes of death for famous musicians?"

"Aren't you little Miss Sunshine and Good Cheer. I thought workin' at the club would liven you up, but that was a vain hope." She leaned in closer and a slow smile crept over her face. "Sometimes a blues singer knows just the right chords to strum, if you get my meaning. If you'd give that cute Scott Hampton half a chance, I'll bet he could have you singing with pleasure."

Oh, I got her meaning. And I ignored it. "You're accusing me of being Debbie Downer? Hell, if I were chewing happy pills, that song would bring me down." I flopped on the piano bench beside Pluto. He was a fat kitty with an attitude. Most of the time he could be mistaken for a stuffed pillow, but when he geared up for action, he was fierce. He and Sweetie Pie were blues lovers and the perfect mystery-solving companions.

"Pain and joy are inseparable. Without love, there wouldn't be the blues." Jitty sank into a club chair beside me. "Sarah Booth, you've had a setback, but there's a long road ahead of you. And you got options. Scott, Coleman, Harold," she ticked them off on her fingers. "Those men know you and they still wanna chance to love you. Plenty of time to love again."

"Great use of sarcasm. And just so you know, I'm not interested in falling for a man. Love should come with a guarantee. I'm not interested in doing this again."

She laughed, and the sound was rich and sultry and delicious, and it made me smile. I had the most sensual ghost on the planet. Even when she was tormenting me, she could be sexy. "Girl, you're all curled up in the fetal position tryin' to protect that big heart, but you can't. Even if you hide out right here in Dahlia House and never love another man, you still get a servin' of pain. You love these animals, and that's loss around the bend."

She was right, so I couldn't argue. And I didn't want to. I wanted to forget, and the best way I knew to do that was to stay in constant motion. "What should I wear to the club tonight?"

"Something slinky, so when you dance, the dress knows it."

I had the perfect outfit in mind. "Thanks, Jitty. Now *that* was helpful."

Sweetie gave an approving yodel of love, and I left the music room feeling more lighthearted than when I'd arrived. Jitty and the blues—who knew such things could improve a broken heart.

The club winked hot blue, purple, and pink neon in the soft Delta sky, and I was thrilled to see the parking lot overflowing with vehicles. Trucks with mud flaps and monster tires, high-end luxury sedans and SUVs, even one electric car everyone knew belonged to Pattie Tierce, one of Zinnia's new lawyers.

I parked beneath a leafless pecan tree across the road and pushed through the door into a wall of sound. Scott had brought the whole county out, and people were laughing and visiting, excited by the prospect of having one of the hottest blues bands working as our very own.

Scott was at the bar, surrounded by a bevy of squealing young women. He was friendly with each of them, but kept his distance. Cece and Jaytee were huddled in a corner and could have been plotting the takeover of the government or a menu for the evening. Whatever they were doing, Cece was radiant.

Coleman slipped up behind me and put a hand on my shoulder. "You okay?"

"Yeah, I'm good." Chin up, smile in place.

"It'll get better," he said.

"Did you learn anything about Scott's former partner?"

"Nothing good. The guy has a reputation for shooting off his mouth, threatening people, trashing people's lives when he can get away with it. The thing is, he's been in Copenhagen for the past six months. There's no indication at all he even knows about this club."

"Aside from threats to the band, do you have anything interesting on your plate?" I'd lost touch with the cases Coleman was working. Graf's shooting, his recovery, his daughter—I'd been so wrapped up in my life with Graf that I'd neglected my friends.

"Mostly run-of-the-mill stuff, except for Ned Gaston's fire. Fire marshal confirmed it was arson, but there isn't a lot of evidence to track the person who set the fire. DeWayne and I won't give up, though."

"Is Ned running the boot shop?"

"He is."

"He's a good man. He made a pair of boots my mother cherished. I still have them." They were beautiful pale leather with stitched designs in hues of turquoise, jade, and coral. She'd worn them everywhere and said they were her favorite dancing shoes.

Coleman reached to touch my lips but stopped. "A good memory because you're smiling."

"Yes." I stepped back slightly. "Any luck tracing the threatening calls made to Scott and the band?"

"They came from different burner phones and pinged off different towers. Whoever did this is very sophisticated, at least with telecommunications."

My frown spoke of my concerns. "Then this may not be a joke."

He nodded. "Someone went to a lot of trouble not to be traced. But why even call and warn Scott? That's the confusing part. If the person is serious about the threat, why warn the band?"

"What if it's all about the club? Maybe they thought he would cancel the opening."

"I wish he had. I did talk to him, but he was adamant. He wouldn't be bulldozed into canceling."

I understood. To give in to blackmail—what would the next demand be? To sell the club? Or only open certain days and times? Blackmail, once yielded to, would only grow in scope and demand. "What can I do to help tonight?"

"Watch the kitchen. I'm a little worried about Curtis back there. I don't want him hurt."

"Got it." I doubted the threatening caller intended to harm the best barbecue chef in six counties, but if that's what Coleman needed me to do, it was as good as done.

"DeWayne is on the front door. And I'll be working the room, trying to keep tabs on anyone who might be contemplating stirring up trouble. You note who goes in and out of the kitchen."

At last I realized what Coleman feared. "You don't think . . . poison?" The idea was horrifying.

"No." Coleman chucked me under the chin. "You are pulling out the worst-case scenarios, aren't you?"

"Life has taught me to be cynical."

"Then save me a dance and I'll teach you how to feel something else." He buried his worry beneath flirtation and his clear eyes held a dare.

"In that case, I might even save you two." I met him tit-for-tat because I refused to be the *poor thing* abandoned almost at the altar.

"I'm sorry for the pain, Sarah Booth. But I'd be lying if I said I was sorry you're single. I'm holding off until Christmas to give you a chance to get your sea legs under you. Fair warning, though. I'm claiming you for the holidays."

It was too soon for me to feel anything for another person. "We'll see about Christmas," I said, unwilling to even hint at my future emotions.

The band took the stage and I positioned myself where I had a clear view of the kitchen door and the band.

The opening song, "Bad to the Bone," had the packed club on its feet and dancing. If the first ten minutes was any indication, Playin' the Bones was going to be a rockin' joint. Scott was electrifying as he finessed pure sex out of his guitar.

"Wow!" Tinkie came up beside me. "They were great at the Black and Orange Ball, but this club is the perfect venue for them. The band is sizzling."

"They are." I scanned the room. Most of the tables had been served their food. Liquor flowed from the bar. Yancy and the two tables of his friends followed every move of the band. Scott had won him over, if I was reading Yancy's body language correctly. "I hear Scott has hired several buses and drivers to take folks home. That was smart."

"He wants to be part of the community. An asset, not a liability."

And yet someone meant to cause him worry, at the very least. Possibly something more deadly.

The kitchen door swung open and two waiters brought trays of barbecue out. Curtis was in the background, his apron stained with his secret sauce. He had a staff of four people helping him, all trusted employees. No one had made any attempt to get into the kitchen, and Curtis knew his food sources. So far, so good.

Despite the fact that Tinkie and I were on guard duty, I found myself being pulled into the music. Mike Hawkins on keyboard and Zeb Kohl on drums each had young ladies putting on a show near the stage. Bass player Davy Joiner, the youngest member of the band, teased the ladies by dancing to the edge of the stage and showing off his Elvis moves.

After the first set finished, I needed some fresh air.

And maybe a cigarette. The band had certainly gotten my blood flowing. Koby Shavers had a Jack on the rocks waiting on the bar and slid it to me like an old western barkeep. "It's good the boss is having some fun. I didn't mean to come on so strong earlier. I like to flirt, but I don't want any hard feelings."

"Not a problem. I like to flirt, too." It was impossible not to like Koby. Beneath his Lothario ways was a man with a good heart.

Customers at the other end of the bar waved for Koby's attention, and I picked up my drink and slipped out the front door. On the side of the club beneath a pecan tree was a small picnic table. I sat down on the weathered bench and lit up a Marlboro. The club, the blues, the joy of the band performing and the audience listening, the friendship offered by so many—all combined to remind me life held so many wonderful gifts.

The back door of the club slammed, and I looked up as Koby Shaver came out the back door. He rolled his shoulders and reached into his pocket for a cigarette. I stood up to walk over as he lit his smoke. A vehicle spun gravel beside the club. I'd only gone about ten steps when the black pickup—running without lights—careened around the corner of the club.

Koby stood perfectly framed in the light from the open back door. I tossed the cigarette and started to run. The shotgun blast rang out into the cold night. The truck skidded past me, a gun barrel hanging out the passenger-side window. I dropped and rolled as a second spray of pellets struck the tree I'd been standing in front of. The truck sped away, a black shadow in a dark night.

I ran toward the back of the club, praying Koby hadn't

been hit, but deep in my heart I knew better. We'd been warned. All of us.

I made it to Koby as the kitchen door banged against the wall. Light fell across the bartender's fallen body. The blast of the shotgun had opened his chest. I felt for a pulse, but he was gone.

5

Coleman firmly maneuvered me away from the body. Within seconds, the security team swarmed the back of the club. The useless security team. Harold and Oscar kept the patrons inside. I couldn't believe everything happened so quickly. I needed a rewind. If I could only go back fifteen minutes and delay Koby at the bar.

"Where the hell were the security men?" I asked Coleman.

"They were checking vehicles at the entrance, and two men were inside."

"Did they see who was driving the black truck? Were they doing their jobs or not?" Fear, anger, and sorrow are a potent mixture.

"DeWayne is questioning the ones on the gate now."

"Sarah Booth, are you okay?" Scott, visibly shaken, vaulted down the steps and came over to us.

"I wasn't hit. I came out for a cigarette." I indicated the picnic table twenty yards away under the tree. "This black truck whipped around the club really fast. I didn't think anything about it, except the lights were off. I thought it was someone who'd had too much to drink." I couldn't stop the rush of words. "I heard the gunshot. They cut Koby down and fired at me. When the truck sped away, a gun barrel was sticking out the passenger-side window."

"Bring her inside," Scott suggested to Coleman. "She's freezing."

Indeed, my teeth were chattering, but I wasn't really cold. I was in shock. Doc Sawyer, the family physician who'd cared for me since birth, would probably give me ammonia to sniff if he were on the scene.

Coleman helped me through the kitchen door of the club and into the interior where he sat me at a table. Tinkie and Cece were immediately beside me, each chafing one of my cold hands.

"Oh, Sarah Booth, thank goodness you weren't shot," Tinkie said. She brushed a tear off her cheek. "What were you doing outside anyway? It's cold." She rubbed my fingers harder.

"I went for a smoke." In the light and warmth of the club, my wits were coming back to me. "I went out the front door and was sitting at the picnic table. I don't think the people in the truck saw me at first."

"Doc Sawyer is on the way to examine . . ." Coleman didn't finish the sentence. "DeWayne is photographing the scene. We'll try for tire tracks, but a lot of vehicles have driven through there in the last few hours. Tinkie, would you make a list of every customer here. Get contact information and tell them to come by the courthouse tomorrow to give a statement."

"Sure thing." She set to work.

Cece came out of the kitchen with a steaming mug of coffee and handed it to me. She stroked my hair, which was almost my undoing. That tiny maternal gesture cracked my rigid control.

"Did you get a look at the truck?" Coleman asked me.

I focused. "It was black, extended cab, long wheel base. Like a F-150 or 1500. I couldn't tell the make or model." I thought hard. "The gun barrel extended out the passenger-side window. I thought it was two people, but it could have just been the driver, using the window frame to rest the gun on. The truck slowed before the shot. When he saw me, he fired again, but the angle was bad."

DeWayne came into the room and signaled for Coleman to follow him outside. My girlfriends immediately swooped in closer. "We should be outside, looking for evidence." I tried to get up, but Cece pushed me back into my chair.

"Not on your life, Nancy Drew. You're staying right here. A man was gunned down in front of you. Coleman will share information. Let him and DeWayne do their jobs. And Doc. You'll have everything you need in the morning."

She was right, but it felt wrong to sit. A man had died— for no reason. The threats whose seriousness I'd questioned had proven deadly. Whoever was after Scott and the band, they meant business, and I feared this was just the beginning.

The other band members put away the equipment and helped Curtis Hebert clean up the kitchen. No one wanted to leave, but there seemed no reason to stay. One by one, the band members and club help left as Coleman talked to them and dismissed them. At last, it was just my friends and me.

"Sarah Booth, let me and Tinkie drive you home," Oscar suggested. "We'll get you in the house and in bed with a toddy. Maybe Doc can give you something to sleep."

It wasn't a bad idea, but I knew I wouldn't sleep. No point worrying my friends. "I'm really good. I'm getting my balance back." I waved everyone away. "Go home. I'll do the same after I talk with Coleman one more time."

Jaytee and Cece were at the bar, talking quietly, waiting to lock the building. I hated to go outside, but I couldn't delay any longer. By now, Doc had probably taken the body to the hospital for the official autopsy.

Tinkie came over with Oscar to check on me one last time before they left. I shooed them home with promises I would go straight to bed. Tinkie leaned down and whispered in my ear, "Take Coleman or Scott with you. You don't need to be alone."

At least she made me smile. "I'll take that under advisement."

She gave me a tight hug before she exited. When I stepped into the night, I saw Coleman talking with De-Wayne and Scott.

"Sarah Booth, I'll drop you home," Coleman said. "I'll need a statement tomorrow, but for right now, you need some rest."

"I can take her," Scott offered.

"I can take myself." I wasn't some helpless damsel who needed a big strong man.

Coleman put a hand on my shoulder. "Go with Scott. I have work to do."

"I'm perfectly fine—"

"Gertrude Strom made bail about three hours ago."

He could have walloped me in the face with a two-by-four and it would have had less impact. "She what?"

"I don't know how she came up with the money, but she did. So I want Scott to take you home and make sure the house is secure. I trust Sweetie Pie and Pluto would alert you to any intruders, but it's best to check and be safe."

"I can stay the night to make sure no one bothers her," Scott said.

It was clear the two men had decided my fate.

"Fine." I said, because I was too angry to say anything else. The woman who had shot my fiancé was out of jail, psychiatric evaluations that proved she was dangerous be damned. She was free to torment me, and she had made it plain, more than once, she meant to harm me.

A thought struck me. "You don't think Gertrude shot Koby, do you?"

Coleman looked as angry as I felt. "It doesn't make sense, but what Gertrude did to you and Graf wasn't exactly the scheme of a balanced person. It's a possibility I have to consider. So yes, it's possible, which is why it would be best if Scott stayed with you. I'd do it myself, but DeWayne and I have some business we can't delay."

"What business?"

"Sarah Booth, go home and stay there. Scott, I'm counting on you to make that happen."

There was no arguing with Coleman when he'd made an executive decision. If I didn't leave, he might arrest me.

Scott had driven me home, and I sat on the steps while he went inside to mix cocktails. I loved the view from the front porch. Looking out over the land, I felt caught in the stream of place and time.

A pale silvery glow extended from the fields of Dahlia House to the far horizon. Moonlight touched the cotton bolls with magic. Far away, I heard the chant of workers in the field.

A clear baritone rang out, "Hy-po-crite and the con-cu-bine, livin' away among the swine."

A chorus of male and female voices answered, "Aunty, did you hear when Jesus rose?"

The baritone returned, "They run to God with their lips and tongue and leave the heart behind."

And the chorus repeated the same line.

The chop of the hoes in the field, the rustle of the cotton plants—I heard it all as the workers moved inch-by-inch down the rows.

Of course it was a fancy. Mechanical pickers now harvested the cotton, and it was the dead of night, the bright moon not discounted. The silvered fields were empty.

The front door creaked open and Sweetie Pie bounded over to where I sat on the front steps and licked my cheek. She flopped beside me and put her head in my lap.

A rattle of ice in a glass signaled Scott's quiet approach. "I should be making drinks for you," I told him as I took the proffered glass. "I'm so sorry about Koby." The reality still hadn't settled in, but I knew Scott had lost a friend.

"It's hard to believe." He sat next to me on the steps and Sweetie gave him a low, mournful groan. Pluto sat a dozen paces back. He missed Graf. He'd lost weight, though he was still a stout kitty, and seemed sluggish and unmotivated.

"What if it was Gertrude? She hates me. If I have brought this tragedy to your door—"

"Stop it." He put a gentle hand on my arm. "Don't do that, Sarah Booth. I was receiving the threatening calls long before that Strom woman got out of jail or the psychiatric ward or wherever she's been."

That was true, but Gertrude had wreaked such damage in my life, I didn't doubt her ability to spread the pain to everyone I cared about. "If she's behind this, I'll kill her."

"You're fierce when you need to be." He sipped his drink. "The best lead Coleman has is your description of the truck."

"Which is freaking generic, at best."

"Maybe DeWayne can get some tire prints."

"Maybe." I held little hope. There'd been over a hundred cars in and out of the parking lot. "That security team was worthless. They didn't see the truck. They said it had to come onto the property from one of the field roads. Weren't they paid to be on top of this?"

"Coleman has some questions for them." Scott rattled the ice in his drink. "I'm going to temporarily close the club."

That made me sit up. "Scott, you can't."

"I won't have any more bloodshed. Until we figure out who's behind this, I won't risk anyone else getting hurt."

"And the person doing this will have won."

"It's not about winning and losing. It's about protecting people."

"I know you put a lot of money into buying the club and bringing the band here. You gave up a successful European tour. How long can you go without income?" I didn't have Tinkie's mind for finance, but I wasn't a total goober. Scott had to be in a tight financial place. Successful blues tours in Europe didn't equate to multi-million-dollar payouts.

"I've had offers from investors, but I haven't wanted to go that route. Now I may have to."

I sipped my drink. "How bad would that be?"

He shrugged. "Depends on the investor. A silent partner wouldn't be awful, but if it were someone who wanted to control the club, it would be hard to swallow. That's the problem I ran into with Wilton Frasbaum, the former band manager. Things were great at first. He booked us into the clubs I wanted to play. He made sure the word got out. He did a great job."

"And then?"

"And then he started trying to shape the band into something else. He wanted us to blend free improvisational jazz into the playlist. You can push the line a little, but we aren't jazz. We're a blues band. Wilton had a nasty temper and a tendency to want to punish anyone who went against him. It ended really badly. He made threats. I never took them seriously, until now."

"I did a bit of checking into his background. I'll push it harder."

"It could have been so much worse if Wilton had had a financial stake in the band. He would have destroyed us. That's why I'm hesitant to take an investor."

I remembered Yancy Bellow's investment offer. "Do you have *anyone* you'd consider?"

"Not off hand. I turned down some Chicago interest. I may have to revisit them."

"What about Yancy?"

"I don't know enough about him to say one way or the other. I have to assume the offer grew from his love of the blues." He rubbed an eyebrow. "The best solution will be to figure out who killed Koby and put the bastard in jail. Then the club can open, and I won't have to concede to any investor demands. I know what the club can be. It will be a success as long as I can hang on to my dream."

"Coleman is on the case, and Tinkie and I will do our best. Give us a few days to turn something up."

"Sarah Booth, maybe it would be best if you let the law handle this."

I didn't have the heart to be affronted. Scott didn't doubt my abilities. He knew I'd suffered great consequences from my last case. Everyone in Sunflower County knew it. No point pretending I was tough and invincible. I was wounded, and Scott was acting as a friend. "I can't hide away in Dahlia House for fear someone is going to injure me or someone I care about."

"Everything you planned has turned upside down. I don't want to be the person responsible for more upheaval."

I leaned against him. "If Graf had not been shot, we would still have confronted the issue of his daughter. That was unavoidable."

"And had Graf not been shot, it may have unfolded in a completely different way."

"Maybe. But maybe not. That's something we won't ever know."

A hoot owl cried from near the barn. In the side pasture, Reveler snorted and Miss Scrapiron answered. Hooves pounded as the horses took off in a game of chase. The crisp November weather infected them with spirit, and they needed to be ridden. I stood up. "Let's go for a moonlight ride. Really. I'm on the case. You're hurting from the loss of a friend. I'm trying to put my life back in order. There are so many things wrong right now, but a ride through the cotton fields would be good for both of us and for Sweetie Pie."

"You're a persuasive woman." Scott stood. "I'm not the most polished horseman."

"Doesn't matter a lick. Just sitting on Lucifer is going to change your attitude. I promise."

We had the horses groomed and tacked up in a matter of minutes, and we set out down the driveway with Sweetie Pie following at our heels. Reveler was eager for a run, but he contained himself as we turned down the road. I'd decided to ride on the Brewer property because the corn and soybeans had already been harvested. Riding the edges of a field didn't bother the crop, but I wanted the cleared field, not the waist-high cotton where someone with a gun could hide. My nerves were edgy and an army could lie in wait in the cotton and never be seen.

Traffic on the road in front of Dahlia House was nonexistent, especially at midnight. We clip-clopped on the right-of-way. The air was brisk, and I let my body relax in the rhythm of Reveler's long stride.

"This is good," Scott said, apparently feeling the same tension release. "I could grow accustomed to this."

"I'm glad you're with me."

"And you with me. I don't want to think about Koby. Not tonight. Tomorrow, when the sun is shining, I'll have to confront the horror of his death. I can't do it now."

"Tomorrow is soon enough, Scott."

We rode for a moment in silence before he spoke again. "I didn't know Koby all that well, but I liked what I knew. We hooked up with him playing in Austin. It was like the hand of fate. He'd just been hired at the bar, and he came up and started talking."

Scott was torn up by Koby's death, and letting him talk was the best thing I could do.

"He was this big, friendly guy who could flirt and tease the ladies. He ran the bar like the captain of a ship. Watching him work, I knew he'd be a terrific asset. When I offered the job, he didn't hesitate. If I hadn't brought him to Mississippi with the band, he'd be alive."

"He came here because he wanted to, Scott. Playing the *if* game only piles guilt on top of sorrow. *If* he hadn't come to Mississippi, *if* a crazy person hadn't had a loaded weapon, *if* it had been raining. There's no way to know how changing one tiny thing could yield a different result." Boy, had I learned hard lessons from personal experience.

"Do you think Koby was the target or was he just convenient? The person who happened to go out the back door just when the shooter was waiting."

"I don't know. That's a question Coleman will also want answered."

We were about to cross the road to the Brewer field when Sweetie bristled and began to growl. The night was velvety black and my vision limited, but I didn't sense anything that might cause my hound concern.

"Sarah Booth. There's a vehicle parked on the verge up ahead."

Before I could respond, headlights not thirty feet away blinded me. Reveler was startled too, and sidestepped away from the vehicle into the center of the road. I heard what sounded like the breach of a shotgun snapping shut.

A really bad feeling rippled down my spine. "Run!" I yelled to Scott, letting Reveler jump the shallow ditch and race into the soft dirt of the field. Lucifer's big hooves pounded behind me.

I turned back and glanced at the vehicle as it roared to life and peeled out down the road. It was a truck, and a dark-colored one. That was all I had time to see. I was focused on saving my neck as the horses raced toward the tree line. When I checked, Scott was leaning down into Lucifer's mane, and he seemed to be managing the ride just fine. I let Reveler run until we reached the far side of the field. When I finally pulled up, breathless, Scott was right beside me.

"It was the same truck, wasn't it?"

I already had my cell phone out and was ringing Coleman's number. "Yeah. I think so. I can't positively ID it, but I would be willing to bet. Maybe Coleman and the highway patrol can stop it."

"Those killers were watching Dahlia House," Scott said.

"Let's not jump to conclusions. It could have been kids parking and we startled them." I didn't believe it, but panicking Scott wouldn't help anything.

"I may have brought more danger to you, Sarah Booth."

"Or vice versa." I signaled him to be quiet but I left the phone on speaker as Coleman answered. When I relayed what had happened, Coleman assured me the state troopers were sending several units to help block the roads. They already had an APB out on the truck. The officers would center the search close to Dahlia House, narrowing the perimeter.

"Did you see anyone in the truck?" Coleman asked.

"The driver blinded us with the headlights, and then we ran. I was afraid they had a gun—I thought I heard a breach snapping into place. I thought they would try to shoot us." I paused. "It could have been the same truck, but I can't say for certain."

"Getting away was smart, Sarah Booth. If that truck tries to leave Sunflower County, we'll get it. Are you and Scott okay?"

"We are."

"Might I suggest you go home and stay in the house? Sarah Booth, you shouldn't be alone." Worry colored his voice. "I'm trusting Scott to be a gentleman."

"You have my word, Coleman. Now isn't the time for rivalries," Scott said. "I'll watch out for her. For both of us."

I'd thought it would be tricky, putting Scott in a guest room, because we'd once shared my bed. But it wasn't. He made everything so easy. He kissed my forehead and closed the door to his room, resolving any awkwardness. When I was piled up in bed, I threw a little pity party for myself. Three weeks earlier, I'd been planning my beach wedding and my future with Graf. I'd visualized our children, our life together, the moments, small and large, that we would share. I'd seen us in the rocking chairs on the front porch of Dahlia House, aging together.

Try as I might to change the mental movie reel in my head, I couldn't. I went to the bathroom and got a wad of toilet tissue to mop up the tears. I hadn't allowed myself any time to grieve the loss of my dreams, and now I couldn't stop crying. I didn't want to wake Scott, but I also couldn't shut down my emotions.

Walking to my bedroom window, I looked out on the barn and the moon-silvered pastures where the horses grazed. That I shared the beauty of the view with no one else made the tears slide down my cheeks faster.

The things that had happened were done. I didn't cling to false hope. I wasn't the kind of person who could ignore the obvious and spin fancies of what might have been. That was a complete waste of time and energy. But I also couldn't close the door on Graf without a proper farewell. Even if I only said it to an empty room.

I had loved Graf twice. The first time I was an idealistic young woman with big dreams of a Broadway career. When I'd left New York to come home to Dahlia House, I'd left my career dreams and the man I loved. That had taken a toll. But when Graf came back to Mississippi, to me, I loved him as much as I had in New York and a little more—*because* he'd come back to me.

And now he was gone. Without any indication he would leave. Intellectually, I knew the abrupt departure hurt him as much as me. He hadn't planned to find his daughter and be confronted with building a life for her. But the truth was he'd gone off to build a new life with his child, and I was left in the shambles of the old life he'd left behind.

"Self-pity is an ugly habit, Sarah Booth Delaney."

I could easily imagine my aunt Loulane's voice in my
head. Folks lived through hard times. That's what people
did. Especially Delaneys. They kept on living and doing
the daily chores. They kept their lives moving forward.
They didn't let a broken romance send them into an
emotional tailspin. Graf was alive. He wasn't dead or
maimed. He had merely taken a path divergent from
mine. At any moment, I could call him and he would
talk to me. It would never be the same, but there were
no truly closed doors. Not like those that death slammed
shut. I blotted my cheeks one more time and resolved to
buck up.

A light touch on the ivories made we whirl around to
face a full-bodied woman standing at the foot of my bed.
A noncorporeal pianist—and instrument—played the in-
tro to the tune about how the blues walk in when a good
man walks out. The words to "Bedroom Blues" suited me
to a tee, and Sippie Wallace was the woman to belt them
out.

I wiped my last tears away and stared at her. She had
a full, round face and a large gap between her teeth. I recognized her from old black-and-white photos. Sippie
Wallace was known as the Texas Nightingale. She hailed
out of Arkansas, but Texas claimed her. She had a voice
that came from deep in her gut.

"I feel you, Sippie," I said. Some folks might be taken
aback by the appearance of a dead blues singer in their
bedroom in the middle of the night. I was just glad for
the company.

"You don't get over a busted love in a few days." Sippie approached me. Her dress rustled as she walked.

"Tell me about it." I wasn't intending to be melodramatic, and I would heal. But each loss changed me. Some days I wondered if I was flexible enough to survive much more.

"Life is a lonesome journey, Sarah Booth Delaney. Especially for women. Men?" She waved one hand in dismissal. "They suffer loss and heartbreak, but they *need* to be loved. They find a new lover. The hard part for a woman who's been hurt is that she can survive alone. It may not be how she wants it, but she can. You can. You can step back into life and travel the road by yourself."

"Jitty?" I knew the pep talk was coming from my haint. "Why are you telling me all this?"

The transformation from plump songbird to slender ghost came in the blink of an eye. "Because you have to know your strengths, Sarah Booth. Miss Alice, your great-great-great grandma and I, we didn't have a choice. We had to be strong for the young'uns. Who are you gonna be strong for?"

An important question. I couldn't hide in my bedroom and mope. A man—a good man to hear Scott tell it—had been gunned down in cold blood. And it had happened when I was on the case. There was no time for self-pity, or pity's partner in crime, self-recrimination. I had to get up and find the person who killed Koby Shaver. I had to climb to my feet and reclaim my life. For my friends. And for myself.

Jitty's smile was a thousand watts. "Now you're onto the right answer, Sarah Booth. Just remember, it's okay to sing the blues sometimes, but you got to pull yourself up and live. Tuck yourself into bed and let me sing you a lullaby like Miss Libby used to do."

Jitty had the most impressive gift of imitation. She chose one of my mother's favorites, the old 1944 standard, "Dream." Just for me, she'd set aside the hard licks of the blues for a song about hope. As I fell asleep, I could only hope my dreams would be happy ones and that one day they would come true.

I was up early the next morning and had the coffee brewing and horses fed by the time Scott got up.

We sat down over an omelet and I asked him questions. Before we were too far into it, Tinkie arrived. To my shock, she wore a cute plaid shirt, tailored, of course, form-fitting jeans, and boots with fleece tops. She looked like Paul Bunyan's very stylish wife. "Going to a tree cutting or log rolling?" I teased her.

She merely sniffed. "We've got a lot of ground to cover. So far, who's on the suspect list?"

"It's a mighty short list," I admitted. "The ex–band manager, from the angle of someone wanting to hurt Scott or the band, but it seems really unlikely a guy living in Europe would take out a hit on a newly hired bartender. This is closer to home, I think. We don't know a lot about Koby's background. Maybe he had enemies. Maybe it's someone with a personal grudge against Scott." I couldn't forget Gertrude. "Or me. Gertrude Strom would hurt the band or the club because Scott's my friend."

"I agree with your line of thinking." Scott cut a bite of omelet but didn't eat it. "Koby enjoyed flirting, but he wasn't the kind to mess with a man's girl or make enemies."

I'd seen Koby's principles in action. He had come on to me strong, but the minute Jaytee had hinted Scott was interested, he'd backed away.

Tinkie shot Scott a look of apology. "We have to check all of the band members and any employees of the club. I'm sorry. I know this is aggravation on top of injury."

Scott pushed his half-eaten breakfast away. "I know. I understand. I don't like it, but I get it. Everyone is a suspect." His gaze caught and held mine. "They'll all check out clean, though. I know these guys. They're musicians and they're completely devoted to the band and the success of the club. Why would any of them do something like this? It could destroy their future security."

"It may not come from them, Scott, but from someone in their past. Some folks drag trouble behind him like a ball and chain."

"And there are the old standbys. Greed, envy, lust, revenge, did I say greed?" Tinkie pushed Scott's plate toward him. "Finish eating. It's going to be a long morning, and you need to take care of yourself."

"What about local people?" I asked. "Has anyone talked against the club?"

Tinkie got up and poured herself some coffee. When she was seated again, she pulled a notepad from the pocket of her jeans. "I made a few calls this morning before I got dressed. I have a list of people who have been outspoken in their opposition to the club. I think it's a waste of time, but we have to check it out."

I scooted my chair so I could read from her notes. "Reverend Jebediah Farley, Angela Bowers, Johnny "Frisco" Evans—who the hell is that?"

"Frisco just moved here from Memphis. Word is, he wanted to buy the club and turn it into a country bar. Angela Bowers wanted to see Playin' the Bones turned into a ballroom kind of place, and it's hard to figure Farley's angle. Apparently he wanted to shut the place down in an attempt to eradicate sin."

"My aching . . ." I left the thought unfinished. "So why didn't one of them buy it?"

Tinkie shifted uncomfortably. "Frisco's the only one with enough money or credit. He tried. It's just that Scott's offer was taken and his wasn't."

Something was off here, but Tinkie's expression warned me not to push too hard.

"I had the better offer, right?" Scott asked.

Tinkie stared deep into her coffee cup. "The owner took the offer he liked best."

Scott was now alarmed. "What do you mean?"

Tinkie sighed. "There's nothing illegal. The owner wanted it to remain a blues club, not country. So he took your offer."

"Was Johnny Evans's offer higher?" I asked.

"It was apples and oranges, as I understand it. Scott had the financial paperwork in place. The owner took the offer he liked. It was at his discretion. But Frisco, as he prefers to be called, was more than a little upset."

"We'll start our investigation with those three." As I picked up dishes and put them in the sink, I filled Tinkie in on the truck lurking outside Dahlia House. "Nothing happened, but we have to be careful," I reminded both of them.

"Get dressed," Tinkie said. "I'll make some calls and set up some appointments for us. We'll knock a few suspects off this list. Let's start with Frisco. He'll be the easiest to pin down."

"Welcome to my world," the tall cowboy sang admittance to his office at Frisco's Fine Autos. "You two ladies come on in," he said with a smile.

Frisco Evans looked like he'd stepped right out of the Wild West. He wore a snap-button shirt and jeans with a big bronc-riding silver belt buckle. His dark hair was shot with gray and he wore it long but neatly trimmed. A cowboy hat, battered and worn, graced his desktop.

The tidy office of the high-end classic car dealership told me a lot about the man we'd come to question. Frisco Evans spent his youth on the rodeo circuit and had the belt buckles to prove it hanging on the wall. He'd been a champion more than a dozen times. A gun cabinet on the far wall displayed two nice shotguns, several expensive rifles, and four handguns. Hunting and shooting trophies lined two shelves.

Frisco played to win at bulls and guns. And now he rode fast cars instead of bulls. Porsches were his specialty. He was a man's man.

Tinkie gave him a high-wattage smile and he sang another line of Jim Reeves's classic song. Frisco Evans had a thing for classic.

"Well, who do you purport to be, Gene Autry?" Tinkie asked. She hit her stride in daddy's girl mode before she even cleared the doorway. "Honey, you can lasso me any day. You've got an impressive baritone."

"Down, tiger!" I grabbed the back of her flannel shirt. Frisco Evans, the cowboy in question, was eyeing her like a bear views a honeycomb.

"Turn the little lady loose," Frisco said in a downhome drawl. "I won't bite her, unless she bites me first."

Tinkie had slayed another dragon, and I feared this one might fall right on top of her. "Mr. Evans, I'm Sarah Booth Delaney and this is my partner, *Mrs.* Oscar Richmond."

The jocularity fled his face. "You're married to the banker?"

"I am," Tinkie said, "but that's no reason we can't be friends."

"Get out." He pointed to the door. "Your husband's bank screwed me out of my future, so you two can take yourselves right out the door and straight to hell."

"Mr. Evans!" Tinkie was all feminine outrage. "I can't believe you blame me for my husband's bank decisions. I have nothing to do with how Oscar runs his business." She pulled her bottom lip in with her teeth and then let it pop out. Frisco Evans was a goner.

"Now, now, Mrs. Bellcase. I didn't mean to upset you." Frisco was flustered, exactly where my partner wanted him.

"Call me Tinkie, please," she said on a deep sigh. "Oscar is my husband, but I don't always agree with what he does. You shouldn't blame me for something I can't help."

"True enough. True enough," Frisco said. He was a man's man who had one weakness—a helpless woman. Tinkie had homed in on that the minute she saw him, and now he was wet clay for her to mold. I could only sit back and admire my partner's technique.

"Mr. Evans—"

"Frisco," he said. His attitude had changed even toward me.

"Frisco," I began again, "Those are some nice weapons. Looks like you're something of a skeet shooter."

"I enjoy competitive shooting." He grinned. "Boys and their toys."

"The bartender at Playin' the Bones was shot and killed last night."

He bristled like a porcupine facing a cougar. "And what is it you think I know about it?"

Tinkie put a hand on his forearm. "Please don't be so mean. We just need to talk."

He backed down immediately and patted her shoulder. "Okay. Let's palaver." He waved us into chairs and went behind his desk and sat down. "I heard the bartender was shot. I can't say I wasn't rooting for the opening to be a disaster, but I never wanted anyone hurt."

"We have a few questions, because of your interest in the bar." I was not the smooth operator Tinkie was. I got straight to business. "Where were you last night?"

Belligerence crossed his face. "I don't need an alibi, but I will tell you I was out with a lady friend."

I pulled out my pad and pen. "We'll have to verify that." When he started to bristle, I said, "It's us or the sheriff. I'm sure he'll be happy to take you down to the courthouse."

"I have nothing to hide. I was with Angela Bowers, if you must know. She had planned on teaching line dancing in my country bar until that Yankee musician bought the club out from under me. Seeing as how I don't have a bar, Angela and I decided to have dinner. We were at the Gardens for drinks and dinner."

Talk about a major sidetrack. The Gardens B&B was owned by none other than Gertrude Strom. "You were at The Gardens? Did you see Gertrude?"

"We were there late. I almost choked when she walked in, just like she'd never been gone a day. Greeted all the customers then went behind the bar and mixed herself some kinda concoction that looked like it would kick like a mule."

"Did you talk to her?" Tinkie asked. "We're interested in her whereabouts, too."

"She spoke to everyone, sashaying around like the Queen of Sheba."

My hand started trembling and I put my pen down.

"Did she say anything?" Tinkie asked. She was as shaken up as I was, but she was better at concealing it.

"Made sort of a general speech to everyone. Said she was back and planned to stay in Zinnia for a good long while."

"What time did she leave?"

Frisco thought. "Like I said, we were dining late. She came in when I ordered and left when the waiter brought dessert, so about eleven o'clock. Angela and I went to Greenwood to Loco Boots bar and danced the night away."

It would be easy to check Frisco's and Angela's alibi at The Gardens, but after leaving there, the two would have had plenty of time and opportunity to drive by Playin' the Bones, which was on the way to Loco Boots. "Can you give us the names of anyone at the bar to verify your alibi?"

"I was dancing with Angela, not everyone at the bar. Ask around. Surely someone saw us."

"We'll be sure to do that. Thanks for your help," Tinkie said, rising. "Where can we find Angela?"

"Probably at the dance studio."

We took our leave but Tinkie caught my wrist in the

parking lot. "Sarah Booth, I know this Gertrude thing is intolerable. She almost killed Graf, and she's out prancing around like nothing happened." Tinkie opened the passenger door for me. "Gertrude has a lot to answer for."

"I can't believe she's really out." I sounded like a broken record.

"Not for long." Tinkie stepped on the gas and squealed out of the parking lot. "Not for long. I promise you."

6

The dance studio had undergone a vast change of direction since the former prima ballerina and instructor known to every young Sunflower County girl as Madame had sold out to Angela. The emphasis was on social dance now, not ballet, jazz, or modern.

As Tinkie and I approached the Dance Salon, toe-tapping country music filtered into the street. We pushed open the door to find children of all ages engrossed in learning the Watermelon Slide. At the front of the room, wearing a wireless mic and calling out the dance steps, Angela Bowers did her best in boots and jeans to outshine Beyoncé. It didn't matter that her moves were blurred, her rhythm just a little off—the kids loved her, and she enjoyed them. This dance studio was about fun, not form.

Frisco had provided Angela an alibi for the past evening, and judging by her personality, I didn't see the first indication that she could harm anyone. But, I'd learned the hard way never to judge a book by its cover.

When the song was over, she waved the youngsters into the hallway for a drink of water. "What can I do for you ladies?" she asked, sizing us up. "You," she pointed at me, "might go for line dancing. The other," she indicated Tinkie, "I can't say. Tap maybe? No! It's ballroom. I'll bet you'd sizzle in the fox-trot."

"Ginger Rogers was always my idol," Tinkie said.

"I have two wonderful male instructors. Mr. Gable and Mr. Aucoin. I could sign you up for private lessons this evening."

"We're here on business," I cut in.

Angela frowned. She was a slender girl with beautiful legs and glossy chestnut hair. "What kind of business?"

"Koby Shavers, the bartender at Playin' the Bones, was killed last night."

She put a hand over her mouth, and for a split second, shock filled her gray eyes. It was quickly replaced with guilt and then suspicion. "I hadn't heard. So why are you talking to me about it? I only met the guy once, at the drugstore. I never went out with him."

"It's come to our attention you made some statements about the blues club." I put it on the line. Tinkie's source, the beautician at Glitz and Glamour, said Angela was in the shop mouthing off.

"Sure, I have an opinion about that club. I said we didn't need another place for men to go and get drunk and screw around on their wives and girlfriends." She planted her hands on her hips. "Why not a dinner club with great music and dancing that requires two people to work together?"

"Is that what you said?" I grilled her. "Because I heard you made some threats against the club. That maybe someone should burn it down."

She paled and then straightened her shoulders. "Yeah, I said it. So what? It's a free country. I can say what I like."

"Not so free if you acted on your threat." Tinkie nodded to the hallway where the whole herd of children watched, eyes wide.

She pushed her bangs out of her eyes. "I'm sorry someone was hurt. I really am. I talked to Koby one time, while I was waiting for a prescription. He seemed like a nice enough guy. I considered saying yes to his offer for dinner, but I had started seeing someone else." She twisted a strand of her shiny hair. "I don't really object to a juke joint, but I'd prefer a place where my students could demonstrate their dance moves, and I think Frisco Evans was cheated out of the club."

"Do you know anyone who might take action against the club or the band?"

"There are still some folks around here who think the blues is Satan's music. I don't hold with such thinking, but I've heard talk. Not about this Playin' the Bones specifically, but in general. People think it's sex music or black music or music inspired by the devil. Ridiculous."

"Any names you'd like to offer?" I asked.

"Put your ear to the ground. You'll hear the gossip."

"My advice to you," Tinkie said, "is not to make any more threats."

I followed with a question—a tactic that kept our quarry off balance. "After your dinner at The Gardens, where did you and Frisco go?"

"We . . . uh . . . we went for a walk around the grounds at the B&B. Such lovely gardens."

"How long were you *walking*?" I asked.

"It was such a beautiful night, we walked for a while."

They were grown-ups with houses and beds—because I had no doubt that walking was just a euphemism for something else. Why have sex on the freezing ground at a B&B where someone could stumble over them? "And after your *walk*?"

"We stopped at a country bar for a drink."

"What time would that be?" Tinkie asked.

"We made a late night of it. Around two."

First, Frisco had lied to us, omitting the time he'd spent canoodling with Angela in the foliage of The Gardens. Second, there was plenty of time between the Gardens and the country bar for them to have killed Koby—and while they were *walking*, they had no alibi.

"This doesn't look good for the two of you," Tinkie said, applying more pressure.

"I don't have to talk to you. You don't have any authority to ask me questions." Her mouth tightened into a thin, stubborn line.

"We can either be your best friend or your worst enemy," Tinkie said softly. "Go with friend. We can help you if you're telling the truth."

Angela leaned closer. "We made love. Okay? Frisco likes to see the stars. He's a cowboy at heart. And if you want to know who was talking against the blues club, it was Bijou LaRoche. She said the club would only bring in riffraff and that a ballroom dance and dinner place would have been much better for her business."

"Thanks." I had what I'd come for. Frisco and Angela weren't off the suspect list, but Angela had given us a more promising lead. "We'll be on our way."

Angela waved the children back into formation. "And I have to get back to work." She took her position in front of the group. "Now let's try the Boot Scootin' Boogie. Who remembers the steps?"

Tinkie and I headed for the door. When we were outside, Tinkie asked, "Do you want to talk to Reverend Farley or let it go?"

"Let's get it over with." I knew Reverend Farley by reputation. He didn't believe in dancing, the blues, drinking alcohol, women holding public office or even a job, blacks and whites living peacefully together, gay marriage, or that anyone except for the twenty people in his congregation would ascend into Heaven. He wasn't affiliated with any of the major Protestant churches, but had declared himself free and independent. His church was the Foundation Rock, the theology picked and culled from the parts of the Bible that suited him. I looked forward to wrangling with him about as much as a toothache.

There are pockets of primitive belief Christian churches all over the world. Most deal with living a life based on a strict interpretation of the Bible, but some, like Foundation Rock and Reverend Farley, had moved from Sunday services to taking action against those they labeled sinners. Picketing, protesting, and other legal forms of expressing an opinion were too soft for Farley.

Congregation members had been caught throwing

rocks through store windows of people who were "ungodly," and a few had gone so far as to deface tombstones in Zinnia's main cemetery. They'd burned effigies of politicians and movie stars they disagreed with. Such events were sporadic and committed mostly by underage members of the group.

While I respected civil disobedience, there was an edge of danger to the Foundation Rock group. Coleman kept an eye on them, and for the most part they remained cloistered on their compound. As far as I knew, they'd never crossed the line from property damage to harming a person.

If I understood the things Foundation Rock opposed, Scott would be high on Farley's list of top ten sinners. Playin' the Bones violated any number of Farley's strict mores. Because blues music delved into the pain of lost love, the primal pull of sexual desires, hard times, and loss some people called it the devil's music. Reverend Farley had been outspoken on the subject, insisting the blues ignited the sex drive and the desire to do bad.

I didn't doubt Farley was a kook, but was he off-center enough to shoot a man in cold blood? I intended to find out.

The church was north of town down a long dirt road that would be treacherous during a good rain. I hadn't expected such a depressing situation, but that was exactly what we found. The tin church, an ugly rusted hull with window slits that made it look more like a fortress than a place of worship, was surrounded by small motor homes and even a few tents where the members of the congregation lived.

A couple of Porta-Potties were set up by the edge of

the woods beside four abandoned vehicles. Several cook fires burned unattended. The place looked depressingly abandoned.

"We shouldn't be here," Tinkie said the minute she saw the terrain.

"Too late."

A man wearing a black suit, starched white shirt, and black hat and carrying a book came toward the car. There was no other sign of a human being. If the RVs and tents were occupied, the inhabitants stayed inside. I thought of a prison yard, empty of inmates, everyone locked away in cells.

"This is private property," the man, who I took to be Jebediah Farley, said as he neared Tinkie's rolled-down window.

"Are you Reverend Farley?" I asked.

"I am and this is my property." He reminded me of a lightning rod, eager for a bolt from the heavens to prove his worthiness.

"I thought this was a church," Tinkie responded.

"You don't look like a believer to me," he said pointedly staring at our jeans. "God doesn't hold with women wearing pants."

"Can you show me where the Bible says women can't wear pants?" Tinkie asked.

Heat jumped in his neck and cheeks. Jebediah Farley had a bad temper, but today he managed to keep it in check. "Please leave before I call the sheriff."

"Please do," Tinkie said. She was tiny but she was tough. She opened the car door with enough force that she would have hurt him had it struck him. She stepped out and stretched. "Actually we're here at the sheriff's behest."

"You are indecent! Showing off your woman parts in those tight britches. Now get in your car and leave!"

Farley's raised voice drew another man out the door of the church. He was tall, lean, and rugged. His arms bulged with muscles, and his black T-shirt stretched tight across his chest. He didn't approach, but he focused on us in a way that was threatening.

"Where were you last night?" Tinkie pressed.

I got out on the passenger side of the car, ready for action. I'd picked up a flashlight, intending to use it as a club if Farley or his minion tried to lay a finger on Tinkie. She was provoking him, which I wished she'd stop doing, but he wasn't going to hurt her as long as I was there to protect her.

"We're in the middle of the fall revival," Farley said. "I was preaching a sermon. I don't owe you an explanation, woman, but I'm giving you one so you'll take your sinful attire away from this temple of the Lord."

Tinkie couldn't hide her disappointment. She knew as well as I did that standing in front of a group of twenty people was a terrific alibi for the time Koby was killed.

"What time did the revival break up?" I asked.

"It was after two in the morning. I had four conversions and six testimonials last night. The Spirit moved through the congregation. It was a powerful thing to witness." Smug was the only word to describe Farley. Well, smug and fervent.

"We hear you have a problem with Playin' the Bones. Folks around town say you've been intimating there may be serious problems there." Tinkie stepped closer, which made him step back.

Farley smiled, but it was ugly. "I don't hold with places that play the devil's music. Serving liquor, creating an atmosphere where sin can set up house and breed. Such places cater to the darkness in the human soul. It was bad enough when the blacks ran it, but now it's pulling in our people and taking them down the road to Hell."

"Our people?" Tinkie pressed him. "What exactly do you mean?"

I was around the car and at her side. I put a restraining hand on her shoulder.

"You know exactly what I mean." Farley's eyes burned with his passion. "There is an order to God's creation. The white man has dominion over the animals, the women, and the other races. The white male was created in God's image and was given the rights and duties to rule. When that order is out of balance, the world is endangered. God will destroy the Earth with fire. It's promised in the Bible. Those who fail to heed God's word will pay the price. I stand against sin, and I do so with pride."

Farley was the most dangerous kind of zealot—one who believed he had God's personal attention and approval. While he might have been in front of a congregation last night, it didn't mean he hadn't sent one of his followers to take action against the blues club. We'd learned what we came for and now it was time to leave before things got out of hand.

"Let's go, Tinkie."

"Good idea." Farley grew louder and louder. "You'd best get out of here, you whores of Babylon. And don't come back. We mind our business here and you'd better mind yours. Next time I see you, I don't doubt you'll both be pillars of salt. Go back to your Sodom and Gomorrah."

I saw movement behind the windows of one of the little

campers. A curtain eased back and the frightened face of a woman stared out at us. Another woman broke from one of the tents and ran toward the church. The long skirt of her dress hampered her ability to move fast, and when she glanced back at us, she was clearly terrified.

Tinkie's fists clenched. She wanted to belt Farley, and that was out of the question. I eased her into the back-seat and jumped behind the wheel. Before I could start the engine, though, Farley had something else to say.

He leaned into the open window and glared at us. "I know who you are, the both of you. You think you're high and mighty, two women running around playing detec-tive and acting like men. There's an uprising coming. Men are tired of women who try to dominate them. You two are headed for a great fall, and when it comes, there won't be anyone willing to offer you a hand. When you feel the ground rumble beneath your feet, that's us coming for you. You will learn your place or perish."

"My place will be dancing on your grave," Tinkie said.

I turned the engine over and rolled up the window before Tinkie could climb through it and scratch out his eyes. I drove out over the bad road with a lot less care than Tinkie had taken coming in. In the rearview mirror I saw the second man approach Farley. They watched us depart. When we were finally on the paved road, I pulled over and took a breath.

"You can't provoke people like them," I chided her. "He's dangerous. You think he's just a fool, but he be-lieves his actions are righteous, and that makes him ca-pable of anything."

"I hate people who use fear to repress others. I was hoping he'd hit me so I could charge him with assault."

"Pushing him to rash action isn't smart."

"Pompous asshole." Tinkie climbed over the seat and into the front. "You should have let me deck him. He'd have blubbered and called for his mama. Men like that are always titty-babies."

"Whoa, I haven't heard that word since second grade." I glanced over at her. The hint of a smile tugged at Tinkie's lips. Her temper was hot, but short-lived. "I wonder what he meant about them coming for us."

Tinkie shook out her blond hair. "Who knows. Who cares. He's a fanatic. As much as I'd like to pin this on him, he has an alibi for the time when Koby was killed. Folks like him talk big but they're usually cowards."

"I fear you're correct. We haven't eliminated him, but we haven't unearthed any evidence."

Tinkie checked her watch. "It's time to take you home," Tinkie said, waving a hand to get the car on the road and moving.

"What are you planning?" Tinkie was up to something.

"Nothing. Just preparing lunch for Oscar."

I didn't believe her for a second, but I knew she'd never tell me anything different.

Sweetie Pie and Pluto met me at the front steps, expecting Tinkie to take a moment to shower them with affection. Instead Tinkie tore down the driveway as soon as I was clear of the car. I could call her and ask again what she was planning, but I'd get the same answer. Nothing. She'd tell me when she was ready.

Weariness weighted my feet as I climbed the steps. I hadn't slept well. I lingered on the porch, taking in the golden light of the afternoon. When I could procrastinate no longer, I went in and started the process of unpacking my clothes from New Orleans, including the beautiful ball gown.

The strains of a favorite old song came to me from the first floor, and I walked to the landing. This was not the style I might have expected from Jitty, but it was a perfect summation of my emotions. She was in the foyer, waif-like with a cloud of dark curls. Instead of the beaded ball gowns of the 1940s, she wore tight jeans, a black and white loose-fitting top, and stiletto boots. Jitty was styling, but it was the song and lyrics that told me who she was impersonating.

". . . to be a diamond . . ." She had the Rosanne Cash visual and vocals down pat. "Blue Moon with Heartache" could have been written just for me.

I sat on the top step, clutching my ball gown. Cinderella and her pumpkin coach had nothing on me.

Jitty finished her song and came to sit beside me. "Don't let anyone make you a victim for free," she advised, borrowing from the song's wisdom. "Ass kickin' is my recommendation. You'll feel a whole lot better."

"I just need a little time."

Jitty blew out a breath. "Sarah Booth, I wish I could tell you life had handed you all the hard knocks you're gonna get. I can't. A successful life is about resilience."

As much as I wanted to get mad, I couldn't muster the emotion. She was correct. Everyone got knocked down and kicked. Success was all in getting back up. "I'll be fine. I have to build new dreams."

"And you will. You got a whole cheerin' section in the Great Beyond ready to back your play." The silver bangles jingling on her arm reminded me of our first encounter.

I'd heard the bracelets only a moment before she first materialized and changed my life forever. "In the next few weeks, you'll have a big choice, Sarah Booth."

Jitty never told me anything about the future. It was against every rule of the Great Beyond. "Why are you sharing this now?"

"This is important. You're gonna want to harden your heart, protect yourself from pain. Choose the opposite. That's what your mama says. Choose to love."

"That's pretty stupid advice. I've just had my heart ripped out and you're telling me to love again."

"Uh-huh. Exactly."

"Well, that's damn fool advice."

She smiled, and I realized that she'd been setting me up to get mad all along.

"Dammit, Jitty!"

The front door opened and Jitty was gone on the last tinkle of her bracelets.

"Sarah Booth," Scott called from the front door. "May I come in?"

I stood up. "Sure. I'm on my way downstairs."

Although I did my best to hide my recent emotional roller coaster, Scott picked up on it. He took my hand and led me to the kitchen.

"Sit while I make us some café au lait." He set to work, chatting about the phone calls and public concern he'd received at the club. He kept it light, but he felt responsible for Koby's death. I saw it in the shadows haunting his blue eyes. It was a heavy, and unnecessary, burden to carry.

When the coffee was brewed and a cup put in front of me, I told Scott about our morning efforts. "If Frisco and

Angela weren't fa-la-la-ing in the shrubbery, they had plenty of time to kill Koby."

"A car salesman?" Scott was skeptical.

"He's a former bull rider and a competitive marksman. His middle name should be Competitive. You beat him out of the club, and he's a man who takes things personally. He wouldn't shirk a physical confrontation and he owns shotguns. Though it would be pretty brassy to display a murder weapon."

Scott rubbed his eyes. "It's impossible to believe a man would kill over a business deal."

"The dance teacher will uphold Frisco's alibi."

Scott sipped his coffee, his shoulders slumping. "I can't believe we're having this conversation. I keep thinking I'll go to the club and Koby will walk out from behind the bar and tell me it's all been a mistake."

Scott was in the denial stage—and I had no desire to push him out of it, but it was my job to update him on my investigation.

"The preacher, Reverend Jebediah Farley, might be capable of inspiring his disciples to kill, but he has an airtight alibi. Coleman is checking it just to be certain, but I think we can rule him out as the killer. Personally, I think he's a blowhard who gets off on bullying and repressing women who have nowhere else to turn. Killing a man doesn't seem to be his style."

"I talked to the band members, and no one can think of a single reason anyone would target Koby." He almost flinched. "His girlfriend is coming to Zinnia," he checked his watch, "any minute now. I don't look forward to this. Koby never mentioned anything about a girlfriend moving here with him."

Based on Koby's flirtatious ways, I was a little surprised too. "Does she know he's been killed?"

"She does. She called to talk to Koby and Jaytee told her. She was halfway here with the U-Haul loaded with all her possessions. She doesn't have anywhere else to go."

"What will you do?"

"She's a bartender. She wants to work."

"Geesh." He was in a tough place.

"There's something I really need to talk to you about."

Why did I feel like the second shoe was about to kick me in the shins? I put down my coffee cup and flattened my hands on the table, possibly for stability. "What?"

"I talked to Coleman about Gertrude."

This wasn't where I expected the conversation to go. "There's nothing Coleman can do until she violates the law."

"I think both you and Tinkie should have some security until the old bat is behind bars. Coleman thinks so too. In fact, he's checking her alibi for the time of Koby's murder."

Their concern was touching but impractical. "I'll stay alert for Gertrude, but I won't have bodyguards following me around." I picked up the coffee and sipped. "Tinkie and I are smart enough to steer clear of a psychopath."

"If she's stalking you, Sarah Booth, she means to hurt you. We've all been trying to figure out why someone is targeting me or the club. What if it's you that's the target? You were outside. You could have been killed as easily as Koby."

He was right, but vigilance was my only option. I couldn't hide in Dahlia House, afraid if I stepped outside, Gertrude would plug me.

"Scott, I appreciate your concern. But—"

"Coleman told me you'd resist common sense."

Instead of getting angry, I laughed out loud. "It's comforting to know the two of you are diagnosing my stubbornness."

"Coleman and I will be adversaries at a later date. We both care about you. And Tinkie. She's in danger too if she's hanging around with you. So you two should stay together and have some protection."

Instead of the divide and conquer, Scott and Coleman had come up with the combine and protect philosophy. "Okay."

Scott's mouth opened and nothing came out. "What?" He was confused. I'd capitulated too easily.

"Okay."

"Are you serious?"

"Would you prefer if I forced you to argue and reason and try to persuade me?"

"This was way too easy." His eyes narrowed. "What are you up to?"

"Tinkie and Oscar have to come here. I'm not leaving the horses. The Bellcases only have Chablis and she lives here half the time anyway. They can move into Dahlia House for a while."

He looked up at the ceiling. "You know Oscar—"

"I'm not leaving the horses. If it's for a few days, they can come to my house. If it's longer, I'll move the horses to Lee's and go to Hilltop. How about that? See, I can compromise."

"I'll take it." He stood just as his phone rang. When he glanced at the number, he frowned. "It's Tatiana Scitz, Koby's girl."

This would be a hard conversation. I signaled him to sit and I picked up the dirty dishes and put them in the sink, then walked out in the backyard to give him some privacy.

In a moment the screen door slammed and he walked with me to the barn. "I have to go to the club. Come with me."

"Sure. Let me check my supplies. I may need to swing by the feed store." We entered the barn, which was dark and chilly. If I had the money for a modern barn, I'd have light and better ventilation, but this old structure had withstood time and the elements. It was as much a part of my home as Dahlia House. I flipped on the light switch and inhaled the scent of fresh hay and leather cleaner. This place soothed my spirit.

"Why are you being so agreeable, Sarah Booth? I don't recall you having a pliant streak."

"I don't want to be hurt and I don't want anyone I care about to find themselves in a bad situation for helping or protecting me."

He stepped closer and I knew he meant to kiss me. I wasn't ready. I pushed lightly on his shoulder and he instantly backed away.

"Sorry, I didn't plan that." He flushed. "I'd promised myself I wouldn't press."

My palm warmed his cheek. "This hard time will pass. I have to rekindle my hope that opening my heart is more than a trap for pain. I have to believe love doesn't always end in being left alone. The only way for me to get there is to find my own path."

"I'll help you find that hope, if you'll let me."

"I can't make any promises, Scott."

"I know you have feelings for the sheriff." His fingers traced my jaw. "The future is something no one can guarantee. You know I care for you, and I think you feel something for me. Now it's time to step back and give you room. *Rebound* is a word I don't care to have a personal relationship with."

"Thank you."

"Let's head to the club. This conversation with Miss Scitz won't be easy."

In deference to the solemnity of the situation, I opted to leave the animals at home, but I wanted to be sure they were safely inside. I whistled up Sweetie Pie. She bounded around the house, long hound ears flapping behind her. It took Pluto a bit longer to arrive. He was a cat and therefore disdained any movement that lessened his dignity. He could be lightning fast when chasing a hummingbird, but he never exceeded a creep when he had the opportunity to make a human wait for him.

"Molasses is slow," Scott said as we waited. "That cat has a definite attitude."

I picked Pluto up and put him in the house with Sweetie and carefully locked the door. "He's a cat. By definition he has an attitude."

Scott climbed behind the wheel and turned on the CD player. The voice of Howlin' Wolf filled the van. As we left Dahlia House, I remembered another trip with blues music playing. When I was in college, I'd traveled with a vanload of fellow students to a blues festival in Memphis. A golden memory.

A hint of sadness settled over me as we pulled up in the parking lot of the blues club. Only a few hours earlier Koby Shaver worked in and owned the space behind the bar. He'd been a giant of a man with a big presence. The place was empty without him. But not for long. A female tall enough to rival Cece came out of the ladies' room. Her black, black hair was shaved on one side and bristled on the other. A dragon tattoo curled around her neck, shooting flames into her cleavage. I couldn't count at first glance how many holes she had pierced in her ears, eyebrows, and nose, but it was at least a dozen.

"Tatiana Scitz," she said, holding out a bejeweled hand banded at the wrist with a studded leather bracelet. Her miniskirt was black leather and her top, little more than a halter, was also leather. Her lushly curved body was blue from the cold, but she seemed impervious. "Have they found the asshole who killed Koby?"

"Not yet," Scott said. "Let's go in the office and talk a minute. This is Sarah Booth Delaney."

We shook, and I realized her grip could break all the bones in my hand. She was tough and strong and proud of it. Her appearance would give Zinnia something to talk about for at least a week.

Scott sat behind an old wooden desk and Tatiana and I took seats in front of it. Photos of famous blues players hung around the room, and a map of Mississippi showing the Blues Trail had been stapled up. Someone had thumbtacked notes on the map with facts about current clubs, performers, and contact information.

"Maybe in the future we'll have a movable blues feast," Scott said, noting my interest. "Change the venue around to different bars. The best thing to fertilize the blues is to soak the soil in plenty of opportunity for talent to rise."

"Tell me what happened to Koby." Tatiana cut to the chase. She was dry-eyed and resolute. She had accepted the facts, and judging from the hardness in her face and voice, she hungered for revenge. I flashed a warning glance at Scott, but it wasn't necessary.

"We're not certain if the attack was targeted at Koby, or if he was simply in the wrong place."

"That's about as comforting as a hole in a condom."

Scott played it straight. "I'm sorry, but we don't have any answers. Not yet. The sheriff is working on it and Sarah Booth and her partner are also helping. She's a private investigator."

Tatiana examined me head to toe but reserved her comments. I had questions, though. "Do you know of anyone who might want to harm Koby?"

"Hell, he'd only been in Mississippi a week. He had a big personality and he liked to flirt, but I doubt he could make a mortal enemy in that time."

She knew about his flirtatiousness and had no concerns. But that didn't mean another woman—or man—might not have taken offense. "Maybe someone from his past?" I suggested.

She shook her head. "We were together for the past year. He never had any trouble at work he couldn't handle with talk. Koby had a knack for saying the right thing, helping people feel better. I told him all the time he should've been a therapist."

"Did Koby have any habits that might have put him in bad company?"

She withered me with a glance. "Koby didn't mix in drugs. He wasn't a violent man. He didn't have dirty secrets or dirty laundry, and we don't have friends who kill each other."

Scott cleared his throat. "I really liked Koby. I still can't believe this has happened. As I told you, you're welcome

to have his bartending job for as long as you want it, assuming the club opens and we can pay our bills."

"I can't thank you enough." At last emotion caught
up with her. She knuckled a tear from the corner of her
eye. "What did Koby tell you about me?" she asked.

Scott shrugged. "Nothing."

"He didn't mention me at all?" Tatiana asked, a little
insulted.

"He didn't," Scott said. "Koby's been in Mississippi
about a week. We met him in Austin on the last leg of
the tour. He knew the bar business backward and forward and he had a personality folks enjoyed. I never
really had a chance to talk with Koby about anything except the bar." Scott shifted to the edge of his seat and
leaned toward Tatiana. "No one talked personal history. We were working too hard to open the bar. There
wasn't time."

"He was so excited about my arrival." Tatiana slumped
in her chair. "He planned to ask if I could be the relief
bartender. We met working in Tristan's Irish Pub. At
first we didn't like each other much, but we grew on
each other." Another tear leaked out and she angrily
brushed it away. "I refuse to cry. Koby wasn't the kind of
man who wanted folks weeping after him. He would
have said to raise a glass at his wake and dance around
the coffin."

"We will find who killed him," I told her.

"Maybe you could speed up the process." Her words
were hard, but her delivery was defeated.

"We're doing our best. A drive-by isn't the easiest
kind of murder to solve, especially since we don't know
if the act was based on personal issues with Koby or directed at the club." I wished I hadn't explained so much,

but the words were out. I'd want all the information possible if I were in Tatiana's shoes.

"Can I go to work?" she asked. "I want to familiarize myself with the bar. Get all the setups in place, review the flow."

"Sure." Scott walked her to the office door. "We've delayed the opening until tomorrow, but there's no reason you can't check the supplies. If anything is missing, just ask. Have you moved into Koby's house?"

"Everything I own is in the U-Haul. I can unload it later, when I'm too tired to be upset. Right now I need to be somewhere with action and other people."

"Let me know if you need anything for the bar. We'll open tomorrow evening."

Scott closed the door and leaned against it. "She's one tough lady."

"She is." I considered how the conversation had gone. "Koby didn't mention anything about her moving here?"

"We didn't really talk personal stuff. I know about Jaytee and Cece, but only because their relationship happened in front of me in New Orleans. Mike is married. I honestly don't know anything about the romantic liaisons of the other band members."

In a bid to make him smile, I said, "Obviously, we need some reporters from the *National Enquirer* or one of the gossip TV shows around here to keep you abreast. Maybe Cece should do a story about the personal lives of the band members."

Scott held up a hand. "That so isn't going to happen." The left side of his mouth lifted slightly. "We've delayed the opening until tomorrow night, but we're going forward come hell or high water."

I slipped out the door and hurried through the bar

into the November sun. I dialed Tinkie and asked for a ride. She was more than happy to escape a planning session for a garden club. I lit a cigarette while I waited for her to fetch me.

7

Huddled deep in my coat, I stomped my feet and finally put out the cigarette because my hands were too cold. To my surprise, Yancy Bellow pulled into the parking lot in a black Land Rover. The woman who got out of the passenger side was none other than Bijou LaRoche. I'd seen them talking at the ball in New Orleans, but apparently it had gone a bit farther than casual chitchat. Bijou looked fantastic, as always, except for the sneer on her face as she came toward me.

"Sarah Booth Delaney," she said, her gaze sweeping my jeans, barn jacket, riding boots, and messy hair. "I'll gladly treat you to a makeover and haircut. It's depressing to see someone my age look so . . . dowdy."

I wanted to blow smoke in her face but I'd tossed my cigarette. "Thanks, but no thanks." I almost added I had important work to do, but such a point would be lost on Bijou, who had nothing to do all day but spend money and torment people.

"Mr. Bellow," I said, "I hear they're giving free vaccinations at the local pharmacy. I doubt rabies is on the list, but you might want to check into it if you're going to hang with mad dogs."

His laughter was gratifying, and so was Bijou's flush. "You're a total bitch," Bijou said under her breath.

"What brings you to Playin' the Bones?" I asked Yancy. It wasn't my business, but I was protective of Scott. He didn't need anyone pressuring him right now, and Yancy had offered to invest.

"Just a friendly visit," Yancy said. "I want this blues club to open in Sunflower County. Having your bartender gunned down in the back of the club isn't exactly the best beginning. I want Mr. Hampton to understand I'm available to help him with whatever he needs."

Bijou put her hand on Yancy's arm. "We both are. I have a number of properties in the county perfectly suited to be excellent B&Bs. If this club takes off, I can keep them booked year round. Yancy wants to start a music festival, maybe bring in some big rockers who trace their musical lineage back to the blues. He'll cover the expenses to get it started."

So the two were hoping to get rich off the club, which was fine with me. "I'm sure Scott will be delighted to hear your plans. He's inside." In the distance I saw Tinkie's Cadillac headed toward us. Rescue was on the way. "There's my ride," I said, edging away.

"Don't rush off," Bijou said. "Maybe we can find some

money to brighten that rambling old hut you live in. It might appeal to the discount traveler."

Bijou could insult me all she wished, but Dahlia House was another matter. "Your point is taken, Bijou. Compared to the whorehouse you grew up in in New Orleans, I guess Dahlia House is a bit sedate."

"Ladies!" Yancy winked at me. "Pull in the claws. We have business, Bijou. Sarah Booth, always a pleasure."

"Oh, Yancy, tell Sarah Booth your good news." She smiled. "Yancy just bought The Gardens. Gertrude Strom needed cash, and Yancy helped her out."

The news hit me hard. I'd wondered where Gertrude got the money for bail, and now I knew.

"With the proper management, it will be a showcase B&B for the region," Yancy said, apparently oblivious to the repercussions of his actions.

"A win-win," Bijou said. "Let's head inside. I'm freezing."

They were gone before I could muster a response.

The highway back to Zinnia was a long stretch of emptiness. I loved the Delta in November, a world both endless and timeless. The fields had provided bounty for generations before me, and I hoped they would for many generations after I was gone. Tinkie drove, and I told her about Tatiana and Gertrude.

"I had no idea The Gardens was up for sale," Tinkie said. "Oscar never mentioned it, but at least now we know *how* she found bail money."

Yancy's role in putting Gertrude back on the street troubled me. "Do you think it was deliberate?" I asked Tinkie. "He knew about Graf."

"Yancy is a businessman first and foremost. I don't think it mattered why Gertrude needed the money. She could have been buying a home in the Bahamas for all he cared. "

"That's not a consolation," I noted.

"No, but if Bijou is chasing Yancy, maybe she's loosened her grip on Harold. Yancy has dealt with women like her all his life. He'll get what he wants from her and then cut her loose. When he does marry, it will be to have an heir. Bijou will never be his wife. She'd eat her own young and she's getting a little long in the tooth for breeding purposes."

Tinkie was hitting too close to Jitty's familiar refrain. I had to change the subject. "I think we should use the rest of the day for background checks on all the band members and see if we can run down Wilton Frasbaum." Scott's former manager, Frasbaum, lived an ocean away, but we still had to eliminate him from our suspect list.

"You're the boss," she said. "Well, actually you aren't."

I had to laugh. "We're partners. There is no boss."

"Let me pick up Chablis. They won't allow her in the garden club meetings so I had to leave her home alone."

The no-dog policy was reason enough for me to avoid such gatherings, but Tinkie had an obligation as Avery Bellcase's daughter and Oscar's wife. Participation in clubs and the organizing of civic events came with the territory as head society belle. Tinkie could whip a committee into shape in five minutes flat, but she'd been unable to get around the no-pets-allowed attitude of some of Zinnia's society ladies.

Chablis was at the door when we got to Hilltop. Before we could get inside, Chablis leaped into Tinkie's arms and then jumped over to me for a lick on my cheek. Cradling Chablis, I settled back in the passenger seat as Tinkie ferried us to the PI office at Dahlia House.

As we turned down the drive, I took comfort in surveying the pastures. The first frost had come early, and though the grass was still green, it wouldn't be long before the brown of winter was everywhere. It was my favorite time to ride.

Tinkie's boots scrunched across the oyster shell drive and gave me an idea. "Want to take an hour and go for a jaunt on the horses?" I asked. She seldom took me up on my offers for a horseback adventure, but this time she stopped on the top step.

"How far is it to The Gardens from here?"

I considered. "About five miles, if we cut across country."

"Let's sneak in from behind and find out what Gertrude is up to."

I couldn't believe my ears. Tinkie didn't hesitate to break the law when necessary, but I wouldn't exactly put this scenario on the list of must-dos.

"Are you sure?" If Gertrude caught us trespassing, it might lessen the impact of my testimony against her when she was finally brought to trial. Then again, she might shoot us, so testifying would be a moot issue.

"She's up to something, Sarah Booth. I want to know if she has a black truck hidden on her property. We can't just drive up and inspect the premises. Coleman doesn't have enough probable cause for a search warrant. It's up to us to sneak in and find out."

I knew from a previous case that Gertrude's cottage was tucked away in the woods behind the B&B. There was access to the back of her property through the fields and a stand of hardwoods, but I'd never actually been

there on horseback. "We may run into some fences or obstacles."

Tinkie shrugged. "Then we can turn around and come
home, can't we? We can talk about the case on the way.
Kill two birds with one stone."

"Good thing you supplemented your lumberjack ward-
robe." I indicated her boots, jeans, and a dark green polar
fleece jacket. Tinkie was normally very chic, but the past
two days she'd worn more woodsy attire. "How did the
garden club take to your rural persona?"

"They hated it." She grinned. "Cece told me to shake
folks up every now and again."

"Cece would be the queen of jolting people out of
their comfort zones. Speaking of which . . ."

I dialed our journalist friend and told her our plans.
"Just in case we don't come home, you'll know where to
find us."

"I gather you didn't call Coleman and tell him what
you're planning because you know he'd have a hissy fit."

"Right."

"Okay. Call me when you head back to Dahlia House.
If you aren't home or answering the phone by five, I'm
calling the National Guard."

Some would think that hyperbole, but I knew better.
Cece would do it in a heartbeat. "We'll be careful and
home by five."

I signaled Tinkie toward the barn. "We'll take Sweetie
Pie, too." I looked at Chablis, who couldn't keep up with
the horses. Her legs were only three or four inches long.

"Never fear," Tinkie said, tucking the dog in her jacket.
Chablis's tufted little ears poked out at the top, giving an
interesting alien look to Tinkie's chest.

We saddled Reveler and Miss Scrapiron and headed out

the back of the property at a nice trot. Although I worried at first, it seemed Chablis enjoyed the rhythmic movement. Sweetie seemed to know we were on assignment. Rather than run ahead, she stayed right beside Reveler.

The horses were fresh and eager for a run. Tinkie sat secure in her seat so we let the horses gallop. They covered the distance in no time. We slowed to a walk at a copse of trees behind Gertrude's property, and my misgivings ripened. My partner deserved protection, not endangerment. This had been her idea, but I should have convinced her it was too dangerous.

"How about you hold the horses here." I suggested.

"I'm not your squire, Sir Sarah Booth." The twitch of her lips said she wasn't offended, but she also didn't intend to cooperate.

"I can be much quieter slipping around by myself. And if I see something suspicious and need to break in, I know the layout of her cottage." I should, I'd been held prisoner there with Graf.

"So do I. *You* hold the horses."

She'd chosen difficult over cooperative. I couldn't blame her, though. I wasn't about to be left behind while she risked her safety. Arguing would bring no satisfaction because Tinkie was every bit as hardheaded as I was.

We walked along the edge of the woods for half a mile, before I found an opening that led to a trail through the trees. I urged Reveler forward. Tinkie followed on Miss Scrapiron.

The moment we stepped into the canopy the temperature dropped by at least ten degrees. We'd been warm riding over the fields in the sunshine at a brisk canter. Now it was cold. Steam rose from Reveler's neck and flanks. Good to keep the horses moving until they cooled down.

The animals seemed to sense our need for quiet. The horses plodded along and Sweetie Pie took the lead, moving unerringly toward the back of Gertrude's property. A few times I paused, breaking a limb that blocked our path. The lower portion of the trail, obviously used heavily by deer, was clear. Tinkie and I had to duck repeatedly to avoid being slapped off our horses by scrub branches or vines.

At last we came to a clearing. Through the thick underbrush I spied Gertrude's cottage. My gut twisted painfully, and I slipped down from Reveler's back. Now one of us would have to hold the horses while the other checked out the premises.

The last time I'd been inside the house, I'd held Graf's hand as he was loaded onto a gurney and rushed to the hospital for surgery. "I'll be right back." I handed Tinkie my reins and took off at a jog before she could protest. I skirted the cottage and checked out the old barn and a garage stuffed full of antique furnishings that could be used in the B&B. But there was no black truck. I returned to Tinkie crestfallen. "Nothing."

"Seems like we ran into a load of bad memories for no reason," Tinkie said. "Dammit, I was certain we'd find the truck. I honestly thought that even if Gertrude wasn't the shooter, she was helping the person who did it."

My disappointment was all out of proportion. In my far-fetched fantasies, I'd daydreamed about finding the truck and the shotgun and proving that letting Gertrude out on bail had been a serious mistake. Reality proved nothing of the kind.

"Let's head back to Dahlia House." Exhaustion tugged at my feet. Even walking was a chore. I leaned against Reveler's stout shoulder.

Tinkie checked behind her at the crackle of a stick. "Let's get out of here before we're caught."

"Good idea." I shifted to turn Reveler around when Sweetie Pie froze. A guttural growl came from deep inside her.

Tinkie and I stopped moving and searched the area. Sweetie sensed something we didn't. Someone who posed a danger to us was near.

"Shit," Tinkie whispered. "We have to go forward to turn around. Once we step into the clearing, we'll be easy to spot."

"So she presses trespassing charges against us," I said, striving for a fearless tone. "It's only a misdemeanor."

"You and I both know she could as easily shoot us dead."

A stick some twenty yards away snapped. Sweetie's growl escalated.

"Run!" I commanded Tinkie. "Run for help. Give me your reins." She'd never get Miss Scrapiron turned and headed out. I could hold the horses while she went for assistance or called for help if we had cell phone reception.

"I'm not leaving you. But take the reins." She stepped up beside me and handed me Scrapiron's reins. The gun in her hand startled me.

"Where did you get the gun?"

"We both have them. You should carry yours. Times like this they come in handy." She stepped in front of me and the horses.

Another limb cracked—closer. Sweetie's hackles rose. Maybe it was a wild animal. There had once been bears and panthers throughout the Delta. I'd rather face a wild animal than Gertrude Strom.

The woman of my nightmares finally stepped out of

the thick underbrush. Sweetie took a defensive stance in front of us. Teeth bared and hackles raised, she let Gertrude know she meant business. But Gertrude's gaze was on Tinkie's gun.

"Well, well," she said, "trespassing and armed. What an interesting combination. How's that gimpy boyfriend of yours, Sarah Booth? I've been incarcerated but I heard he dumped you."

"Shut your piehole." Tinkie chambered a round in the pistol. "It would give me immense pleasure to put a bullet right between your eyes."

Tinkie was a good shot. She could do it. But she wouldn't kill Gertrude in cold blood no matter how much the old witch deserved it. Gertrude was unarmed. I brought out my cell phone only to discover there was no service so far from the main road. "I'm calling Coleman," I bluffed.

"How will it look? One of the primary witnesses against me is caught trespassing on my property. Have you considered how that will refute any testimony you might give?"

"That's ridiculous." I lowered the phone. The problem was, I had thought about it. Yet I'd trespassed anyway. Coleman would be mightily pissed off at me and Tinkie.

"Not so ridiculous. It's obvious you have a burn on for me. You're stalking me, tormenting me. Maybe you fabricated some of the details." Gertrude didn't bother to hide her pleasure at my situation. "What are you hunting that's worth all of this?"

"Do you have a black pickup?" Tinkie asked.

"What?" Gertrude looked from Tinkie to me. "What's she talking about?"

"Do you own or drive a black pickup? It's a simple question."

"No. And that's a one-syllable answer. You snuck in on horseback to see what kind of vehicle I was driving?"

Gertrude was mean but she wasn't dumb. Her expression brightened as she figured out why we were on her property. "You think I had something to do with the murder at Scott Hampton's club." She patted her abundant bright red hair. "I'm like the Al Capone of Sunflower County. If a crime is committed, it has to roost at my door."

When I started to say something sarcastic, Tinkie stomped my foot. Hard. "Gertrude, we're leaving. Call the sheriff if you want." She took Scrapiron's reins from me and clucked to Sweetie Pie. "Let's get out of here."

"I'll see you in court, Sarah Booth. I look forward to it."

For the life of me I couldn't figure out why she wanted to goad me. She stood to spend the rest of her life in prison. And yet she couldn't stop herself. "Gertrude, you won't be my problem for long. You're about to end your days at the women's prison. Not exactly a vacation spa."

"Don't count on it. I have a new lawyer."

Something clicked. The whole conversation, Gertrude's changed attitude, suddenly made sense. She'd been dying to tell me this. For some reason, she thought a new lawyer would get my goat. "How nice for you. I hate to break it to you, but not even F. Lee Bailey could help your case. Graf will testify about what you did to him, and Coleman has evidence you killed the graduate student."

"Don't be too sure." She was aggravatingly smug.

Tinkie bit. "Who's your new lawyer?"

"Alton James."

I almost choked. Alton James was the most high-profile defense lawyer in the nation. He didn't walk into a courtroom without a half-million-dollar retainer. He represented the worst of the worst and more often than not got them acquitted.

"Oh, you've heard of him." Gertrude gloated. There was no other word for it. She brought out a cell phone and snapped a dozen photos. "Proof that you were on my property."

"How can you afford James?" Tinkie asked. "You sold the B&B, but the proceeds won't come close to paying his fee."

"I have a benefactor." Gertrude patted her hair back into place. "I've been dying to see your face when you heard the news. So gratifying! Now I suggest you get off my property. Immediately."

We didn't need a second invitation. I turned the horses around and Tinkie and Sweetie Pie led the way out. When we were out of earshot, Tinkie stopped. "How is she paying for Alton James? Oscar wouldn't be able to afford him and we're the wealthiest people in Sunflower County. Or I thought we were."

"I don't know." My fear subsided and had been replaced with rage. Gertrude had wantonly injured a number of people. A young grad student was dead because she'd poisoned him. And she possibly had the best lawyer on the planet, one known to prevent guilty people from paying for their crimes? It wasn't right.

"She might have a big-name lawyer, but Coleman has the evidence," Tinkie said. "And you witnessed her torturing Graf and trying to kill you. For heaven's sake, Graf almost lost his leg because of her. She won't get away with this. Your testimony alone will put her in prison."

"I just tainted my testimony." It was true. By trespassing on her property, I'd played into the role of obsessed stalker. I'd weakened anything I might say in court. Tinkie didn't deny it. "I'm not leaving here without something to connect her to what's happening at the club. I know she's behind it. Her hatred of me is irrational."

"What are you going to do?" Tinkie asked.

"Search her cottage."

"You can't." Tinkie tried to grab my wrist. "That's breaking and entering. That's a felony. You could get jail time. Or worse. You go in there alone without a witness and she may try to kill you."

I didn't care. I'd risked and lost. Now it was double or nothing. "Will you wait for me here?"

Tinkie chewed her lip as she thought. "Yes." She pushed the gun into my hand. "You've got thirty minutes. After that, I'll ride until I get a signal and then call the sheriff."

Gertrude was not just mean and determined to ruin my life—she was guilty. I believed it to the bone. I had to find evidence of her part in what was happening at Playin' the Bones.

I ran down the trail with Sweetie Pie at my side, the gun tucked in my waistband. Panting from exertion, I circled the cottage. Gertrude was gone. But for how long? I pulled my car keys from my pocket and used a key to remove the screen from a back window and eased the old-fashioned window open. I had to find something. I couldn't walk away empty-handed.

Once I was inside, I went to the small library and began my search. The B&B financial records were on the desk, along with an appraisal. To my surprise, Yancy had paid two hundred thousand dollars more than the property was valued at. Why? I skimmed through more papers but found nothing.

I had to get out of there. Tinkie would have Coleman tracking me down, if Gertrude didn't come home and shoot me first. I tidied up her desk to hide my intrusion. A business card fell from the stack of papers. Bijou LaRoche. It wasn't evidence, but it sure led to speculation.

I snapped photos of the financials with my phone and then went back out the window where Sweetie Pie waited patiently, her attention on the path from the B&B. "Let's go home," I said to my dog, who eagerly led the way out of the woods.

Tinkie had her cell phone in hand when I hailed her from the edge of the trees. We mounted the horses and headed toward Dahlia House at a gentle canter. It was too much action to allow chitchat, which was fine with me. I wanted to get home, put the horses safely in the pasture, have a drink, and get Tinkie to examine the financials.

At the boundary of Dahlia House land, Tinkie pulled Miss Scrapiron to a walk. "Sarah Booth, Alton James is a celebrity lawyer. We need to poke into this. Gertrude paid her mortgage on the B&B each month. The place provided a decent living. Now she sold the property to Yancy to make bond. She doesn't have the income stream to pay a big-name lawyer. Who is funding her? And why?"

Those were great questions, and ones I hoped I could at least partially answer once we were in the office. "Gertrude has obviously attracted some special interest. Alton James is a gun for hire. He's defended Nazis, child molesters, serial killers. If they have the money, he'll take the case."

"So who's behind hiring him for Gertrude? It isn't like she's innocent and being railroaded by corrupt law enforcement. She's guilty as sin, and twice as ugly."

"I found something." I was eager to tell her.

"As luck would have it, you can tell me and Coleman at the same time," Tinkie said. We'd walked up a slight rise and Dahlia House was a vision in the distance. The brown patrol car Coleman drove was parked in front of the house. He sat on the steps, obviously waiting for us.

"Do you think Gertrude called him?" I asked. He was going to be really, really pissed off at us.

"We'll find out soon enough."

I didn't like the sound of that, but there was no running from it. We'd escaped Gertrude's property without injury. If she pressed trespassing charges, it wouldn't be the worst that could have happened.

Coleman prepared coffee while Tinkie and I untacked and gave the horses a good rubdown. Sweetie and Chablis abandoned us and went inside for some warmed up chicken and dumplings from Millie's Café—cooked especially for my hound. Coleman had been kind enough to heat the snacks for the dogs while Tinkie and I dealt with the horses.

Tinkie put the English saddle back on the rack and then ran an oil-soaked cloth over it. For a nonhorsewoman, she knew how to care for leather. "I don't think Gertrude called Coleman. He's too laid back. If she'd told him about the trespassing, he'd be on our asses like a duck on a June bug."

"The ethical dilemma is whether we should confess." I wiped down the bridles and hung them on pegs. The horses' grain was soaking in warm water and a little molasses—a nice hot mash. "We found—"

"No." Tinkie brought her manicured hand down emphatically through the air. "End of story. No confessing."

I fed the horses and let her persuade me. She had a good point. Telling Coleman of our actions would only worry him, which meant Oscar would be worried. Never a good turn of events. "Okay, mum's the word," I conceded. "We won't tell. But we'll get Harold to help us with the financial stuff. And Gertrude's connection to Bijou."

We entered the back door to the delicious aroma of coffee and a wonderful cinnamon smell. Sweet rolls!

Coleman brought a pan from the oven filled with Millie's homemade cinnamon buns. Tinkie fell on one with gusto. "Oh, this is good," she said with her mouth full. We were starved after our brisk ride. I hadn't realized how hungry I was until I smelled those tantalizing baked goods.

Coleman's gaze caught mine and held. "What's going on?" I asked.

"I don't want you to get broadsided by this. Gertrude has a new attorney. Alton James."

I pretended to be surprised and choked on the sweet roll. Tinkie slapped me on the back to dislodge it and we managed to get through the moment.

"James sent notice he intends to speak with all of the prosecution witnesses," Coleman continued. "You and Tinkie are on the list."

"We don't have to talk to him." I wasn't a lawyer, but I knew a few of my rights.

"No, you don't." Coleman sat down at the table and

picked up my cold hand. "It's up to the two of you. Some-times, though, you can learn a lot by the questions asked."

Coleman wanted to send us on a fishing expedition. His reasoning was obvious, but I didn't know if I could do it. I didn't want to think about Gertrude's trial. Or her high-dollar lawyer. Or the horror that hung over my head with the court case. Maybe I should have just shot her when I had the chance.

My tactic was to change the subject. "What's new in the Koby Shaver murder?"

Coleman got down to business. "Based on the crime scene, we feel the driver of the truck *could* also be the shooter. The angle of the shot would indicate the gun was resting on the window ledge."

"Driving and shooting simultaneously, they had to be pretty darn good." Tinkie ate the last bite of her sweet roll. "There are an awful lot of good shots around these parts. Lots of shotguns, too, what with the hunters and skeet shooters. Frisco Evans has some trophies to prove his shooting skills. And his only alibi is Angela, and she has a reason to want Scott to fail, too."

"DeWayne is talking with those two right now," Coleman said. "This case is going to be solved by motive rather than forensic evidence. Have you turned up anything?"

"Nothing solid." I hated lying about the things I'd found at Gertrude's, but I wasn't sure they were relevant. "Farley is problematic. He's a zealot and filled with righteousness, but he has the best alibi of the lot."

"Tell me about the preacher," Coleman said.

"Farley is running a cult. It's a scary place," Tinkie said. "You might check in on it when you get time. I have a bad feeling that something's wrong there, and I wouldn't be surprised to find domestic abuse. Very patriarchal place."

"I read you loud and clear," Coleman said. "I've heard some complaints in the past, but I could never pin anything on Jebediah. When I went to investigate, not a single member of his congregation would speak out. Farley is pious and filled with God's rules and regulations, except they don't apply to him."

"What do you know?" Tinkie asked. She had caught the scent of good gossip.

"Farley grew up in Greenwood. He was in the police academy with me, but he didn't finish. Dropped out to preach. He said he could make more money working on Sunday than I could working seven days a week. He used to tell me how he could herd people like sheep. He said a slick preacher could part a widow from her pension and make her glad to go hungry."

"What a total creep." Tinkie was indignant.

I held up a hand. "Wait a minute. That doesn't sound like the guy I met." I wasn't defending Farley, but he'd appeared to be a man who turned away from material things. He lived in what I considered poverty conditions. "The compound is bleak. A hobo wouldn't be thrilled to live in that campsite. They don't have running water or electricity. It's pretty basic."

"The question to ask is whether Farley actually lives at the compound." Coleman arched one eyebrow. "Sometimes, Sarah Booth, your naivety is just refreshing."

I punched him in the arm, hard. I'd fallen for Farley's game and I hated it. "Where does he live?"

Coleman's grin was pure devilment. "You'll love this."

"Dammit, tell us." Tinkie was as curious as I was.

"Last spring he was the guest of Jewel Kelner."

Tinkie and I both were gape jawed. Coleman took his finger and lifted my chin. "Don't catch flies, Sarah Booth."

"You are lying." Not in my wildest imagination could I put Reverend Farley and the Delta's most notorious prostitute on the same planet, much less the same room—or even more unbelievable, the same bed.

Tinkie recovered from the shock first. "Coleman Peters, I don't like Farley, but that is slander. You can't say such things about a woman like Jewel. She's a sexual predator. Farley would stick in her craw."

Coleman was out and out laughing at our shock. "You two are a pair. You're old enough to know folks and their sexual proclivities are never predictable."

"Oh, my," Tinkie covered her eyes. "The idea of it has made me ill. Jewel and Farley coupling—unspeakable."

When he tired of mocking us, Coleman had more to tell. "Before Farley took up the Bible, he was well-known around Greenwood as something of a . . . woman pleaser."

Tinkie covered her ears. "Stop now before I sue for punitive damages."

Now I was laughing. The two of them were awful. "Farley was a stud?"

"He was. He had quite the reputation."

"Who knew?" I found the whole thing amazing. Distasteful, but amazing. Farley and Jewel, who ran a brothel just across the Arkansas line, would be like pairing a spider and a shark.

"How do you know all this?" I asked Coleman. The dark suspicion he'd been friendly with Jewel crossed my mind. She was a beautiful woman and her talents were highly touted by the men who'd made her acquaintance.

"I have an in at the church."

"Who?" Tinkie and I asked together.

"DeWayne's cousin, Amanda Tyree, attends services there. Her husband is a true follower of Farley. Amanda is young and foolish and thinks she can change Clemont Tyree. Amanda goes along with the dictates Farley puts out every day, and she's a good source of information while she's there. She's bought into the whole business of the Rapture Farley is selling and until she wakes up, De-Wayne can't influence her. But she still talks to him. Clemont tries to stop her for seeing DeWayne, but Amanda has some will left in her."

"If she were my cousin, I'd drag her out by the hair of her head."

"Folks have to come to life decisions on their own, Sarah Booth. Otherwise I'd be able to make more head-way with you."

"Bada bing!" Tinkie said, high-fiving Coleman.

"You and DeWayne know Farley's nothing more than a poser and a hypocrite. You should get the girl away from him before irreparable damage is done." They could make fun of my hardheadedness if they wished, but the stakes were high for Amanda.

Coleman was finally serious. "DeWayne can't make Amanda see the light. She truly believes Farley speaks to God and that he's the way to the Rapture."

"And he's been in the sack with a madam," Tinkie said. She sighed. "The whole thing is just nuts. But nonetheless, I agree with what Sarah Booth said. The club is the perfect target for Farley's crusade. He whips his followers into a frenzy. One of them could easily have taken matters into his own hands and decided to kill sinners."

Tinkie was dead-on. "Frisco Evans wanted to buy the

club, but killing Koby wouldn't bring him closer to his goal," I said.

"Unless he hopes to cripple Scott's business. How many people want to go to a club where folks get shot?" Coleman said.

"Good point. And the same could be said about Angela Bowers. She just wanted somewhere to ballroom dance. Running off Scott's business could work to her advantage. And it's possible the shooting was a scare tactic gone wrong."

"There's a real problem with this case," Coleman said. "We have plenty of suspects but no real evidence to prove who did it. So far we've run down nine new black extended cab pickups. Every single owner was somewhere other than Zinnia the evening Koby was shot."

"Tinkie and I will call Wilton Frasbaum tomorrow." The day had slipped away and darkness had fallen.

Coleman stood. "Walk me to the car, Sarah Booth."

Tinkie gave me a knowing look as I followed the lean, tall lawman out of the house, more aware than I should have been of the play of muscles beneath his tan patrol shirt. As Aunt Loulane would say, I was wounded but I wasn't dead. When he turned to face me, he wore his stern expression. "What in the hell were you doing riding horses at Gertrude's?"

For a moment I couldn't think of anything to say. Finally, I blurted, "The old bitch tattled on us when she said she wouldn't."

"She may press charges. If she does, that's going to put you on the defensive when you testify at the trial. Alton James will make you out to be a psycho stalker or the equivalent. I would have given you credit for more sense than to poke that snake."

He was right. I couldn't even muster a thin defense. "I was hunting for the black truck."

Coleman sighed. "This is hard for you. Gertrude's running around loose and may have shot Koby and been snooping in front of your property. I understand. But you can't break the law where she's concerned. Not now. You're too important to the case against her."

"I'm sorry." I felt like I was ten.

"Did you find the truck?"

"It could be hidden in the woods, but it wasn't parked at her cottage."

"I'll check the parking lots around the B&B, but don't you go back there, Sarah Booth. I want your word."

"You have it." I had learned my lesson. I'd risked a great deal. "I found a connection between Gertrude and Bijou. And Yancy Bellow paid more for The Gardens than it was appraised for. That's strange, since he's supposed to be such an astute businessman."

"When were you going to share this with me?"

"After I'd checked it more thoroughly, because you'd ask how I got the information and I'd have to tell you."

Coleman's hands gripped my shoulders. For a long moment he studied me, then stepped back when my cell phone rang. He resettled his hat. "Better answer that." With a nod of his head, he got into his patrol car.

I checked the ID. Harold was calling. I answered, and he launched into a frantic story of Roscoe disappearing and how he suspected Bijou was at the bottom of it. I wanted to ask how Bijou had gotten hold of Roscoe, but Harold never paused. At last he took a breath and I jumped in. "Come get me. I'll help you find Roscoe."

"I'm already on the way."

Coleman watched me with the strangest expression.

I felt the need to explain. "Roscoe is missing. Harold's coming to fetch me to help hunt for the dog. Nothing dangerous."

"Good for Harold. He'll keep you busy. I'm sending a couple of Scott's security men over here to watch over the place tonight. I agree with Scott that you should move to Hilltop, but I understand about the horses. We'll work it this way for tonight. Once Harold brings you home, stay inside. Promise me."

I held up my three-finger salute like the good Girl Scout I'd once been. "On my honor, I will stay in the house."

"I'll hold you to it." Coleman drove away before I could even respond. I was left with my witty retort hanging unsaid and my partner hanging out the parlor window spying on us.

8

Harold's emergency call came as no surprise. Roscoe, the demonic little terrier I'd given him, merged the personalities of Richard Pryor and Charles Manson. Short, wiry and with a goatee, Roscoe peed on people's feet. He stole items from neighbors' yards and even their bedrooms. Generally personal items he had no business grabbing. Had Harold wanted to work as a blackmailer, Roscoe was the perfect partner. He zeroed in on a person's secrets and dragged them into the daylight. I adored him, of course.

Knowing that Harold would arrive to serve as my keeper, Tinkie left to check on Oscar. She seldom cooked, because she had staff who loved doing it. While she might not prepare the meals, she made it a point to be at the table to share her day with her husband and to take an interest in what happened with him.

Since I was alone, I anticipated a visit from Jitty. I was positive she'd comment on my lack of action with Coleman. And comment. And comment. I was both disappointed and relieved when she didn't show up. But Sweetie Pie and Pluto filled the gap. The cat rubbed my legs and headbutted my knees, then bit me. Hard. He wasn't shy about making his feelings known. Sweetie, as always, flopped on her side and let out a low moan. She was full of chicken and dumplings and happy after a long run with the horses. Her pleasure with life was audible in her deep sighs.

I hated to do it, but I put my critters in the house—Bijou's place wasn't safe for them. Sweetie voiced no complaint, merely went to a corner and faced away from me. Pluto, though, would have his pound of flesh. He'd been left alone far too much in the past two days, but Bijou hated animals, and Sweetie and Pluto would instantly pick up on it and go into mayhem mode. They were safer at home.

Harold's new matador-red Lexus convertible whipped down the driveway. I waited on the porch. I couldn't take the condemnation in Pluto's glare.

"Let's hit it," I said as Harold pulled to a halt. "So where is Roscoe? You said something about Bijou's." Harold had been circumspect on the phone. "Do you think she abducted him?"

"Not exactly."

"Harold." He was being deliberately evasive.

"It's a long story."

"You'd better tell me or I'm not going anywhere."

"Bijou stopped by the house this morning before I left

for work. Roscoe hates her. While she was in the house, he got in the window of her car and peed all over the driver's seat. She was completely furious and she promised he'd pay."

"She should be careful. Roscoe is no one to mess with." A hundred images flashed in my brain, all of them wonderfully amusing. If Roscoe had it in for Bijou, I wanted to be there to film it. YouTube would never be the same.

"She's a mean woman."

"Did she hurt Roscoe?"

Harold considered his answer as he took a curve really fast. The car handled like a dream. "No, he's fine, but someone shot him with a pellet gun. They hit his rump, and it stung him, but no permanent damage."

Oh, I would be happy to kick her ass. "In all fairness, Roscoe goes a lot of places he shouldn't." The dog seemed able to either teleport or hitchhike. He covered an amazing amount of territory in Sunflower County. He'd be sniffing the mayor's garbage and twenty minutes later stealing jockstraps from the high school football team.

"I found a pellet gun in Bijou's car. I can't prove it, but I can put two and two together. I think she parked down the street and shot him."

"Let's find her and beat her senseless."

"I'm concerned Roscoe has taken it on himself to exact revenge. I've searched everywhere and no one has seen hide nor hair of him for the past six hours. I'm afraid if Bijou trapped him, she'll kill him and pretend to know nothing about it."

I almost told Harold to drive faster so I could whip her butt sooner. "You know she's been running around with Yancy Bellow. And Gertrude had her business card."

"Yancy and Bijou are starting a business. B&Bs to capitalize on the new music emphasis."

I filled him in on the financial statements I'd seen on Gertrude's desk. They were on my phone, but he couldn't look and drive.

"Yancy isn't tight, but he also isn't a fool. He wouldn't overpay for The Gardens out of a generous soul. That's suspicious. You're right about that. I'll examine the documents after we save Roscoe."

I couldn't read Harold's expression in the dark. "Are you interested in Bijou?"

He shook his head. "No. She was fun the first few dates, and don't say it. I knew she was a predator. What I didn't expect was how possessive she became. It was like she owned me. I'm a status symbol. Someone she caught. I don't like that. I know how you women feel when a man is only out to notch his belt."

"Of all the men I know, you're the one who didn't need to learn that lesson."

We were ten minutes from Bijou's estate and the night sky was breathtaking. Stars spread across the wide-open horizon. Night or day, the Delta offered a vista that never grew old.

"I've never understood Bijou," I said. "Money abounds. She's beautiful. Why is she such a witch? And if she would hurt a dog because she's jealous—she has some deep psychological problems."

"You're not telling me anything I don't already know."

"So what's the game plan?"

"We'll pay a call on Bijou and determine if she's captured Roscoe. Which means I'll divert her while you search the premises for my boy. Once Roscoe sniffs your scent, he'll let you know if he's imprisoned there."

Rushing around the LaRoche plantation in the cold and dark wasn't my idea of a great time, but I'd do anything for Harold and Roscoe. "You're going to owe me a fine dinner with a lot of expensive wine," I told him.

"Find my dog and help me drive a stake through Bijou's heart and I'll fly you to Venice for dinner."

Harold would do it too. He was that kind of guy. "Are you telling her I'm with you?"

"Sure. We'll go in and have a drink. Then you step outside to smoke."

"Show time," I said as we pulled up in front of the Taraesque plantation house where the LaRoches had homesteaded since before the Civil War. This operation would take some time because there were stables, barns, and the slave quarters to search. At most plantations, the small houses where slaves had once lived had been destroyed or moved. Bijou had more than a dozen of the shotgun houses intact. Bijou undoubtedly planned to turn those into rental cottages as part of the B&B movement. Dollar signs flipped in my brain. She was a vampire of romance, but she was a smart businesswoman.

Before I could get out of the car, a big man approached my side. "What's your business?" he asked. Harold joined me, standing slightly in front.

"We're here to see Bijou," Harold said. "Have you seen a little—"

I whacked him in the back of the heel. "Tell her Harold Erkwell and his date are here." There was something familiar about the man, but I couldn't see him clearly.

"She didn't say she was expecting company."

"We're surprising her. And who are you?" I asked sweetly, doing my best to use the frisky, interested tone Tinkie managed so well.

"None of your business," he answered.

Obviously I had a lot of work to do on smooth-talking men.

"Come with me." He led us to the front porch where the light illuminated his face. I almost gasped. I did recognize him. From Reverend Farley's camp. He was the man who'd come out of the church and watched us.

"What's your name?" I asked in a less friendly tone.

"Mason Britt, Miss Delaney," he said, pressing the point that he knew me. "I'm Ms. LaRoche's farm foreman."

I was about to ask him if he belonged to Farley's congregation when Bijou opened the door. "Harold!" Then she caught sight of me. "And you."

"We were in the neighborhood and thought we'd stop by for a drink," Harold said.

Oh, right. Awkward, much? I could have brained Harold for not having a better excuse. Bijou loathed me and I couldn't stand her. Stopping by for a social visit was a bit hard to swallow.

"Fascinating," Bijou said. She linked her arm through Harold's and totally ignored me. "I'll mix you a nice bourbon," Bijou said to him. "I'm sorry, Sarah Booth, but I'm all out of drain cleaner."

"Bourbon is fine," I said brightly.

Bijou's home was an interesting blend of the past and the modern. She had a good eye for paintings, even though I hated to admit it. While she pressed Harold into an overstuffed leather sofa, I wandered around the parlor appreciating the artwork she'd accumulated. A vase that looked as if it had been cut from a tree trunk caught my eye. The work of DeWitt Lobrano was distinctive. And highly sought after. Bijou had paid a pretty penny for his pieces.

She had lowered her voice and was murmuring something to Harold, but I ignored them. If she wanted to suck the juices out of him and he was fool enough to sit there and let her, more power to them. Because it was clear Bijou had no intention of preparing drinks, I helped myself to her bar and also took Harold a libation. Just to show a little class, I served her one, too.

He winked at me and put his arm around Bijou. "Isn't she a special creature?" he asked.

"Oh, definitely," I agreed. "You have some nice art, Bijou."

"I can't believe you recognize fine art," she said.

"I like good wine, too. Harold can tell you." It wasn't a great dig, but I had Roscoe on my mind. As soon as I could escape to search for him, I'd do so. I didn't want to arouse Bijou's suspicions and I also had to beware of Mason Britt lurking about in the night.

Harold eased back from her. "Bijou, the strangest thing has happened. Roscoe has disappeared. Now I'll be free to squire you all over the country."

"Really!" She sat up, victory in her eyes. "I know you loved the little guy, but he really did impede your lifestyle."

"He did," Harold agreed, though I watched his grip on his drink glass turn his knuckles white.

It was the past tense of *love* that had gotten to him. If Bijou had harmed Roscoe and Harold discovered it, she would suffer.

"I just can't believe he left by choice." Harold put his drink down and pulled Bijou closer. "I'm so glad I have you to offer solace. I've come to realize, Bijou, my life is empty without you in it. I can live without Roscoe, but I'm not certain I can live without you."

"Though she isn't nearly as cute or smart as the dog," I said under my breath.

I thought Harold might choke, but he regained control and frowned at me. "I need to tell Bijou something private. Would you mind, Sarah Booth?"

"And I need a cigarette," I said. "I'll be back in," I checked my watch, "ten minutes. Whatever it is you need to do, please be finished when I get back."

"Make it twenty minutes," Bijou said. "There's a coat in the closet by the door."

She wanted me out of there badly. Harold had played her like a Stradivarius.

Because I wanted to snoop, I made a production of opening the closet door, getting the coat, and then going back to the parlor. "Maybe I could just smoke in here?" I asked. "It's cold out there."

"Even a country bumpkin knows not to smoke around fine art. These paintings don't need your vile nicotine."

"Okay, I guess it's outside then."

I slammed the door behind me and stepped out of the front porch light. I pulled out a cig and lit up just in case Bijou was watching. After a few minutes, I edged farther and farther into the darkness until I'd cloaked myself in the night. Then I hauled ass to the barn.

"Roscoe!" I whisper-hissed his name. "Roscoe?"

Silence answered me. Bijou wasn't the type to have horses or cows. She had no pets on the property at all. Except for Mason Britt. And he was a serious worry. But finding Roscoe was my only concern.

I worked my way to the slave quarters. Nothing alive answered my calls as I opened doors and whistled for the dog. What I did find in the last cabin, though, was a small office set up. Desks, computers, printers, a copy machine, scanners. It was an impressive operation. A stack of flyers had been left on a desk. I picked one up.

"Satan loves a sinner, and sinners love the blues."

The flyer went on to link blues music with everything from Satan to pedophilia. The most outrageous propaganda. It didn't take a mathematician to add crazy talk with Mason Britt and come up with Jebediah Farley. I just wondered if the sophisticated Bijou knew Mason was using her equipment to spew hatred. Bijou supported the blues club. This was directly against her stated interest. She might not know what her employee was using her copiers, printers, and time to produce.

I grabbed a few of the flyers and folded them into my jeans pocket. These deserved some study. I wanted to read the fine print. Roscoe, though, was my first priority. I headed back into the night.

The last structure was a long low building I would have used for an equipment shed. When I got there I realized that the back of it had once kenneled hunting dogs.

"Roscoe?"

A whine answered me.

"Roscoe, where are you?"

Another whine led me deep into the interior. I couldn't see worth a crap so I brought out my phone and used the light from it to find the little guy. Roscoe was curled, trembling and whining, in a pile of old feed sacks in the far rear of a kennel. My heart pounded with anger. He was hurt, scared, and freezing.

I crawled into the kennel and did a quick examination of his back and legs, holding my phone in my mouth to give me light. There were no open wounds, no gashes, no gunshots, but when I touched his ribs he moaned in pain. I tried to coax him to stand, but he didn't want to move.

I picked him up and tucked him into my coat as I duck-walked out of the kennel. When I could stand up straight, I hurried to the car. "Stay here," I said as I settled him onto the floorboard. I got a quilt out of the trunk and thanked the heavens Harold was prone to impromptu picnics. He keeps quilts, blankets, bug spray—all the necessities of outdoor life in the South—in the trunk of his car.

I covered Roscoe. "Don't make a sound," I told him. "I'll rescue Harold and we'll take you to the vet."

My impulse was to rush into the house and snatch Bijou by the hair of her head, drag her outside, and kick her ass all the way to the wretched kennel she'd stuffed Roscoe into. Then I wanted to shut her in there, lock the door, and leave her to freeze. Wisdom tamped down my fury. Such action would give me emotional gratification, but I'd lose the upper hand.

Instead I rushed into the house and flopped on the sofa where Harold and Bijou cuddled. "I'm sick," I said. "I think Bijou poisoned the alcohol."

"You stupid beast, you poured your own drink. I didn't touch it."

"Oh, no, I'm going to barf." I got on my knees and made gagging noises as I leaned over Bijou's lap.

"Get away from me." She tried to push me aside, but I collapsed on her, wallowing and gagging and moaning.

"Remove her," Bijou said, "and don't ever bring her back."

"I'm so sorry," Harold told her. "I'd better take her home. Why don't you come over to my house in half an hour?"

If she did, Harold would find some inventive way to torture her once he learned what she'd done to Roscoe.

"Okay," she said. "We'll pick up where we left off."

"What about Yancy?" I asked. "Isn't he your lover?"

Bijou was a little taken aback, but she had a ready answer. "I don't owe you an explanation, but Yancy is a business partner."

"Is Gertrude Strom a partner, too?"

"Get out of my house." She'd had enough of me.

Harold helped me to my feet and supported me out the door. I decided to keep the warm coat I'd borrowed. Screw Bijou. It might come in handy at the voodoo shop when I found time to vacation in New Orleans. Didn't they need an article of clothing or some hair to make the curse work properly? If so, I could meet the need.

At the car, I gripped Harold's arm. "Roscoe is hurt. We need to go straight to the emergency clinic."

He tried to turn around and go back in the house, but I stopped him. "Roscoe needs you, Harold. Bijou can wait."

"I intend to hurt her like she's never been hurt."

"And I'll help. Now drive." I snuggled the dog in my arms as we roared down the darkened driveway.

9

The emergency clinic was staffed by a young vet I didn't know but who took Roscoe into an exam room with Harold as soon as we walked in the door. The minutes ticked slowly by. A few whimpers came from behind the closed door and I cringed. Roscoe had to be okay. He couldn't be seriously hurt. Harold would blame himself until the cows came home.

He'd left his jacket and cell phone in the chair beside me, and when his phone rang I remembered that Bijou was supposed to meet him at his house. She would be enraged. Good. I picked up the phone. "Darling, Harold and I are busy. What do you want?" I panted and moaned. "Oh, yes, right there, Harold. That's the spot. Oh, baby, yes, I know I'm the sexiest woman around."

"I'll get you both for this." Bijou hung up.

Whatever Harold had planned for her, my little prank wouldn't mess it up. He'd wait. He understood the old maxim was based on truth: revenge was best served cold. Bijou had a serious comeuppance in her future. And she'd be totally unprepared when it hit.

I pulled out the fliers I'd liberated from the slave cabin. The ugliness and hatred spewed across the page nauseated me. Bijou might not know what her foreman was up to, but I found it hard to believe. Yet, give the devil his due, as Aunt Loulane would say, it didn't make sense, if Bijou wanted to capitalize on the upswing in tourism that a real blues club would bring into Sunflower County, that she was participating in printing handbills that decried the music, saying it "reeked of the devil" and would do all kinds of evil, including bring down democracy and destroy the earth.

At last Harold and Roscoe came out of the exam room. Harold was wrung out, and Roscoe rested, relieved of his pain for the time being. "What?"

"Someone kicked him and broke two of his ribs. He was lucky they didn't puncture a lung."

Beneath the expression of worry and exhaustion, fire crackled in Harold's eyes. There would be blood. "Will he be okay?" I asked.

"Yes. Dr. Knizley wrapped his ribs to give him a little support and protection. I have to keep him quiet and still."

"Good luck with that." Roscoe cannonballed through life like he'd been charged with jet fuel.

"We'll do just fine. He's my boy." Harold stroked his head.

"Let me drive you to Dahlia House. You and Roscoe can stay with me if you'd like. Sweetie Pie will mother him."

"Maybe just for tonight." Harold bumped me with his shoulder. "Thank you for saving him."

"It was your plan. I'm just glad it worked. Oh, and Bijou called. I pretended we were having sex."

Harold's smile was slow, but it arrived nonetheless. "I reserve further comment because I don't want you to know what I have planned. You can cling to your innocence."

"The first time in history. Let's head home."

I drove slowly, glad Roscoe had been sedated and now slept. I still had on Bijou's coat, and I reached into the pocket to search for gloves she might have left. My fingers found a small card. I handed it to Harold. "What does it say?"

He switched on the interior light. "It's a business card from Alton James, the attorney."

"Now that's a damn twist of events." I filled him in on Gertrude and the lawyer, wondering the whole time how Bijou was involved. The heiress seemed to have her finger in everyone's pies. "Do you think she's paying for Gertrude's legal defense?"

"I wouldn't put it past her. Bijou has a streak of perversity. She seems to support Scott and the club, but that could be a façade. A vibrant blues club would help her B&B business, but it would be a lot more lucrative if she owned and controlled the club."

"She told Angela Bowers she'd prefer a ballroom dancing and dinner club. A better class of clientele was how she put it. She is devious."

"Not to worry. I have a few tricks up my sleeve, too."

"How about a burger from the Sweetheart Café?" Millie's was closed, but the drive-through was still open.

"My treat," Harold said. "It isn't dinner in Venice, but it will have to suffice until Roscoe heals."

"You're on."

We ate our burgers and milkshakes, then, stressed to the max, Harold and Roscoe collapsed in the green guest room the minute we got back to Dahlia House. I paced my bedroom. The cruelty of Roscoe's treatment left me fueled with a desire to exact revenge. Now! But there were other demands on my time. Namely, doing more research on Mason Britt.

I doubted that Bijou had used her Manolo Blahnik–clad foot to kick Roscoe, but Mason Britt wouldn't hesitate if the order were given. They both epitomized the word *vile*. What else could I unearth on Bijou's foreman?

I fired my laptop up and was sitting down to work when I heard something moving around the house. Two security men, compliments of Scott's team, were on the premises. I'd seen them step out of the trees lining the driveway when Harold and I pulled up. They were on the grounds, but not in the house. The noise I'd heard came from inside.

I put aside the laptop and roused Sweetie Pie with my bare foot. She lifted her head, eyes bloodshot as if she'd been on a bender, and flopped back down. She snored softly.

"Fine watchdog you are," I told her. I crept to the bedroom door and listened.

The sharp sound of a trumpet combined with a plunking six-string guitar. Jitty was in the house. Judging from the music, she was downstairs. She scared me senseless when she materialized behind me.

"Wanna set the world on fire?" she sang, and continued with talk of mad desire and devils in disguise. And murder.

She was slender and beautiful and her dark hair was cut in a pageboy with bangs that hung straight into her eyebrows. "Who are you?" I loved the song, but I didn't recognize her.

"Josie Miles." She sat on the bed, the slit in her long skirt revealing an elegant leg. "She could belt out a song about revenge."

"I don't want to sing about it. I want to act on it."

Jitty chuckled, a sound so warm and real it was hard to believe it came from a ghost. "Karma works in its own good time, Sarah Booth. Remember that. It isn't your job to hurry it along."

"Not my job, maybe my destiny."

"Girl, your mama is havin' a hissy fit. She wants to come down here and slap a knot on some people right beside you. One thing about Miss Libby and Mr. Franklin, they didn't hold with hurtin' helpless animals, not that Roscoe could be called helpless. That dog is too smart."

Talking about my parents always calmed me down. Jitty knew it and played it to advantage. "Mama would think of something to do. You know she would."

"Yeah, something like a batch of Ex-Lax brownies. I could tell you stories about Libby Delaney. She was an evil genius when it came to payback."

The brilliance of her suggestion struck home. "Perfect!" If Bijou LaRoche wanted to talk shit, she'd have it coming out of both ends.

"Thank you, Jitty."

"I shouldn't encourage you."

"No, I can sleep tonight knowing tomorrow karma will have a little assist."

A slight chill touched my cheek, almost like a kiss, and she was gone. Sweetie rolled to her back with a moan. Tomorrow I would research Mason Britt and Ex-Lax brownies. Now I would sleep. While vengeance belonged to the Lord, payback was headed to Bijou.

Massive cloud formations tinted peach, fuchsia, and gold filled the sky as I drove to the pharmacy at the butt-crack of dawn. I was on a mission. Sweetie rode in the passenger seat beside me wearing her signature sunglasses and scarf to keep the wind out of her ears and her identity hidden.

Watching the sky, I imagined a dragon, an angel with spread wings, and what looked like a panel truck. The clouds shifted and changed forms as wind currents caught them. The clouds were magnificent, but they also brought a warning. Rain would be upon us within the next twenty-four hours. Koby's funeral service was set for the afternoon, and the club reopening for seven.

Scott was an early riser, as I knew well. Since I was running errands, I called to ask if he needed any supplies from the local megastore. It wasn't a place I normally shopped, but it was also the only place open at six thirty in the morning.

Plastic bowls to serve the jambalaya Curtis Hebert was cooking, sporks, paper towels. The list was short but important.

"I worried about you last night, Sarah Booth. The

security team reported to me every few hours, though. I knew you were safe."

"Harold and Roscoe are still asleep in a guest room." I told him the whole sordid tale of Roscoe's abduction and torture. "But don't you worry, karma is headed to Hemlock Manor, which is the nickname I've given Bijou's house. With enough repetition, I can make it stick, too." Cece would help me. In every newspaper article she wrote from now on, Bijou's home would be Hemlock Manor. Oh, the load of caca about to descend on Bijou's styled head was just getting started.

I pulled into the store parking lot, amazed at the people already out shopping on a Wednesday morning. America had become a land of zombie shoppers. They were out all the time, wandering down aisles crowded with bad food products, loading carts, and hauling it all home. And I had become one of them!

I gathered up the items for the club opening and my few purchases and drove home.

Harold greeted me on the porch with a cup of coffee and a very subdued Roscoe.

"He's in some pain," Harold said. He was still in the sad mode. Soon he'd hit revenge and we could partner up to show Bijou a thing or two.

He followed me to the kitchen and didn't ask a single question when I brought out the laxative and dumped it in the brownie mix, along with some chopped walnuts and extra chocolate chips. Bijou would definitely bite into this prank.

"How will you deliver them to her?" Harold asked as he stirred the batter while I greased the baking pan.

"A gift from an anonymous admirer. It's a perfect play to her ego."

"She's going to kill us if she figures it out." Harold was pleased rather than concerned.

"There may be nothing left of her but fancy shoes."

He laughed heartily. "You make me feel so much better, Sarah Booth. You know, we make a great team." He captured my hand and squeezed it.

My thumb gave a tiny throb of pleasure at his compliment. Harold and I had a complex relationship. He supported me no matter what. When Graf or Coleman had tried to control me "for my own good," Harold had helped me. He trusted me to know what was best for me. No other man in my life had ever believed in me as much as Harold did. And he was a damn accomplished man with more polish than anyone else I knew. And sometimes the most questionable taste in women.

"How did you get involved with Bijou? You've both been single for years. Why suddenly date her now?"

"She stalked me at the bank."

I laughed out loud. Harold was blunt—but accurate. "How dangerous do you think she really is?"

He didn't answer quickly. "At first I thought she was merely a huntress. One of those women who love the chase. Once they catch their prey, they kill it and move on. I went into the game understanding that, at the conclusion, she wouldn't care what happened to me, figuratively speaking. I knew there were no real feelings between us, but what I failed to grasp was how she literally did not care if I lived or died. And to hurt Roscoe as some juvenile form of revenge—she is sick."

"She's a classic narcissist."

"To the tenth degree." He pushed the bowl of batter to me so I could pour it in the pan and bake it. "Something is missing from Bijou's personality. Maybe it is narcissism. Or maybe she's a sociopath. What *she* wants is all that matters. Once the want is gone, there's nothing left but a black void."

I brought up the flyers I'd found and showed him. "Sarah Booth, this is vile. And dangerous. And beyond ignorant."

"I know. Would Bijou work against her own self-interest?"

"What we don't know for a fact is what her interest is. She's gadding about with Yancy Bellow now, but is it because they share a business interest in developing B&Bs or because she wants to bed him?" He examined the flyer. "Or some other reason we have yet to uncover."

Harold's blunt assessment wasn't the sentiment of a man who had feelings for a woman. "You don't care a thing about her, do you?"

"I don't even like her. I shouldn't have slept with her, but it was exciting." He shrugged. "One of the few times I let the little head do the thinking and it almost got my dog killed. Lesson learned."

I leaned over and kissed Harold's cheek. "You are a very special man, Harold Erkwell."

"Not as smart as I once thought." His gaze searched mine. "When the dust clears, I do want to take you to Venice for dinner."

"It's a date. As long as you know I'm not able to care about anyone now. Not in the way you deserve."

"Heard and understood. I want you to play. There hasn't been enough of that in your life, Sarah Booth. Play is vastly underrated."

I poured the brownie batter into the glass pan and put

it in the oven. Roscoe gave a low whine so we took the dogs outside while our secret weapon baked. Roscoe was pitiful. He could hardly hike his leg to water my favorite lily. Anger burned fresh in my chest, and when I glanced at Harold, I knew he felt it too.

"Never tell a soul about the brownies, Sarah Booth. Not Tinkie or anyone else. This is between us. Most folks are caught because they blab. Bond of silence." He held out his pinky finger, which I hooked with my own.

"Bond of silence."

When the brownies were baked, I let them cool, slipped on some crime scene gloves to keep from leaving fingerprints, and cut them into squares. I'd purchased a beautiful Victorian painted tin and lacy tissue paper. When Harold and I finished, the brownies resembled a gourmet delight. I printed out a note on card stock: "I've admired you from afar, but I sense the time is right for a closer acquaintance. Enjoy these handmade sweets from Memphis. I'll be in touch." We settled on the initials P.P. It was our little joke for poopy pants.

"Do you think she'll really eat the brownies?" I asked.

"She loves chocolate. And she's greedy. She won't share."

"Karma is sometimes a load in your pants."

We both laughed as I gave Harold the tin. He had a trusted friend who would put the confections in Bijou's mailbox.

Our work complete, Harold went home to dress for work. Roscoe would accompany him to the bank, though I offered to mind the little demon. Harold wanted him close. I sent the files I'd photographed to Harold's phone so he could study them at the bank. Then I called Tinkie and suggested we research the band members and the ex-manager, Wilton Frasbaum. Tinkie took the former band manager while I did background on Jaytee and the gang. Tinkie was simply better with financial matters, so it made sense she'd tackle Wilton from a business angle.

Scott had given me a list of former friends and associates of the band members. At the top of my list to call was Jaytee's brother, Beegee. The family had a real issue with spelling out initials as names. From all accounts, the brothers weren't close. A pissed-off relative could be a great source of information, and I intended to find out if Prince Jaytee had any warts. Protecting Cece was my first concern, but I had to be certain Jaytee didn't figure into what was happening in Scott's life.

A bit of Internet sleuthing turned up a Beegee Johnson in Cleveland, Ohio. He was thirty-nine, a chemist, and Jaytee's brother. He'd been employed by a pharmaceutical company but had no current employer. My call was picked up by an answering service that said Beegee Johnson was out of the country on business. I left a message for him to call me back about his brother.

Next up for excavation was Mason Britt's background. Payback for Roscoe was coming his way as well.

The Internet yielded little of interest, but I had a few sources who could help me out. Millie Roberts would be at the café, and I needed a big stack of french toast to get my brain cells churning. Because the café was gossip central, I could find out a lot about local people from Millie.

Sweetie had gone for a run, and Pluto was sound asleep on my bed. I slipped out and drove to the café. It was after the breakfast rush, so Millie was able to sit and talk after she served my french toast, bacon, and coffee.

I asked about Mason Britt, and she hesitated. "I knew

his sister very well. She worked for me for over five years. Mason, I don't know if anyone knows him now."

"What happened?"

"Beth died of cancer. She was so young and it took her slow and ugly. It was toughest on Mason. He was only seventeen and it broke him. He joined the marines after that and headed to the Middle East. As I recall, he did several tours there and in Afghanistan. It was like he wanted to get killed. Then he disappeared. He's back in the area, but he doesn't come around the café. I don't think he's renewed a single old friendship."

While the story plucked the sympathy strings, I couldn't forgive Mason for his part in hurting Roscoe. "He's foreman for Bijou LaRoche's operation over at Hemlock Manor."

"Hemlock Manor?" Millie cut a sideways glance at me. "You made that up."

I nodded.

"I like it. I'll use it every chance I get. Bijou is a man cannibal. She puts them in her pot and cooks them alive."

Laughter erupted from me, startling the few remaining customers in a corner of the café. Millie grinned. "I knew you'd like that."

"Harold escaped only parboiled."

"That man needs a wife. He's at an age where trouble is about the only thing he's going to find if he keeps poking at fast women."

Millie and Jitty shared a common vein of wisdom when it came to men. Millie loved Harold, but she held his feet to the fire, just as she did mine. "Harold's working through things." I didn't want to go into more detail. "So what else can you tell me about Mason?"

"He played baseball in high school. Must have been the years you were in New York or up at the college. He was a standout. Then after Beth died, he left Sunflower County." Her eyebrows arched. "I did hear mention of him involved in some religious cult."

"Jebediah Farley's church. I saw Mason at what passes for their church grounds."

Millie shook her head. "He was a decent young man. Had a bright future. I don't know Reverend Farley, but I've heard some things I don't like. Abusive toward women is what I'd call it. Females in the church have no say in anything. They bear children, do the work, and don't dare open their mouths. Beth Britt would have spit in Farley's face. It hurts me to think Mason has taken up with someone like him."

Now she was really making it hard for me to think of taking vengeful actions against Mason. But a tragic life didn't give a man the right to harm innocent creatures. Everyone had troubles. Rich and poor, smart and dull. Hard times visited each one. Compassion was the lesson, not cruelty.

"Thanks, Millie. This is a big help." I could try to get his military records, though Coleman would have more success than a PI. "Any clue how he hooked up with Bijou?"

"No," she said. "I do know he's been working for her for a while. Must be doing a good job. Bijou doesn't suffer a fool, except in the sack. She has a lot of business-people coming in and out of town." She signaled one of the waitresses for a coffee refill for both of us. "She has a little airstrip for the crop dusters and the gentlemen who come in on private planes. She's sharp when it comes to business. And treacherous. She'd sell her mama for a profit."

I had to hand it to Millie. She nailed Bijou and then hammered it home.

"What's the story on Yancy Bellow?" Millie knew a little bit about everyone in the county and a lot about some.

"Wealthy and quiet about it. Likes to do cultural things. Never been married, and most of the women he's dated have been in New York. Folks think he's too big for his britches, but he donates to the battered women's center, a healthy chunk of money. And he's done a lot for the youth of the county. Cece may know better than anyone. And speaking of Cece, how is she doing with that hot harmonica player?"

"She's really happy."

"She's a special woman and deserves a good man." Millie rose. "I have to chop onions and peppers for the jambalaya tonight. Curtis is cooking, but I'm helping out a little." She leaned down to kiss my cheek and whispered in my ear. "I expect Elvis to make an appearance tonight."

Millie loved reading the *National Enquirer.* Elvis sightings were mentioned frequently in the tabloid, and Millie believed the King was alive, that he'd simply decided to walk out of the pressures of his life and assume a quiet existence. Sometimes I thought she might be right.

"I hope he does. I'd love to meet him."

"Me, too. Just keep your eyes and heart open, Sarah Booth. Scott Hampton may not be dark-haired like Elvis but when he plays his guitar he makes my gizzard quiver."

I gave Millie a hard hug. "You are incorrigible."

"I'm old enough that I can be whatever I wish. You

watch your back. I don't know what's at stake with all the meanness directed at Scott's club. An innocent man gunned down, it's just more than I can comprehend."

"You and me both," I told her. I grabbed my jacket and purse and set off.

10

Sitting in the Delaney Detective Agency office at Dahlia House, I pored over Internet articles and consumed the facts. Around me the house had settled into quiet. Sweetie was running through the fields and Pluto slept on my computer desk, snoring lightly. I'd thought he'd lost weight, but from this angle, he seemed to have gained heft. A diet might be in his future.

I'd barely thought the word when one green eye opened and zeroed in on me. If Pluto could talk, I was sure he'd say, "Try to put me on a diet and see what happens to you."

Perhaps he was just a large-boned kitty.

My method of digging up information on the band involved newspaper articles and some music magazine stories that detailed the beginning of Bad to the Bone. Because the band wrote a lot of music, magazine writers were always finding threads of the band members' pasts in each song and extrapolating. It wasn't scientific, but it gave me a lot of personal information.

Reading about blues musicians was easy duty. Jaytee Johnson, especially. He grew up in Chicago and started his first band at the age of eight. He taught himself to play the harmonica. A record producer heard him play and Jaytee was given a scholarship to a fancy arts high school where he excelled academically and musically. His family supported him, an unusual situation for most musicians, especially those who claimed the blues as their genre. Jaytee was a golden child. Whatever he turned his hand to, he excelled at.

Where other boys his age were getting jail time, bullet wounds, expulsions from school, Jaytee took home scholarship grades, civic awards, and musical opportunities. It was the story a fairy godmother would concoct to create the perfect musician—talent, motivation, hard work.

I found nothing to indicate Jaytee would betray Scott and the club. Or Cece for that matter. Jaytee was linked with several A-list celebrities as an escort or date or travel companion, but there wasn't a hint of a serious relationship.

The same could not be said for Mike Hawkins, the keyboard player in the band. Mike carried the weight of musical training and production experience for Bad to the Bone. He'd learned to play the piano from an elderly woman at a local church in an Arkansas town of three thousand people. His love of the blues put an end to access to the church's upright when he was fifteen. Devil music couldn't be played on an instrument in the Lord's house and Mike was jettisoned from the church.

Chicago was the happening city for the blues, and Mike moved there on his own. He was only fifteen, his only talent was his ability to play a keyboard. He fell into the drug scene and gang life. Two close calls with death from overdoses finally sent him into rehab, where he met Zeb Kohler, who'd sat in as drummer for a few tour dates with Scott's band. The young musicians determined to clean up their acts and join Bad to the Bone. They'd both achieved their goal. In more than one article, Mike attributed turning his life around to Scott, the band, and his wife, Danni. His loyalty to Scott since appeared unswerving, and Mike had an additional anchor, his wife and their daughter.

Zeb's past was the darkest of all the band members. He'd grown up in the system in Memphis, passed from foster home to foster home. When he hit eighteen, he left for the Chicago music scene. For a kid without connections getting gigs was tough, and he ended up on the street with two choices—sell drugs or sell himself. He chose the former and became valuable in a gang for his intelligence. He put together schemes and plans for raising profits and laundering money that impressed his boss.

By the age of twenty-two, he was driving a Ferrari and living the life of a drug lord. He had everything he wanted. Women, money, cars, clothes—everything except the blues. There was no room in his life for playing music. No legitimate band wanted him. He was too high profile, too dangerous. Drummers without such baggage could be found in abundance.

Scott ended up playing a gig in Chicago and took Zeb on for one show. He liked the kid's style, his ability to give everything he had to the drums. He hired him for two additional shows. It was the lifeline Zeb needed. His love for music was stronger than his love for drugs and violence, and he changed his life. In the end, Scott had given him the job that saved him.

The newest member of the band was Davy Joiner, a kid who laid down a bass line with such confidence he sounded like he'd been playing for fifty years. He was only twenty-one, a graduate of Georgia Tech with a degree in engineering. Job security and a life of comfort were no counterweight to the lure of the blues. He'd walked away from job offers with salaries in the six figures to play in the band.

While a lot of the information I gathered could be put at the door of PR and hype, it gave me an understanding of the band members. Both Mike and Zeb had connections to crime and drugs. The threats against the band could easily come from their past. As much as I hated doing it, Delaney Detective Agency would have to probe those connections. Mike or Zeb could have unwittingly brought the element of violence into Zinnia.

When I was done, I e-mailed the files I'd put together to Tinkie. The phone rang almost instantly. "Frasbaum is such a smug bastard. And he's not in Europe. He's in Chicago. He moved back about two months ago."

"Do tell."

She'd spent over an hour on the phone with the former manager, who accused Scott of stealing and hiding money from the other band members and of sabotaging the Spanish leg of the last tour on which Frasbaum had served as band manager. "He said Scott owed him money."

"Did he have anything to support those charges?"

"Not that he was willing to show me. To be honest,

he sounds more like an extortionist than a murderer. He thinks he can say whatever he wishes, make allegations, and Scott will pay him off to shut him up. Also, Coleman made a few calls for me and it turns out Frasbaum is wanted on domestic abuse charges. He beat up his girlfriend pretty badly before he fled for Europe with the band."

"Did Scott know about the abuse?" I couldn't believe the man I knew would help a felon flee, especially for hurting a woman.

"Of course I can't know for sure, but I'd say no. Piecing the situation together, it looks like Frasbaum had a set-to with his girlfriend about the European tour. He beat her up pretty good, and he was already on the plane and flying to Germany when she went to the police. I don't see how Scott could have known. Frasbaum denied it when I confronted him with the facts. And then he hung up."

"Damn."

"He's really mad at Scott, Sarah Booth. I'd go so far as to say he hates him. He can't stand it that Scott ditched him and then became a success. And he let it slip that he knew about the blues club in Zinnia."

"Great job, Tinkie." I'd just moved Wilton Frasbaum to *numero uno* on my suspect list. Revenge, payback, jealousy, malice—he had a number of key motives to try to hurt Scott and the club. And he had a known record for violent action.

"Coleman is working with the Chicago PD. There's not really much we can do down here." Tinkie sounded glum at our lack of ability to nail Frasbaum. A beep on the phone line let me know she had an incoming call. "Hey, wait a minute. It's Coleman."

I powered down my computer as I waited for Tinkie to come back on the line. When she did, she had big news.

"Chicago PD let Coleman know that Frasbaum has fled. They went to talk to him about the assault charges and he escaped out a back window. There's an APB out for him. Do you think he'll head down here to Zinnia? Maybe he's going to try to intimidate Scott for cash. When I talked to him, he offered to give me some dirt on Scott if I would pay for it, so I'd say he's short on funds and may be looking for an easy mark."

"He doesn't know Scott very well if he thinks that tactic will work." Scott was one of the easiest going people I knew, but he'd never stand still for blackmail.

"We've done what we can for the moment, Sarah Booth. Koby's funeral is in an hour. Shall I pick you up?"

"That would be great. I would have thought he'd have his service in his hometown."

"His girlfriend is here. He's estranged from his family."

Tinkie had done the background work on Koby, which had turned up nothing suspicious. Just sadness. From everything we could find, he'd been an on-again, off-again college student studying anthropology on the GI bill, who happened to make great money as a bartender.

She continued. "After he got out of the marines, he moved around a lot, bartending, working as a bouncer. I think Tatiana is the only person who loved him." Tinkie sniffed. She was too tender for her own good. "I checked with Scott. Koby was cremated, so there's a memorial service. I don't know what they'll do with the ashes."

This was going to be a hard afternoon. "Swing by for me. I'll be ready and waiting." I'd been to far too many funerals in my life, but I had to attend Koby's. For Scott's sake. For the band. And for the case. Sometimes the strangest people showed at a final service.

The small group that gathered at Freeman's Funeral Home chapel consisted of the band members, Mike Hawkin's wife and young daughter, Coleman, DeWayne, Oscar, Harold, Millie, Cece, and Madame Tomeeka.

When Tatiana Scitz entered the room, all small talk ceased. She wore a black leather miniskirt and motor-cycle jacket. Thick black liner rimmed her eyes, complete with flash lashes. Her boots were thigh high. It wasn't tra-ditional funeral attire in Zinnia, but Tatiana wasn't a traditional girl. I put a hand on her shoulder. "Come and sit with me and Tinkie."

The band had chosen an informal service. There was no minister. Scott invited all attendees to take the podium and speak about Koby. "We didn't know him well," Scott said, "but we liked everything we knew. He had big plans for the bar and for making the club a success."

Tatiana spoke first. She blinked back tears as she talked about how she met Koby and how quickly they'd realized they were meant for each other. "I should have come with him when he left Austin," she said. "I stayed behind to pack up our belongings. I shouldn't have waited." She sat down, wiping away tears.

Zeb was about to tell his stories when the back door of the chapel opened. To my shock, Mason Britt entered. He wore camo pants and a black T-shirt. He strode to the podium and faced us. If he was there out of fondness for Koby, it didn't show on his face. He was furious and didn't hide it well.

"I served in Afghanistan with Koby. We were like brothers. He was a good man, deeply religious, a man who'd given his soul to Jesus. Until he fell in with a pack of musicians. Blues musicians. The devil's music took him straight to hell. Now, he'll burn in eternal flames because of you. This is on you." He pointed around the room. "On each and every one of you. Tempters, debauchers, fornicators, whores. A good man is dead because of your treacherous lies."

All the members of the band, Coleman, and DeWayne stood. "Leave now." Coleman was calm but steel threaded his voice. "Mason, this isn't the time or the place."

"What better time and place? Koby is dead because of that juke joint and these people." He stepped down and walked to stand directly in front of Scott. "You're responsible for his death."

"The person responsible is the one who pulled the trigger," Scott said calmly. "You've got a wire loose, buddy. My suggestion is to get some help. I appreciate your service to this country, and I'm sorry you're so afraid you have to believe in a god who punishes people who love music and a good time. But don't bring that crap in here."

Mason drew back a fist, but Coleman caught his arm before he could swing. "Come outside with me," Coleman said softly. I could clearly see his white knuckles. His grip on Mason's wrist had to be punishing.

"You're as bad as the rest of them," Mason said to Coleman. "God is going to punish all of you. There's a price to pay for sin."

"There's a price to pay for shooting someone in cold blood," Scott said. He wasn't about to back down. "Whoever killed Koby snuffed out the life of a good man. I will see that person punished."

Coleman twisted Mason's arm behind his back and

pushed him down the aisle and out of the chapel. For a moment no one knew what to do. Cece had the presence of mind to begin to speak.

"Let me tell you what I know about Koby Shaver." She launched into a funny story about stocking the bar with various tequilas and how Koby knew details and anecdotes about different musicians and what they drank. Slowly the tension faded from the room.

"We have to investigate Farley much more closely," Tinkie whispered to me. "I thought for sure we had Frasbaum in our sights. Now, though, even if Farley didn't pull the trigger, he's mongered fear and hatred."

"And Bijou. We haven't determined what her influence over Mason might be. Everywhere I turn, her name pops up." Thoughts of the female barracuda made me wonder how the brownies had gone down. As if I had a psychic connection, my phone vibrated. Doc Sawyer was calling. "Excuse me," I said, leaving the chapel and going outside where Coleman had Mason pressed against the patrol car and was talking to him. I watched but stayed out of earshot so they couldn't overhear my conversation.

"What's happening, Doc?" The elderly doctor, who looked remarkably like Albert Einstein with his cloud of white hair, had saved my life more than once. He'd been my family doctor until he retired from private practice and took over the emergency room at the local hospital. Now instead of working twelve-hour days, he worked 24/7. He also performed the autopsies for the county.

"Bijou LaRoche is in an exam room. She's asked the nursing staff to call Coleman." Even as I talked to Doc, Coleman dismissed Mason and reached for his cell phone. He nailed me with a glare as he began to talk.

"And?" I wasn't admitting to anything.

"She's claiming you tried to poison her."

"Oh, really?" It was hard not to laugh. "What kind of poison?"

"She says you put something in brownies and then gave them to her as a gift."

"She sounds crazy. Does she have any evidence?"

The long pause indicated Doc had confirmed his worst suspicions about me. "What was in the brownies? She's in bad shape. She can't get more than six inches from a toilet."

"Which might indicate how full of shit she is."

"Sarah Booth!"

"Oh, quit pretending, Doc. She isn't hurt. She's begged for something like this for a long time. And remember, this conversation is protected by doctor-client privilege."

Doc's chuckle told me everything I needed to know. "She's a bitch," he agreed. "This won't kill her, but right now she's having a really bad experience. Re-al-ly bad."

"Boo-hoo."

"Might I ask what brought this on?"

"Roscoe was held prisoner in a filthy cage in her barn. He has two broken ribs where someone kicked him. Bijou meant to have him destroyed. I can't prove it, but I'd stake my life on it."

Doc sighed. "I have to treat her. I took an oath."

"I know," I said. "Just maybe slow down the remedy as much as you can."

"You're a pistol, Sarah Booth. Your mama would approve, and your daddy would keep you out of the hoosegow. You'd be his only client, you know. He wouldn't have time for anyone else."

"I love you, Doc." And I did. He connected me to my childhood with one sentence, bringing my parents back to me even if the visit was brief. "Here comes Coleman, gotta go."

The look on Coleman's face warned me that the phone call he'd received had indeed come from the hospital regarding Bijou's accusation. How she'd known so quickly I was the culprit, I couldn't say. In a way I was glad she knew—as long as she couldn't prove it. Now I wondered what Coleman would do.

"Did you send Bijou a box of brownies?"

"Me?"

"Are you denying it?"

I had to think quick. I didn't mind lying, but I didn't like doing it to those who loved me. I faked a frown, as if I were thinking hard. "Brownies? You know I don't bake."

"She's in the emergency room with intense intestinal distress. She says you're responsible."

I shrugged. "Perhaps it's merely a case of karma. She's a real pain in the ass to a bunch of people. Maybe the karmic boomerang has struck her down."

Coleman put an arm around my shoulders and ushered me back inside the funeral home. "You know if Bijou decides to press charges I'll have to investigate. There'd better not be any evidence tying you to her problems."

"When would I have time to bake brownies?" I asked.

His arm squeezed me tight. "You are a one-woman force of trouble. Trespassing, bad brownies. Just beware. You've been warned," he whispered in my ear, making goose bumps pop up on my neck and arms.

We entered the chapel in the middle of Cece leading the gathering in an a cappella rendition of "Amazing Grace." It was a joy to watch her with Jaytee, who stood slightly behind her, singing along, but proud to let Cece have center stage. So many horrid things had happened in the past few weeks, so much loss, but Cece had found someone to love who seemed to love her back. Her affair with Jaytee was whirlwind and irrational and possibly a danger to her heart, but I couldn't fault her for going for it full bore. She'd spent years changing her gender to become the woman she knew in her heart she was destined to be. She'd accepted that her life choices were difficult for some people to accept. Yet she'd honored her inner truth, courageously changed her body to match her heart, and now she had let Jaytee into her life without reservation. Her passion and trust in the future put me to shame.

The service concluded and Scott led us out into a day where massive thunderclouds loomed in a front on the western horizon. Sometimes the clouds formed and floated over the Delta, but my predicting ability said a storm was settling in for a hard stay.

"Come to the bar for a drink," Scott said. "In honor of Koby."

It was a fitting conclusion for a bartender.

11

My sleep roiled with nightmare images, gunshots, and Gertrude Strom. I awoke in midmorning more exhausted than when I'd gone to bed. Tonight was the reopening of the club, and I had much to do.

Tinkie blasted out of Zinnia at daybreak to chair a national meeting of her Ole Miss sorority in Memphis, but she would be back by midafternoon. A horseback ride was in order if I wanted my brain to function. To that end, I checked in with the two security men and told them my route, saddled Lucifer, and trotted off around the fields with Sweetie Pie at my side. Riding clarified my thoughts and simplified my emotions.

As the sun beat down on my shoulders and Lucifer

surged beneath me, I allowed my thoughts to return to Koby's death. Senseless. I was pissed off and worried for my friends. Now I had to push emotions aside and sort facts, but I took a moment to savor the success of my culinary prank.

Revenge, though sweet, could have a bitter aftertaste. I didn't feel bad about what I'd done to Bijou, but it wasn't an appropriate punishment. She needed to do jail time, suffer public humiliation. For her, I'd vote to bring back the stocks, complete with rotten vegetable pelting. My hard emotions were provoked by the suffering of an innocent animal. Well, not innocent, but one who hadn't deserved such brutal treatment.

At last I was able to push my angry thoughts away and ride. A mass of clouds marched on the western horizon. The fat underbellies hung low, promising a drenching when the storm front finally arrived. I gave Lucifer his head and we settled into a rocking-chair canter. He covered the ground with incredible speed. When we came to a brake and small stream, he sailed over the water without missing a stride. Yes, bad things had happened in my world, but there was also a tremendous joy.

Hunger finally drove me home to discover Tinkie idling her Caddy at the front door. "I got halfway to Memphis and blew off the meeting," she said. "Are you okay, Sarah Booth?"

"I am." We hadn't really had a chance to talk, and there was a lot I had to tell her. "Want to come in for coffee?"

"When I drove in, Gertrude Strom was parked about a hundred yards down the road from your driveway. When she saw me, she took off. There was someone in the car with her."

"Who?"

"I couldn't get a good look. I called Coleman. He's speaking with the security men."

"Let's put the coffee on."

Tinkie checked her watch. "Sure, I have this crazy urge to go home. It's like we've been trapped in a bog of people being hurt for a year, but it's only been four days. It makes me want to hide in my house and hunker down." She turned off the car and picked up Chablis.

"I know." We entered the house to the joy of Sweetie Pie greeting Chablis and the disdain of Pluto, who sat on the stairs and licked a front paw.

Instead of the kitchen, we aimed for the office. "I have a confession." I told her about the adventure Harold and I had at Hemlock Manor, and about Roscoe. I kept the brownie part to myself. I didn't want to implicate her in Brownie Blowout, but I wanted her to understand the situation had been successfully resolved.

She grabbed up her car keys. "I'm going over to Bijou's right now." Her cheeks were hot pink—never a good sign. "She will not hurt Roscoe without consequence."

I took the keys away and gripped her hands. "It's been handled. I promise. And there will be more retribution in the future, but you can't get involved in it."

She cocked an eyebrow. "What did you do?"

"If I tell you, it may come back to haunt both of us."

"I gather you wish to withhold the details. Which means it must be something illegal." She bit her bottom lip in concentration. When it popped out of her mouth, I couldn't help but think of the effect that simple maneuver had on men. Tinkie could bring Samson to his knees and never have to touch his hair.

"I promise, I'll tell you later. I don't want to taint you

with knowledge, in case there are legal repercussions. If I get in trouble, you have to be free to help Scott."

"This sounds delicious!"

"In a manner of speaking," I said.

"Curiosity is killing me."

"I'll give you a hint." If she didn't get the info from me, she could draw her own conclusions. "Talk to Doc Sawyer. You'll put it together and I won't have to tell you anything."

"I'll do that. Now let's figure out what's going on with Koby's awful death."

For the next twenty minutes we laid out the pieces of the case, trying to fit the facts into a coherent pattern. Mason Britt's audacious appearance at the funeral home colored our perception of the facts. Mason was a zealot in a church that hated the blues. Koby, though, was a bartender, not a musician. And Koby and Mason were friends. Or had been close. They'd survived a terrible war, a bond sometimes closer than blood.

"Mason Britt may hate the blues and think Satan has us by the shirttails, but would he really gun down his combat buddy?" Tinkie asked. "I can't buy that. He'd be more likely to kill Scott or a band member, someone he felt dragged Koby into sin."

"I agree. Maybe the shooter wasn't Mason but someone else in the church. Or, it's possible the shooter, if it was Mason, didn't see Koby clearly and thought he was a musician. I still think Frasbaum looks like the best choice. Or maybe Frisco Evans."

"Good points. Coleman will have to investigate Frasbaum. The Chicago PD won't work with us. And I have to say, if Frisco and Angela were doing it in the bushes, I think they should both be put in jail for bad taste." She shuddered. "How could that be fun? It's cold, and there are bugs."

"You are not a nature girl, Tinkie." My partner was more the five-star-hotel type. "If we could get someone from Farley's church to talk to us . . ." I was thinking out loud. "Maybe one of the women."

"They never let the women off the compound, Sarah Booth. Coleman should handle Farley."

Tinkie wasn't afraid, but she recognized we'd have little influence on Farley and his group. Our gender rendered us ineffective there.

"What troubles me are the warning calls. Those seemed designed to scare Scott away from Sunflower County, to force him *not* to open the club. Mason works for a woman who plans on using a resurgence of interest in the blues to further her business holdings. Whether she knows it or not, her office equipment is being used to stir up hard feelings toward Scott and the club. And Bijou told Angela she'd prefer a different kind of club. Let me add that I don't think a single thing happens at Hemlock Manor that Bijou isn't aware of. She's playing both ends of this dance club thing. Maybe that's smart business, but it sure looks like she's manipulating the situation to get the outcome she wants."

"Her motives and actions are at odds," Tinkie said, summing it up neatly. "You're right."

"So where does that leave us?"

"Worried about tonight." Tinkie yawned. Though she was perfectly turned out, it was evident she hadn't slept well either. "If someone is truly opposed to Scott opening his club, he'll do something awful to destroy the big show. A terrible feeling is churning in my gut."

Tinkie wasn't prone to premonitions or even bad attitudes. "Have you talked to Madame Tomeeka lately?"

Tammy Odom, also known as Madame Tomeeka, was a former classmate and Zinnia's full-time psychic. While some might scoff at Madame Tommeka's dreams, visions, and ability to see the past and future as well as communicate with the departed, I knew her gift was real. Sometimes she was able to warn us when danger stalked. She'd saved my bacon more than once.

"I haven't had a chance. She went to Memphis to visit little Dahlia and just got back. I barely had time to say hi at the funeral."

"Let's give her a call."

I had Tammy on speed dial. When she answered, she said, "What worry brings you to my door, Sarah Booth?"

"How did you know it was me?" I fed her the joke line.

"I *am* psychic, but it was caller ID," she said, but she didn't laugh. "You and Tinkie have been on my mind for the past four days."

I didn't care for what that implied. "Can you come over? Tinkie is here and we're working on a new case."

"I'll be there as soon as I can."

I had concerns that Tammy might be able to sense Jitty in the house. Tammy was sensitive and sometimes Jitty liked to tease my guests, fluttering a curtain or rattling a pan. Jitty always claimed it was a breeze, but I suspected otherwise. Now I had to have a word with my haint. If she showed up singing the blues, Tammy would surely sense her. Best to nip this problem in the bud.

"I'll put on some coffee. Back in a minute," I told Tinkie.

"I'm creating a flow chart of our suspects. So far, we don't have a damn thing."

"I know." I left her to it and hurried to the kitchen.

"Jitty! Jitty!" Calling my ghost was about like spitting into the wind. She arrived when she wanted, and she left when she felt like it.

The irresistible sound of a plunky guitar filled the kitchen. Jitty, carrying a bit more weight than normal and wearing trousers and a man's shirt, sashayed into the room. "You a hound dog." She sang the blues number Elvis Presley had sent to the top of the rock 'n' roll charts. "You gotta quit that snoopin'," she said.

She was dazzling and sassy and I instantly recognized her—Willie Mae "Big Mama" Thornton. I couldn't resist tapping my toes and I wanted to shake my hips. Big Mama inspired my body to dance. But I knew the dark side to Big Mama's spectacular talent. She was often overshadowed by other singers performing the songs she wrote. I couldn't help but wonder if this was another way Jitty was trying to warn me.

"Madame Tomeeka is on the way over," I said. "Don't mess around, okay? You know she can sense you're here."

"Maybe we could collaborate and start a 1–900 hotline to the spirit world." Jitty was full of herself.

"I'd appreciate it if you cooled your jets. She's here to help with the case."

"I wish I could sing at Playin' the Bones."

It was the first time Jitty had ever expressed a wish to participate in an activity of the living. It pierced me. She came and went between my world and the Great Beyond, but she could never fully be in the here and now.

"I wish you could sing at the club, too. You'd be excellent. Scott and the band would love you."

She smiled. "I would be good, wouldn't I?"

"You would indeed."

"Sometimes bein' dead is a real pain." She tucked in

the tail of her shirt, which had slipped out when she danced. "Don't worry. I'll steer clear of Tammy Odom. She's more aware than the average human, and I don't want to scratch her suspicions. Though I could have a little fun with her." The twinkle in her eye was dangerous.

"Thanks."

"Have fun at the club tonight. And Sarah Booth, be careful. There's mischief afoot."

I knew better than to ask her what was happening or who was behind it. The Great Beyond had a whole lot of rules, and a big one was not tipping off mortals. We were supposed to find our own way without guidance from a ghost. Jitty did everything she could to help me, but there were limits. And I didn't press her. Over the past year I'd grown to rely on her. If she got recalled from Dahlia House, I would be all alone.

"Sarah Booth!" Tinkie's voice echoed in the house. "Where's the coffee? Tammy is here!"

"Coming." The kitchen was empty. Jitty had departed. I put three mugs of hot coffee on a tray with sugar and cream and headed back to the offices of Delaney Detective Agency.

Madame Tomeeka and Tinkie commandeered the rolling office chairs, so I perched on the edge of a desk. "How's the bundle of joy?" I asked Tammy. Babies weren't really my thing, but this baby had won my heart when she was born.

Tammy, who was close to my age, wore the serenity of grandmotherhood. Her face held an inner glow when she spoke of her daughter and grandchild. "Growing too fast, Sarah Booth. She's a beautiful baby. One day she's going to be someone great."

I didn't doubt it for an instant.

We shared a few more pleasantries before Tammy broached the subject I knew she'd come to talk about. Something was off-kilter.

"I'm worried about you two," she said, putting her empty mug on the desk. She folded her hands in her lap, and I couldn't help but admire the long, elegant fingers and the calluses. Tammy's life had been hard. We'd both been marked by early tragedy, but I'd had the cushion of family money. She'd had determination and her ability to see things others didn't. For a long time she'd worked as a maid as she built up her clientele. Now she read tarot cards, listened to her intuition when people asked questions, and interpreted her dreams and the dreams of others. In the past she'd been a big help on several cases.

"Do you have something to tell us?" Tinkie asked. She was more direct when dealing with the unknown. I hadn't realized how much I dreaded what Tammy might say until Tinkie popped the question.

"There'll be trouble at the club." Tammy wasn't happy with her job as bearer of bad news, either. "I'm sorry. I hate having a dream like this, but it's been the same dream for the past three nights. I had no choice but to tell you."

"It isn't your fault, Tammy. Just give us the details." Tinkie would yank out a troublesome tooth. She faced things head-on. I preferred to hide under the bed and hope things got better. Now I had to push back my fear and listen to my friend. Tammy's dreams occasionally offered a solution, if I could only open myself to different options.

Tammy's left hand tapped nervously on her thigh. "Last night I dreamed about the club opening. It was raining outside, and the neon lights reflected in puddles in the parking lot. Music swelled out into the darkness, along with laughter. Folks were having a good time. I was eager to get inside and party with y'all, but as I opened the door, I smelled something."

I could only hope it involved the spicy jambalaya Curtis was cooking. "What?"

"I smelled Death."

"Oh, no." Death had stalked me since I was a child. Tonight all of my closest friends would be gathered in Playin' the Bones, and if Tammy's dream was precognitive, this wasn't good. "Are you sure?"

"I am. I don't often get an olfactory warning that Death is riding his black horse into town, but it was strong this time. Blood and fear mingled together in this sharp, coppery odor." She inhaled and let it out. "I don't like saying this, but something bad is coming down at that club tonight."

"Tell us the dream," Tinkie said. "If we're prepared, maybe we can stop it."

Tammy focused inward, remembering. "Keep in mind I see what *can* happen in my dreams. It doesn't mean it has to happen. External factors change things. Maybe this can be prevented. I don't know. Nothing is carved into the book of life until it happens. Even Death changes directions sometimes."

I felt slightly better. "Tammy, no one blames you for what you see," I said. "We appreciate your talents and your willingness to share. This may help us save a life."

She nodded. "In the dream, I walked into the club and it was like a tide of good sound, delicious smells, laughter, and joy. Folks were having a fine time. The dance floor was crowded, the music was hot." She paused to gather herself. "Then a black shadow passed over the club. It doesn't make any sense, because I was inside and couldn't see outside, but I felt it. I knew right then Death had brushed my soul. All the bright colors were drained from the room, and faces went from joy to horror, like they were all witnessing a terrible event. The smell changed. Rot was close by."

I didn't want to hear this. My first impulse was to excuse myself to brew more coffee, but Tinkie's face told me to sit my butt still and not break Tammy's concentration. "Maybe it was Koby's murder you're sensing. A death already past."

"Maybe," Tammy said, but I knew from her expression she didn't believe my interpretation.

"Go on," Tinkie urged her. "Tell us the rest."

"The shadow passed over the club and everyone looked up. A gunshot came close and very loud, then a scream, a woman I think. When I turned to the stage, all the band members wore blank masks and stood together, but one was missing. There was an empty spot."

"Which man?" It couldn't be Scott.

"I don't know, Sarah Booth. They were lined up on the stage—all alike, but I couldn't say who wasn't there. When I walked up to the stage, blood pooled in a big circle. Outside the club, an eagle shrieked, and a small creature squealed in fright. Another loud scream came from inside the club, then silence, and I woke up."

"What a terrible dream," Tinkie said. She stood and went to Tammy, pulling her into a hug. "I'm so sorry you had to relive it, but thank you for telling us. Are you okay?"

Leave it to Tinkie to do the kind, compassionate thing. I was so busy worrying about Scott and the band, I hadn't considered what a toll this would take on Tammy. I picked up her cold hands and chafed them to bring back the circulation. "Ditto what Tinkie said, and thank you for warning us."

"I don't always know what the dreams mean, and this one is confusing. There's danger at the club, but also danger outside the club."

"We'll be very careful," Tinkie promised. "And we'll warn everyone else. Nightshade Security has roadblocks set up at the front entrance and another team at the farm road near the back. I don't think anyone will be able to get close to the club with a gun. They're checking every person and car that tries to enter. Anyone with weapons or a crappy attitude will be sent packing."

Tammy didn't seem comforted. "Mean folks can always find a way. Coleman's hands are tied. He can't stop folks from carrying guns. Or from using them."

"No, but Scott can stop them from coming onto the club property. You'd think people would have enough sense not to bring loaded weapons to a place that serves liquor, but folks don't think. They assume everyone will behave. They don't consider individuals with anger issues or a hothead who's just looking for an excuse to light his fuse." Tinkie was getting agitated herself.

"Now hush that fretting," Tammy said. "We're putting on a brave face and hanging hard to the belief that this will be a stellar event." Tammy couldn't hide her worry, though she was doing her all to be supportive.

I considered calling Scott and urging him not to open, but the threat wouldn't go away. Not next week or next month. If a person was determined to prevent the club from opening, he could wait us out. Scott would lose his investment if the doors didn't open soon.

"Let's put away the doom talk. We're all aware now.

We'll be on the lookout. What are you wearing?" Tammy asked me. "Something sexy, I hope. Now that you're a free filly, you have to get out there and shake your moneymaker."

I pretended insult. "Moneymaker?"

"Don't play coy," Tinkie threw in. "You know you've got a handful of men waiting for a chance to make change."

Tammy yelped with delight, and I took an outraged tone. "As if I'd sell myself to a man just for security."

"I would!" Tammy threw both hands in the air.

"Sarah Booth would, too," Tinkie said. "It's just got to be the right man. But as my mama used to say—and I'm sure Aunt Loulane would agree—you can love a rich man just as easily as a poor man."

I'd heard such wisdom from Aunt Loulane more than once. "I'm not in the market to be loving any man," I said, arms akimbo. "I was bitten by the python of love and I'm not going back to play with more snakes."

"Oh, my lord," Tinkie gasped. "Python of love? Where did that come from?"

"I think I'm off sex for the rest of my life." Tammy pretended to swoon.

"Just remember, when you start to tease me, I have the power to destroy your love life with a simple turn of phrase." I leaned toward them. "One-eyed wonder muscle!"

"I submit." Tammy rose and put her arm around my shoulders. "No more love advice from me. Just promise me, you'll stay inside the club tonight. No going outside to smoke cigarettes."

I wasn't aware Tammy knew I smoked, but why should

I be surprised? Everyone in Zinnia knew everyone else's vices. "I'll stay inside. You have my word."

"You, too." Tammy drilled Tinkie with a glare. "We'll stick together and enjoy the music and hope my dream was anxiety tapping at my subconscious."

I nodded, but the chances of Tammy having a mere anxiety attack were slim. Her dreams were precognitive.

With grit I could only admire, Tammy turned the conversation. Her tone was girlish and excited. "I'm wearing this wonderful blouse I got in Memphis while I was visiting little Dahlia. It's red-and-black striped and sparkly. And I'm bringing a date, so you two don't embarrass me."

"Who?" Tinkie asked. She looked at me and I shrugged. I wasn't aware Tammy was dating. She meddled in my love life, like all the rest of my friends, but she'd never hinted she was interested in a particular man.

"Parker French."

"*The* Parker French?" Tinkie and I said in unison.

"None other." Tammy tried hard not to preen, but she was totally unsuccessful.

I swept a bow to her. "My, oh, my!" Parker French was a highly regarded music critic for *Rolling Stone*. "How the heck did you arrange to get Mr. French down here?"

Tammy posed with a coy look over her shoulder. "I just batted my eyelashes and—"

"Give it a rest," Tinkie said. "Tell us the truth."

"Parker is a friend of the Mount Sinai Methodist minister. I was telling Reverend John Hillet about the troubles Scott was having at the club, so John called Parker and asked him to come. They went to seminary together. Parker studied to be a minister until he realized writing about music was his calling. Anyway, I said I'd be Parker's chauffeur. I brought him back from the Memphis airport on my way home."

"And you've kept it a secret all this time!" Tinkie shook a finger at Tammy. "You are a sly one, aren't you?"

"This is amazing." Scott would be over the moon when he heard. A big-city music critic coming to Podunk, Mississippi, was big news for Cece too. I had to let her know ASAP.

"I left a message for Cece." Tammy gave me a crooked grin, letting me know she could read my mind as well as predict my future. "We're arriving at the club a little early so Cece can talk to Parker. And Reverend Hillet has asked the entire congregation of the church to come, too. We're showing strong support for Scott. The blues have nothing to do with Satan, and we're sick of hearing it."

"You are an amazing friend, Tammy." I kissed her cheek. "Amazing!"

"This club is important to me and my friends. We don't practice voodoo or worship Satan and the blues are no more sexual or suggestive than country or rock and roll. I'm a little tired of hearing cheap talk from ignorant mouths."

"What have you heard about the club and the devil?"

"Whoever is working against Scott is organized and has financial backing. There were flyers all over downtown Zinnia. Millie and her waitresses were hustling up and down the street, pulling them down. She said she got every one she saw, but who knows where they were distributed."

So Mason had actually put up his hateful flyers. No wonder Tammy was having bad dreams about the club. Who would have thought we'd end up waging a PR campaign about a form of music born in the cotton fields right outside my door. The blues were part of the Delta. A few legends about Robert Johnson trading his soul to the devil at the crossroads and people went nuts. I had a deep and ugly suspicion this attack on the blues had a lot more to do with race than any devil's bargain.

"This makes me mad as a hornet," Tinkie said. "There's nothing satanic about this music. The blues grew from the old field hollers where one person or group sang a line and another group answered. The blues are about drinking and loving and dancing and temptation and revenge and jealousy and joy and every other human emotion—just like any other music."

"My church group is already handing out *our* flyers," Tammy said. "We'll have a good turnout. I promise. We won't let Scott down. We have to get dressed to the nines and put on the dog. That's what we can do. We can be there and take photos and put it all up on social media. We'll make this opening the biggest thing to ever hit Sunflower County."

Tammy was right. "I've got to pull together a hot outfit." Tammy had her clothes planned and Tinkie never looked less than perfect. I had work to do. "I can't be the ugly duckling while all of you are strutting your stuff."

"That's the ticket," Tammy said. "See you both tonight!"

For three hours, Tinkie and I labored over the suspect list. No matter how we approached it, we simply didn't have the evidence necessary for an arrest. We ate lunch and worked until the clock struck four.

Coleman's call gave us a chance to take a break. "I

talked with Gertrude, who claims she was alone and had stopped on the road to let a bee out of her car."

"A bee?"

"She's up to something, Sarah Booth. Watch out. I can't arrest her, and we have security men at Dahlia House, but you're going to have to be vigilant. I'm worried."

"I'll use extra precautions," I promised. "See you to-night."

Tinkie stretched and yawned. "I'm going home and taking a nap. I don't know if our brains aren't working or if we're simply exhausted. But it's pointless to go through the facts again."

I wanted to disagree, but I couldn't. Tomorrow, after the club opening, we'd take another run at Foundation Rock. Our plan was to slip in and try to speak with one of the females. It wasn't a brilliant strategy, but at least we had a plan of action.

As Tinkie drove away, Chablis's little red bow bobbed in the breeze from the open window. Pluto at last rubbed my legs. I was forgiven. Together the cat, Sweetie Pie, and I tumbled into bed for a snooze.

12

Based on the enthusiasm of the crowd and the fact that Scott had to open the doors and let the music pour out into the parking lot where the overflow crowd tailgated and camped in lawn chairs brought from home, I judged the club a smashing success. Curtis Hebert's jambalaya ran out by nine o'clock—just as the band cranked up to full-tilt boogie. I'd never seen a bigger collection of sparkle, dazzle, and dance moves. While the dress was casual, it didn't prevent the women from wearing a fancy blouse over jeans and styling shoes. A few men even wore suits. And everyone danced!

Cece sang a few numbers, wowing everyone in the audience. She was the belle of the ball, and enjoyed every moment. Yancy Bellow was in the front row with another bit of arm candy, an elegant blonde who spoke with a Dutch accent. The surprising thing about her was not her looks but her encyclopedic knowledge of the blues. I wondered if Yancy's interest in the music came first or if Chantal Noordeloos inspired his willingness to invest in Playin' the Bones. She was certainly beautiful and interesting to talk to. And Yancy had the money to indulge her passions. I hoped Scott wouldn't have to take an investor, but the fact Yancy and Chantal were there boded well if that turned out to be the case.

At ten o'clock, Scott took the microphone and settled the crowd. "While this is a celebration tonight, Koby Shaver is very much on our minds here at Playin' the Bones. Koby had only been a part of the club for a short time, but we'd all grown to care about him. His death is a loss—a cruel and unnecessary loss."

I watched the crowd, searching for a wrong expression. The people in the club had been vetted by the security team out front and I knew many of them. No one showed a suspicious reaction to Scott's words. My gaze strayed to Tatiana, who wiped at her cheeks with a bar napkin. For a gal who looked so tough, she teared up easily.

Scott scanned the room as if seeking someone. "Now I want to acknowledge a local man who has made an extraordinary donation. Mr. Bellow, would you stand?"

Yancy tried to deflect the attention, but Scott waited him out. The businessman finally stood.

"Mr. Bellow has given ten thousand dollars as a reward for information leading to the arrest of the person who shot Koby."

The crowd rose to its feet, clapping and whistling. Yancy blushed, waved at everyone, and quickly sat down. Chantal leaned over and kissed his cheek.

"Would you care to say anything, Mr. Bellow?" Scott asked.

Yancy stood and cleared his throat. "I hope this reward money will bring forth new leads," he said. "There are many rumors about why Mr. Shavers was killed. Only the person who pulled the trigger can know for certain why such an act was committed. Our heritage is under attack. If I can contribute to justice in some small way, I'm happy to do so."

He sat down and Scott took pity on his discomfort and pulled the crowd's attention back to the stage. "Now, I want you to dance and enjoy the evening, but don't forget Koby and the injustice done to him and those who loved him."

The band picked up an old tune, and the party atmosphere returned.

After five dances in a row, I went to the bar to get another Jack and water and evaluate how Tatiana was holding up. If necessary, I could take her place. She looked like she'd be more at home in a grunge bar than a juke, but she knew her stuff when it came to mixing drinks. She was a virtuoso, pouring several liquors at once, plopping lime wedges and lemon slices as garnishes, chatting up the patrons.

When she saw me approaching, she took a deep breath, as if she'd been working hard to hide her sadness and could now relax. "Sarah Booth, it's been a day, hasn't it?"

"Indeed. Do you need a break? I can take over. I'm not as quick or flashy as you are, but I can mix a drink."

"Working keeps my mind occupied. Part of me wants to crawl to Koby's house and hide, but I'm doing this for him. He would've wanted me to help open the club." She nodded toward the packed room. "I think Scott has a hit on his hands. I thought the murder would scare off the customers."

"Everything is moving like clockwork. Even the rain has held off."

"The band is hot. I see why Koby moved down here. It's like a family. The sad truth is, most of us are have no strong ties to blood relatives."

"Do you think you'll stay?"

"I don't know. For a while, at least. Zinnia is such a small town and I stand out like a sore thumb. I went to buy groceries and the Piggly Wiggly manager followed me around like he thought I'd steal his beans."

She almost made me laugh. "Folks will adjust to you. It is a small town with a measure of narrow thinking. Once folks know you, they'll stop judging you based on appearances."

"Except I work at the club where the band has a contract with Satan. The checkout clerk at the grocery was almost afraid of me. She said my mortal soul was in danger. People don't like the idea of this club. She had a flyer saying we worshipped the devil and had orgies and wanted to blend the races into one."

Mason Britt and his damn flyers. "I wouldn't say a lot of people feel that way, Tatiana. Superstition and ignorance are everywhere, not just here in the Delta. Once folks adjust to a successful blues club, the stupidity will die down. I love Zinnia, but anything new is always suspect. This whole blues-equals-contract-with-Satan campaign isn't really about the music."

"Yeah?" She leaned her arms on the bar and stretched her back. "What's it about?"

"History that's been twisted. And prejudice. Against blacks and women."

"Good to know." She stood up. "I guess my appearance fits right in with the Satan worship idea."

I couldn't deny it, but I also wouldn't say it. Once folks met and talked to Tatiana, they'd learn she was a girl grieving the death of her boyfriend. The tattoos, leather, and piercings didn't define her. Like everyone else, only her conduct mattered.

Yancy stepped up to the bar and ordered an old-fashioned. "Sarah Booth, it appears Mr. Hampton has opened with great success. Even the weather has cooperated. The torrential downpours predicted haven't materialized. Scott must walk under the auspices of a protective star."

"He's a good man. Sometimes good things happen to good people."

"Well said. I was afraid the death of his bartender might negatively impact attendance. The power of a great band overcomes the biggest obstacles." He held up his drink. "To the blues."

We tipped glasses and drank.

"To a very generous action." We clinked and drank again. To be honest, the way Yancy stared at me gave me a little gut twist. He had the reputation of a man who loved women, and he looked at me like I was a juicy little hunk of sausage. "Where's Bijou?" I couldn't help myself. I really couldn't.

"She had health issues." One side of his mouth twitched in what could have been a hastily controlled smile.

"Too bad. You two make a handsome couple."

"Bijou is a lovely little cannibal."

At first I didn't believe I'd heard him. Then I almost choked on my drink. He gallantly slapped my back until I caught my breath. "There, there, Sarah Booth," he said,

"I'm not in Sunflower County a great amount of time, but Bijou's reputation precedes her." He laughed at me and leaned closer. "As does yours. What did you put in those brownies?"

"I don't know what you're referring to." I got the denial out with as much conviction as I could muster around the impulse to laugh. Yancy had pegged me, and nothing I could say would change his mind.

"Very well." He signaled Tatiana for more drinks. "Are there any new developments in the search for Mr. Shaver's killer?"

"No." I hated to admit it, but there was no point lying, especially not to a man who'd just donated so generously. "I hope the reward money helps."

"Me, too. Sarah Booth, I was very sorry to hear about your troubles with Gertrude Strom. It was terrible what she did. I realize by buying her B&B I complicated things for you and I'm sorry."

"Gertrude is unbalanced and dangerous." And out on bail, I could have added but didn't.

"Your mother tried to be good to her. She helped Gertrude through a time of personal turmoil and even spoke with me about hiring Gertrude for clerical work. At the time, I had closed my office in Sunflower County. I can't remember the details of Gertrude's distress. Something like an unwanted pregnancy, as I recall. Strange Gertrude would focus all of her ire on you. It appears she's brought out the big guns for her legal defense."

He knew an awful lot about my family background. And about Gertrude's motivation and her legal maneuvers. Someone had been talking about Gertrude's private business, but I knew my mother had never betrayed a confidence. I sipped my drink. "You're well informed."

"I was at The Gardens for dinner tonight. I'd made plans to meet Bijou, but she wasn't inclined to venture out in public. I ended up dining with Alton James. I met him last year at a cocktail party in New York, so it was natural for me to ask why he was in Zinnia."

"I heard he was representing Gertrude. He's a very expensive lawyer."

He put his glass on the bar. "Yes, he is. He's also a legal shark. I'm afraid I played a role in bringing him here."

I couldn't hide my shock and anger. "You gave Gertrude money for a top defense lawyer? Why?"

"It wasn't what I intended. Gertrude contacted me and offered to sell the B&B. You know my interest in building tourism. I agreed to buy it on the spot. The property has tremendous potential, and I overpaid. I acted quickly, without thinking of the repercussions, because I wanted to close the deal before other investors heard the place was going on the market. I wanted you to hear this from me before my name got all tied up in Gertrude's legal mess."

My anger simmered, but not at Yancy. At least he'd had the *huevos* to tell me to my face. "Thanks for telling me."

"This is a small community. My dinner with Mr. James will be all over town by tomorrow. I wanted to get ahead of the gossip. Sarah Booth, I had great affection for your mother. She was remarkable. There were those who felt she was too outspoken, too much a champion for justice, but I admired her courage."

"She was passionate about her beliefs."

"And you are cut from the same cloth."

"That's a compliment I'm not sure I deserve."

"Let's put this unpleasantness aside. Would you care to—"

Coleman appeared at my elbow, putting a hand on my shoulder. "May I have this dance?" he asked.

"Sheriff, enjoy your dance." Yancy picked up his drink. "I need to speak with Ms. Falcon about an article on the rise of five-star B&Bs in the Delta. We need to generate a buzz."

I smiled my appreciation for his classy conduct. "Thank you for the reward money, Yancy."

He eased through the crowd, greeting people as he passed. While he appeared to be shy, he had a bit of the country politician in him as well. "He's an interesting man," I said. "He wanted to tell me about buying The Gardens and how Gertrude managed to make bail. I think he felt guilty, but he shouldn't. He was merely conducting business."

"No shop talk for four minutes while we dance," Coleman said. "You know this is a rare occasion for me. I'm not all that comfortable on the dance floor."

I would have goose-stepped to a wind-up monkey slamming cymbals for a chance to dance with Coleman. All the years I'd known him, he'd avoided the dance floor like the plague. I linked my arm through his and led the way to the center of the floor.

I put my hand in his and we faced each other. The first notes of Percy Sledge's classic, "When a Man Loves a Woman" slid down my body like an intimate touch.

Scott's voice, crisp and clear and sexy, did justice to the lyrics of the love ballad. While the song wallowed in sexual overtones, it was also filled with sadness. It epitomized yearning, an emotion I had extensive personal experience with. It was also a song I'd cherished for years. My parents often danced to it, loving each other so much their love spilled over onto me. Watching them bonded in a musical embrace, I'd wanted the same kind of love. I had to wonder if such a thing existed now, or if a special magic had fallen over my folks giving them such intense, wonderful passion and understanding because their lives were destined to be cut so short.

"You okay, Sarah Booth?" Coleman asked.

"I am. Right this moment I'm very okay."

"Hold on."

He swept me into his arms, pulling me tight against him. I had no objection. I didn't try to talk. I simply let the music sway me, and Coleman's arms support me. For the first time in weeks, I felt safe. It would last only the length of the song, but it was a welcome relief.

Although I wasn't the most graceful dancer around, I loved trying, and Coleman was a strong lead. We swept past Madame Tomeeka dancing with the debonair Mr. French, who looked more than a little taken with his chauffeur. The music critic held Tammy in his arms, his eyes closed, as he moved her about the dance floor with technique and style.

Coleman maneuvered me to the back of the room, his strong hands on my back. I was acutely aware of the smell of sunshine and fresh laundry that always clung to him, the rasp of his beard against my cheek.

Moving among the crowd of dancing couples, I glimpsed Tinkie and Oscar, and Harold and Cece. Jaytee was on the stage, blowing the harp to a fare-thee-well. Yancy danced with the lovely Chantal.

Folks had come from as far away as Chicago and New Orleans. They came to listen to the music and dance. While I knew a lot of the people attending, there were also many strangers. A few I didn't recognize had come costumed as the Blues Brothers or as famous blues singers.

My heart skipped at beat at a mocha-skinned beauty, who had fashioned her attire after the incredible Billie Holiday. I feared for a moment that Jitty had acted on her stated desire and showed up to attend the opening. A closer inspection revealed the young woman as a local, Panky Street, an aspiring rapper who'd gone to school with Madame Tomeeka's daughter.

The band's reputation, and Scott's raw sex appeal, brought many of the people to Zinnia, but the club itself had magic. The junction of Highways 61 and 49 at Clarksdale was traditionally thought to be the crossroads where bluesman Robert Johnson traded his soul to the devil for musical ability. Once that deal was signed and word spread, legend had it that several other bluesmen followed in Johnson's footsteps here at the junction of Sawmill and Pentecost roads.

This had been a gathering spot for field workers from all over the Delta. In the early days, someone with a wagon would ride along the road, allowing those on foot to jump aboard for an evening of music, dance, and drink. It was a place where the hard work of sharecropping could be forgotten for an evening of pleasure.

The rural South of the early 1900s held little hope for blacks. The rich Delta land was owned by wealthy whites, and sharecropping, for poor blacks and whites alike, was a hard life filled with scarcity. Music was the ticket to a better life. Desperation, the legend noted, drove more than one man to trade his soul for talent and the ability to earn a living.

Many, like Robert Johnson, who died at the age of twenty-seven, found the bargain to be a hard one. But some of the most remarkable music ever created had also been played here.

A blues club had stood near the crossroads since 1870, and though the building had twice burned to the ground, a new club always rose again. Stories had it that the ground had been saturated with talent, and those who sought a career in the blues would do well to play here, to soak in the magic.

Judging from Bad to the Bone's performance, the superstition was true. I'd never heard Scott play and sing better, and the other band members were equally on fire. Even the audience shared in the intensity. Folks from all different backgrounds had come together. Everyone looked happy.

I took mental snapshots of my friends, something Cece had been doing all evening with a real camera. The next edition of the *Zinnia Dispatch* would put to rest some of the stupid rumors Mason Britt and his faction had instigated. People would see the harmless fun everyone was having, the joy. How could anyone find fault with a place where people danced and laughed and let the music wash away all their differences?

This was a night to remember, a celebration of the sound that was a part of the land we cherished and the rootstock of rock 'n' roll. For one evening, what mattered most was music and friendship. We'd come together: black and white, old and young, religious and non, and we were celebrating our history and love of the blues.

The song ended and Coleman dropped me at the table with my friends. "I'll take a spin around the exterior," he said. "The security team reports everything is calm, but I like to check it out myself. You ladies have fun."

When Scott shut down the bar at two A.M., I'd had more than enough to drink, and I'd danced so much my legs were numb. "It was a spectacular show," I told Scott.

We'd had the last dance together, a belly rubber called "What Can You Do?" Jaytee and Cece had performed it together to a standing ovation that brought the house down. "I believe the launch was a huge success."

"It was." He took my hand and we joined my friends. "Thank you all. Tammy, I owe you big time. I so appreciate meeting Parker French and having a chance to talk to him."

Parker interrupted an intense conversation with Oscar. "It was my pleasure, Scott. For a white boy, you sure can sing the blues."

Tammy slapped him playfully on the arm. "We don't see color here, Parker. We're just people. Neighbors who care about each other."

"Mississippi has taken big steps," Parker said. "I'm proud to see it. Proud to be here and participate in this opening. Living away from the South for the last twenty years, I've failed to see the progress. Old stereotypes are hard to destroy. I'm glad to meet all of you. I owe Reverend Hillet more than he knows." His hand on Tammy's shoulder said plenty. "And I'll be sure and let Wilton Frasbaum know that his evaluation of Playin' the Bones is way, way off track. Some would even call it sour grapes."

"What exactly did Wilton say?" I kept my tone conversational though my heart had begun to pound.

"He said he'd once managed the band and that Scott had cheated him. He made a few other allegations, including that the talent was second tier. He also said this venue would never work out. Too rural, he said. Too rustic." Parker watched Scott's face. After all, Parker was a journalist, and a good one. He was here for the story, whatever that might be.

"Parker?" Tammy was in shock.

"Mr. French, did Wilton Frasbaum say he'd *seen* the club?"

Parker hesitated. "Not in so many words, but he clearly implied he'd been down here investigating."

"When did you talk to him?"

"He called me this morning," Parker said.

"Did he say where he was?" I pressed.

"No, but I half expected to see him here tonight."

Oh, not on a bet, I wanted to say. Coleman would pop him in jail so fast his head would spin. "Thanks," I said, eager to pass the news to Coleman. If Wilton Frasbaum was in the area, Coleman needed to know.

Waiting for a chance to speak with Coleman, I reviewed the night. I'd danced with Harold and DeWayne, and even the band members when they could break away from the stage. I'd danced with men whose names I didn't know. I'd spent the night as a dancing fool. The bar was shutting down, and so far, so good.

Coleman and DeWayne were in the parking lot checking to be sure each guest was safely buckled in his or her car and on the road home—with full driving faculties.

Zinnia didn't have a taxi service, but Scott had engaged drivers to ferry those too inebriated to drive. I'd kept my word to Tammy and stayed strictly inside. Now I finally went out for a smoke. The event was over. If someone had intended to do something terrible, the moment had passed.

I lit up, enjoying the cigarette as I observed Coleman and DeWayne. The four security men came up from the roadblock and reported nothing had given them reason for concern. The grand opening had gone off without a hitch, and I, for one, was relieved. And ready to go home.

Sweetie and Pluto would have to be pacified before I could sleep. They weren't used to being excluded from my cases, but a juke joint was no place for a cat and dog. When I crawled out of bed in the morning, I'd take Sweetie for an ice cream and stop at the seafood place for a treat for Pluto.

First and foremost, though, Tinkie and I had to determine if Frasbaum was in the area, and if he was a threat or just a blowhard. News of the reward money would spread quickly and I hoped callers would give us new information.

Gertrude hung over me like a thundercloud, but she'd wisely stayed out of my sight. Lurking on my road was an intimidation tactic, but she'd failed to file trespassing charges against me and Tinkie, which was a curious thing. Her lawyer should have advised her to do so, because it would have damaged my credibility as a witness against her. Yet she'd taken no action. If she was spying on me, I hadn't caught her at it. I could only hope that her trial date would arrive soon, a conviction would be handed down, and she'd spend the next twenty years behind bars, Alton James or no Alton James.

A low rumble of thunder warned that while the storm didn't ruin the opening, I might not be so lucky. It felt like the sky would unzip at any moment. When Graf and I were together, I'd loved Dahlia House in the rain. We'd prop ourselves up in bed and talk and daydream. The rain had sealed us in the house, given us an excuse to shut out the rest of the world and attend to each other. The thought of going home alone, especially after dancing the night away, was depressing.

A flurry of rain splashed down, and I stepped under the eaves of the blues club to finish my cigarette. Movement at the oak that shaded the picnic table caught my attention. A silhouette stood, watching the club. In the darkness I couldn't discern any detail, but the way the figure watched the club was ominous. It was almost as if he or she waited for something to happen.

I crushed out the cigarette in preparation to challenge the watcher. As I turned I bumped into a broad chest and let out a startled yelp.

Scott had come out to check on me. "You okay?"

"Yeah." The watcher was gone, and the branches of a small shrub swayed in the wind. Could I have imagined the figure? "How about you?"

"That bit about Wilton threw me for a loop. A year has passed and he can't seem to let it go. That he'd go to the trouble of calling Parker French and have knowledge of the club here. It's just a little unsettling."

"There's a lot about Frasbaum you don't know." I filled him in on the sexual assault charges.

Scott was suitably angered. "He hid all of it. You think he's here?" He scanned the velvety night. "Waiting to hurt me or someone else?"

"I don't know, but it never hurts to be careful." Scott's nerves were stretched to the snapping point. I'd tell Coleman what I'd seen.

"At least the opening is behind us," he said.

Scott should have been celebrating, but he was down. "It was a great night, Scott. The band is incredible. You're sex on a stick. I think this place does have a special mojo."

"I knew it was the right place for us. Gut instinct. I'm so relieved. The opening was better than I ever anticipated. Parker French in the audience. The night went better than I'd dared to hope." He pumped himself up.

I couldn't help teasing him a little. "I watched all the

women getting hot and bothered for you." Scott had every right to be on top of the world. His opening had been stellar. Despite Madame Tomeeka's dream and the intrusion from Wilton, we'd concluded the night without bloodshed.

He laughed and ducked his chin. For a man who could summon unending stage presence and make his guitar moan like a woman to his touch, Scott had a shy streak. "Can I give you a lift home?"

Tinkie had picked me up and brought me to the club. She and Oscar were still inside talking with Tammy and Parker French. Cece and Jaytee had beat it out the door like their tail feathers were on fire—and I had no doubt when they got home a few sparks would fly. Almost everyone else had left, except Tatiana and the three waitresses, and they were putting the club in order.

"That would be great. You sure you don't need to stay?"

"That's why I earn the big bucks," he said. "I'm the boss."

We headed toward Scott's van when the back door of the club flew open and Tatiana ran out calling Scott's name. Her panic was like a live electrical wire, twisting and sparking.

"What is it?" Scott tried for calm, but his nerves had been stretched to the max, opening the club and expecting an attack at any time.

"I was helping clean up the kitchen, and I heard the phone in your office. I shouldn't have, I guess, but I answered it." She was frantic. "It was a woman. She said blood would be spilled. She said you'd been warned, and now the price would be paid."

"Coleman!" I called him and the tone of my voice brought both lawmen over. Tatiana repeated what had happened. "There's been another threat to Scott and the club."

We went back inside where it was warm and Tatiana went over what had happened several times while Coleman began the process of tracing the call, which proved to be futile. The caller had used a drop phone, just as in prior calls. The difference was this time the caller was female. Tatiana was positive about it. When I reluctantly reported the elusive watcher, Scott stood.

"This is stupid, but I can't risk another person's life," he said. "I have to consider closing the club, at least for a few weeks."

"And that will bankrupt you," Oscar said quietly.

Tinkie put her hands on her hips. "I don't understand why a juke joint has become such a controversy. They've existed in the Delta since the slaves were freed. Sensible people really can't believe there's a connection between this music and the devil. Sure, this location has a reputation, but for heaven's sake, it's a legend, a story to bring tourists to town."

"Never underestimate the stupidity of people," Coleman said wearily. "They're sheep. It's an old story. When someone preys on the fears of ignorant people, their reaction is predictable. That's how lynch mobs are whipped into a frenzy and how gangs stay in power."

"Whoever is behind this is slick," I said. "It's almost as if they had eyes on us."

"Tatiana, can you think of anything distinctive about the caller's voice?"

"I was too scared to pay close attention. I'm sorry." She slumped in her chair. "I've been thinking, though, and she said, 'We will spill their blood.' It was strange, the way the words were put together."

Coleman rolled his shoulders. "Everyone should go home. We'll tackle this in the morning. The security team will stay here until the cleanup is complete. Let's hope that reward money Yancy Bellow put up brings a few grubs out from under rocks."

Scott started to say something but I touched his arm. "Don't make any decisions until tomorrow," I said.

13

As it turned out, Scott gave me a ride home, but Tinkie, Oscar, and Coleman also came along. DeWayne stayed at the club until the doors were locked. At Coleman's request, Tatiana had written down the words of the threat, as exactly as she could remember them.

"It's almost as if this person is taking pleasure in torturing us," Tinkie said. "She or they or whoever wants us to suffer. They call to tell us they intend to hurt someone so we can fret and go nuts trying to figure it out."

Tinkie's words silenced everyone sitting around the kitchen table. I'd poured fresh coffee and served the apple pie Millie had dropped by earlier. She'd let most of her staff off to attend the club opening, which meant she'd had to stay at the café. Always thinking of others, she provided pie for the after-opening gathering.

"Tatiana said the woman sounded ordinary, but muffled, like she meant to disguise her voice," Tinkie said. "What she remembered was the strange phrasing. 'We will spill their blood. You were warned and now the price will be paid.' "

" 'We will spill their blood,' " Scott repeated the words. "Sounds like movie dialogue."

"It's poetic, in its way," Tinkie said.

"Money isn't the motivation here. It's strictly the club. Someone wants Scott to fail," Oscar added.

"Because they hate me or because they hate the blues?" Scott asked.

"I wish I could say for certain." Oscar rubbed his eyes wearily. "The only thing I know is that this isn't an empty threat. Koby Shavers is dead. Everyone associated with the club has to use extreme caution, and that includes you, Tinkie, and you, Sarah Booth."

"Agreed," Tinkie and I said in unison.

"At this point, we have to move forward assuming everyone associated with the club is in danger," Coleman said. "Before we do anything else, call everyone in the band and all the serving staff at the club including Curtis Hebert and warn them to be alert." He was frustrated and angry, high spots of color on his cheekbones.

"I should simply close down. Give it a few weeks," Scott said. "It isn't worth risking my friends."

The cost to Scott would be high. "Surely we can figure this out."

"We will, Sarah Booth," Coleman said. "But right now, I agree with Scott. I think he should take out an ad in the local paper and say the club is on hiatus. Folks had a great time tonight. They'll remember and return when the club reopens."

"How will Scott pay the bills without income?" I asked.

"I can provide a personal loan," Oscar offered. "You have to meet payroll and pay the liquor distributors. If your credit is bad there, you'll be in trouble."

"Thank you." Scott looked around the room. "If I ever doubted how much I would love living here in Zinnia, you've put all my concerns to rest. The offer of the loan is very generous. I'll consider it, along with other options."

He meant taking a partner, the thing he didn't want to do. Scott was a proud man and he wouldn't take on a debt he wasn't absolutely positive he could repay. Especially not from someone he viewed as a friend.

Coleman stood up, effectively shutting the meeting down. "Scott, talk to your employees. Tatiana was shaken up. She may know more than she realizes. Try to jog her memory, she may be more comfortable talking to you. Sarah Booth, you and Tinkie put together a list of all the people who were there tonight. Cece will have photographs, and that's a great place to start. I had the security team write down every license plate. I have a sense that whoever is behind this has a plant inside the club. These threatening calls are timed in a way that leads me to believe they know everything happening in the club."

"If there is a spy on the inside, we need to ferret him or her out," Tinkie said grimly.

Coleman signaled me to walk out with him. I slid into my jacket and stepped into the cold night. Sweetie Pie had come out with me, and Pluto sat in the window, watching.

"You checked the background on the band members?" he asked.

"I did. I told you Zeb and Mike both had tough beginnings, but they seemed to have left that behind. Jaytee was clean as a whistle."

"Did you check Tatiana?"

I hadn't. "She wasn't in town when Koby was killed."

"Check her."

"Okay. Do you suspect something?"

He sighed. "I don't. But I don't really have a lot to go on here. Think about it. The killer is calling and warning Scott about impending death. What's the point? Why do that? It isn't logical."

I couldn't argue.

"I'll check Tatiana's background tomorrow and let you know." I had a possibility I didn't want to bring up, but I had to. "Do you think it was Gertrude calling tonight? To create worry and unhappiness. Her hatred of me is irrational. She really believes my mother told people about her pregnancy, which is ridiculous. My mother never opened her mouth, and even if she had, why should Gertrude hate me so much?"

"Sins of the mother," he shrugged. "Gertrude knows you and Scott were once involved. She might be behind all of this, Sarah Booth. I've asked surrounding counties to send a few deputies over to help me out. If I get the manpower, I'll put an officer on her."

"I wouldn't have suspected Gertrude would know about burner phones and such." The depth of hatred required to kill an innocent man just to hurt me was staggering, but she'd almost crippled a man who'd done her no harm—because she wanted to hurt me.

"We greatly underestimated Gertrude in the past. We won't let that happen a second time. And she's irrational where you're concerned, Sarah Booth. I'll have a word with her."

"Thank you." The old bat should be behind bars, but I had no power to change the situation until her trial came up.

"I'll make sure she knows I'm watching her close—" Coleman's cell phone interrupted his reply. His face tightened. "Scott is here," he said into the phone. "I'll let him know."

Something awful had happened. "What is it?" I asked.

"Come back inside. Mike Hawkins has been shot."

His tone propelled me in the door with him. He went straight to the kitchen. "Scott, come with me. Someone in a black truck drove by Mike Hawkins's house and gunned him down in his front yard. He's still alive and being transported to the hospital. I'll take you there."

"How bad is he?" Scott bolted to his feet.

"Bad. You need to hurry to the hospital."

The rest of us stood, unmoving, stunned by the news. Oscar recovered first and whipped out his phone. In a moment he had Cece on the line. "You and Jaytee watch your step," Oscar said, filling her in. "Stay inside. Don't go out. Coleman will be in touch with any information. Scott is headed to the hospital. No, Cece. Stay inside your house."

Oscar's dire tone galvanized me to action. "We'll call the rest of the band members and staff. Come on, Tinkie."

Coleman and Scott rushed out after promising to call the minute they had news. As he left, Coleman called the security men to go to Mike's house and secure the scene until he could get there. Oscar offered to help us, but when we assured him we could handle calling the others, he went home to check on Chablis. Basking in the success of the club opening was over.

When Tinkie and I were finally alone, I slumped into a chair. "Oh, Sarah Booth," she said, comforting me. "This is terrible."

I wanted to cry, but I couldn't. As if the sky sympathized, it opened up with a crack of lightning and a boom of thunder. I felt like the bones had been sucked out of my body. Sweetie put her head in my lap and Pluto jumped on the kitchen table and headbutted me.

"I'm sorry," I said, "I can't believe this has happened again." I accidentally swept a coffee cup off the table. The cup crashed to the floor. "Dammit to hell and back." I picked up another cup and threw it at the wall. It broke too. "I want to beat the snot out of the person responsible for this."

"If cursing would help, I'd cut loose." Tinkie wiped at the coffee that had spattered on my blouse. "We can dress you up but we can't take you anywhere."

At last I chuckled.

"There it is," she said. "Nothing wrong with anger, but follow with a laugh. You don't want your emotional gauge to get stuck in the hot zone."

My lack of emotional control embarrassed me, but Tinkie took it right in stride. "I'm okay now." I picked up the broken cup. "This is just unfair. I'm worried for Scott. He'll close the club now and lose everything. It's better than risking the band, but it's just not right."

"I hear you. Let's get the band members on the phone. The sooner we do it, the safer they'll be."

She took Davy Joiner, the bass player, and I called Zeb

Kohl, the drummer with the gangster past. He sounded like he was asleep when he answered.

"Zeb, I have some bad news. Mike was gunned down outside his house. I don't know how bad it is, but he's on the way to the hospital."

"Damn. Let me grab some clothes."

"Don't." I cut him off. "Stay where you are. Lock the doors. Be alert. It won't do any good to be at the hospital right now. Stay inside."

"How about his wife and kid? Are they okay?"

"I'm pretty sure they are. I believe Danni called the ambulance and the sheriff. When I get news I'll call. I promise. Just stay put."

"This is my fault." Zeb's voice cracked. "I'm responsible."

"The person responsible is the person who pulled the trigger. But tell me what you're talking about." Calm settled over me. "Why are you to blame?"

"I owe money to bad people. A lot of money." He squeezed the words out.

I'd done the background on Zeb, and I knew he'd once run with a gang, but all indications were he'd made a clean break. "You could have told us this sooner." I couldn't help the snap in my voice.

"I didn't want Scott to know. I got mixed up with bad people and I owe them money. All of this happened before I hooked up with the band. I thought I'd taken care of this, but about a week ago, I got a call."

I struggled with the impulse to say something cutting and mean. Koby Shaver was dead. Mike Hawkins wounded, and from the sounds of it critically. Now Zeb was finally speaking up. "Was it a threat?"

"Yeah." He sounded defeated. "I'm so sorry. I never thought they'd hurt anyone but me. And I assured them I'd have the money for them soon. Once the club opened, Scott said we'd all get big bonuses."

"If you're dead you can't pay the money back."

Tinkie had hung up and whipped around, shock on her face. "What's going on?"

I held up a hand to silence her. "Tell me what they said. Exactly."

"The guy who called said they knew where I was and if I didn't bring them the money I owed, I'd find out what hell was all about."

"How much do you owe?"

"Two hundred thousand."

"Holy shit, Zeb." It was a staggering amount. "How did you get in so deep?"

"I stole some dope. Not that much, but I stole it. It was back when I was shooting up and I had to have it. You know, dopeheads don't think. They need the drug and they do what's necessary to get it. So I stole from people I knew would kill me. And then I split town."

I waved Tinkie to pick up the other phone. I'd called on the landline, and there was an extension right beside her. "Zeb, I'm surprised they didn't track you down and kill you long before now. Nobody steals two hundred thousand from a gang and expects to live."

"It was only about five thousand dollars' worth of heroin."

"Then why do you owe—"

"It's the interest. They compound it. I could have gone back to work for the gang, come up with financial plans and ways to move money. I could have paid off the debt, but that's when Scott gave me a chance. I quit using, cleaned myself up. I thought as soon as I saved enough, I'd repay them. I didn't realize how the debt would grow. Then it was too much to ever pay back and we left for Europe."

"Folks don't walk away from a gang. And you moved right back in their neighborhood. Memphis is two hours north at best." He was in a mess. Tinkie shook her head, warning me not to speak so rashly. She'd quickly picked up on what Zeb was talking about.

"I've avoided them for over a year. I thought . . . man, I guess I didn't think clearly at all."

I had to remind myself I was dealing with a man who'd walked away from a million-dollar income as an outlaw to play the drums in a band. It was the rare musician who earned more than poverty wages.

"Zeb, this is Tinkie Bellcase Richmond. You have to tell this to Sheriff Peters," she said, but her tone was sympathetic.

"I'll tell Scott at the hospital. I'll turn myself in to the sheriff and he can take me back to Memphis. I'll do whatever I have to do to prevent anyone else getting hurt."

"Don't go anywhere!" If drug money was truly behind the shootings, the worst thing Zeb could do was run around in the open where he was an easy target. "It may have gone beyond the money you owe, Zeb."

"Stay where you are," Tinkie threw in. "Rushing out will only endanger other people. We don't know your debt is behind the shootings."

"What else could it be? Scott's a great guy. The other band members—" His voice broke.

"Zeb, you have to pull yourself together and stay safe. There's no proof this is the reason Mike was shot. Or

Koby. Did any of the gang show up at the club during the performance?"

"No."

"When was the last time you heard from them?" Tinkie asked.

"Monday."

"Did they give you a deadline?" It wouldn't matter if they gave him until the cows came home. He'd never raise that kind of money unless he sold his own organs.

"Yeah. Friday."

"Not much time to raise two hundred thousand dollars."

"Tell me about it." Fear and self-loathing lingered in his tone. "At this point I don't care if they kill me. I just want them to leave the band and my friends alone."

"Now you listen to me," Tinkie said. "You stay right where you are. We'll send a patrol car to get you just as soon as an officer can break loose. An officer will escort you to the hospital so you can talk to Scott. Do not *move* until a deputy shows up. If you care about your friends, do as I say. Stay put. We don't need to waste manpower chasing after you. Understand?"

"Yes, ma'am. I'll be right here."

"Good. Now there's no proof any of this traces back to you. Keep that thought. The calls Scott received seemed to point to an enemy who wants to wreck the club, not a debt you owe. Try not to beat up on yourself and just hang tight."

Tinkie put me to shame. Instead of heaping guilt on Zeb, she offered compassion and possible absolution. And she was right. We had no evidence a Memphis gang was picking off club employees to settle a drug score.

"We'll call you as soon as we have word about Mike," I added.

"Thank you." He sounded like a kicked dog.

Tinkie and I hung up. We didn't need to talk. We were running on raw nerves and anger. "What's the story on Davy Joiner?" I asked.

"Jump in the shower and change clothes, then we'll take Sweetie Pie and Pluto to Oscar at Hilltop and I can freshen up. On the way, I'll fill you in on Davy."

"Give me fifteen minutes," I said.

Tinkie slumped in her chair. "I'll snatch a few winks while I wait for you."

The hot shower helped, but fatigue had settled over both of us. We were dragging as we pushed ourselves down the stairs and toward the car.

Tinkie's conversation with Davy Joiner had been simple and to the point. The kid had never been in any trouble and he understood that keeping himself safe kept others from risking injury. He agreed to stay in his room at The Gardens, a rather expensive place for a twenty-one-year-old musician to be staying.

"His father's a doctor," Tinkie explained, covering a yawn with her hand. "He's a good kid. I suggested he might want to visit his parents for a few days."

"And?"

"He's a young man with more sense than most, but he won't run away from this. He's staying to support Scott and the band."

I couldn't blame him, though I wanted to pack his bags and send him home to his mama before he got hurt. "Are you sure he isn't hiding any dark secrets. Like that he builds bombs for a terrorist group? He does have an engineering degree."

The news about Zeb and his drug debt to a gang had kicked me in the gut. I should have been on top of that. My blasé attitude and superficial sleuthing might have cost Mike Hawkins his life.

"Davy's exactly what he appears to be. A talented young man. My gut tells me he's not part of this." Tinkie pushed me out the door and into the car.

At Hilltop, Tinkie accomplished a quick toilette and settled the pets in an interior bedroom upstairs. No one was going to drive by Hilltop and shoot our critters. We were ready for action.

I'd retrieved my pistol from the Roadster. I generally kept it in the trunk of the car, but I put it in my purse. I'd had enough. Settling things with a gun had never been my first choice, but if it was forced on me, to protect those I cared about, I would do whatever was necessary. Tinkie, too, retrieved her gun.

Oscar was sound asleep, and Tinkie kissed his cheek and left him, safe in an upstairs bedroom. I was impressed that he trusted her enough not to fret and worry when he knew she was working a case. Somehow, after a rocky patch in their marriage, they had become the power couple.

Tinkie hadn't really wanted to marry Oscar. Her marriage had, essentially, been arranged—the melding of two families with great wealth. Tinkie was a princess and Oscar a prince, and the marriage brought her more money and security and him a wife who was a social asset, which translated into more wealth and security. I'd thought the whole idea of such a marriage abhorrent—until I saw them together. Call it fate or luck or kismet, but they had grown to truly love each other.

We stepped into the darkness with extra care. A long, curved drive led to the Richmond home, and from the front door we had a fair view of the terrain around us. No strange cars lurked near Hilltop. In fact, the roads were empty as we drove to the hospital. The solitude evaporated as we turned in to Sunflower County Hospital. The place was a zoo. About twenty blues fans had heard about the shooting and were in the waiting room, weeping and wailing. Emo women! Coleman and Mike's wife, Danni, waited with Scott to hear the doctor's verdict.

Tinkie assessed the situation and took charge. "Ladies, you have to leave this area."

They reacted as if she'd turned into an ogre.

"We're here for Mike," a plump young lady said. "You can't force us to leave. We're holding a vigil for him. We love him."

Tinkie bit her lip. "If you want to help him, pack it up and take it home."

"You can't make us."

Now the plump woman was joined by another tall, thin young fan.

"Oh, I think I can." Tinkie leaned forward so she could whisper. "Scott Hampton told me if you ladies would go home, he'd arrange a dinner for you all with Mike and the whole band when he recovers. We need to clear this room right now."

They whispered for a minute and the first woman nodded. "Okay."

Tinkie pulled a pad from her purse. "Sign your names and as soon as Mike is well enough, we'll have a friendly dinner and you can tell him how you all stood vigil at the hospital, praying for his recovery."

Tinkie was a damn genius.

As soon as the ladies cleared the room a nurse, who worked the sign-in desk, brought us coffee. "Thank you. I was about to commit bodily harm on those weeping Wandas."

"How is Mike?" Tinkie asked.

"We can't share medical information. It's against the law. But I can tell you he's in surgery. And he's in good hands. Doc Sawyer stabilized him and Mr. Bellow flew in a thoracic surgeon from Memphis. They're working on him now."

"Yancy Bellow flew a doctor here?" He was a rich man, but this really went over the top.

"Yes. On his private plane."

We thanked the nurse and took a seat beside Danni, Mike's slender young wife. Her hazel eyes were red from crying. After expressing our condolences, I asked about the black truck.

Still torn up by witnessing her husband being gunned down, Danni gathered herself. "Mike called me to say he was headed home, and the night had been a huge success. I was so worried. I'd just gotten a phone call saying someone would be hurt—"

"What phone call?"

"Mike forgot his cell phone. He must have dropped it beside the bed. I heard it ringing and answered. This man said Scott and the band had been warned and now someone would suffer the consequences."

Tinkie and I exchanged glances. This was nuts. Why was a man calling Mike's cell phone and a woman calling the club?

"Are you sure it was a man?" Tinkie asked.

"No doubt about it," Danni said. "He was very clear. I was so worried about Mike. Then he called to say everything was okay. I didn't tell him about the threat. I wanted to wait until he was home. If I'd told him, he might have been more alert. He might—"

"Don't do that to yourself," Tinkie said. "The person to blame is the person who pulled the trigger. Not you."

"Why didn't you come to the opening?" I asked.

"I'm pregnant and I'm at the stage where everything makes me queasy. I wanted Mike to play and not constantly be worried about me. So I stayed home with our little girl, Kiley." She inhaled and fought to steady her voice. "I heard Mike pull up, so I went to the front door to welcome him. I was standing there as he crossed the lawn. I heard the truck—it was loud, like a diesel. But I didn't think anything about it. To me, the club had shut down for the night and the danger was over. I convinced myself the caller was pulling a prank."

"We should have sent security to every band member's house," Scott said.

"No." Danni put a hand on Scott's arm. "It isn't your fault. How could you know what a maniac will do? There's no way to predict crazy."

I hadn't had a chance to really talk with Danni before, but I liked her. A lot. "Can you remember any more details?" I asked.

"The truck roared up to the house and then slowed. There was a very bright cue-beam aimed out the passenger window, like illegal night hunters use. It came on, highlighting Mike. He yelled at me to get inside and he dove to the right. The truck jerked, like the driver lost control for a minute. Otherwise Mike would have taken the shot directly in the chest."

"And what happened next?" I asked.

"The truck drove off. I went to Mike. He was hurt so bad. I called 911. They must have called the sheriff's department."

"Can you describe the truck?" Tinkie asked.

"Black, extended cab, late model. I think it's a diesel. I couldn't really see anything else. It didn't have any lights on. It came out of the dark and then lit up Mike with the cue-beam and shot him. It drove away fast."

If other details became available, Coleman would share. Now it was best not to grill the poor woman further. Her husband's life hung in the balance and she was pregnant with their second child. Talk about a world of hurt.

Tinkie engaged Danni and Scott in casual conversation, and Coleman spoke with the nurse at the desk. When he finished, he tilted his head toward the hallway. I joined him there.

"Do you have any insight into why would Yancy Bellow fly a specialist in from Memphis for a musician he doesn't even know?" Coleman asked.

"He offered to buy into the club, to give Scott some operating cash."

"So he views the band members as an investment." Coleman digested that information.

"Yancy thinks Playin' the Bones can be a big asset to the community. Especially the tourism business. I got the impression the blues club is a means to an end for him. He bought The Gardens and he's looking to acquire more property that could be turned into B&Bs. The club will bring in tourists."

Coleman caught Scott's attention and indicated he

should join us. He walked over and Coleman put the same question to him.

Scott rubbed his eyes. He was exhausted. "This is an amazing community. Folks step up to help each other. I don't know what this specialist costs, but I can only promise to try to repay Mr. Bellow. That is, if I can keep the club open. If not . . . touring in Europe builds a reputation but it isn't exactly a ticket to wealth. I want to stay here, in Zinnia."

"Few businessmen are motivated by compassion," Coleman said. "Yancy may be the exception, but I wouldn't bet the farm on it."

"He stands to make a lot of money if the music takes off," I said.

"I need to head to the crime scene," Coleman said. "DeWayne is there, but he's been hampered by the darkness. Dawn is breaking and we need to get to work. If there's evidence, we have to retrieve it."

"We'll stay here with Scott and Danni," Tinkie said. "We'll call as soon as we hear anything about Mike."

After Coleman's departure, we simply sat in silence. My brain sent jumbles of incoherent images chasing each other. We were all exhausted but unable to rest. The minutes ticked by. I got fresh coffee for us, and we sat more.

At last, Doc came into the waiting room. He wore fresh scrubs, but his face told me how seriously Mike was hurt. We jumped to our feet, as if taking the news upright would be easier.

"How is he?" Danni asked, doing her best not to weep. Tinkie put a protective arm around her.

"The shotgun blast did some damage. Dr. Lee was able to repair his lungs. Thank goodness he arrived here so quickly. I'm a fair surgeon, but he's amazing." He found a worn smile. "Now there's nothing to do but wait and see."

"What are the odds?" Tinkie asked.

"Mr. Hawkins was lucky. The blast hit his lungs but spared his heart. If he doesn't throw a clot, his chances are pretty good. He's young and healthy." Doc took Danni's hand and patted it kindly. "He's a strong man. I'd put my money on him."

Pretty good didn't sound like the odds I'd want. I favored exceptionally good. Damn near a hundred percent was what I wanted to hear, but I kept that to myself. Instead, I maneuvered Doc away from the others.

"Was he shot in the back?" I asked.

Doc shook his head. "No, he was facing the person who shot him."

If he lived, he might remember something more than Danni did.

Doc patted his cloud of wild white hair. "I'll see Dr. Lee off. There's a private plane waiting for him and he has patients to see in Memphis."

"I'd like to thank him," Scott said.

"Sure." Doc motioned for Scott and Danni to follow him into the medical staff area. He gave Tinkie and me a thumbs-up. "Keep good thoughts. I'll be back in a few minutes."

We sat down. Again. I couldn't tell if I was relieved or simply dead beat. Numbness reached from my butt to my brain. "Dr. Lee saved Mike's life."

"Yancy Bellow is a peculiar man," Tinkie said. "I asked Oscar what he knew about him. Not much more than we know. It's strange, because Oscar knows everyone with money in Sunflower County. Well, actually in the Delta.

Yancy travels under the radar. Old family, lots of land, but he's never been active in local events. His holdings are international and mostly handled in New York, where he spends the greatest part of the year, though he throws some business to Oscar."

"Is that unusual?" Having no money to invest, I wasn't up to speed on how the upper crust managed money.

"No. The Delta has a fair number of extremely wealthy people. They bank out of Memphis and other big cities. Money goes to money. The law of attraction. Yancy's interests are far-flung. But I refuse to look a gift horse in the mouth. I'm confident Mike would have died without this specialist. Thank God he took action."

"Yeah. Yancy has been a good friend to the club." I didn't say it, but maybe he would still invest and help Scott keep the club alive, if it came to that.

"I can say one negative thing about Yancy." Tinkie's voice was glum.

"What?"

"He could exercise better taste in women. A lot better."

"Bijou!" I'd actually forgotten she existed. "Why would he spend his valuable time with her?"

"She's pretty, wealthy, probably a shark in the sack," Tinkie counted off her attributes on her fingers. "And he's a man. He couldn't care less about her moral or ethical character. He's not going to marry her."

"She's not interested in marriage." Bijou seemed to be a new breed of Delta woman. She didn't need a man for her identity. Wealth had passed to her directly, through no accomplishment of her own I might point out. She didn't need a husband to provide endless security or luxuries. She could afford to indulge every whim. With her personality, she wouldn't yield to the pressures of society to wed. In a way, I could actually admire her. If she wasn't such a total and complete bitch.

"I like his new girlfriend, Chantal. Classy," Tinkie said. "Maybe he's done with Bijou."

"Maybe." The question to ask would be was Bijou done with him.

Doc returned alone and sat wearily beside us. He had to be in his late sixties or early seventies and he put in longer hours than anyone I knew except maybe Millie. Doc and Millie came from hardy stock—people who worked steadily without complaint.

"What did Sarah Booth do to Bijou?" Tinkie asked him right off the bat.

"Nothing I know of." Doc focused on the floor. He couldn't risk a glance at me or he might rat me out or burst into laughter.

"Doc Sawyer!" Tinkie's curiosity demanded an answer. "Sarah Booth won't tell me. She said you'd know."

"Correction!" Tinkie was slick, but I couldn't let her buffalo Doc into thinking I wanted him to tell my secret. "I *said* for you to ask Doc what was wrong with Bijou. I never said I had a thing to do with it."

Doc's eyes crackled with amusement. "Let's just say when she came out of the bathroom, I was surprised there was anything left of her."

The conversation stopped when Scott and Danni returned. He looked worse than before, if that was possible. "Dr. Lee did a remarkable job. And you, too, Doc Sawyer. They aren't letting anyone sit with Mike. There's nothing we can do until he comes out of recovery. They said four or five hours. I think we should go home and try to rest."

"I'm staying here," Danni insisted. "Tatiana helped me find a sitter. She's a sweet and helpful girl, and she was so upset about Mike. More even than Koby." She pushed her hair from her face. "I can't leave Mike alone. I want to be here, in case . . . I promise I'll call with any news at all."

"You do what you feel is best," Tinkie told her. "Just call if you need us."

Sitting in the waiting room, fretting and worrying, was a waste of time for us, but it might give Danni a tiny sense of control. "Scott, please stay at Dahlia House. We can grab a few hours of sleep."

"I will." Every lick of fight had been sucked out of Scott.

I kissed Doc on the cheek and whispered in his ear. "Thank you."

He patted my shoulder. "I don't disagree with your actions." He leaned close and whispered. "Just don't get careless, Sarah Booth, or there will be consequences, no matter that you're on the side of the angels. What you did to Bijou might be considered assault." His soft laughter tickled my ear. "Assault on an ass. An excellent description of Bijou."

We left the hospital, stepping into the promise of a new day. The sun glinted between the horizon and a mass of enormous clouds that promised rain. I thought of Coleman and the crime scene. By all rights I should have gone to help him, but I didn't know if I could put one foot in front of the other.

We dropped off Tinkie at Hilltop and picked up Sweetie and Pluto. Always willing to forgive, Sweetie bounded toward me, yodeling her joy. Pluto was another matter altogether. Every time I reached to pet him, he hissed and gave me his butt. He reserved his affections for Scott.

"He knows how to emphasize his point," Scott said, cradling him as I drove home.

"Cats." One word said it all.

"He knows he's superior and now he's letting you know it, too."

We both needed the laugh. At Dahlia House, Scott declined breakfast. "I'm going to sleep. Can we set an alarm for three hours? I need to be up and moving."

I obliged and took myself upstairs for a nap. Before I conked out, though, I made a few calls regarding Tatiana, per Coleman's instructions. Koby had worked at Mike's Molotov Cocktails, a popular Austin bar. The general manager wasn't in until five, so I left a message asking for a callback.

And then I collapsed. Pluto deigned to sleep on the foot of the bed, but he refused any cuddling. Sweetie Pie was strangely wound up. She paced the bedroom.

I checked her over, concerned she might have pulled a muscle or hurt herself playing with Chablis, but I found no evidence of physical discomfort. She was simply tense and anxious. And so was I. I tried to sleep, and though my body demanded shut-eye, my brain wouldn't cooperate.

At last I got up and went downstairs for coffee. I rummaged through the refrigerator and found fresh spinach, bacon, eggs, and cheese and whipped up a quiche. While it baked, I dressed for the day and went to my office to go over the notes on the case.

Guilt was my problem. It ate at me. I was five days into this case, and I'd turned up not a single lead that Coleman could use for an arrest. Koby was dead, and Mike gravely wounded. Scott had been effectively blackmailed into shutting down the club, which would bankrupt him shortly. Who was behind this? Was the perpetrator willing to kill innocent people to make a point about the blues and some ignorant belief involving Satan? I honestly couldn't wrap my brain around such a crazy thing.

It seemed more likely that someone meant to harm Scott, but I hadn't been able to dig up any reason. Or possibly to get back at Zeb for his actions. But that didn't ring true, either. And what gave with two separate warning calls. A man calling Danni and a female calling the club landline. Other calls had come into the band members' cell phones, as if the caller were taunting them with the fact that he'd obtained private cell phone numbers. The landline for the club was listed and it was no big deal for the female caller to obtain the number. A woman caller.

I sensed this was important, but I couldn't figure out how.

Was this about money?

I had three classic motives for the shootings—religion, revenge, or greed.

The frustrating thing was that I'd found no evidence to lead me in any direction. Sure, Farley's church railed against the blues club, but shaking a finger at Satan and shooting people were miles apart. I disliked everything Farley stood for, but I was having difficulty believing he deliberately orchestrated a murder and a shooting because he didn't like a style of music.

Without a motive, it would be nigh on impossible to find this drive-by assassin who seemed to select his victims at random, drawing from the pool of those involved with the blues club. Did Gertrude or Bijou figure into this? They hated me, but that, too, was a stretch. Frisco Evans needed a closer look.

The timer on the quiche went off and as I passed the front porch headed to the kitchen, I saw a car in the driveway. Harold had stopped by. I unlocked the front door and let him in before he could knock.

He gave me a peck on the cheek, but he wasn't there for romance or conversation. Harold wore his worried expression, and that upset me. "What's wrong?" It was nine thirty in the morning. The bank had been open for half an hour and Harold never missed work.

"Oscar got a call this morning the moment the doors unlocked. A conglomerate out of Tennessee wants to buy Playin' the Bones and the six hundred acres around it. Their plan is to develop a blues theme park."

"Money."

Harold put a hand on my forehead to check for fever. "Connect the dots, Sarah Booth, you're making me think you've had a stroke. What are you saying?"

"Money is the motive for trying to shut down Scott." This was so much better than sin or personal animosity. Money. "Someone realizes if the juke joint is a huge success, Scott'll never sell. If he has the best venue in the state—an original juke, not a Disney version—they won't be able to compete with him." It clicked into place. "And that place, that one spot on planet Earth, has the blues mojo and is worth millions in advertising. It is the primo location for a club. And if there's that much land for sale around the club . . ."

"Those exact thoughts occurred to me," Harold said. "That's why I'm here. Oscar is doing his best to find out who's behind this conglomerate offer, but it's not as easy as it should be. Oscar took the call from a lawyer, Vito Martine. He is, naturally, refusing to disclose whom he represents. He merely says an 'offshore interest.'"

"Which means the money has been stockpiled in the Cayman Islands or another country with thick privacy shields. It could be anyone."

"Yes, that's true."

"And if this conglomerate wants the club badly enough, they'd kill to force Scott out."

"I don't know that, but I do know such tactics have been used before in high stakes investments."

I signaled Harold to follow me to the kitchen before I burned the quiche to a crisp. Coffee was brewed and waiting, and I pulled the egg dish from the oven and put it on a trivet to cool while I filled two mugs.

"Where's Scott?" Harold asked.

"Asleep. He was dead on his feet. I couldn't relax, though."

Harold stepped behind me and rubbed my shoulders, his strong thumbs digging into the tight muscles with just the perfect amount of pressure. "If these muscles ever truly relax, your head will pop off and splatter like a fat tick."

"Thanks for the image." It was gruesome but funny. "What's Oscar planning to do about the property offer?"

Harold ceased the massage and sat down across from me. "The entertainment center they're proposing would bring a lot of money into Sunflower County. Lots of money. They could put a facility anywhere in the Delta, but it's the location for Playin' the Bones they want. The legend of the crossroads at Pentecost and Sawmill roads. They asked Oscar to broker the deal with Scott, and they want an answer in twenty-four hours. They're offering six times what Scott paid for the club. He could get out of debt and start over."

"I'm envisioning the Dollywood of the blues." I wasn't

being catty or sarcastic. The Delta was one of the most economically depressed areas in the nation. Such a vast development would bring jobs, entertainment, tax revenues. The theme park in the Great Smoky Mountains near Gatlinburg, named after a country singer I adored, had brought jobs, health care, better schooling, and much more to a very impoverished population. Zinnia would benefit from such a venture.

"There's an ugly side to it, potentially." Harold played devil's advocate well. "This type of development kills off authenticity. It will become a mockery of what it intends to portray. Sanitized blues. Authentic music approved for the whole family. Soul food prepared in microwaves and served to those who don't know any better. Whenever you put profits ahead of anything else, what you get is . . . sad. But amazingly lucrative."

"I can see that." My concern was far more personal and immediate. "If Scott has to close the club for longer than a week, he'll lose it. Oscar's offered a loan, but Scott won't take it. He won't risk Oscar's capital. If Scott can't meet his mortgage, that'll open the door for the bank to sell the club to this huge concern."

"I'm afraid that's true." Harold wasn't happy. "Scott is over a barrel. The one bright spot is that he has the option of investors," Harold said. "If someone with enough money to cover his operating costs steps in, that would buy him time to get past these murderous threats."

"Yes, but a partner brings other complications."

"I know." Harold wasn't there to sugarcoat things. "Any leads on who is killing off his friends? If you and Tinkie and Coleman could find out who's behind the attacks . . ."

"I turned up something, but I haven't determined if

it's a solid lead." I told him about Zeb's financial problems and the sudden reemergence of Wilton Frasbaum in Scott's life and business. "The folks behind this club takeover have the most to gain, financially, and money is generally the most reliable motive for murder." But why not just kill Scott and be done with it? That would accomplish the same thing and with far less bloodshed. "This doesn't parse. None of it fits. Not the international investors building Bluesorama or the Memphis gang connection to Zeb, or the idea a lone wolf is stalking and killing men for cheating or some kooky religious belief where women are second class and music is Satan's tool."

"I agree, Sarah Booth. But we work with what we have. By eliminating suspects, we are accomplishing something. I'll try to break down the shield of protection on this conglomerate, but it's difficult even when the government steps in. It takes time."

"And that's the one thing Scott doesn't have."

"Any news on Mike Hawkins?" Harold asked.

"HIPAA laws—they couldn't tell us much. If his condition heads south, Doc will call, though. He can't give details but he can warn us to be there."

"I should return to the bank." Harold leaned down and kissed my cheek. "You'll figure this out and save the day. I have complete faith in you."

Harold's words warmed the cockles of my black little heart, but they were also a burden to carry. I didn't have any magic or even leverage. It occurred to me that when Graf left, he might have taken my detective mojo right along with my heart. What if I now sucked at PI work? My only marketable skill might have evaporated.

"Sarah Booth, are you okay?"

"I'm not sure."

Harold pulled his chair beside me and put an arm around me. "You've had a rough few months. Why don't you call Doc and check on Mike? Oscar and I will put our heads together and take this offer apart. Maybe we'll be able to trace it back to the people behind it. If Coleman has to call in the feds, I think he can make that happen."

Harold was doing everything he could to reassure me. I had many good friends, but Harold had turned into the staunchest supporter of my PI work. And for Tinkie, too. He valued what we did, and he viewed our abilities as true talent, not just as Lucy and Ethel floundering into a resolution.

"How's Roscoe?" I had to get the focus off me.

"Feeling much friskier. He's supposed to stay quiet for another week, but it's driving him nuts, which means he's driving me to drink. Heaven forbid when the vet cuts him loose from restricted movement. I fear for those in the vicinity."

I didn't doubt it for a moment. Roscoe terrorized people he didn't like. It was fifteen miles to Bijou's place, Hemlock Manor, and Roscoe would attempt to get there as soon as he escaped from the house. Roscoe carried a grudge in a way I couldn't help but admire.

"You have to keep him contained."

"How well I know. Care to offer any tips on how to accomplish that, other than a kennel?"

"Frontal lobotomy?"

"Very clever but not helpful."

"Sorry. Roscoe is a force of nature. Maybe he can come out to Dahlia House and play with Sweetie Pie."

"More likely he'd convince her to plot mischief with him."

"True." Harold loved Roscoe. He loved him because of and despite his uncanny ability to create trouble and to lampoon people he sensed were pompous or arrogant. In certain ways, Roscoe and I were much alike, a point that wasn't lost on me.

"The important thing is Roscoe is home with you and will suffer no lasting damage."

"None," Harold said. "Thanks to you. The vet said if he'd laid out on the cement in the cold for the whole night, he might not be with us."

"Have you considered filing cruelty charges? Or at least dog theft." I wanted Bijou in jail.

"I've thought of something better." He grinned and the glint in his eye was worthy of Clyde Barrow. "Even better than laxative brownies."

"Do tell."

"I've invited all of the members of Mason Britt's church to camp in the slave quarters at Hemlock Manor. For a two-week revival. And I sent the invitations in Bijou's name."

"Harold! You are a genius. Mason is her right-hand man, so she'll be reluctant to run them off because of him. Oh, I love this. What if she realizes it was you?"

He shrugged. "What will she do? She crossed the line when she hurt Roscoe, or allowed him to be hurt. This is war. The rest of my productive days will be spent figuring out ways to screw her."

"I love you!" And I did. Harold fought for the helpless and the innocent far harder than he'd fight for himself.

"If I'd known sooner that messing with Bijou turned you on, I could have started years back."

And like Roscoe, Harold could be incorrigible. I lightly punched his shoulder. "Grow up!"

He kissed my cheek and gave my shoulders a last squeeze. "The bank demands my presence. You should try to sleep. Even a couple of hours would refresh you."

I pointed to the quiche. "I need to eat. Can I send some to the bank with you?"

He patted his stomach. "I cooked Una Mae Denison's campout breakfast casserole this morning, so I'm full up. Call me if you need me. And never doubt yourself, Sarah Booth. Never."

14

At ten o'clock, I woke Scott, fed him, and dropped him at the club, which stood forlorn, as if a black cloud had settled over it. The day was dreary, but that didn't completely explain the closed and shuttered look that made me think the wooden structure itself was saddened by recent events. The club had aged fifty years overnight. The empty parking lot was a sharp contrast to the successful opening.

"Are you sure you want to be here?" I asked.

"Coleman said it was okay."

He displayed a talent for evasion. "Have you changed your mind? Are you going to open?" A million questions popped into my head. Who would play keyboard? Should the band all stay together in the club for the evening? Even if Scott opened, would people come? Playin' the Bones was getting a dangerous reputation.

"No. We aren't opening." Scott's tone was conclusive. "I came to check over the building. We need to be sure the band equipment is safe, the kitchen shut down. I don't need a fire or for a thief to break in and steal the band's instruments."

I didn't want to, but I told him about the proposal that had come to Oscar at the bank. It shook him, literally, to his shoes. "How much did they offer?"

"A lot of money. Enough to give you a solid start somewhere else. They also want to purchase a large tract of land around the club. It sounds like a multi-billion-dollar investment, and this club is the hub of it all. Because of the legend about the crossroads out front."

"If I close the club for longer than a week, I'll have to let it go. I took a big risk putting the money down on the property, paying for the band members to move here, renovating the kitchen and stocking the bar. I can't sustain the debt if I don't have money coming in."

"I find the offer and the shootings strangely coincidental."

"I know." Scott was almost defeated. "But what can we do about it?"

"The timing with this offer, the way disaster follows immediately on the heels of any success—there has to be local involvement, Scott. Someone here in Sunflower County is working to bring the club down. Are any of the band members still . . . friends with Frasbaum?"

"No. Wilton didn't inspire friendship. He was about control and money."

"Would he push things so far as to shoot someone?"

"I wish I knew." Defeat laced through his words.

"Look, I'm headed to the newspaper to check out the photos Cece took. Maybe I can spot someone who shouldn't have been at the opening."

"I'll review the club inventory and see what we need to order, should we open this weekend. I want to hang around here."

I almost went to him to offer comfort, but Scott didn't want to be comforted. He wanted to save his club. That was my mission.

"Check on Tatiana." I was worried about her, too. Mike's shooting would bring every horrid second of Koby's murder back with a fiery ferocity. "If you hear anything from Coleman and DeWayne, please call me."

"Sarah Booth, you have the heart of a lion. I admire your courage. This is my dream, and you've bought into making it real as if it were your own. I can survive this. If I lose the bar, it won't kill me. Don't put yourself in danger for the club. Or for me." Scott rumpled my hair and walked into the bar, his lean hips churning up memories of a time not so long past.

The *Zinnia Dispatch* was one of the last locally owned newspapers in the nation, and as such, it relied on real reporters committed to the community to dig up and report on the news that mattered to Sunflower Countians.

I loved the smell of paper and ink, and the sense of stepping back in time that came with a visit. When my father worked at the courthouse, I'd often accompanied him to the newspaper for a quick interview or to give the editor his legal advice on whether a story was libelous or not.

Back then, the newspaper had been printed on-site with hot type. I'd wander around the back shop where lead was melted, and then set into letters, words, and sentences, then locked into a page that was placed on the printing press. The rush of the press, forward and back as the pages were printed, four at a time, both terrified and excited me.

Now it had all changed to offset. There were no type-writers, only computers. No Linotypes or roaring presses. The process of printing a paper was so much faster and less labor-intensive. Still, I had great memories.

Cece's cubbyhole was in the very back of the front office, past the desks and cubicles of the other reporters and photographers. Most nodded a greeting or called out a hello as I passed by on the way to her inner sanctum. The reporting staff adored Cece, but they also loathed her a tad. She was the society editor, but more often than not, she broke the big stories because she was dead set in the middle of them—helping me and Tinkie.

I opened the door to her office and stepped inside. Clutter reigned, and while I couldn't see her behind the stacks of newspapers and magazines, I heard her clacking away at her keyboard. "Cece?"

"What?"

"Do you have the photos from last night?"

"Sure. Let me pull them up on the screen for you. How's Mike?"

"No word, yet."

My organized and industrious friend had uploaded all of the images from the club opening onto her computer. Before I could concentrate on identifying faces, I had a question. "Where's Jaytee?" I had to be sure he was tucked safely away and not roaming around the town, an easy target.

"He's still in bed. He's a musician, Sarah Booth. He

doesn't get up until noon. I told him if he left my house I'd get a chain and dog collar and fix him right up." She grinned. "He thought it sounded like fun."

"Oh, for God's sake, stop it." I made the sign of the cross with my fingers. "I don't want to hear about your sex life until I have details to spill, too."

"You could have your pick of men and you know it. You just aren't finished grieving."

I couldn't argue. "Did you find anything odd in the photos?"

"I've been over them three times. I didn't recognize anyone who might be capable of such an awful deed. I know most of the people."

Cece, because of her work at the paper, had a far better breadth of knowledge of local residents than I did. "Can you show me the people you didn't recognize?"

"Already created a file and sent it to Coleman, but let's take a look."

It was worth a shot. A lot of the folks at the club opening were good friends or friends of good friends, but there had been plenty of strangers. Somewhere in that mix was the person I sought.

While I went through the photos, Cece called Tinkie to join us. Ten minutes later, my partner breezed into the newspaper office glowing as if she'd been on a two-week vacation at a spa. No matter how tired, Tinkie came off looking like a million bucks.

Against all the newspaper rules prohibiting dogs, she brought Chablis with her, tucked under her arm. The little Yorkie with the sun-glitzed hair and ferocious underbite leaped four feet from Tinkie's arms into mine, kissing my face as if I were her long lost relative.

"Good, you hold her," Tinkie said, dropping into the

chair in front of the computer screen. "Let's me scroll through these."

For the next hour, we examined a thousand photos. Chablis tired of my lap and sniffed around the floor for morsels of interesting lunches past. Cece was well known for her ability to suck down sugary carbs and never gain an ounce of weight.

"That's a lot of pictures," Tinkie said. "My eyes are glazing over."

Cece had covered the event from top to bottom, including photos of those tailgating in the parking lot. While we perused the pix, Cece wrote her story for the next edition.

"Who is this?" Tinkie asked, pointing to a man in the far corner of one picture. Strangely enough, he wore sunglasses indoors at night. And they weren't Blues Brothers–style sunglasses. These were big aviator glasses, circa 1970. His straight dark hair hung around his face and he sported a thick, bushy beard that obscured his features. A tuque was pulled low on his forehead. He seemed to deliberately recede into the darkest corner of the club.

"I don't know him." I magnified the photo, but the image became a grainy blur. In the dim light of the club, a lot of detail was lost.

"Who is this?" Tinkie signaled Cece over. "Do you know?"

"I don't remember him at all." Cece clicked forward and back to see if he appeared in other photographs. There was no trace. "It's almost like he's a ghost."

I had a terrible thought. Jitty! Had my haint showed up at the club opening wearing a beard and disguised as a man? I enlarged the image. Of course Jitty could take on the persona of anyone she chose, but this wasn't her.

This was someone else who didn't want to be documented. The photos were shot in sequence with only a few moments between. He was there, and then gone.

"He must have realized I was photographing that part of the room and disappeared," Cece said.

"Or hid."

"What would be the benefit of spying?" Tinkie asked. "It's all over town how wonderful the opening was."

"More likely a jealous lover checking up on a cheating spouse," Cece said. "Trust me, those musicians have seen plenty. Jaytee has some fine stories. Those blues boys aren't angels."

"He wouldn't rat out his buddies," Tinkie said.

"Guys talk." Cece shrugged. "They do. Pillow talk. They always want to accuse women of being gossips, but they are the *worst*. I've gotten a few of my best stories in the throes of amore."

"Isn't that illegal?" I asked.

"Not if you do it right." Cece laughed at my expression. "If you don't lighten up and have fun sex, you're going to be an old maid in britches."

"Oh, for pity's sake. I'm not the story here. The shootings are. Leave me and my dying eggs alone."

"You just need some old banty rooster to strut into your bedroom and give you a good pecking." Cece stuck out her head and used her arms for wings, doing the chicken around the room.

She was full of herself since she'd taken up with Jaytee. I couldn't begrudge her feeling terrific. "Take your barnyard wisdom back to your computer and finish your story," I said.

"Amen," Tinkie added. "We have a murder and a shooting to solve. Sex has to come in second place."

"Only for you," Cece said.

"Quit bickering and keep working," Tinkie ordered.

My cell phone rang—Doc Sawyer was calling. "Mike Hawkins is waking up, Sarah Booth. I've called Coleman to talk to him, but I thought you'd want to know."

"How is he?"

"The next few days will be tricky, but the fact he's awake and able to understand what is said to him is a good sign."

"Thank you, Doc, be sure to let Scott know." I didn't have to share the good news with my two associates, Tinkie and Cece had jumped to the correct conclusion. They beamed and demanded details. "Mike is awake. Coleman is with him now."

"Let's finish the photos. We may be needed," Tinkie said.

The strange man with sunglasses and thick beard didn't reappear, an oddity in itself. Until the last few shots. Cece had caught him near the door of the kitchen.

"Here he is again." Cece enlarged the picture.

The pixilation was bad, but it looked to me as if the beard didn't match his natural hair color. "I think his beard's a fake."

"Me, too, but even if I try to ignore the beard, I can't tell enough about him to determine if I know him. He's right beside the kitchen. Maybe it's one of Curtis Hebert's helpers."

"We can find out!" Cece hit the print button on the photo. Her printer churned out a color image. "It's not as good as a print, but it'll do. Curtis lives about three blocks from my house. He and his wife, Patricia Ann, are good people."

"I hope Curtis can help us." Tinkie lifted Chablis into her arms and we were on our way like three ducks in a row.

Curtis Herbert was a slender, wiry man with arm muscles like Popeye. His wife said we could find him at the Golden Age fund-raiser, a gathering of folks interested in 1950s cars, music, movies, and paraphernalia. Curtis was behind a small concession stand selling pulled pork, beef, and chicken sandwiches faster than he could cook the meat on his four big grills.

"Ladies, what can I do for you?" he asked, mopping the meat with a barbecue sauce that held the tang of vinegar and the sweetness of brown sugar.

"Do you recognize this man?" I could hardly ask the question because my mouth watered profusely. The barbecue smelled delicious.

Curtis examined the print. "I saw him at the club last night. He was hanging around the kitchen door. "You think he had something to do with the keyboard player getting shot?"

"Maybe. I wish we could find out his identity. No one seems to know him."

"Ask Nandy, she's my new . . . helper and a wonderful girl. She came by the club to deliver more cornmeal and I asked her to chase him away from the kitchen door. I shouldn't have asked her to speak to him—she's underage and shouldn't be in the club. The dude standing right in the way was a liability, though. If someone flew through the swinging door and barreled into him, they might have been hurt. You know how sue happy the world has become."

"Indeed. Good thinking, Curtis. Do you think Nandy knew him?" Cece asked.

"Could be. She's a shy thing. Doesn't say two words, but she's a hard worker. She can lift, carry, and clean better than any man I've ever had helping me. She does a good job, too." He walked around the grill area and surveyed the parking lot. "She'll be back in a minute. She went to buy more brown sugar for the sauce."

"She's here?" Tinkie asked. We hadn't expected such a stroke of luck.

"Actually, she went to the Pig. Like I said, I need more sugar. Who knew we'd sell four hundred sandwiches today." He closed the lid on the grill and wiped the sweat from his face with his shirtsleeve. It was a chill November day, gray and damp, but working over the grills was hot even in the coldest weather. His red face concerned me.

I went to the front of the stand and got a water for Curtis and took it to him while we waited for Nandy to return.

"Thanks," he said. "Don't frighten the girl, okay?"

"Of course not," Tinkie said sweetly. "We wouldn't do such a thing."

"She's been dealt a rough hand. She's liable to bolt and run if you get too aggressive."

"How so?" Cece asked. She was always sniffing for a good story.

"Her parents belong to some crazy religious cult. She didn't attend high school. They homeschooled her." He drew air quotes around the words. "She showed up at an event I was cooking for nearly starved to death and asking if she could work for a sandwich. I took her home to Patricia Ann, who discovered Nandy was illiterate for all practical purposes. In three weeks, she takes her GED, thanks to Ned Gaston. Such a shame about his house burning to the ground. I hope the sheriff finds the arsonist."

"Ned worked with her? I thought he focused on the migrant workers." Cece had the scent of a great human-interest story.

"Mostly, but Ned helps anyone who needs it. When I asked him, he didn't bat an eye. That's just the way he is."

I couldn't recall Nandy from the bar, but she'd only stopped by the kitchen to deliver the cornmeal. "Is Nandy a relative?"

"No, no, she's not related, but she's like our daughter. Patricia Ann took a real liking to her. She let her move in with us, and she's been there ever since. About two years now. Like I said, she'll get her GED and Patricia determined Nandy needs a degree. We're looking at Delta State for her."

Whoever she was, Nandy had stumbled on the pot of gold at the end of the rainbow when she approached Curtis Hebert for work. The Heberts intended to help her through college. Folks could truly be amazing sometimes.

"She never really wanted to talk about her life before us. She said her parents were brainwashed by a religious cult and she got away. No one ever came hunting her. No one asked. She moved in and it was like she'd always been a part of our family. Patricia couldn't have children. Nandy was a gift from God."

I saw the young girl walking down the row toward the concession stand carrying two grocery bags equally weighted. She was pretty in a plain way, and she walked in a manner that shunned attention and screamed lack of self-confidence. "Was she with Reverend Jebediah Farley?" I asked Curtis.

"Could be. She didn't want to talk about it and I didn't push it. She doesn't have to help me cook. She likes it. She does little things for Patricia that are thoughtful and kind. This girl deserves an education and a chance at life, and we're going to give it to her."

"Does she have a last name?" I asked.

"She goes by Hebert now. When she gets ready for college we'll have to get her legal birth certificate, but so far, there's been no need to probe into her past. She's skittish. We didn't want to scare her and send her running."

Curtis hadn't exactly broken the law, but he'd skirted it. He'd failed to involve the authorities, and obviously Nandy's parents hadn't bothered to file a missing person report on her. While the law might not agree, I could say things had worked out perfectly.

She came up to us and handed Curtis the sugar. "Nandy, these are friends of mine. They're trying to help the band from the blues club. They want to ask you some questions."

She looked like a wild animal caught in a trap. "I don't know anything. I wasn't there but a minute. I went home before anything happened."

"That's true," Curtis said. "We were both home and tucked in bed before Mike was shot."

"We understand," Tinkie said soothingly. "But we need your help." She was the same height as Nandy, who might be close to eighteen but could be mistaken for a child. "We have a photograph of a man. If you can tell us who he is—"

"I don't know anything," she said, fear in her voice.

She sidled closer to Curtis as if he would physically protect her.

"We won't hurt you," I said.

"Girl, they're trying to find out who killed that bartender, Koby. You met him one day in the grocery store and liked him. You want to help find the people who shot him. And they shot Mike Hawkins, too. Just take a look at the photo. If you can help, do it."

Tinkie offered her the picture. She took a quick look and twisted around as if she expected someone to jump out and grab her. "I can't say. They'll hurt Curtis or Patricia."

"Who will hurt them?" Tinkie asked in a gentle voice.

Nandy shook her head. "I won't say. I can't. You can't make me."

Curtis pulled her against his side. "I know you're scared, Nandy, but Patricia and I can take care of ourselves. I promise you. And we'll take care of you. Why are you so afraid?"

"They hurt people. They do it all the time and no one ever stops them."

"Who is they?" I asked.

"The church. Not the church people, but the big shots. The men who run it."

Heat jumped into Tinkie's cheeks. "Reverend Farley?" she asked Nandy.

The girl nodded, so miserable she couldn't even face us. "Him and those bigwigs. They got private planes and they come in big black cars and off they go to do business. They hate that kind of music, and they hate places where black and white people mix. They hate women. They hate everything." She started crying. "They burned

Mr. Ned's house because he helps the migrant children. But mostly they burned it because he helped me study to go to college." She grabbed Curtis's arm. "They'll hurt you and Patricia, too. They don't believe girls should have an education. Reverend Farley says an education is a ticket for the weaker sex to go straight to hell."

"Farley is a total asswipe." I couldn't stop myself. "He's wrong, Nandy. He's wrong about everything he says. You can't let crazy talk influence you."

"He hurts everyone except for his chosen. That's who was at the club last night. That's the man in the picture. Fred Doleman. He was there snooping for Reverend Farley. Fred can do things none of the others can because Reverend Farley says he's impervious to temptation. He said he's been tested and passed. He was at the club spying. That's why I couldn't chase him away from the door. I didn't want him to know I was there."

Beneath her fear, anger bubbled. If she was ever going to break free of the training she'd been subjected to, she'd have to hold on to her anger and wield it like a sword. "What they taught you and did to you is a crime."

Cece knelt down, able to remain graceful in her miniskirt and high heels. "Honey, each one of us has a right to be who we are. No matter what they told you, the man upstairs loves each of us just the way we are. All he asks is that we're kind to one another."

Nandy's tears fell silently. "Fred says the people in the club will pay for their sins. Reverend Farley and his friends have so much money. Before I left the church, I overheard the reverend talking with one of the rich people who fly in to see him. He was talking about millions of dollars and shipments and such. How can he have so much money when the people who follow him don't have enough to eat sometimes?"

"Did he say what was being shipped in?"

Nandy shook her head. "It's all a big secret, but it was hinted that this was food to be sent to different groups surviving in the wild. A network of folks living off the grid and ready to take back America from the socialists. Sometimes the women and teenagers help unload trucks late at night. Mostly into old sheds hidden around local farms. We were never told what we were doing, just that it was God's work."

"Can you take us to some of the sheds?" I asked.

She shook her head. "We never saw where we were going, and it was always at night. We knew not to ask."

What Nandy described amounted to little more than slavery. "We'll handle this," I promised her.

"They'll burn that blues club down like they did Ned's house."

"You know they burned Mr. Gaston's house?" I pulled my cell phone from my pocket to call Coleman.

"It had to be them. They were mad, because I told them I was going to college." She was crying so hard it was difficult to understand her. "I saw them at the store one day. Fred and Wanda. They're always the ones who get to leave the compound and act like normal people. I didn't run. Instead, I stood up to them. I told them I was going to college, that I was going to be someone. They said the people who corrupted me would pay. They said a woman's place was to be obedient to her father and husband. I shouldn't have gotten in their face. I should have run away. Now they'll hurt Curtis and Patricia, too."

"Do you have any proof they set fire to Ned's house?"

The question calmed her tears. "No. I just know it."

Unfortunately, that wasn't good enough for an arrest. Nandy had a lot of suspicions based on the terrible treatment she'd received. But it wasn't evidence.

While Tinkie comforted Nandy and Cece made some notes, I called Coleman. I recounted what Nandy had told us, and he asked to speak to Curtis.

"We'll be along as soon as I finish the concession here. I can't leave these people in the lurch. Maybe another hour. Would you send someone to check on Patricia? Listening to Nandy talk, I'm worried now."

He handed me the phone.

"Good work, Sarah Booth," Coleman said.

"I can't take credit for stumbling over this." Another instance where fate, not my sleuthing abilities, handed me a piece of the puzzle.

"Would you stop by Mrs. Hebert's and alert her to potential trouble?" Coleman asked. "I've known Patricia Ann for a long, long time and I feel sorry for anyone who tries to cross her. But let her know there's a risk."

"Ten-four."

While Curtis finished with the barbecue, we chatted with Nandy. She calmed down as she talked about the church. "The men are everything. They make all the decisions. The women do the work and obey. If a woman tried to speak out or even say what she felt, she was punished. My mother," she teared up again, "Daddy cut her hair. In front of the church. And then he whipped her with everyone watching."

"Why would he do that?" Tinkie asked.

"She said I was smart and maybe I should go to a church school. He said she defied him by questioning his authority."

"How did you get away from them?"

"I saw Reverend Farley and Wanda Tatum having sex. I stole Wanda's cell phone and took pictures of them. Then I hid the phone. I told them I had the pictures and I'd sent them to a friend who would give them to the police if anything happened to me."

I wanted to clap and applaud Nandy. She'd learned meek behavior to survive, but she was smart and strong and brave. "And so they let you go."

She nodded. "I thought they had. Then Mr. Ned's house burned, and I knew it was them, getting back at me." Her chin trembled. "I have to go back. If I don't, they'll hurt more people."

"No, they won't," Cece assured her. "Why did your mother agree to join Farley's group in the first place?"

"My little sister drowned while we were swimming. Mama was smoking weed and sunbathing down at the river. Daddy told Mama it was God's punishment for her sinful ways. He said God took Julie because Mama was sinning. He made her believe she was bad. Something happened to her. It was like she broke. She just quit fighting. Daddy had been going to meetings with Reverend Farley and the Midnight Templars, and he said we were selling the house, joining the church, and living a godly life from now on. We sold everything and moved into a tent."

"How old were you?" Cece asked.

"I was eleven. They pulled me from school, and I lived on the church property in a tent until I ran away."

"Tell us about the Midnight Templars," I requested. I'd never heard of the organization, and I had a very, very bad feeling I wasn't going to like a single thing Nandy offered.

"I don't know much. Only men can belong. Sometimes Reverend Farley and the head people go to New York or Washington for business meetings. Those are the rich people. A few of the church men belong, but in a different way. Men like Fred and Mason Britt train and practice in the woods with weapons. They teach the children about all the conspiracies in the government, how America is becoming a country of sinners."

"Sinners as defined by Reverend Farley?"

She nodded.

"Nandy, Sheriff Peters will take care of this, and I promise you he'll do whatever is necessary to keep you and the Heberts safe."

We dropped Cece back at the newspaper and a cooperative Patricia Ann Hebert at the courthouse. Tinkie and I stopped at the hospital. Coleman, as promised, had called to fill us in after talking with a very groggy Mike Hawkins. Mike had been moved to a room, and when we tapped on the door, his wife invited us in.

"He's gaining strength," Danni told us. She was ghostly pale and shaky, but her smile was a million watts. "Every hour puts him more in the black."

"Is he strong enough for questions?" I asked.

"He told the sheriff everything he could remember." Danni didn't want to say no, but protecting Mike was her first duty. "Just a few."

"I know Coleman asked, but do you remember anything about the truck?" I hated to be blunt, but the day was slipping from us. Night was only a few hours away, and I dreaded the possibility another band member would be attacked.

Mike closed his eyes. "I got out of the van and started toward the house. I saw Danni in the doorway, waiting for me. I was so excited about the opening and how well it went. Since Danni was pregnant she had to miss the big night, and I couldn't wait to share the evening with her."

Danni picked up his hand and kissed it.

"So you were walking toward the house, yet you turned back to face the street. Why? Did you hear something?"

"I *did* hear something." A light touched his face. "I didn't tell the sheriff this because I'd forgotten. I heard music."

"The blues?"

He shook his head. "No—"

"It was the national anthem, 'The Star Spangled Banner,'" Danni said, leaning forward. "I'd forgotten, too, but it was strange. The music was so loud, coming from the truck, except I didn't see the truck. It was like the music came out of the darkness because the truck was parked there, idling, without any lights."

Mike was excited. "I heard the music and then the loud muffler, and then the diesel engine when the truck roared past the house and the gun went off."

"You turned at the sound of the truck's muffler?"

"At the music. That's why I was shot in the chest instead of the back." Mike looked shaky but triumphant that he'd remembered.

"Thank you," I said. "We're going to find the person, Mike. You're already in the healing process. Scott will save the club. Before you know it, Bad to the Bone will be on the stage and playing the blues."

"The person who did this has to be caught," Mike said. "This is bigger than me or Koby or Scott and Playin' the

Bones. This is about intimidation and people who are willfully ignorant. It makes me mad they're using our national anthem when they commit acts of terror, and that's what this is. We aren't going to let them win."

"No we're not," Tinkie said. "Now you rest. This has been a lot of help."

"How's Jaytee? And Davy? And Zeb?" Mike asked. "Are they safe?"

"They are." Tinkie checked her watch. "Davy's in his B&B and Zeb is at his place. Both promised to stay put. Jaytee is at Cece's house. She'll make sure he stays right there, so no worries."

"Keep us posted," Danni said.

"Absolutely," I promised. We left before we tired Mike.

Tinkie and I ran by Millie's for a quick bite and then headed to Hilltop to pick up the critters. Dahlia House and Delaney Detective Agency was our destination. We had work to do researching the Midnight Templars. The crazy thing Mike and Danni had remembered—the playing of the national anthem—was a very loose connection to what Nandy had told us about the Midnight Templars and survivalists who felt they were losing control of "their" country. We needed to solidify that connection with real evidence, not my gut feelings.

But the very first thing I had to do was let Harold know his prank against Bijou might have dire consequences. He meant to inconvenience Bijou by cluttering her life with the Foundation Rock people. He'd invited them to hold a revival on her property, and while I was positive Bijou was tough enough to deal with pit vipers, Harold might want to reconsider his action. The problem was I didn't want to tip Tinkie to what Harold had done. He could tell her, if he chose to.

We were almost home when Cece called. Tinkie answered, and in a few seconds, she grabbed my arm. "Turn around. We have to go to Cece's."

"Why?"

"Jaytee is missing and it appears there was a fight in the house. Cece just got there from the newspaper. She's almost hysterical."

"Damn," I said inelegantly, as I whipped the car around in a U-turn and pressed the accelerator to the floor.

15

Harold was on the scene by the time we arrived. He and Roscoe were doing their best to comfort a distraught Cece, with no success.

"There's not a sign of him. And look!" She pointed at the overturned sofa, a broken lamp, the laptop on the floor, spitting and sizzling. I reached over and unplugged it from the wall where it had been charging.

"We'll find him, won't we, Sarah Booth?" Tinkie kicked my foot, but gently.

"Sure we will." I pulled my thoughts back to the immediate moment. "When did you last talk to Jaytee?"

Cece didn't have to think. "After you dropped me at the paper, I called and told him I'd be home within the hour. I had to do the edits on my story about the club opening. I finished and came straight home. To find him gone!"

Cece wasn't a wailer or a whiner, but she was on the verge of losing control. I couldn't blame her. I knew what it felt like to have your beloved taken by a crazy person. But I wouldn't think of Graf and Gertrude. I wouldn't bring that bad karma to this door. Jaytee would be fine. He had to be. Cece deserved a shot at happiness, and Jaytee was the man for her.

Coleman, haggard and exhausted, arrived with De-Wayne and began the tedious process of searching for forensic evidence. The TV shows that depict finding DNA or trace evidence in a blur of magical whirring machines and technicians who can spot a molecule on a dust mote are so far from the truth of how most small, underfunded crime units worked that it is laughable.

But I did have a little good news for Coleman. I pulled him aside and told him about my talk with Nandy and Curtis Hebert.

"Midnight Templars," he said. "What the hell is that?"

"Tinkie and I are checking into it. Nandy wasn't clear and she couldn't distinguish between Farley's activities and this secret organization of rich men. Of course, it could be Farley blowing smoke to appear to be more important than he really is. Or someone could be using Farley as a beard—taking actions they hope the church will be blamed for."

"I'm sick to death of crazy people." Coleman's anger was quiet, and far more lethal than loud anger.

"Couldn't you just shoot them?" I was only half-kidding.

"I'd like to. Talk about a way to save tax dollars, that would be my choice."

I had plenty to add, but ranting wouldn't help. "You can't fix stupid."

"Amen. But I can damn sure put it in jail."

"I'll investigate the Midnight Templars, but first we have to find Jaytee. Please, for Cece's sake."

"We'll find him, and Sarah Booth, Gertrude has filed trespassing charges against you and Tinkie. I don't understand why she didn't do it immediately."

I didn't even care. "So, I'll pay the fine."

"It's a bit more complicated, but don't worry about that right now. There's something else."

"What?"

"Frisco Evans has disappeared. He hasn't been at the car dealership since yesterday afternoon. He was last seen showing a Mercedes roadster to Gertrude. The same model car that you drive."

"My mother's car."

"Exactly."

"Do you think Gertrude did something to Frisco?"

"It's possible. It's also possible he's behind the new offer to buy the club. He's a wealthy man. Oscar helped me out a little, and Frisco made some terrific investments. He's got a lot of disposable cash. I don't know how he's involved with Gertrude, or if he's involved at all. He's still a viable suspect in the club shootings. He's used to getting what he wants."

"He had an alibi." I sounded pitiful.

"So many things have happened in such a short time frame, we're both playing catch-up instead of offense. This is a crime wave. I need at least ten more deputies. You and Tinkie are a great help, but we can't cover the ground we need to cover. What strikes me is that all of this started *after* Gertrude was released."

"There is no end to Gertrude's involvement, is there?"

"Her finger is in this pie, I'm just not sure how. Instead of focusing on her, though, finding Jaytee is the top priority. Now you buck up. I need you strong and alert."

"Okay." I met his gaze with calm. Coleman had enough on his plate. He didn't need to worry I was melting down. "I'm good."

"You're amazing, but let's put that talent toward finding Jaytee."

DeWayne took the fingerprints he found to the sheriff's office to run against those on file. It was a long shot, but it was something. I pulled Harold aside and urged him to rescind the invitation to Foundation Rock to gather at Bijou's property.

"There's a small problem. I'm not certain I *can* rescind the invitation. What will be, will be."

Harold was far too blasé for my taste. "I wouldn't object if they used Bijou for human sacrifice, but I don't want it to splash back on *you*."

"No worries. If Bijou doesn't want them on her property, they'll be gone. Bijou truly can take care of herself, and she isn't hampered by the law, ethics, or what's right and wrong. I fear for the person who crosses her. But enough about her." He pushed my hair out of my eyes. "You look like shit."

"Such a sweet talker."

"When this is over, consider my offer of dinner in Venice. You could use a vacation away from everything familiar."

"You, sir, are a tempter. I might have to report you to Reverend Farley for trying to lure me into bad behavior."

"That's only the tip of the iceberg." He winked at me and went to talk to Cece.

Looking around Cece's home, I tried to imagine what had happened to Jaytee. The door hadn't been kicked in, so the harmonica player had opened it to someone. Or perhaps he'd been on the way outside when someone attacked.

The place had been trashed, as if the kidnapper was hunting for something. What did Cece have the kidnapper might want? She was comfortable, but not rich. The likelihood of finding great wealth or even expensive electronics was slim. What could she have of value? Was someone looking for the photos from the club opening? I thought the answer was a firm yes, based on the evidence—her files had been scattered around the room and the intruder had taken the memory cards from the two cameras on her bookcase.

Anyone who knew Cece would know she'd downloaded her photos as soon as she got home and sent them to the paper. It was SOP for her. That ensured a triplicate set of photos—one on her camera, one on the cloud, and one at the newspaper. But a person who'd never worked in journalism or met daily deadlines wouldn't realize that. If the intruder had meant to destroy the photos from the club opening—and Fred Doleman had behaved as if he didn't want to be photographed and possibly identified—then I could make a deduction that might lead to Jaytee's location.

I caught Coleman alone and told him what I suspected. "They might be holding Jaytee at the church compound."

"That's a damn good lead, Sarah Booth."

"I don't have solid evidence. Just a hunch."

"It'll be difficult to get a judge to give me a search warrant for a church. Everyone on the bench has to run for reelection, and invading church property . . . not going to happen without major probable cause."

He didn't have to explain. I knew the political climate. "It's a sensitive area, especially these days." I could have gone into another rant about how justice shouldn't be held hostage to politics, but none of this was Coleman's fault. We were all victims of a system out of kilter. "I can go in."

"Oh, no." Coleman was having none of that. "If these people are kidnapping, setting fires, and shooting musicians, they wouldn't think twice about doing something to you. You'd open your mouth and send them into a frenzy. You are absolutely not doing anything that risky."

"Do you have an alternative plan?"

"We'll come up with something. Just stay away from Farley's compound. Promise me."

"Okay." I smiled. I had no intention of lying to Coleman. I wasn't that kind of girl.

Tinkie was busy comforting Cece, and Harold left for home. Cece would give Tinkie a ride back to Hilltop when they realized I was gone. I hated to set off without my partner, but Tinkie would insist on accompanying me. She was dead-eye Pete with a pistol, but she didn't need to be involved in my plan.

I'd promised Coleman I wouldn't go to the church compound. And I didn't intend to. Bijou's property, Hemlock

Manor, was my destination. It stood to reason that Farley, if he was behind Jaytee's abduction, wouldn't hold him at the church compound. Too obvious. Harold's fake invitation to Hemlock Manor would give him the perfect opportunity to imprison Jaytee there. As I knew from searching the premises for Roscoe, there were plenty of places to keep someone captive. Bijou's complicity in all of this could be determined later.

A rescue attempt wasn't my plan. I would stay hidden and photograph Jaytee, if he was there. I would gather the evidence Coleman needed for a search warrant.

The person I had to be careful of was Mason Britt. Bijou's foreman acted like a true believer of the propaganda Farley was selling. And if Koby's murderer came from the church, Mason Britt would be my first choice as shooter. He had the training and the temper.

My backup plan, should I fail to photograph Jaytee, included finding Nandy's parents and squeezing them until they coughed up useful information.

To that end, I slipped from Cece's house and hurried to my car. Like a land shark, Roscoe came up behind me, growling his evil little growl, eyes crackling with intelligence, little goatee aquiver with anticipation.

"Go home." I stopped to point in the direction of Harold's. "You're injured and you need to stay home."

"Grrr-rrr-rrr-rrrrr." His beady little eyes danced.

"Roscoe, go home. You have broken ribs. You can't go with me."

"Grrr-rrrrr-rrrr—ahhhh!" He sounded positively possessed.

I ignored him and walked to the driver's side.

"Aaarrrrffffff!"

His sharp bark was like a bullet crack. Holy moly, he'd have everyone in Cece's house out in the yard if he kept it up.

"Shut up!" I knelt down and took his face in my hands. "I know what you're doing. You're blackmailing me into taking you. I can't do it. You're injured. If something happened to you, Harold would never forgive me. Now go home." I pointed again. I had no doubt Roscoe understood every word I said. The thing was, he chose to disobey.

Roscoe held his ground.

At any moment Coleman or Tinkie would come out of Cece's house and find me trying to make a getaway. I tried once more to open the car door and Roscoe tilted his head and barked—softly. As if to say, "I can make it loud if I really have to."

"You demented little beast!" I waved him into the car. "Come on." I would take him with me and lock him in Dahlia House. As my aunt Loulane would opine, there was more than one way to skin a cat, or an impish little dog.

Roscoe hopped gleefully into the front seat and sat down like royalty waiting to be chauffeured. I had to run by Dahlia House to check on Sweetie and Pluto, and to get some tools, namely my camera and telephoto lens. My pistol was already in my purse.

Graf had once accused me of excellent rationalization skills. Perhaps. Or maybe I was just an optimist. My mission to Hemlock Manor was dangerous, but I had faith I could pull it off.

I had to believe that if the kidnappers meant to kill Jaytee, he would have been dead on Cece's floor. His abductors wanted leverage. For what I didn't know, but I couldn't wait around to find out. There was a troubling aspect to my theory that Farley and his cult were behind Koby's murder, Mike's shooting, and the abduction of Jaytee. Summed up, it was simple. Why? Could they really hate the blues that much and think a nightclub was a danger to their American way of life? It didn't make sense. Sure, they were crazy. And crazy bred crazy. But Farley, for all of his willful ignorance and backwoods mentality, wasn't stupid. There was a big old world out there with hip-hop, jazz, R&B, rock, classical—lots of music that might not suit his taste. He couldn't eradicate it all.

Bottom line, I just couldn't believe Farley was that dumb. Then again, perhaps I overestimated his intelligence. No, I had shifted my focus to Mason Britt and the high-stakes offer to buy the club. I didn't have a clear picture, but it seemed far more likely to me that someone— maybe Frisco Evans—was determined to run Scott out of Sunflower County. And Mason Britt was a powerful weapon to aim.

I pulled up at Dahlia House to find Sweetie and Pluto on the porch waiting for me, almost as if they'd communicated psychically with Roscoe. I glared at Roscoe, who was wearing his innocent face. Who? Me? When I opened the passenger door to get him out, he refused to budge and growled at me.

"Roscoe!" I wasn't afraid of him. Exactly. He was known to snap when he didn't get his way, but this was one battle he wasn't winning. "Out of the car."

"Grrrrr-rrrrrr." With his bushy eyebrows and beard, he looked demented.

"You have to get out."

A breeze blew by me as Sweetie Pie sailed past the front seat and into the back. Pluto, who could not be hurried if his tail were on fire, sauntered up to the car and jumped into the front seat with Roscoe.

Roscoe growled at the cat, then licked his head.

"Out!" I pointed to Dahlia House. "All of you. Out!" They refused to budge.

I picked Roscoe up in my arms and took him to the front door and put him inside, then went back to deal with the mutiny taking place among my own animals. I was in a hurry. I didn't have time to fight with recalcitrant critters.

Sweetie refused to leave the backseat, and when I leaned over to get Pluto, something vile and wicked jumped on my back and flattened me in the seat. Roscoe was back. Sitting on my head. He'd rushed out the kitchen doggie door.

For a dog with broken ribs who wasn't supposed to exert himself, Roscoe was not being a good patient.

"Fine." I had to hurry before Coleman got the report I was MIA and figured out where I was headed. "I can lock you all in the car. You can just sit and wait—"

My lecture was cut off by the mournful sound of minor piano chords. I froze as the sweet, musky scent of gardenias filled the air. I knew what was coming. "Not now!" I said aloud. "Time is crucial!"

A rich, distinctive voice sang lyrics I knew by heart. "Southern trees, bear a strange fruit . . ." The words painted the legacy of violence and blood that had scarred the South for too many generations.

I pivoted and faced Billie Holiday on the front lawn of

my home. Thin as a rail, elegant in sequins, and tired, she sang the song written by a Brooklyn schoolteacher that never failed to move me.

My father had told me the history of "Strange Fruit," and the courage of the composer and the performer who took on racism at a time when such things could be deadly. Daddy had lectured me on the price for standing up for justice, and he had instilled in me that good people took a stand. Like Abel Meeropol, the songwriter, and Atticus Finch, a fictional attorney. Doing the right thing always came with a price tag.

Jitty, as Billie Holiday, sang the lyrics with grit and passion. I needed to hurry, but time had to be taken to hear this song. And with each line, my fear for Jaytee grew. Was Jitty telling me the harmonica player had been killed? A victim of senseless violence?

"Tell me he's okay," I begged as soon as she'd finished.

"Be careful, Sarah Booth."

"Jitty, just tell me. If something has happened to Jaytee, it will kill Cece." My own life had been upturned by loss, but what confronted Cece was so much worse. Graf was alive and living his life in Hollywood. I could imagine him happy and healthy. Such would not be the case if a cult of crazies killed Jaytee to drive home a point about music or race or gender or whatever their warped agenda might be.

"Hurry, Sarah Booth. There's no time for talk or second guessing. Be careful and hurry."

I didn't wait for a second command. I rushed inside for the camera, made sure I had my gun, climbed behind the wheel, and fishtailed down the drive. Whatever Jitty's purpose in my life might be, she'd galvanized me to action. I had my equipment and my four-legged posse.

I would find Jaytee and I would do whatever was necessary. Coleman was right about that. The one thing I would take from this season of loss was a true knowledge of myself and my ability to defend what I loved and believed in.

16

The drive to Hemlock Manor took me past peanut, corn, and soybean fields. Another two weeks would bring Thanksgiving. I wanted to have a party, like my mother used to have. A celebration of friends on the one holiday devoted to harvest and homecoming. Pumpkin pies, turkey with dressing, all the trimmings. I could cook most of it, but Millie, Tinkie, and Cece would bring dishes. Or at least advice. Tinkie had been banned from the Hilltop kitchen because her last experiment with doggie treats almost required the EPA for disposal. Alcohol might be a safer choice for her.

I tried to think of pleasant things as I drove toward a dangerous encounter. Jaytee was in danger. I'd underestimated the people who'd taken him. My fingers traced the outline of the telephone in my jeans pocket, but I didn't call Coleman. He was hampered by the law, and if he arrived too soon, he would prevent me from getting the evidence he needed to act.

I could do this quicker, better, and with no legal entanglements other than a possible trespassing charge. I seemed to be acquiring a slew of those.

All I needed was one clear photo of Jaytee on the premises.

I replayed the layout of Hemlock Manor, piecing together the places most likely to hide a human hostage. The wild card was whether Bijou was involved in this. The logical answer was no—Harold had invited the church congregation onto her property without her knowledge or consent. Yet I couldn't discount the fact that Mason Britt, her foreman, had been copying flyers for Farley's organization on her equipment. That proved nothing, but it ignited my suspicions and tickled my gut instinct.

If I couldn't find Jaytee outright, I had my fallback plan. Nandy's parents were likely still members of the church. Finding them would be trickier and would require a lot more risk.

I'd never studied the deeper psychology of cults, but I understood the participants yielded their individuality to be accepted into the whole. The hallmark of a cult was the loss of personal identity. The Manson cult was the famous example. They rampaged and killed "the rich and beautiful" at the behest of their leader. Charles Manson vilified a particular segment of society and his followers savagely killed them.

And the Reverend Jim Jones's Kool-Aid mass suicide was another example of people who'd fallen under the sway of a man who used what he called religion to control others. Over three hundred people, most willingly, drank poison. They gave it to their children.

Members of both Manson and Jones's cults were willing to kill and be killed to protect their leader.

The power one charismatic leader could wield over a group of adults amazed me. In a belief system where one race or gender was treated as inferior, the bond could be even stronger. Adolf Hitler launched a world war based on such insanity.

I couldn't imagine letting someone break me down and make me believe I deserved second-class treatment— or that I should treat anyone else as inferior—but I'd seen it more than I cared to in abusive marriages. Women who cried for help while their husbands beat them and then turned on the police who arrived to save them. Domestic calls were most cops' worst nightmare.

And it cut across both genders. But mostly women were oppressed, and especially those in a religion or culture that fostered a woman-as-servant philosophy.

Turning down the private road to Hemlock Manor, I could only hope my supposition was correct—that the cult ringleaders had shifted from the church grounds to Bijou's more accommodating property and brought their hostage with them.

Sweetie's soft yodel came from the backseat. She, too, was singing the blues. Somehow the animals sensed I was driving into danger. They were anxious and attentive.

"It'll be fine. I'm already one trespassing charge in the hole, why not go two for two?" Talking to the animals was becoming a bad habit. Jabbering clearly showed nervousness. I was afraid. No way around it. Too much hung in the balance.

Torn between a need to rush and a desire to play it

safe, I parked in the woods on the grounds of Hemlock Manor. Now I wished I hadn't nicknamed the place for a poison. I didn't need a premonition of death. Not even for Bijou. I disliked her enormously, but I didn't want her dead. I didn't want anyone else to die.

I pulled deep enough into the trees where no one could see my car if they drove past. I grabbed my handgun and my camera. "Stay here," I warned the animals. "I'll be back." It was a promise I meant to keep.

I slipped out the door and closed it before any of the critters could follow me. Sweetie Pie sent up a heartrending howl. Roscoe bounced in the passenger seat like a possessed bobble toy. But it was Pluto who sent an icy chill through my heart. He put his front paws on the dashboard and glared at me. The hair along his spine and tail stood on end, and he arched like a Halloween caricature.

He was one angry pussycat.

Before I lost my resolve, I headed through the woods, glad the day was bitter cold and all the ticks, yellow flies, and mosquitoes were long dead.

Any Delta girl worth her salt can navigate through woods and fields using the sky for directions. I angled ever eastward, jogging until I was out of breath, and then walking. I would start a fitness routine the minute this case was solved. The very second! Wheezing and blowing, I leaned against a tree trunk to catch my breath. I'd calculated that my route would stretch about a mile. I had to be close.

The woods around me were alive with birds and small creatures crackling in the leaves. The wild things fell silent when danger approached. They'd learned how to survive by being still. I had to be as canny.

A male voice stopped me on an inhale. I froze.

"Mason, you're needed in the tractor shed."

It was a completely normal thing to hear on a working farm, yet my lungs tightened with fear. Mason Britt had to be within shouting distance. I'd closed in on the house quicker than I'd calculated. I couldn't see the person who spoke because of the thicket of trees, unusual on a Delta plantation where the rich topsoil was so valuable for growing crops. I thanked my lucky stars, though, that I had cover to hide in.

Success depended on caution and the ability to slip around the property without getting caught. First I had to ascertain where everyone was situated. I eased forward, the camera ready, the gun tucked into the waist of my jeans. After I started my fitness regime, I would purchase a shoulder holster. And take shooting lessons. And ballroom dancing. And definitely jump on that diet. Right after I took down these creeps.

Inching forward toward the clearing where several pickup trucks, three tractors, a cotton picker, and assorted vehicles were parked, I realized I'd come upon the place where farmworkers parked and reported for duty. From this central location, they'd be sent into the fields to till, harvest, cut—whatever was necessary. I judged Hemlock Manor to contain at least four thousand acres. The land would be in production year-round, with cotton the primary money crop. Still Bijou would grow corn, soybeans, peanuts, any number of other crops, just in smaller acreage. The work would keep a team of farmers busy all year.

And Mason was in charge of organizing the farm. Which meant that if he did his job properly, he would be constantly on the move, overseeing projects, making sure things were done right. If I were really, really lucky, he would leave the main house property and head to the fields, taking most of the men with him.

"What about the winter rye? We should get that seed out. I can take Juan and his crew and get started on it," the same man asked Mason.

I'd crept close enough that I could see Mason behind a pickup. He was talking with another young man who wore short sleeves in the bitter cold. His arms bulged with muscles and tats.

"Yeah, good idea," Mason said. "I have errands to do for Ms. LaRoche."

"I thought the errands you did for her took place in the main house," the man said. "Until she started hanging around with that old man. He can't give her what you can, but he can buy a lot of shit you can't. You'd best be careful or you'll lose a really good thing. If he catches on to what you and the missus do together, he won't tolerate it."

He had to be referring to Yancy Bellow. He was older, and he was also very wealthy. Money attracted money, and if I knew a thing about Bijou, she wouldn't hesitate to marry Yancy and keep her boy toys on the side.

"I'm not worried." Mason sounded as arrogant as ever. "I've got what she needs. The old man is a mark."

The other man laughed. "We'll see about that. Where did those church people come from? They showed up here this morning and took over the slave cabins like they'd been invited in. The women, hell, they look like something from a pioneer history book with those dresses down to the ground and their hair all done up. Are they Amish or something?"

Mason visibly tensed. If his reaction was any indication, it would seem the other farmworkers didn't know of his affiliation with Reverend Farley and his church. This exchange should prove interesting.

"They're not Amish. They're God-fearing women who know how to dress not to provoke lustful thoughts in men."

Okay, I was officially pissed. Now women were responsible for men's thoughts. Really? The farmhand was taken aback. This wasn't the reaction he'd anticipated.

"Sorry, man. Didn't mean to step on any toes. I'll round up the crews and get them off to the fields. We're running late for the afternoon chores as it is." He was walking away when Mason spoke.

"No offense taken. This has been a mess. Folks coming and going and no one where they're supposed to be." He was so tense the muscles of his neck stood out like cords. "You haven't seen any more strangers around here, have you?"

"No, just the work crew. Should I be on the lookout?"

Mason shook his head. "The church people are leaving. It was a mistake they came here. Someone got their wires crossed." He loosened up and grinned. "Ms. LaRoche was fit to be tied. Someone sent out an invite for them to move into the slave quarters and use the main barn for their church. When she finds out who did that, she's going to put a whuppin' on them. Just be careful what you say about folks and their religion, Jimbo."

"I hear ya, Mason. I didn't mean any harm."

"Keep the fact the congregation was on the LaRoche property under your hat. Folks wouldn't understand. And leave Lon here. Tell him to be sure none of the church people wander around the utility sheds. There's some dangerous chemicals stored there. Wouldn't want anyone to get hurt."

"I'll send Lon down there. See ya this evening." Jimbo hopped in a truck, gunned the engine, and took off.

Mason stood for a moment, his hands clenching and unclenching. He took his church business seriously. Now I prayed he'd climb in a vehicle and leave too. My prayers were granted when he opened the door of a red Dodge Ram and drove away. I had a clear path to search for Jaytee and whatever evidence I could find.

Using the telephoto camera lens, I checked around the area as best I could, zeroing in on places where Jaytee might be hidden. My cell phone vibrated in my pocket. I didn't have to look to know Tinkie, Cece, and Coleman were all calling. Pissed and calling. I had no intention of answering.

The coast was clear, and I had to make a move. Mason might be back in twenty minutes or four hours. I didn't know, so I had to take the opportunity in front of me.

I dodged around the vehicles, using them for cover from the main house. I didn't think Bijou was the kind of woman who sat at her bedroom window looking out over the utility barns and shed, but I couldn't say for positive. She might be up there with a rifle and scope ready to pick off any trespassers.

My grand scheme to stay on the fringes and use the camera wasn't working out the way I'd planned. The only option was to rush the premises and do a building-to-building search. This area of the farm would take time, and I knew from a Google aerial of the property that out-buildings were scattered about the vast acreage; places to store fertilizer, chemicals, equipment, even a hangar for the private planes that landed at Bijou's small private land-ing strip. Many of the working plantations maintained facilities for crop dusters to touch down to refuel and restock the pesticides they sprayed. The Delta, a vast expanse of fertile land, was also geographically isolated from business centers. Private planes made trips to Memphis, Atlanta, and New Orleans much more convenient.

Ducking and weaving, I made my way to the first shed. The smell of old hay and mold was strong. The structure contained four horse stalls, now empty except for tractors in various states of disrepair. Several closed doors held promise, but they led to rooms with shelves containing parts. There was no sign of Jaytee.

The next shed was twenty yards away. I'd have to run across open ground. I hit it before I gave it too much thought. Fertilizers and chemicals filled this building—the tools of large-scale farming.

Though I looked in every possible spot, the man I sought wasn't in evidence. In fact, the only activity I saw was around the old slave quarters where the demurely clad women Jimbo had mentioned were packing things into the bed of an old truck. They worked methodically, the skirts of their long dresses catching the November wind and billowing out. They had to be cold in those skirts. I wore jeans, boots, a thick, heavy jacket, gloves, and a scarf and the wind still cut into me. Winter had come early to the Delta this year, and it promised to be bitter.

Avoiding the packing activity, I sprinted to the big barn where I'd found Roscoe in a cage. I'd pinned my hopes that Jaytee would be there. I searched the place from top to bottom, even climbing into the hayloft, which was filled with sweet, fresh square bales that offered many possibilities for hiding places.

I found no indication Jaytee had been held there. My heart sank. If he wasn't here, I didn't know where he might be. The utility sheds were scattered far and wide. The one thought I couldn't entertain was that Jaytee was dead. That wasn't acceptable. I had to look harder.

About thirty yards from the big barn was the house where Mason lived. In my search for Roscoe, I hadn't investigated the cottage. Mason didn't strike me as the kind of man who allowed a dog in the house, but he wouldn't blink an eye at holding a prisoner there. Now I didn't have a choice. I was in for a penny, so I might as well jump in for a pound. Aunt Loulane might not approve of my activities, but she'd dig the fact I remembered so many of her adages.

I scuttled across the barnyard and almost stopped dead in the middle of the open area when I saw a Chinese-red Mercedes roadster parked at Bijou's front door. Gertrude had been looking at a car exactly like my mother's. And there it was—parked at Bijou's. Either Gertrude or Frisco, or maybe both, were on the premises.

I couldn't risk storming the main house. I pressed myself against Mason's cottage. It occurred to me after I committed to the action that I hadn't a clue if Mason had a girlfriend or wife or lover or roommate. I'd assumed he and Bijou had something going on, and I knew where such assumptions could lead me. Big trouble. Anyone could be waiting inside the house. I was taking a huge risk.

Peeping in the window, I saw an old iron-framed bed covered in a worn quilt. The patchwork was stitched by hand with tiny, perfect little stitches. That homey touch hit me hard when I remembered his dead sister. I had no time to ponder Mason's personality. I wanted to find Jaytee safe and sound. I eased around the house, checking through the windows. As best I could determine, there was no sign of the harp player. My hope hit the ground. I was so positive I'd be able to find Jaytee, clearing the way for Coleman to bring him back to Cece.

Before I gave up, I tried the back door. It wasn't locked, and I entered the cottage. A quick walk-through was all I had time for.

Dirty dishes were piled in the kitchen sink. Nothing out of the ordinary. I went through the house and it wasn't until I was in the front room that I saw a billfold laying on the coffee table. Mason wouldn't leave his billfold behind. I opened it and saw Jaytee's driver's license, credit cards, and about eighty dollars.

He'd been here. I wasn't wrong, I was just too late. Had they killed him?

I had the camera, but I used my cell phone to snap a photo of the open billfold on the table. I prepared a text to send to Coleman with the photo of the billfold and my location. My thumb hovered over the send button when cruel fingers closed around the back of my neck. I was so startled I dropped the phone before I could press send. The cell phone hit the floor and my attacker kicked it across the room. He snatched the camera from my hand.

"I heard you had a yen for trespassing. This time you won't get away with it."

I didn't have to see the person holding me in a painful grip to know Mason Britt had returned and I was in a world of hurt.

"Where's Jaytee?" I rasped.

"Oh, you'll connect with him before you know it. I don't suspect it'll be a happy reunion, either."

"Is he dead?" I had to know one way or the other.

"You'll find out soon enough."

"Take me to Bijou." I didn't expect her to be thrilled to see me, but she was too smart to harm me. I hoped. She knew my relationship with Coleman. If I disappeared he wouldn't rest until he found out what happened to me. And truthfully, I couldn't see Bijou tied up in Foundation Rock Church. She wasn't the type to put up with Farley's belief system.

"Bijou's indisposed."

"What are she and Gertrude Strom cooking up?"

My little distraction worked and I broke free of Mason's grip and dove for the cell phone. I only had to hit one key. One tiny tap. Mason caught me again, and his fingers on my neck paralyzed my limbs. He shook me like a dog with a rag doll. My phone skittered across the floor and disappeared.

The bitterness of defeat overwhelmed me. If only I'd been able to press the send button, the cavalry would be on the way. Mason's death hold on my throat was slowly choking me, and my only hope of help was gone. I had few options left.

"Why are you doing this, Mason? You served with Koby Shaver in a combat zone. You were friends. And now he's dead. Why would you kill him?" I had to keep him off balance, and I had to get free of his fingers.

Footsteps sounded on his front porch. They didn't belong to friends of mine.

"Mason! You in there?"

"Shut up before I silence you for good," he warned me. "Be out in a minute," he called. "Check the Big Branch Field and make sure those guys are working and not sitting in the shade."

He didn't want the person outside to know I was inside.

Should I scream? His fingers tightened to the point I couldn't. "Koby never did a thing to anyone," I squeezed out. "He was a good guy trying to make a living. He was an employee, like Jaytee and Mike. They work for a paycheck. You shouldn't hold them responsible."

"Musicians play the devil's music and lure the lambs to the slaughter. Koby knew better. He was consorting with sinners. I warned him. I told him what would happen. He laughed at me and—" He broke off abruptly.

"And who?"

"You're not so clever."

"I know Farley is in this up to his eyebrows. Where is he? I want to talk to him."

"Before this is over, you'll want a lot of things. Mostly to meet your maker and beg for forgiveness. Sometimes an example needs to be made."

That didn't sound promising. I struggled to free myself, but Mason only tightened his fingers. Holding me from behind, he had every advantage. I couldn't thrash too desperately or he'd feel the gun tucked into my jeans.

I went limp and he dragged me to the sofa and threw me onto it with enough force to knock the breath from my lungs. When I hit, I felt the gun in the back of my pants. I let myself slide to the floor, so that I was wedged between the coffee table and the couch.

Mason held a gun leveled at me while he flipped through the photos I'd taken with the camera, which didn't amount to diddly. I'd snapped some shots of farm equipment, hay, tools, and fertilizer. Nothing incriminating or even interesting. He tossed the camera at me. "You risked your life for nothing. You don't have any evidence."

"So let me go." I sat up, shifting so that the gun didn't

dig into my spine. If I could reach it, I'd shoot him in the leg. Or maybe someplace a lot more devastating.

"Funny," he said. "You'll pay for the part you played in bringing that music here, encouraging folks to rub on each other, to socialize with the wrong people."

"Wrong people?" I knew what he meant, but I wanted to make him say it.

"God didn't intend for the races to mix."

There it was, the ugly bigot showing his face. Misogynistic and racist—lovely combo. "You're wrong, Mason." If I could work him up, distract him, send him into a rage where he wasn't watching me so closely maybe I'd stand a chance to retrieve the gun from my back. "You're going to be *dead* wrong when the sheriff gets here."

"God will protect us. We follow his rules, not the laws of man." He spoke loudly, as if he had an audience of one hundred instead of one. "Our women know their place and they are obedient. Reverend Farley leads us on the righteous path. America has lost its way. Families are destroyed by indecent women and disobedient children who've forgotten how to support the head of the family. Women flaunt themselves and compete against men in the workplace. It's against the natural order. You're a harlot and a Jezebel, and I do believe Reverend Farley will take pleasure in using you as an example."

The footsteps on the porch paced back and forth. Could whoever was out there hear Mason's insane ranting? If so, would he think to check inside and maybe call the law? I didn't dare hope for such. I gigged Mason again.

"What are you planning to do, cut my hair? Shame me in public?"

"You're a foolish woman, but I will tell you God promised he would never punish humanity again with a flood. Fire is his tool. Fire is your punishment. You'll face a great conflagration."

For a moment I thought he meant to burn me at the stake, but then something else occurred to me. He meant to burn Dahlia House. Just as he'd burned Ned Gaston's home.

17

Panic nearly choked me, but I didn't have time to react. Mason grabbed my arm and pulled me upright. My foot caught the coffee table leg and I went down on one knee and fell forward onto my hands. Terrified that he would see the gun in my waistband beneath my shirt, I rolled onto my back. Something under the sofa glinted. My cell phone! I had to buy some time.

"If Fred Doleman is outside, I want to talk to him."

Mason reached down and for a moment I thought he might slug me. Instead he yanked my arm hard. "How do you know him?"

"I know a lot more than you think I do. And so does Coleman Peters."

"You don't know squat. You and that rich bitch partner

of yours run around the county setting the worst example for women. At least she has a husband, though he can't control her. You think you can do whatever you want. You brought yourself onto sacred property wearing pants, nosing into things that are none of your business. You brought pain and suffering to people."

"I didn't even talk to anyone but the preacher."

"They saw you. The women and girls. Your example had to be cut out of their brains, like a cancer. You and Mrs. Richmond are responsible."

I had hoped to reason with Mason. It wasn't possible. And it was unlikely the men who worked for him, even if they didn't share his views, would defy him. Help wouldn't come from anyone at Hemlock Manor. I had to get my hands on my phone.

"Speaking of my partner, where do you suppose she is right now?"

"We have folks watching her and know exactly where she is. Searching for that harmonica player. And now she's looking for you, too. She won't find either one of you until you've paid the price for your sinful ways." He was smug.

"Where is Jaytee?"

"You'll see him soon enough, but you might not like what you find. You're an ignorant woman. You were born ignorant and your parents failed to teach you."

Mason Britt was a true believer, and if I destroyed his notion of superiority there was no telling what he might do. I was on a tightrope, and I couldn't slip or falter or Jaytee and I would pay the ultimate price. I edged my hand closer to the phone, but I kept my gaze on Mason. I searched his face for any reveal, any chink that could help me.

"How did you come to know Reverend Farley?" I couched it as an innocuous question.

"What do you care?"

"Farley said something the other day that hit home." I'd done some research on Mason Britt, and I knew a few of his secrets. His father had abandoned him and Mrs. Britt when Mason was young. His mother, who died when he was seventeen, had done what she had to do to feed her son and daughter. Sally Mason had been a pretty woman, and the men had been willing to pay to spend time with her. The fatal blow of Mason's life was the death of his sister to cancer. There had been no one left for him.

One way or another, the women in his life had abandoned him. I could see how that twisted him against women. He'd joined the service, gone to the Middle East for four tours. There he'd seen segments of society that often repressed women, forcing them to wear clothes concealing their features. Patriarchal was an understatement.

When he came home, he fell under Reverend Farley's influence, which solidified a lot of his attitudes about women. He was a prime case of how to make a zealot in three easy steps.

"What could the Reverend say that you would pay any attention to?" he asked.

At least he was curious, and every second was one in my favor. "He said that Tinkie and I were lost. That resonated with me."

"The Reverend is a kind man who tries to give everyone a chance. Even a harlot. He offers those who follow him illumination in the darkness."

"I hear what you're saying." If I had ever had any acting skills, now was the time to employ them. "I can't explain it, but there's something missing in my life."

He grinned, but not with amusement. "You can't play me, Sarah Booth Delaney."

"I'm not playing you or anyone else. My fiancé dumped me. For the second time. I live alone in an old family house I can barely pay the taxes on. My life is not right. I don't know how to fix it."

"Maybe we should just sit down and have a good cry. Maybe give Oprah a call."

Sarcastic, superior bastard. I wanted nothing more than to jump up and punch him in the nose, but I forced myself into a demure posture. "Crying doesn't help. I need . . . a path."

"Wouldn't a rich husband who indulged your every whim—like your partner has—wouldn't that be better than learning obedience and serving man?"

He wanted me to grovel. Okay, whatever kept him talking. The longer we stayed in his living room chewing the fat, the more time Coleman had to find me. Even though I couldn't reach for my phone while he watched me like an eagle, I knew the phone was on and Coleman could track the GPS chip. Given enough time, help would come for me and I wouldn't have to lift a finger.

Of course, if Mason gave me half a chance, I'd get the pistol from my waistband and shoot him. Cramped between the sofa and the coffee table, I wouldn't be able to maneuver fast enough to pull this off with him two feet away. I had no choice but to keep up the charade.

"A rich husband would be nice, but what I really want is a husband who has a direction, who has a calling and who can help me find that path."

"You're a sly thing, aren't you? Thinking you can con me."

"Con you?" I was all wide-eyed innocence. "I want a husband and family. Children. That's the truth. Those things have eluded me and I have to accept my life choices are to blame. I'm doing something wrong, and I need to change before it's too late."

"Get up."

My acting skills had obviously abandoned me. "Why?"

"Women don't ask why. They obey. That's the first rule to learn."

"May I speak with Reverend Farley?"

"Not a chance."

"Where are you taking me?"

"And women don't ask where or when or how. They obey. You ask too many questions. It's a bad habit that will lead you straight to the fiery lake of hell."

I wondered if he was sincerely attempting to teach me his lessons or if I would soon be marched to my death. I studied his face, aware that frowning was his natural expression. He would expect me to try something else. I had to outfox him. "If you'd listen to me, maybe try to help me, there are benefits."

He shook his head. "You are a sinful woman. You think you can change what's going to happen by offering sex?"

The idea of it shocked me. "Don't be ridiculous. I was offering no such thing. I meant—"

"Women like you always think their bodies are coin to trade. There's a word for that. Whore."

Now I was honestly offended. *He'd* taken an innocent statement and turned it into something sexual, not me. "Get over yourself. I was thinking what a wonderful church Dahlia House would make." It was a crazy ploy, but I had no idea if he'd sent people to burn down my home. Holding out my ancestral property as a gathering place for his nutcase group knotted my stomach, but playing pretend about the future with Mason was all I had, until I could get my gun. And it might save my home.

My suggestion gave him pause.

"Women like you don't convert so easily. This is a trick."

Give the guy a slice of pie.

"I'm not converting to anything. I'm seeking answers to my life. I'd be willing to try things your way. Maybe I would find peace and serenity. Having a man to take charge would be . . . wonderful. I have everything on my shoulders at Dahlia House. I would love to have someone I could lean on and trust to make the big decisions."

Mason's jaw clenched. "You think I'm a fool, don't you?"

"You don't know much about women if you don't understand that no matter how rich or independent or accomplished, every woman wants a man to look up to. Every single one. Do you have a woman, Mason?"

Thin ice! The danger signs were posted everywhere. If I hinted at his hypocrisy, bedding Bijou while he espoused purity, Mason would never work with me.

"That's none of your damn business."

I sat taller, pushing my hand under the sofa for support. My fingers grazed the cell phone. Another inch and I'd have it.

"I want to make it my business. A good woman, one who truly wants a partner, can bring wonderful things into a relationship. It isn't all taking, you know. The right woman can give. Some women can give a lot."

"Are you talking about yourself?"

I realized too late the ice was also emotionally thin for me. I had to be honest enough to sell it. That had always been the trick of acting. To bring my emotions to the characters. When I was younger and trying for Broadway, I'd been afraid to really reveal myself. Now, I had to be emotionally true or he would smell my deceit. "I'm afraid to talk about myself. I've had to be strong for such a long time. Now, I'm scared to be vulnerable. I don't know if you remember, but I lost my parents when I was young. A car accident. Everything I'd thought of as secure and safe disappeared overnight." The painful lump in my throat wasn't pretend.

His eyes registered shock for one split second before he covered it. "Stop the yakking and get on your feet now. You're so curious about Jaytee, I think it's time for a reunion." He tugged me upright just as a knock came at the door.

"Mason," a female voice called out. "It's me, Amanda. Reverend Farley sent me to get you. Mr. Doleman is on the porch waiting for you. There's a big meeting up at the main house. Two men just got here in a real nice sports car. Red and—" she broke off. "Sorry. I know that's not important. Reverend Farley isn't here, and Mrs. LaRoche sent me to get you."

"Shut up!" Mason snapped. "Get in here."

"I'm not supposed to enter your house. Reverend Farley said no woman should step into a man's home without the proper chaperone."

"Get in this room right now."

A young woman in her early twenties slipped into the room, her eyes downcast. She wore a dress at least a size too large for her that covered her from her neck to her ankles, but it still couldn't hide how pretty she was. She cast a furtive glance at me. The false hope that had arisen at the sound of her voice died a quick death. The women of the church were so browbeaten, none would risk punishment to help me.

She hovered at the edge of the room. "Ms. LaRoche said to come to the big house. She got rid of her company." She cast a another sidelong glance at me. "Now."

"Get me something to tie her hands," Mason ordered.

"Mason, I—"

"Shut up and do what I said."

"I guess I could cut a piece of the clothesline out back."

"Do that." He reached into his pocket for a knife and held it out to her. She hesitated but came deeper into the room to get it. Once she had it in her hand, she scurried back to the doorway.

The split second he was distracted, I eased the gun out of my waistband and held it behind my back. I hoped the girl would leave, but I couldn't control the situation. I wasn't about to let Mason tie my hands.

"Didn't I tell you to do something?" Mason asked her.

"Yes, sir." She disappeared and I heard the front door close.

It was now or never. Mason was ten feet away from me. I brought out the gun and aimed it at his chest. Coleman had taught me to go for the chest area, the largest target.

"What the—" At least he was shocked by my maneuver. "Put that thing away."

"I'm leaving, and if you try to stop me, I'll shoot you. I swear it."

"You're not going anywhere."

"I am. And when the sheriff arrives, he'll find Jaytee."

"Not likely." Mason wasn't afraid, and that worried me. Most people looking down the barrel of a deadly weapon exhibited more nerves.

"I'm walking out the door. You stay put." I edged around the coffee table and moved sideways to the front door. The cottage was shotgun style so the exit was close. The problem was the open ground between the house and the woods. I would be an easy target for any of Mason's confederates to pick off.

"Here's the clothesline." The girl entered and stopped. She held out her hand, frozen in place. "What are you doing?" she asked me.

"I'm leaving," I said, easing behind her. "Mason is staying here in this room, or I'll have to shoot him."

She didn't budge.

"You won't get to the barn," Mason said. His assurance gave me great concern, but escape was all I had.

I reached the door and opened it wide but kept Mason in my sight. The girl watched me. Her eyes widened and she almost called out, but no sound left her mouth. Something, or someone, was behind me.

I never saw the blow coming. The attacker struck me on the head hard. I staggered, fighting the loss of balance, the encroaching darkness. Then I went down.

18

Returning to consciousness, I discovered my hands were tied behind my back. I was lying on the sofa. I kept my eyes closed, listening. I was in big trouble. If Coleman was riding to the rescue, he was way late. I had to assume that no one was coming to help me. I'd lost my gun and, with my hands tied, I'd never be able to use the cell phone not two feet from me. *If* it was still under the sofa.

"I never signed on to break the law," said a male voice, younger than Mason.

"Don't worry about the laws of man. We serve the laws of God." That was Mason, selling the party line. I'd underestimated him and now I would pay the price.

I opened my eyes a slit and saw Mason and another

man I didn't know sitting at the kitchen table. The young woman had obviously been sent about her chores.

"This is getting out of hand," the younger man said. "Mason, I want to be godly, but I don't want to hurt people. Fred was sitting out on your porch, and he said we were going to hang that blues fellow. He said we'd make an example of him to all who wanted to come to Sunflower County and listen to Satan's music. He said the Midnight Templars needed an example, to show the world what we believed."

"True believers do what's necessary. You don't believe enough, Silas. Reverend Farley will be disappointed when I tell him how he's failed you."

"He hasn't failed me. But burning a man's house? Tying up women? Kidnapping? Lynching a man? That's not part of following the Lord."

"Who are you to question the reverend's orders?"

"I'm nobody." Silas was defeated. "I guess you know best."

I wanted to scream out that Mason didn't know anything except crimes that would land him in prison for the next forty years.

"Finally you're talking sense," Mason said, but I could tell by his voice he wasn't satisfied with Silas. "And just a little secret between the two of us—that blues fellow isn't all that he seems to be. Put your faith in Reverend Farley's plan. I do believe we may have us a convert."

"What are you planning for her?" Silas asked, pointing at me. "Sheriff Peters is a close friend of hers. He won't ever stop trying to find her. He'll never give up. I want to follow the Lord, but I don't want to go to prison."

"The sheriff won't find a trace of her. Not until we're

ready for him to. By then it'll be too late to stop us. Look, Silas, we're conducting some business tonight that will provide for the church and its followers for years to come. Reverend Farley is tending to that right now. You need to put your faith in his leadership and in the plans handed down to us from the Midnight Templars. If we prove our loyalty in this, we'll be welcomed into the fold of a great organization, a moment in time when we can change the path of America. This country is headed in the wrong direction, and we can be the agent of change. When the Rapture comes, we'll be called through the pearly gates by name."

"Seems we could live a godly life on the compound and stay out of all of this . . . violence. Why are we doing this?" Silas asked. "I mean we have our church grounds, and we have our jobs. We make ends meet in the congregation. You talk about how important our work is, but I don't see it. Why are we fighting a music club? We don't have to go there and listen. Let the blasphemers have their pleasures. We'll be triumphant when the Rapture comes."

A chair scraped back and I peeked. Mason was standing. "That music is corrupting our community. We are God's warriors, Silas. We live according to his dictates, and now it's time to show others the way. Destroying the club will bring media attention. We'll have a platform to tell the rest of the country how God wants us to live. We will bring the Word, exhibited by our lifestyle, to the rest of the people. This will become a movement, a resurrection of godly ways and teachings. You have to believe this, Silas. We are God's warriors. God's gladiators."

Listening to Mason rant, I thought of Charlie Manson and his belief that he was Jesus Christ. He'd convinced a handful of young people, through hallucinogens and physical brutality, that he was literally Jesus returned to Earth. He ordered his followers to steal from and murder an eight-months-pregnant woman, among others. To underestimate the power of belonging was a very dangerous thing. Reverend Farley was no Charles Manson, but what he offered these lost people was potent. And he had an effective enforcer; Mason was his right-hand man.

"I'm humbled to be here," Silas said.

"Has the church ever failed you?" Mason asked.

"Reverend Farley said the church would find a wife for me."

"Yes, a man and a woman together is God's plan."

"Amanda is pretty." The desire in Silas's voice was clear.

"Tell me about her," Mason said. "What's her story?"

"She showed up with the man who claims to be her husband and the clothes on her back, which were unsuitable, by the way. Rawley Gomes took her in and her husband, Clemont, went to live in the men's barrack. Reverend Farley said they had to be counseled for six months before he would marry them in the church, to be certain they were both practicing the faith."

"That's the rules," Mason said. "Some women need a stronger man. They need a firm hand, guidance in the true path. Reverend Farley must have some concerns about the power of her man to control her and keep her safe. So she's been put under Rawley Gomes's supervision. How is that working out?"

"Amanda helps Mrs. Gomes teach the school lessons. She's smart. She loves children."

"Reverend Farley hasn't married Amanda and Clemont.

They aren't *truly* married until *he* performs the cere-
mony."

Silas shifted in his chair, clearly uncomfortable at the
direction the conversation had taken.

Mason put his elbows on the table and leaned forward.
"Silas, I want you to spend some time with her. I'll make
certain you're together next week. You make sure she's
on the path. What she saw today might frighten her, make
her question her commitment to the church. Bob Doleman gave our little snoop a real bonk on the head and it
upset Amanda. I'm trusting you to help her through this."

"Okay." Silas sounded eager.

Amanda was a pretty girl, and it made me sick to hear
these two men talking about her as if she were property
to be parceled out to whomever they chose. They were
obsessed with forcing women to obey. To be reduced to
a slave and breeder was intolerable. I had to get loose and
call in the reinforcements.

Mason put his hand on Silas's shoulder. "When Reverend Farley returns to the church compound, talk to
him about Amanda. See what he thinks about the idea
that you might make a better husband. Things here need
cleaning up, and I need to help the women pack up their
belongings. I'll be finished in time for the evening worship service."

Silas glanced at me, but he'd raised all the objections
he had in him. Mason had put him in his place and given
him a reward, a pretty girl. He'd take the spoils of war
and forget those who perished.

Silas stood up. "Mason, do I tell Amanda I'm interested in a future with her?"

"You can. Obedience is a woman's lot. She needs to

learn now if she hasn't already. But maybe it would be a better surprise down the road."

"Thank you. You're so right. I want her to know me and like me before I tell her."

Silas went out the front door and spoke to someone waiting on the porch. Though my eyes were closed, Mason knew I was awake. He stood over me, waiting for me to break, to move or say something. I swung out with my foot, hoping to connect with his groin, but all I accomplished was falling off the sofa onto the floor. I couldn't use my arms to break my fall, and I hit hard on my cheekbone.

"Shit." I tried to roll over but couldn't.

"A little bit of rope can teach a woman a lot of patience."

"You are a sicko, and I wish I'd shot you."

"So the mask of the repentant woman has fallen off." He laughed as he hauled me to my feet. "It's more fun to break a feisty woman."

Now he was provoking me, and very successfully. I lunged at him, but he used one hand on my head to push me back to the floor. I fell with my face aimed under the sofa. My cell phone was gone. They'd obviously found and taken it. Probably destroyed it. My last hope for rescue died.

He righted me. "Don't look so sad, Ms. Delaney. This could be the very path you were asking me to help you find. The Lord works in mysterious ways. Now that's not a Bible verse. Some folks get confused and think it is. A true student of the Bible knows better. But while it isn't God's word, today I believe it suits my purposes."

He pushed me roughly toward the front door. At least

I was on my feet—with a throbbing head—and we were moving outside. A tall man in a dark suit stepped off the porch and walked away. He'd heard every abusive thing Mason had done to me and never lifted a finger to help me. No one here would help. I had only my wits.

"Does Bijou know you're holding people hostage on her property?"

"I don't think she's overly fond of you, Ms. Delaney. She's been in terrible distress ever since someone sent her poisoned brownies. She's pretty sure you're the culprit. I don't think she'd much care what I did with you."

He had a point. Sort of. "She might care when she realizes she's an accessory to kidnapping."

"You came here all on your own. No one kidnapped you. I caught you trespassing, and by the way, that seems to be a real bad habit of yours."

"How do you know about my trespassing?" He'd been talking to Gertrude Strom. The car I'd seen—like my mother's. Gertrude had bought it, and she'd been here. If she was behind all of this in some sick attempt to hurt me . . .

"Never you mind. Now, as I was saying, I found you here and restrained you. If you happen to meet an untimely end, it won't be a hard sell to Sheriff Coleman Peters. The man knows you're a loose cannon."

"If you let me go now, we can settle this without involving the law."

He shoved me across the porch. I stumbled down the three steps and nearly sprawled in the dirt. It was hard to walk without using my arms for balance.

"Where are you taking me?" I tried to present a bold, assertive attitude, but my gut was twisting with fear. Mason Britt had convinced me he was capable of anything.

He enjoyed hurting women. He liked exerting his power over me.

A couple of men crossed the yard and entered an equipment shed. If they saw me, they ignored my plight. No help from that quarter.

"Move it," he said, pushing me off balance. Each step caused my head to pound harder and took me toward a fate I wasn't ready to meet. I spun to face him and stopped, gob-smacked. Jaytee came out of an outbuilding. He wasn't restrained in any way. In fact he walked across the yard and stopped to talk with a young woman who demurely kept her gaze on the ground.

Mason's words about a convert hit me hard. Jaytee hadn't been taken. He'd come here voluntarily. The whole thing was a setup. Jaytee was the convert who would prove Farley's godly powers. And Jaytee was the inside man, feeding information to Mason and Farley.

I started to call out to him, but Mason clamped a hand over my mouth. He saw them too. Anger infused his face. "You had to know we had someone on the inside of the club helping us." He was almost gloating. "Shut up and move!" He pushed me so hard I had to run several steps to keep the momentum from tumbling me again. When I regained my footing, Jaytee was gone.

I thought he might have been a figment of my imagination, a hallucination brought on by the blow to my head. I was damn good at making believe, but I couldn't deny the truth. Jaytee wasn't a prisoner. He was here voluntarily. Which meant everything about him was a lie.

This would kill Cece. As I knew from personal experience, betrayal rode the top of the list for soul-destroying experiences. Jaytee was the first man Cece had really trusted. She'd let him into her life and into her dreams for the future. Their relationship exploded like a starburst, because Cece had wanted love for such a long time. Jaytee had accepted her—a transsexual—and he'd shown her fun and joy and pleasure. Their affair happened too fast, with too much passion, but no one could have predicted that Jaytee would betray Cece, Scott, and the band.

I would kill him.

A murderous rage sparked inside me. I had no weapon and couldn't even use my hands but I meant to hurt him. Bastard. He used Cece and Scott and everyone else. He was in cahoots with the crazy people.

As mad as I was at Jaytee, I was equally furious with myself. I should have checked closer, run down more leads, somehow found out Jaytee was a poser and a scumbag before we let our friend fall so deeply in love with him. Koby was dead, Mike wounded. Cece, in particular, would pay a terrible emotional price.

I dodged to the right, running toward the shed where I'd seen Jaytee. Blinded by fury and a desire to do bodily harm, I evaded Mason's reach. I was halfway across the barnyard when a tug at my bound wrists almost pulled my arms from the sockets.

"Stop, Sarah Booth," Mason said quietly.

"I will kill him." To my utter horror, I sounded like I was about to cry.

"Get moving." He turned me about and nudged me, this time more gently.

To my surprise, Mason herded me away from the buildings and toward the woods. For a moment, I felt hope bubble up inside me, but then I realized that the woods offered seclusion for whatever he wanted to subject me to.

The red tide of rage had subsided a bit, and I knew I

had to think fast and creatively if I meant to stay alive. "Mason, we can talk about this."

"Keep moving."

We gained the trees, and he indicated I should walk along the edge of the fallow field, heading always away from the barn area of Hemlock Manor and any potential help.

When we were hidden from view, his fingers dug into my shoulder. "Now you listen to me." He jerked me around to face him. "I—"

He never got a chance to finish. Seventy pounds of hound catapulted out of the woods and hit him full on in the chest. He stumbled backward into the field, his boots immediately clotting up with the thick topsoil that stuck to his soles in clumps. Sweetie Pie hit him again and he went down.

The rain from the night before had been heavy, and the resulting mud, called gumbo in the Delta, weighed down Mason's arms and legs. He struggled like a turtle flipped onto its back. And I ran.

"Sarah Booth! Come back!"

What kind of a fool did he think I was? Did he believe I'd wait around for him to pull himself out of the quagmire so he could abuse me again? Running with my arms tied behind my back was awkward as hell, especially after I ducked into the woods. Limbs slapped me in the face and there was nothing I could do to protect myself. I tucked my head and bulldozed on.

Behind me, Mason called my name, and then I heard a sound like a Tasmanian devil. And Mason yelled. Roscoe had joined Sweetie Pie, and while my hound had a gentle mouth, Roscoe was another matter. Mason had a world of hurt coming his way.

I was free.

I angled toward the car, hoping I could find a sharp edge to cut the bonds tying my hands. I was safe from Mason for the moment. Sweetie and Roscoe would keep him down in the dirt until they tired of the game or someone came to call them off. But what of the other members of the church? They could be anywhere. I had no doubt that if they saw me, they would take me prisoner again. They all marched to the orders of Jebediah Farley.

Limbs stung my face and neck as I slammed through the woods. Buck vines, some as thick as my wrist with huge thorns, grabbed at my flesh and clothes. One cut my cheek and blood traced a path down my face, dripping onto my jacket. I pushed on, focused on the car. The keys were still in my pocket. I was all but home free.

Up ahead I saw a clearing. I tried to remember if I'd passed it on the way into the estate, but I was panicked and tired. My head throbbed and dizziness assaulted me. If I lived through this, I vowed to give up cigarettes and really start a fitness program. I would excel at Zumba and P-69 or whatever the super-workout was called. I would organize my underwear drawer and throw away my hidden supply of dark chocolate. I would be a better person and a better friend.

I stumbled and went down on both knees. My head swam and nausea churned in my stomach. I couldn't faint. I. Could. Not. Faint. Not now. Not when freedom was so close.

Something rustled in the deadfall behind me. It tramped through the thicket, unconcerned that it alerted me to its progress. All around me the birds fell silent. The wild creatures knew danger stalked.

In the distance I could hear the dogs, and I had to believe Mason was still pinned down by them. Whatever was moving around the woods, circling me, wasn't Mason Britt. This was a new danger.

Leaves crackled, limbs broke. The person drew near.

I tried to propel myself to my feet, but I couldn't. I rolled to my stomach and tried to push up on my knees. I wasn't strong enough. Dizziness washed over me and I refused to think about concussions or aneurysms. There was more at stake here than just saving myself. I couldn't quit.

The creature moving through the underbrush could be a person, a bear, or a wildcat. At one time such creatures were plentiful but now they were almost extinct in the Delta. *Almost.* It didn't really matter if it was a bear or a Chihuahua, because I didn't have any fight left in me. I pushed myself against a tree trunk and waited for the worst.

When Pluto stepped out of the woods, his shiny black fur covered in leaves and brambles, I almost laughed. "Pluto!"

He sauntered over and headbutted my chin, then turned his attention to nuzzling my left hip. I appreciated the affection, but I needed help, not love.

"Pluto, untie my hands."

Even if he could understand me, Pluto had no thumbs. Highly unlikely he could untie the knots Mason had used. The clothesline I was bound with wasn't thick, but it was strong. Pluto, always game to help, slipped behind me and pulled at the rope. He got an A for effort, though it didn't help. Tired of the rope, he headbutted my lower back. When he dug his claws into my butt, I'd had enough.

"I'm getting up." The cat wouldn't let me quit.

The sound of the dogs harassing Mason ceased, adding another layer of urgency. I had to fight. I couldn't let Mason catch me and take me back to the kooks.

The sound of a dog crying out in pain or surprise forced me to try harder to stand. I managed to get to my knees and stagger to my feet. I pushed on through the brambles. I couldn't help Sweetie Pie and Roscoe until I got my hands free and surely there was something at the car I could use to cut my bonds.

Struggling through the undergrowth I arrived at my car. The dogs had chewed a hole in the convertible top to escape. I didn't care. Thank goodness they'd gotten out and come to my rescue. Now I had to figure out how to get home.

In the distance I heard the sweetest music. Sirens. Somehow, someway, Coleman had figured out where I was and he was coming, along with the cavalry.

19

"Do not untie her hands until she explains herself." Tinkie stood before me, hands on hips, as she tapped her boot-clad foot on the ground. "You ran off and left me. You got yourself in big trouble and no one knew where you were." She stood on tiptoe and got in my face. "You are irresponsible and you worried me sick."

I had no defense, except I was trying to protect her and that would *not* be a good thing to say right now. "How did you find me?"

"There's no time for this," Coleman said angrily. He was furious with me too. "Did you see Jaytee? Is he here at Bijou's? Is he injured?" he asked.

My face must have given me away.

"What?" Tinkie and Coleman asked in unison.

I had to swallow before I could tell them. "Jaytee isn't a prisoner. He's here of his own free will. I saw him. And Gertrude—or at least I saw the convertible parked at Bijou's front door."

It took Tinkie all of three seconds to absorb the implications of my statements. "I don't give a damn about Bijou, but I will kill Jaytee with my bare hands," she said softly.

"Get in line," Coleman said.

Tinkie didn't want to give up so easily on Cece's love. "Before we jump to the wrong conclusion, someone tore up Cece's house and made it seem like there was a struggle. That doesn't make any sense. Why would Jaytee go to such trouble? He was there alone. No one to stop him. He could just take what he wanted and leave. Cece—" She broke off because her voice had started to quaver.

"He's the man on the inside. I don't know how or why. I didn't get a chance to talk to him. But I did see him, and there's more going on here than just a backwoods minister fighting against music he doesn't like. Now, please cut these freaking ropes." I turned around and Coleman sliced the clothesline. At last my hands were free, and I leaned against my car. "Sweetie and Roscoe had Mason Britt down in a field. Maybe they've hurt him, and if so, good. But I heard one of the dogs cry out. If he did anything to them—let's take the fight to Mason and his minions!" I had my second wind and I was ready to find Sweetie and Roscoe.

"Stop right there." Coleman's tone brooked no argument. "Tell me everything."

I relayed what I had witnessed and what had transpired and how someone had struck me and Mason had bullied me. "I'm pressing charges."

"He'll counter with trespassing," Coleman noted.

"He can't. It isn't his property. Bijou would have to." I was feeling smug until I remembered the whole brownie incident.

"Bijou has no love lost for you," Coleman said.

"Yeah, you're right." If I pressed any number of charges against Mason, Bijou would surely nail me for trespassing since she couldn't *prove* I'd sent the brownies. The term *boomerang karma* came to me. Madame Tomeeka had warned me more than once that whenever I did anything nasty, it would come back to me tenfold. And here it was, sitting right on my doorstep.

Tinkie whipped her handgun out of the top of her boot. She was the only woman I knew who could turn the phrase "armed and deadly" into a fashion statement. "It's time to retrieve the dogs and confront Jaytee." Tinkie wanted her pound of flesh, and I didn't blame her.

"Put that thing away," Coleman ordered her. "I'll question Bijou and I'll find Jaytee. And if Gertrude is there, I hope to tie her into some illegal activity and get her back in jail." Coleman was angry, but he'd long ago learned how to tamp down his feelings and think with his brain, not his heart.

"We'll go too," I volunteered.

Coleman shook his head. "You're rounding up the dogs and getting off Bijou's property this instant."

As if they'd been summoned, Sweetie Pie and Roscoe raced down the drive to the car. They were caked in mud but seemed none the worse for wear. With his pointed Vandyke and wiry eyebrows, Roscoe looked like some horrific animated voodoo doll made of clay. Sweetie resembled a big gray tick with her ears plastered to her narrow head by the mud.

"Thank goodness they're riding in your car," Tinkie said with just a hint of malice. She was still angry, but Jaytee was the primary target for her ire.

"What should we tell Cece?" I asked Coleman. "And where is Cece?"

"She's at the club with Scott and the rest of the band. I convinced her to stay there until I found you. And Jaytee. The security men have the road barricaded."

"This is going to kill her," Tinkie said. "The band is like part of her family. She won't only lose Jaytee, she'll lose singing at the club and all of it. She'll think Jaytee only liked her because he was using her."

"Jaytee will have a lot to answer for when we do find him," I said. My anger had cooled. Jaytee deserved a chance to tell his side of things. And I was eager for him to start talking.

"Load up and get moving," Coleman ordered.

"How did you know where I was?" I asked. "Just tell me that. Did you track my phone's GPS?"

"You texted me a photo of Jaytee's billfold with your location," Coleman said.

I shook my head. "I was about to when Mason caught me. I'd punched in the number, but I never got to hit the send button."

The implications struck all of us at once. Someone else had sent the text I'd begun. "My phone has to be in Mason's cottage," I added.

Pluto took that opportunity to swat me on the butt. I reached back and felt the bulge in my hip pocket. My phone. "How—?"

I'd been unconscious for an undetermined amount of time. It could have been someone who came into the cottage while I was out of it, but somehow I didn't see Mason being that careless. The bottom line, though, was that someone at Hemlock Manor had sent a text to Coleman on my behalf.

"We'll puzzle this out later." Coleman walked around the cruiser to the driver's door. "Do not come back here unless I call you. Understood?"

We nodded.

"Tinkie, I'm deputizing you and putting you in charge of Sarah Booth. If she doesn't do exactly what you say, arrest her."

"You can't do that." They were treating me like a troublesome two-year-old.

"By the time you get out of jail, it won't matter whether I can or can't," Coleman said. "I can't do my job and rush all over the county plucking you out of trouble." Coleman slammed the door and drove toward Hemlock Manor.

Tinkie had ridden to the scene with Coleman so she had no choice but to ride with me and the mud-dogs. Pluto used the hole the dogs had chewed in the ragtop and was already in the front seat, ready for home and dinner. Roscoe and Sweetie jumped in the back, a long smear of mud rubbing across the leather of the backseat. It would all clean up.

For an awkward moment, Tinkie and I stood at the car. "I'm sorry," I finally said. "I thought I could sneak in, snap a photo of Jaytee being held prisoner, and it would give Coleman probable cause to get a search warrant."

"Because you were being held here, he had probable cause." Tinkie wouldn't look at me. "And just so you know, he could have gotten a warrant for Bijou's place. It was the church property that had his hands tied. Your excuses don't hold water."

"I shouldn't have come here without telling anyone. It was a mistake in judgment. And before you say not the first one, I know. I can't undo what happened. But we still have to find the person who killed Koby and shot Mike. Whatever else Jaytee did, he couldn't have done those two things because he was with Cece."

"You're right there."

She would forgive me, but I needed it to be now, not later. "Tinkie, if you want me to grovel, I'm groveling."

"They could have killed you, Sarah Booth, and no one knew where to start looking. We were frantic. Coleman wasted precious time worried about you."

"I'm sorry. This wasn't how I expected it to go, obviously. Now, please! Let's put this aside until we resolve the case."

I gave her the rundown of my time as a captive, and she reminded me that Amanda Tyree was DeWayne's cousin. "He's been secretly talking with her and learning about the Foundation Rock group. She told DeWayne she thinks there's a lot more going on than religious repression."

"She said there was a meeting tonight. People from out of town and Bijou. Mason was talking with another member of the congregation about a plan to unite this country in some kind of godly reform. It didn't make sense."

"Coleman has been worried about Farley's group for a while, but mostly because of the treatment of the female members of the congregation. There is clearly abuse, but unless the women will come forward and testify, there's not a lot the law can do."

"Do you think we should try to get Amanda out?"

"Oh, hell, no! Get in the car and drive. I promised Coleman I'd get you off the premises and I intend to honor my word. At least one of the people in Delaney Detective Agency should be able to stand for something."

Holy cow, she was like a dog with a bone. She wasn't going to quit chewing on me until she was good and ready.

I didn't argue but backed into the drive and headed out the gate. On the way Tinkie told me that Coleman had checked into Zeb and the Memphis gangs. "Zeb's past doesn't appear to be involved in the shootings in Sunflower County, but the Memphis Police Department have been monitoring gang-related activities in north Mississippi. There's been a lot of gang activity in the rural areas. If there's a connection, they'll find it."

It was a relief to hear Coleman had some help. "What gang-related activities?"

"Smuggling guns and drugs," Tinkie said. "The Memphis PD told Coleman they believe gangs are using farm buildings to hold the contraband until they pull together a megashipment for transport north. But this has nothing to do with Zeb."

"That's pretty smart. There are sheds and barns all over the county that no one checks for months, until it's time to fertilize or harvest. Free storage *and* no legal responsibility."

"And the contraband is easily accessible," Tinkie said. "You don't have any outbuildings around Dahlia House, do you? Coleman said it can happen and the property owners never know."

"A few." I leased my fields to Butch Watson, and he kept a sharp eye out, but I would give him a heads-up, just in case. "This should greatly relieve Zeb. He was carrying a heavy load of guilt."

"While you were busy being held hostage, Zeb talked with Davy's family. They've made arrangements to pay off his debt. He'll pay them back, without the risk of being kneecapped or shot. Let's hit the road. We have to talk to Cece."

"You got it." I'd hoped to go home. The dogs were a wretched mess, my head throbbed, and my body ached. But home wasn't an option. Coleman had asked Tinkie to stop by the club and fill in Cece and Scott.

It had been a long day and I didn't look forward to what lay in our path.

Security guards stopped us at the crossroads near Playin' the Bones. In the day of the original blues club built at that location, the roads had been only dirt—impassable in heavy rains and as hot as asphalt in the summer sun. A clear vista stretched in all directions. The lights of Playin' the Bones shimmered like a mirage in the distance. The tin roof winked in the starlight.

The guards insisted on searching us and the car. While the delay annoyed me, I was gladdened by the extra security precautions. Night had fallen, and the sky glittered with stars. There was little light pollution in the Delta, making the sky a rich, black backdrop highlighting the Milky Way and other constellations.

Tinkie and I had reached a precarious agreement. We would not tell Cece about Jaytee being free. We would simply tell her I'd seen him and he was uninjured. That would relieve her mind without breaking her heart. While we couldn't prevent future pain, we could delay it. Coward that I was, delay sounded like the better option.

Our friends were at the bar, and an air of desolation lingered over the club. We filled Scott, the band, and Cece in on what had happened at Hemlock Manor. Cece took the news of Jaytee's safety with joy. She was grilling Tinkie for details when I escaped outside with a bottle of dish soap, buckets of hot water, and some kitchen towels that I would replace. Sweetie and Roscoe, if the mud dried completely on them, wouldn't be able to move. It was tempting to let that happen to keep them out of mischief, but the rascals had come to my rescue once again and I owed them.

Koby Shavers's death was very much on my mind as I set to work cleaning up the dogs. Tinkie had called Harold, who was on his way to retrieve Roscoe, so I washed him first.

The entire time I lathered him up, Roscoe growled. He was the most cantankerous creature I'd ever met, and I still adored him.

To my surprise someone in the club picked up a guitar. I recognized the song instantly. The rough, powerful female voice that picked up the lyrics to "St. James Infirmary Blues," surprised me. Cece could sing, but this didn't sound like her.

The song tickled down my back and arms. Chill bumps danced, even though I was up to my elbows in hot water and suds.

"I went down to the St. James Infirmary, I saw my baby there. She was stretched out on a long white table, so cold, and fine, and fair. Let her go, let her go, God bless her, wherever she may be. She can search this world over, never find another man like me."

The classic blues song touched me with dread, and when I saw a woman standing in the dim light from the back windows of the club, I recognized the wild hair, the ring-covered fingers gripping the microphone, and a voice that died too young. Janis Joplin, a Texas girl who tried too hard and never knew her own worth.

I held the squirming Roscoe in the tub of water as I sat on the steps and listened to a song I'd loved from the first moment I heard it.

"Not a good song for tonight," I told Jitty when she'd finished singing. "No one here is going to die. We'll get to the bottom of this."

"Watch your back, Sarah Booth. Folks aren't what they seem."

"Tell me about it." I thought of Jaytee.

"Folks are never what they seem. Not a one of 'em."

"Boy, didn't I learn that the hard way." I scrubbed at Roscoe a little more. The mud had bonded with his coat.

Jitty's bracelets chinked on her wrist as she sat down beside me on the steps. Roscoe growled, but it was more at the fact he was immersed in hot water than at Jitty. I wanted to ask my ghostly comrade why she was singing a funeral dirge, but I knew it was pointless. She never told me what the future held, if she knew herself. I was just glad for her company. I finished rubbing the mud off Harold's dog.

"Things are always darkest before the dawn, Sarah Booth."

"You're hanging out with Aunt Loulane."

Jitty laughed. "I take good company where I can find it."

"Riddle me this, Jitty. What is the point of falling in love, because it always, always ends in hurt. Cece is the prime example. She's been so careful. She's worked so hard to be who she is, and she's held her trust in check. It's so hard for her to allow intimacy. She risked so much with Jaytee, and I am afraid she'll suffer now."

"Caring for others is risky, whether it's romantic or the love of a mother for a child. You know all this. So does Cece. The stakes are high, but the rewards . . ." Jitty chuckled. "It's been over a hundred and fifty years, and I can still remember sitting with Coker on the front porch of our house on a night just like this. The moonlight on the curve of his cheek, the flash of his eyes, his long fingers laced with mine. Those memories are worth a lot of pain, Sarah Booth. Time takes away a lot of the sting and leaves most of the pleasure. Think how terrible to end up an old woman without those memories to sustain you."

She was right. Even with all the pain Graf had caused me, he'd also given me wonderful memories. And the knowledge I could love so deeply. Whatever happened with Jaytee, Cece would have the same.

"Gotta go," Jitty said, standing abruptly. She'd returned to her regular appearance. Janis had faded away.

"Stay while I wash Sweetie Pie." It was time to finish the doggy baths.

"Be alert. Stay strong. Keep your heart open."

She was gone that fast.

The back door of the club opened and Scott was silhouetted in the light. My nerves were so on edge I almost yelled at him to get out of the doorway. He was perfectly framed for someone to shoot. I held my peace, and he closed the door and came down the steps into the darkness.

"Need help?" he asked.

"Sure."

He grabbed one of the empty buckets and went inside, returning in a few moments with more warm water. He slowly poured it over the grumbling Roscoe as I rinsed out the soap. Squeaky clean, Roscoe took off running and shaking and giving little yips of pleasure or discontent, it was impossible to tell.

"What really happened at Bijou's?" Scott asked.

"Pretty much what we said."

"Okay, then tell me the part you left out, because your face tells a different story."

Sweetie responded to my whistle, and I set to work on her. "How much do you really know about Jaytee?" I asked.

"He's a fine harmonica player."

I couldn't argue that point, but it wasn't what I was after and Scott knew it. "Just tell me."

"He had some trouble when he was younger. I know about it. Why are you asking about Jaytee?"

While I wouldn't tell Cece—yet—I did tell Scott what I'd seen. We finished bathing Sweetie Pie in silence. In the light falling from the kitchen window, I couldn't clearly see his face so I couldn't judge his reaction. Rinsed and freed from my grip on her collar, Sweetie shook water over both of us and then hauled boogie after Roscoe. A little more filth didn't faze me at all.

"Tell me about Jaytee's trouble."

"He asked me to keep it to myself, but Jaytee worked as an investment broker on Wall Street for a year. He got in over his head with bad investments."

"I checked into his background. I didn't find a mention of a career in finance, much less inappropriate behavior." Was I that terrible of an investigator? "Not a word."

"Jaytee ended up testifying for the feds. He's in witness protection. Changed his name, gave him a new identity."

"You have got to be kidding me. The whole background, with the brother, Beegee, Teepee, whatever—"

"It's all a fake."

Well no damn wonder I wasn't getting any callbacks from Beegee Johnson. "How can he be in witness protection and be part of a blues band?"

"It's not like we're the Rolling Stones, Sarah Booth. And he's changed, physically. He lost sixty pounds of desk flab once he started playing music, and when he accidentally broke his nose in a bar fight in a Paris club, he had plastic surgery. Changed his appearance completely."

I didn't say anything because I felt gut-punched. At last, I managed, "You should have told me."

"The whole point of witness protection is to build a new identity. He didn't intend to tell me. I stumbled on some passport issues he was having and he finally told me. I chose to protect his identity because I thought I knew him."

Thought being the operative word. "Scott, I'm worried the attacks on the club are all much bigger than just a religious cult having a hate on for music or liquor or sin. Or Frisco Evans being mad because you one-upped him and bought the club, or even Gertrude being out to hurt anyone I care about because she thinks my mother betrayed a secret. Somehow this blues club is sitting in the middle of something else."

"What do you think it is?" Scott asked.

"I don't know. But I have to find out before another innocent person is hurt."

Harold arrived, and we all went inside the club together, including the dogs. Tired and happy for a warm place to rest, they curled on the floor near the kitchen door. Pluto paced the bar. The health department would be on Scott's ass if they saw the cat, but in the long list of worries we faced, a health code violation was barely a blip.

I desperately needed to tell Coleman what I'd learned about Jaytee's new identity, but I knew better than to call him. He'd find me when he was finished at Hemlock Manor. Until then, I had no choice but to cool my jets and support my friends.

Scott had news from the hospital. Mike had shown improvement during the day. The doctor was talking about letting him go home in a day or two if he continued to heal. The extreme emotions of the day had taken a toll on all of us, and we lined up along the bar for a drink. Cece played the role of bartender. She was so happy that Jaytee wasn't hurt she almost sparkled. I plastered a smile on my face and kept it there—after Tinkie had taken me to the ladies' room to wash the blood off my face. My scratches were only superficial, but I felt better with a clean face.

Tinkie was still angry with me, but it was wearing off. She sat beside me at the bar. I was busting to tell her about Jaytee's financial background, but I'd promised Scott. Things were so complicated between friends and the secrets we shared. Scott hadn't revealed Jaytee's real name, and if he panned out to be a good guy, I wasn't interested in knowing anything else.

The bar's back door cracked open and Sweetie and Roscoe went nuts. Tatiana stuck her head inside. "Everything okay?"

I felt guilty I hadn't contacted her. Someone should have called and asked her to join us. Scott stepped forward and brought her into the bar with his arm around her shoulders. "A lot's been going on, Tatiana. We were catching up."

"Tell me," she said. She took her place behind the bar. "What happened to your face, Sarah Booth?"

"I tripped and fell." I didn't want to go into detail.

"That's too bad." She looked around. "Where's Jay-tee?"

"He had some business to take care of." It was Cece who offered the explanation.

"Are you going to open the bar this weekend?" Tatiana asked Scott. "I need to stay busy. When I'm at the apartment, all I think about is Koby."

"My plans are to open Saturday night," Scott said.

The news cheered all of us. "Who'll play keyboard?" Zeb asked.

"There are a couple of local guys who came by and offered to fill in until Mike was back at it. The community has been really supportive."

"Except for the jackass who keeps shooting people," Zeb said.

"I somehow don't think the people behind the shootings are local," Scott said, taking everyone by surprise.

"Do you have a lead?" Tatiana asked. "When I find the people behind killing Koby . . . bad things are in store for them."

"We all feel the same way," Cece said. "When Coleman finds the shooter, and he will, the criminals will go to prison for a long time."

"I hope they burn in hell," Tatiana said.

"Tatiana, this has been horrible for you. I worry because you don't have people here." Tinkie spoke gently. "Maybe it would be easier on you if you went back to Austin. We love having you here, but this must be hard."

"I come to the bar late at night when I can't sleep. I feel closer to Koby here. When he called to talk to me, he was so excited about what the club could be and how he was proud to be a part of it. He said he'd found a home for us, and a place where we both could fit together in a bigger picture."

Tatiana wasn't a crier, but Tinkie teared up. I picked up a bar napkin and passed it to my partner.

"How did you and Koby meet?" Cece asked. "It may help to talk. We didn't know Koby that well, but we liked what we knew."

I didn't think I was ready for a therapy session, but there seemed no way to avoid it. Besides, I was behind the curve on checking into the bartender's background. If the manager at the Austin bar had returned my call, I'd missed it while I was tied up on Mason's floor. Better to get the info from the source, anyway.

"Oh, we met in a bar. Didn't Koby tell you?"

"No," Scott said. "He didn't. But we didn't really have a lot of time to talk. We were all so busy preparing to open, and we were in New Orleans to play for the Black and Orange Ball. I left Koby to handle the details of the club. A lot of the personal information got pushed to the back row."

"We'd like to hear it now, though," Cece said.

Not me. I didn't want to hear a sob story. I had struggled to bury my own feelings, and I feared listening to Tatiana's grief would ignite my own. I couldn't get up and walk outside. Not right now. In a moment I would escape, using a cigarette for an excuse. Now I would simply endure.

"Koby and I met at this biker bar," Tatiana began. The story of their courtship unfolded, two people with the same occupation who liked the same music. There was nothing remarkable in the story, except they'd found deeper feelings.

Tatiana poured another round of drinks for everyone

and Cece snapped photos with her phone. "I'll make an album for the bar," she said.

"Good idea," Harold said. "I have a camera in the car. Let me take a few, too."

"Now that I've refreshed all of your drinks, I think I'll head home." Tatiana came out from behind the bar. "You've made me feel better. I want to go home and rest. The bar is reopening tomorrow. It's a big event. I'll be available, Scott, to help with any last minute details."

He gave her a hug. "Thanks. You know you're part of the bar family."

"I appreciate it." She was at the door when Harold snapped a photo of her. The flash made her flinch, and he apologized.

"Not a problem," she said. "See you guys Saturday evening."

20

By the time Harold finished with the photos, we'd downed our drinks and stood to leave. My cell phone rang, and I checked the number. It was local, but I didn't recognize it.

"Ms. Delaney?" A female voice asked.

"Yes?"

"This is Nandy. You have to help me. Someone beat up Curtis. He's hurt pretty bad but he won't let us call an ambulance or go to the hospital."

"We'll be right there." I hung up and signaled Tinkie. "We have to go."

"What's up?" Harold asked.

"Someone attacked Curtis Hebert. Nandy called. We need to get over there."

"We can all go," Scott offered.

"No. Tinkie and I will check it out. I don't think we should show up en masse. I don't know how badly Curtis is hurt, or how he wants to handle it. Just be careful. Everyone."

"Take my camera," Harold said. "Be sure and document his injuries. The prosecution will be able to use the photos."

"Excellent idea." I took the camera. Mine was still at Bijou's place. Hopefully, Coleman would retrieve it. Speaking of Coleman, I checked my watch. Like it or not I meant to call him while I was driving. He should have finished at Hemlock Manor by now.

Harold agreed to take Sweetie and Pluto to his house until I could retrieve them, and Tinkie and I set off. I was dirty, tired, and had a bump on my head. I didn't have a lot of reserve to deal with another person who'd been hurt because of Farley and his miscreants.

Coleman didn't answer his phone when I called. Tinkie even tried, thinking perhaps he was still annoyed with me. Both calls went straight to voice mail, which led me to believe he was occupied.

"We'll handle this," Tinkie said. "But we'll call De-Wayne, too. No more running into danger without someone knowing where we are."

The Heberts lived on the outskirts of Zinnia in a modest brick home that showed a lot of love and attention to detail. The yard, filled with mums and fruit trees, won Lawn of the Month from the local garden club at least four times a year.

I pulled to a stop, and Nandy came flying out of the front door to meet us. "Curtis won't go to the hospital. I tried to convince him, but he won't."

We followed her inside. Curtis sat at the kitchen table, an ice pack on his right eye and blood on his shirt from cuts on his face. Someone had worked him over.

"Did you see who attacked you?" Tinkie asked as Patricia Ann made coffee for us.

"He came from behind. He put a cloth sack over my head and then whaled away on me. I never got a look at him."

"Where did it happen?" I asked.

"I was taking the garbage can out to the street. I guess he was hiding in the bushes."

Curtis was hurt, but not seriously. Nandy was my bigger concern. She was about to come apart at the seams.

"This is all my fault," she said. "I never should have let Curtis and Patricia Ann help me. I dragged them into my mess."

Patricia Ann put her arms around the girl and held her. "None of this is your fault. You can't be responsible for the meanness of others."

"We'll check around and see if we can find anything outside," I offered. "Would you mind if we took pictures of your injuries?"

"Go ahead." Curtis lowered the ice pack while I snapped photos from every angle. "I'm not hurt that bad. I'm just ready to knock some heads. I would have gotten some good licks in if I hadn't been blindsided."

Tinkie put the camera on the table. "I wish you'd let us take you to the hospital. Doc Sawyer should check you over, just to be on the safe side."

Curtis shook his head. "I'm not hurt. But next time I'll be prepared."

Nandy picked up the camera. "Mind if I look through the pictures?"

Tinkie waved approval. "Have at it."

She blinked against the tears as she scanned backward. When her face paled, I was staring right at her.

"What?"

"That's Wanda Tatum. She and Fred Doleman are Farley's right-hand helpers. How did you get a picture of her?"

I rushed to look and Tinkie was right beside me. Tatiana stood in the doorway of the bar as she prepared to leave. "*That's* Wanda Tatum?" Tinkie asked.

"She looks different, but that's her. She has on makeup and shaved her head."

"The tattoos?" I asked.

"Yeah, she was a biker babe before she came to Zinnia and met Reverend Farley. He uses her as an example in his sermons about how anyone can turn her life around."

Moments from the past few days cascaded in my brain. Where I ended was a mental image of Tatiana standing behind the bar asking Scott if he intended to open. I put the heel of my hand on my forehead. It was all right there. Tatiana showing up when no one knew about her, Koby's flirtatiousness with me when he allegedly had a girlfriend on the way to live with him, Tatiana's lack of tears or emotion. I'd racked it up to her being stoic or hard. Hell, no, she'd never met Koby and didn't give a fig about him. We'd been infiltrated and not a single one of us had ever suspected. The asp had been clasped to our bosom. And maybe it wasn't Jaytee.

"You were at the bar opening," I said. "You didn't recognize Wanda then?"

Curtis answered. "Nandy was only in the kitchen for five minutes. She brought more cornmeal. She's under-age. I was out of line to ask her to run off that creep wearing sunglasses and blocking the kitchen door, and Nandy refused. She never had an opportunity to see the bartender."

"We have to get back to Playin' the Bones," I told Tinkie.

"Tatiana is up to no good." The same thoughts had obviously been coursing through her mind.

"She's planning something terrible! Call DeWayne while I drive. Tell him Coleman has to come. And call the fire department. Send them out there now. If it isn't on fire, it will be." I wasn't a psychic, but it didn't take a fortune-teller to add up the clues and come to the conclusion that the blues club would be the perfect target to torch. Mason had said something about fire when he was holding me captive on Bijou's property, and I'd thought it was Dahlia House he meant to burn, but now it seemed more likely he'd meant the club. If the club was gone, Scott couldn't open. If he couldn't open, he'd lose his investment and never be able to recoup it. The property at the crossroads so valued by blues aficionados would soon be on the market again.

Curtis Hebert's beating might have been just a diversion, a way to assure Tatiana and her co-creeps that we'd leave the club so they could do their dirty work. The shocking part was that they didn't just lock us in the club and burn it to the ground with us in it. They'd killed one person and tried to kill another. What were a few more bodies?

"Be careful," Nandy whispered to us as we hurried out the door.

"I promise," I told her with as much assurance as I could muster.

———

The first sign of trouble was the empty security post. The paid guards, who were supposed to man the barricade 24/7, had vanished. Nightshade Security had come highly recommended to Scott. And yet they'd allowed someone to drive onto the premises with a shotgun and kill Koby Shaver. Now they were gone. Another example of how easily we were wooed into a sense of safety that never existed.

"We should wait for Coleman," Tinkie said. She had her gun in her lap. Mine was still somewhere at Bijou's. It struck me that it would be a bitter moment if my gun was used to harm someone I loved.

I pulled off the road. The dark outline of the club was about a hundred yards in the distance. "We have the element of surprise," I reminded Tinkie.

"And we don't have the dogs or cat to help us," she pointed out to me.

"We do have the gun and Harold's camera."

She snorted. "What's your plan? To snap bad photos and humiliate them on social media?"

"At least you still have a sense of humor."

"It's required to put up with you."

And with that statement, I knew our friendship was back on track. "Let's sneak down to the club and spy."

"If we get caught, they could very well put us in the building and roast us like suckling piglets."

I thumped Tinkie's arm. "What an awful image."

"What? You'd rather be a Boston butt? Maybe a shoulder roast."

"Stop it." It felt good to giggle, but we had to keep our concentration to avoid being caught. "Ready?"

She checked the gun. "Yeah. I'm as ready as I'll ever be."

The stars gave us enough light to navigate the rutted road without injury, and we reached the bar in silence. The stench of gasoline hit me like a fist. I saw movement and managed to pick out a black-clad figure hauling a heavy jug of what could only be gasoline around the side of the club.

Playin' the Bones was a new building created out of weathered and worn lumber to look old. It would go up like a haystack, especially with accelerant poured all around it. Beside me, Tinkie raised the pistol she carried and pointed at the figure. I put a hand on her wrist. "Don't."

"I thought we came to stop them from burning the club."

"In the movies, if you shoot someone who is holding gasoline, the spark sets off an explosion. We could blow the club up."

"My memory of science class tells me that isn't right, but I'm not willing to risk it," Tinkie said, lowering the gun.

"Let's get closer. If that's Tatiana and she's working alone, the two of us can take her. At least until Coleman gets here."

"It would be a lot easier to shoot her in the leg."

"Then let me lure her away from the club. I don't care if you blow her up, just not the building."

"Details, details."

The black-clad figure had disappeared, and I signaled Tinkie to go right. I went left. If Tatiana spotted one of us, the other could attack from behind her. Having a partner was one of the best things in the world. I crept to the edge of the building and got down on my hands and knees to peek around from a low vantage point. I saw her soaking the wood with the gasoline. It almost pushed me into rushing her, but I controlled myself.

It was only when I saw movement behind Tatiana and knew Tinkie was in position that I gathered myself to tackle the little arsonist. I launched myself like a sprinter coming off the block at the Olympics just as Tatiana reached into her pocket for a cigarette lighter and struck the flint.

I hit her low and hard, knocking her so hard the plastic gas tank flew up in the air and spilled over both of us. Gasoline rained on us and the Zippo's flame caught the fumes. I wasn't certain what happened because the concussion of the explosion sent me flying. I heard Tinkie scream, and I felt heat on my arms and back.

I was on fire!

I hit the dirt and rolled, trying to smother the flames in the cold Delta soil. Someone else was screaming, a woman, and an awful smell surrounded me. When the wave of soapy water splashed over me, it was almost more of a shock than the explosion.

"Get up, Sarah Booth! *She's* on fire!" Tinkie said. "*You're* just smoldering. Help me put her out!"

I scrambled upright. Pulling off my water-soaked coat, I ran at Tatiana and used the coat to suffocate the flames.

"Here comes the fire truck." Tinkie pointed toward the club's driveway as we rolled Tatiana in the dirt. The flames had been extinguished, but she'd suffered burns on her hands and face. Her clothes had protected the majority of her body. The stench of burning feathers from her down jacket made me want to puke.

"You put me out with dirty dog water?" I asked Tinkie.

"You're lucky you left the water out here."

I turned to the club, relieved to see that the fire hadn't caught there. The building would have gone up like fat lighter. When the gas container exploded, it had pushed us away from the club instead of toward it. The cloud of flames had missed the fuel-soaked wood.

Tinkie's lips moved, but my hearing was fading in and out. A ringing sound roared in my eardrums. Gee. How in the hell did I go from being abducted and abused to blown up? The day had not improved.

The firemen arrived and quickly took over care of Tatiana. Tinkie hustled me toward one of the young men who examined me and pronounced me okay. I had miraculously escaped serious injury. My heavy coat and gloves had taken the punishment.

"I'm not hurt," I assured Tinkie, speaking really loud because my hearing was still impaired.

"I wouldn't go that far," Tinkie said. "Wait until you see your hair."

I ripped off my gloves and patted my head. She wasn't lying. My hair was mostly gone. Singed off. In a panic, I felt my ears. Both were intact. Hair would regrow, though I'd look pretty pitiful for the next few months.

"Sarah Booth, you saved the club."

The ringing had begun to diminish. "It was a team effort."

"You figured out that Tatiana would burn the club and you stopped her." She took a blanket from one of the firemen and covered me in it. She leaned down to whisper, "Coleman is going to be so pissed at you. You almost blew yourself up."

"I know. I get to have all the fun." If anyone dared to fuss at me about anything, I would throw a hissy fit on the spot. "Why was Tatiana burning the club?"

"I don't know. I've been a little busy, watching my best friend blow up, but I'll get on it right away."

"Ha, ha!" This was going to be a joke that grew old quickly.

"You should have seen yourself flying through the air."

I held up one hand, palm facing her. "Stop it, before I have to hurt you."

"You're sort of cute in a Sinead O'Connor way. If only you could sing."

"Stop it!" My ribs were sore and it hurt to laugh.

"You are so bald if a mosquito tried to land on your head it would skid and break its neck."

"Tinkie!"

We both laughed, a welcome release, the insane joy at being alive. The story could have had a much different ending.

"I love you," Tinkie said, hugging me hard. "There are days I want to kill you, but I love you."

"The feeling is mutual."

"Doc Sawyer will be relieved that we made it through a case without one of us ending up at the hospital."

She was right, up to a point. "This case isn't complete. A lot of things aren't clear. Let's see what Tatiana . . . Wanda can tell us."

Wanda sat on a cot in the back of the EMT van as a paramedic worked on her burns. Two stout firemen blocked any attempt at escape. I motioned for Tinkie to follow me to the van. The firemen stepped back when I requested some privacy. I had some questions for the pretend fiancée.

"You almost blew me up," she said angrily.

"Right. I was the one holding a plastic gas tank with fuel still in it and flicking a Bic."

"It was a Zippo." She had to be hurting but I gave her credit for not crying. One cheek had blistered, and her hands looked scalded. She was in for a painful recovery.

"Oh, yeah, the technicalities make it so different," Tinkie said.

"What's going on with Farley? He may hate the blues and Scott's band, but there's more to this."

"Sinners have to be punished." She refused to look at either of us.

"Don't be a fool," Tinkie said softly. "You're going to take the blame for a lot of serious crimes and Farley and the men of the church are going to walk away scot-free."

"Leave me alone." The slightest quaver in her voice gave me hope.

"You don't have to talk, but I think you will," I said. "Let me put it to you plain. You're a female, and Reverend Farley and his associates will be more than glad to let you take the blame for all of this. Think about it. You're here, caught red-handed. You think they'll voluntarily step up and cop to their part? If you believe that, you're delusional. In the end, this will be all *your* idea, your plan, you acting alone."

"They wouldn't do that." Worry darkened her eyes.

"Have you seen the way the rest of the women are

treated? Do you really think they view you differently? They let you think you're one of the men, but get real. They used you. They used you worse than any other female in the church. They got you to hurt people who would have been your friends."

"My friends . . ." Her bravado slipped and she tucked her chin into her chest. Her hands trembled, either from shock or pain.

"Why didn't they send a man to help you?" Tinkie asked. "They let you try to burn down a building by yourself, and they didn't even teach you to do it properly. Does that sound like they care what happens to you? You almost died, and do you honestly think Farley or Mason Britt care? Now you're caught, and you'll take all the weight. You'll go to prison. The people who wanted to be your friends, the people who would be standing here with you now if you hadn't betrayed them, are the members of the band and Scott. You could have had a real family with them instead of being a disposable tool."

The pain from her hands and face and the emotional pain of betrayal were too much. A tear fell into her lap.

Tinkie and I shared a glance. It was now or never. I'd have preferred to wait for Coleman so it would be official, but this moment might never come again.

"Who killed Koby Shaver?" I asked.

She spoke slowly, but clearly. "I drove the truck. Fred Doleman pulled the trigger."

"And Mike Hawkins?"

"The same." She wouldn't look at us. "The club had to be destroyed. I watched all those people, drinking and dancing, all of them letting the devil get into them. Some of them were almost having sex on the dance floor. Reverend Farley was right about the power of Satan in the music. You felt it. I saw you." She pointed at me. Then Tinkie. "You too."

"We were dancing and having fun."

"I know where such things lead. I know plenty. Before I found Reverend Farley and the church I was passed around by men who drank and used me. They were bikers and I was their property. Fred found me on the streets in Memphis, and he took me to the church. They saved me."

She struggled to control her voice and continued. "Reverend Farley taught me to respect myself. I wanted to get the tattoos removed, to take away the stain of my past life, but Reverend Farley said I should use them for good. He said my past should be the example to show the young girls of the church what could happen if they left the protection of their families. He gave me a home and taught me to serve."

I recalled what Nandy had said about how Farley used Wanda Tatum as his living example, capitalizing on her tattoos and sad past. What Wanda didn't see was that she'd been used by Farley just like the men before him. Sexually and in ways equally as awful.

"Where are your parents, your family?" I asked.

"The church is my family."

Wanda started to stand up from the cot, but I shook my head. "Don't. You need to wait here until the sheriff arrives. Tell us how to contact your parents or a sibling, a relative who can help you."

She glared at me. "There is no one. Reverend Farley will come."

"No, he won't," Tinkie said softly. "Did he tell you to pretend to be Koby's girlfriend?"

Wanda held on to her defiance, but I suspected fear was at the root of it. "When he asked me to find a way to work at the club, I was glad to do it. The reverend wants to save people, to keep them from burning in hell. And that's where all of you are headed."

"Because we like to dance?" Tinkie asked.

"Because you love to sin," she said. The fire was back in her eyes. "Don't you see? Everything about this place is against God."

"You've been brainwashed," Tinkie said bluntly. "I don't know what Farley did to you, but you aren't using the good sense God gave you. Think, Wanda! Why would you give yourself over to—"

"It isn't my place to think. That's what's wrong with the modern world. Women want to think and be the boss and run the family and compete at the job and act like they're smarter and know better than the men. That's not God's way. Women are weak and should cleave to the man for his strength and guidance. We women are incapable of caring for ourselves. We are like children. I have lived in a world where I had to care for myself and it ended up in pain and drugs and sin. The man is the head of the household. He has dominion over the animals, the women and children, and the other races."

It was hard to watch a young woman spout such nonsense so sincerely. If Farley wasn't punished for any other crime, he had to go down for what he'd done to Wanda and others in his congregation.

"So, killing an innocent person is the right thing to do?" I asked.

"No one is innocent. We are all sinners. Reverend Farley had a plan to rid Sunflower County of temptation and the source of sin. It would be a sign from God to rally people to the cause of righteousness."

"You were okay with killing Koby Shaver, a decent man who did no harm to you or anyone else?"

She didn't answer.

"Koby was gunned down in cold blood. He never had a chance."

"It isn't my place to question what I'm told."

"Wanda, you're facing a murder-one charge. That's a death sentence." Tinkie didn't mince her words. "Did you know they meant to kill Koby?"

Her eyes were large and scared. "I didn't."

"What happened? You'd better tell us right now. If you were duped into this, I promise Sarah Booth and I will try to help you."

"No one ever really helps me." Another tear soaked her lap.

"You have my word," Tinkie said. "It's the only thing you have right now."

Wanda used a shoulder to rub her eye. "Fred went in the club. He reported back that it was filled with sin. It was just like the reverend said. So he called Reverend Farley, who sent me in the truck with the shotgun. He told me to drive and give the gun to Fred. The security men had been paid off, so they let me in."

"And you didn't know what was going to happen?" Tinkie held out the slimmest hope. "If you didn't know, you can help yourself."

"I thought Fred intended to shoot the building. I didn't know he meant to kill. It didn't matter to him who, just the first person who walked out the door. It was the bartender. The second time I was told to drive, I couldn't let him kill Mike. I liked Mike. His wife came up to the club and we talked. She was so excited about the baby coming. I couldn't let Fred shoot him down in his front yard so I jerked the wheel. Fred missed his shot. He was really mad. I told him the wheel slipped."

Danni had said the truck jerked as the shot was fired. Tatiana was telling the truth about that, at least.

"I don't hold with sinning, but killing isn't right," she said.

"How did you know to say you were Koby's girlfriend?" Tinkie asked.

"Fred said the club would be shorthanded for a bartender. I'd worked in bars before, so it was easy to pretend to be Koby's girl. No one really knew him, so it wasn't too much of a risk. We made some calls to the bar where he used to work, found out he was single." She shrugged.

"Wanda, you are not a stupid girl." Pink stained Tinkie's cheeks. "How could you fall for all of this? How could you give your life over to men who treated you like a cow?"

Wanda pulled her shoulders back. "Because I had a place where I belonged. A place where no one hurt me, and they said I was good and one day a man would take me for his wife and I would have a home forever."

Never underestimate the power of belonging—the secret weapon of the cult.

"What role does Mason Britt play in all of this?" I asked.

"He's the enforcer. He punishes those who fall by the wayside. Farley gives the orders and Mason enforces them.

He goes with Farley to his big meetings. Sometimes Fred goes too."

"And Jaytee?" I would make that weasel pay.

She finally looked up. "I don't know about him."

She'd never been part of the inner circle. Always an outsider, she hadn't a clue what it was all about. After all, she was just a woman.

"What about Bijou LaRoche?" Tinkie asked.

Wanda avoided eye contact, but not before I saw her features harden. "She is a vile creature. She tempted Jebediah and Mason. She flaunted herself before them. She called them to her home and offered them sex. She is a Jezebel."

"Bijou never does anything unless she gains something. What did she want?"

"Ask Jebediah. She was his friend. She gave Mason a job so he could work in the community. He grew up around here and knew all the old farms and the barns. They had a real thing about those old buildings and moving the food shipments out there so the small planes could pick them up."

Tinkie and I exchanged glances. "Food? What kind of food?"

"Who knows? Reverend Farley and Mason would go off at night to meet people. It was secret stuff, not for women. Sometimes they would come to the church and get us up to go and unload food boxes into the farm sheds." Her eyebrows rose. "Reverend Farley told me once he was involved in changing the world order. God touched him! He told us all about it, how he was up early writing his sermon and God spoke to him and gave him an important role to play. He's a special man. And he said I had a role to play as well. Reverend Farley said God had marked me as special, too. We were gladiators and we would change the world."

This was a girl who'd never had a moment where she felt like she was important or valuable until she joined a cult. Jebediah Farley had exploited her fear, self-loathing, lack of confidence—he'd played on every negative thing that made her life a misery.

"Was Farley interested in Bijou's buildings?" Tinkie asked.

Wanda shrugged. "Fred told me Farley was shocked when they got the invitation to move to Bijou's place, but the women were excited. They'd have houses to live in, even if it was an old slave shack and we were only staying a week or two. It would have been so much better than what we had. Those tents get cold and winter is coming. The men meet in the lodge, but women aren't allowed there."

I had more questions, but Coleman arrived with two other men. It took a moment for me to recognize Jaytee and Mason Britt. Mason wasn't wearing handcuffs, and Jaytee had a lot of nerve showing up here. I jumped down from the back of the EMT van just as the paramedics came to close the door

Coleman arrested Wanda, read her her rights, and sent her on to the hospital. DeWayne would meet her there so she could be treated for her burns, and then taken into custody. When she was well enough, she'd be transferred to the Sunflower County jail. I did feel a little sorry for her. She'd been the dupe, and I certainly knew how that felt. Not pleasant.

I might be in jail beside her too because I intended to hurt Mason Britt and Jaytee. The only weapon I had was Harold's camera, and I grabbed it by the strap with the intention of swinging it directly into Mason Britt's face. I was almost on him when strong arms encircled me and pulled into a giant bear hug that immobilized me.

"Hold on, Sarah Booth," Coleman said.

I struggled like a wild thing. "You have no idea what he did to me. He—" Words failed me. I wanted action, and I wanted to hurt him. Then I remembered Mason wasn't cuffed. "Why isn't he under arrest?"

"If you will stop acting like a pissed-off grizzly, I'll tell you."

His tone was so reasonable it settled me more than anything else. "Tell me what?"

"Yeah, you'd better start talking." Tinkie was unrestrained, and she was eyeing Mason and Jaytee with anger. "Coleman can't control both of us at the same time."

Coleman pulled us aside, out of hearing from the firemen, who were putting their hoses away. They'd finished spraying the outside of the building with water to dilute the gasoline. Their work was complete.

Mason and Jaytee wisely hung back, and I had to wonder at the way they stood, so casual and at ease with each other. It made me want to hurt them more. They'd abused and humiliated women and gotten away with it, and if Jaytee wasn't in it up to his hairline, he was still a jackass for not calling Cece to say he wasn't hurt.

"Sarah Booth, Mason is an undercover agent from the ATF."

I stared at Coleman. "Say that again."

He did, and I read his lips because I didn't trust my ears.

"Are you saying he's a fed?"

"That's exactly what he's saying," Mason said, stepping forward. "I'm sorry for roughing you up, but I had to be convincing. Fred Doleman was waiting on the porch, listening to everything I said to you. So much was at stake. There was to be a big meeting tonight, and at last I was going to be allowed to attend. I've worked undercover two years for that moment. If I hadn't been so harsh, Sarah Booth, Fred would have suspected. Doleman is the one who clocked you from behind, though. I couldn't react to protect you."

"And you!" I turned on Jaytee. "I told you if you hurt my friend, I'd make you pay. You're in this—"

"He's working for Mason," Coleman explained.

"I'm sure he's *undercover*, too." Tinkie was as mad as I was.

"Liaison with the FBI," Jaytee said, "but only for this case."

"Very freaking clever." I was pissed. "How is it I got beat up, tied up, tossed around, and he walks around like Caesar?"

"You were poking around where you didn't belong," Mason said. "You could have blown my cover."

If Mason was trying to be obnoxious, he had succeeded.

"How does Bijou figure into this?" Tinkie asked.

Coleman put a hand on my shoulder. "Let's go inside the club. I called Scott. He's on the way. He was with Harold so they're both coming. And they're bringing Cece."

"If she forgives you, you're a lucky man," I said to Jaytee as I walked past him and followed Coleman into the club. I was still angry. It had been a long, hard day, and the Johnny-come-lately facts I was receiving only served to frustrate me more.

I'd risked my life. The club had almost been burned down. Koby Shaver was dead. Mike Hawkins was shot. Curtis Hebert was beaten. Ned Gaston's house was burned to the ground. All of this had happened with federal agents right in the middle of it. How had they failed to stop it?

Coleman had a key to the club and opened the door. We filed in. Tinkie and I sat at the end of the bar, away from Jaytee and Mason. Coleman went behind the bar and quickly poured a round of drinks.

When he served me and Tinkie, I grabbed his wrist. "How can you let them get away with this? Did you know?"

"I did not," he said. "And I'm angry. But it's the system, not the fault of these guys. The feds often don't clue in the locals. It's a serious problem, and this time I believe people were hurt because of the lack of communication. But this is something to address tomorrow. Tonight," he increased the volume of his voice, "I raise a glass to Sarah Booth and Tinkie, who saved the club from being torched."

A flash went off at the door, followed by a squeal of delight as Cece dropped her camera to a tabletop and rushed into Jaytee's arms. His kiss appeared to be the real thing, but I wouldn't bet good money on it. He was a deceptive man. Cece would hear the truth from me, and then she could make up her own mind. Witness protection, double agent, spy, James Freaking Bond—I wasn't impressed with a man who would lie to his beloved.

Before Coleman could pour Cece a drink, Harold and

Oscar came in the door, followed by thundering dogs. Petite Chablis nipped Sweetie and Roscoe on the back legs as she chased them around the bar. It seemed everyone had forgiven everyone else, except me and Pluto. I was angry at Mason and Jaytee, and Pluto was angry at me. He jumped on the bar and came toward me. His green gaze zeroed in on me like a heat-seeking missile. His black paw knocked my drink into my lap.

"Uh-oh," Coleman said. "Someone is pissy."

"Indeed we are."

"Love the new hairdo, dah-link," Cece said as she sauntered over, leading Jaytee by the hand. "I never realized you had such a big head, Sarah Booth. You know when the West was being settled, men would advertise for brides. Often they included the measurements of their heads in the advertisement. A big head was much sought after."

"Now, now. She sacrificed her hair to save the club," Jaytee said.

"Fascinating." I burned him with a glare.

"Dah-link, we can have seams tattooed on her head and nickname her Spalding."

It was funny, but instead of laughing I shot a death-ray at Jaytee. "Fess up now," I told him.

"What's the matter with her?" Cece asked her boy-friend.

"There are things we have to tell you, and chances are you're about to become extremely mad, too," Jaytee said. "We're waiting for Scott and Zeb to get here. We'll tell it all once and be done with it."

The dogs had settled down and Pluto had allowed me to hold him in my soggy lap when Mason and Jaytee began the story.

"There are a lot of things I'm not proud of in this case," Mason said. "Koby Shaver and I served together in the marines. Koby signed on as bartender for the club because he was helping me work this case. In that respect, he's dead because I asked for his help. I will point out that Koby believed in what we were doing. I regret I didn't take this threat more seriously. If I had, Koby might be alive right now."

"What case?" Tinkie interrupted.

"We were investigating the Midnight Templars, a national organization with a focus on isolationism, a church-based state, and a hatred of the federal government, which they intend to overthrow. They're involved in weapons, drugs, and counterfeiting," Mason said. "Their goal is to take down the U.S. government and drugs are their weapon of choice. To that end, they bring in heroin from Mexico and the Middle East. They sell it to buy guns to arm their survivalist militia. The Delta, because of the isolation and the numerous small landing strips on the farms, has become a hub of the operation."

"The boxes of food." I suddenly saw the bigger picture. "It isn't food."

"That's right," Mason said. "They launder drug money through legitimate businesses. They also move weapons, using local farm buildings to store the guns and drugs until they can fly them out from the farms' landing strips. They use local isolationist groups like Jebediah Farley's because they're cultish, and the cult members obey without question and are easily manipulated."

"You know all of this and you didn't stop it?" Fury pounded in my head. "Koby is dead and Mike is shot."

"I had no idea anyone would be hurt," Mason said. "Attacking the blues club was a way to rally the church members. It was a ploy, and Farley intended it to work as motivation, not bring about serious injury. That's standard for cults. To unite the congregation, Farley needed a symbol of sin and evil. I never thought he'd send assassins to kill folks associated with the club."

"Then you thought wrong."

Coleman put a hand on my arm and Scott grasped my shoulder.

"What's the bottom line?" I demanded. "Who's headed to jail? And don't tell me Wanda is going to take the fall for all of this."

"Farley, Fred Doleman, Wanda Tatum, or Tatiana, as you knew her, and that's just the beginning, are in custody. We'll clean up this local cell of the Midnight Templars, but I had hoped to infiltrate the top financial ring." Mason's jaw clenched. "That's why I pulled Jaytee into this. And why I didn't act before now. Farley is the local level. This involves powerful people. Very powerful. But my plan didn't happen, and my cover is blown. In a rather spectacular way."

"My part is done," Jaytee said. "I didn't really get off the ground as a spy. It's just as well. I can go back to being a musician. And be with my gal." He put his arm around Cece and led her over to me and Tinkie. "I didn't want to be involved in this, but Mason needed my help. He'd hoped to introduce me to Farley, and through Farley get to the big money. I would reveal my background in finance, my past history and hatred of the government, and offer to help launder the money. My role wasn't that big, and I certainly didn't mean to hurt Cece. I do love her. I know it's fast and impetuous and all the things our parents warned us against. Here we are, nonetheless, and I intend to love and care for her for as long as she'll let me."

I had to admit, it was hard to stay mad at him when Cece looked so happy. "Couldn't you have called her and reassured her you were okay?"

"He wanted to, but they were watching him so closely," Mason answered the question. "I would have called Cece, but I didn't dare do anything to tip our hand. We were so damn close to infiltrating the top rung of the Midnight Templars. The meeting was set for tonight. Obviously, it's been canceled."

"Who was attending?" I had a sudden suspicion.

"We'd enlisted Bijou LaRoche to help us," Mason said. "Which is how I ended up as her foreman."

"I can't believe Bijou volunteered to help you."

"She didn't exactly volunteer," Mason said. "She needed money."

"And yet you took a dog captive, mistreated him, and—" I got off the barstool. Just thinking about poor Roscoe, who appeared no worse for the wear, actually, refueled my anger.

"Hold on a minute," Mason said. "Roscoe showed up at Bijou's. He went out in the pasture and was chasing one of the bulls. He got kicked. I picked him up and confined him, and to be honest, I meant to drop him off at Harold's, but you came after him before I got the chance."

He had an answer for everything, but I didn't believe him. It was all too convenient. "And Bijou is a federal agent, too?"

"Not exactly." Mason said. "She'll be charged with tax fraud and drug sales. It seems Ms. LaRoche has been cooking her books for a long time where the farm is concerned. Lots of expenses, none of them legit. She owes the IRS at least half a million dollars."

For the first time, I thought I might be able to forgive Mason for tying me up, pushing me onto the floor, leading me to think I was going to die, and forcing me to worry that my friend's future happiness would be shattered. Not! I drew back and slugged him in the jaw. The shock slammed from my knuckles to my elbow and up to my shoulder.

Mason rubbed his jaw, and I thought my arm would fall off.

"That's enough," Coleman said, but I could tell he sort of wanted to slug Mason, too.

"Can I take a swing?" Tinkie asked.

"No!" Coleman grabbed her wrist. "Don't force Oscar to keep you in line. You need to learn your place."

Steam rose from the top of Tinkie's head. "How dare you—"

Coleman burst into laughter, along with everyone else, even me. "Sorry, Tinkie," he said, "but I knew you'd see the humor once you got over being mad."

"I don't find that humorous. Not really." Tinkie was pensive, not angry. "Why would women participate in such a repressive belief system? What about those people who believed in Jebediah Farley? Their lives are ruined. Or at least upturned. Some of them will never be able to find their old lives. To believe in someone and something and then realize it's all about power and money . . ."

She'd summed it up far better than I could.

"This is a tragedy," Coleman said. "For a lot of people. Most of all for those who cared about Koby Shavers."

"And Bijou?" I asked. "Will she see jail time?"

"It's out of my hands," Mason said.

"Because she cooperated?" Tinkie asked.

"She did. She allowed us to use her property, which gave us an edge. And she set up meetings with wealthy men. We'll follow up on those and hopefully round up some of the big money people, but we really don't have any solid evidence and I never infiltrated the top rungs. Farley is a bottom-feeder."

"Was the bid to buy Playin' the Bones real?" I asked.

Mason nodded to Oscar.

"There was money in play, but I could never get a firm lead on where it was coming from," Oscar said.

"Who owned the black pickup truck?" That was a final puzzle piece.

"It belonged to Farley. He bought it in Memphis and never registered it in Mississippi. He kept it in a shed on the church grounds."

"And who was making the threatening phone calls to the band members?" I asked.

"Fred Doleman made most of them. The female caller—we haven't cleared that up. We will before it's over."

Mason had answered most of my questions. "Will you let us know if you take down the big money people?"

"It won't be me," Mason said. "I've been recalled to D.C., where I'll get a new assignment. We think the Midnight Templars will be dissolved here. At least for a while. But they have cells all over the country. There are always people who want to believe they're superior to others, and a new leader will show up to enslave them. It's the way of the world."

"Not comforting," Tinkie said.

Oscar put his arm around her. "And you and Sarah Booth will be here to stop it from taking root."

21

Sitting in the two A.M. cold, smoking a cigarette on the front porch at Dahlia House, I tried to recognize the constellations in a black sky spangled with stardust. My father had taught them to me long ago: Orion's Belt, the Seven Sisters, the Archer, Taurus, Scorpio. Each had a legend, a story he told, often while we were sitting in the spot I now occupied.

Sweetie Pie snoozed beside me, and Pluto sat at my feet, his little kitty brain conjuring his next revenge plot. He was mostly over being miffed, but not completely. A word to the wise—a miffed cat is not your friend.

Headlights turned down the drive, and for one moment my heart lifted before I reality checked myself. Graf was not coming home.

The florist van pulled up at the front door and a young male in jeans and a coat hopped out and retrieved an enormous vase of red roses—at least three dozen.

"Miss Delaney?" he asked, hidden behind the flowers.

"Yes, bring them in." I jumped up and opened the door. He placed them on the side table near the mirror. The bouquet was incredible. I'd never seen roses so big and fragrant.

"Who sent them?" I asked.

"There should be a card. I didn't take the order. I'm simply the delivery guy."

I tipped him and he left. No florist shop in Zinnia made deliveries this late at night, so they hadn't been sent locally. By the time I thought about checking the tag on the van, it had pulled down the drive. I couldn't read the license plate but I did see the name of the florist. Bountiful Bouquets. I'd never heard of them. Whatever, they did lovely work.

I went back inside and opened the card, which was typed on plain white stock. "Congratulations. Until next time."

A chill traced down my spine. I read the card again. The only way to interpret it was as a challenge. I considered throwing the flowers away, but they were so beautiful, and I wanted to show Coleman in the morning. I would not call anyone tonight. It was too late and everyone was exhausted. Tomorrow would be soon enough. A vase of flowers didn't seem like an imminent threat, even if the card was weird.

A soft voice spoke behind me. "Company's comin'. Don't dress for bed yet."

I didn't have to turn around to know that Jitty was with me. "Sing me a song," I requested. Now that I'd discovered Jitty could mimic all the blues greats, I had plans to keep her busy.

"What would you like to hear?" she asked.

Amazingly, she let me pick the song. Jitty never gave me choices. She was all about ultimatums.

"I'd like to hear 'Voodoo Woman,' the Koko Taylor version."

"A perfect selection." Jitty morphed into the full-cheeked diva with the mischievous eyes and big smile. She sang away, a heavenly musical accompaniment coming from somewhere. I'd learned not to ask too many questions.

Jitty got down on my favorite part that listed all of the charms from a rabbit foot, a toad, and a crawfish to rattlesnake dust and spider bone and "if that don't do it baby, you'd better leave it all alone." Yes, Jitty was a voodoo woman.

Nobody was around to watch and I got up and danced, first with Jitty and then Sweetie Pie, who cut loose with a howl that made Jitty squeal with laughter. Jitty finished the song and we tumbled out the door and collapsed onto the front steps, panting and chuckling.

"Your dog knows good blues when she hears them," Jitty said.

"It's in her blood. She's a Delta hound. It's in my blood too."

"Girl, you cut loose and juke. Time is short and youth is gone in the whisper of a sigh. Don't set up in this house grievin' what's past."

"I promise you, Jitty, I'll get back in action. I do need to think. Maybe this is a chance for me to define what I truly want. A bicoastal marriage was never my dream.

I think about Hamilton Garrett V. I could have married him and helped him with the wonderful causes he takes on. I just couldn't live in Paris or Europe. In my heart, I knew it."

Her smile was a little sad.

"I want to live here in Dahlia House," I continued. "I would have forced the bicoastal thing to work with Graf. It would have been hard, but I would have done it. Now, though, maybe I don't want that life."

"Most people find happiness like a blind hog after an acorn. You put some thought into it. That's the right thing. I won't nag at you to marry, Sarah Booth."

"Why, Jitty, thank you. You're so understanding."

"Like I said, company's comin' any minute now. And just to be clear, you don't have to marry the man, but your eggs are dryin' up fast. So grab some viable sperm, fertilize that moldy egg, and let's get this show on the road. I need an heir to haunt. Marriage can come at your leisure."

"Dammit!" I stood up to confront her, but she had vanished. And another pair of headlights came down the driveway. What now? A poison bonbon delivery from Bijou?

The brown cruiser alerted me it was either Coleman or DeWayne, and my bets were on the high sheriff himself. I hoped he was over being mad at me for spying at Bijou's without telling anyone.

"Coleman," I said, "what brings you here?"

"I'd like to say pleasure, but . . ." He came up the steps. Pluto really liked Coleman and rushed to rub against his legs. He picked up the cat and held him. "You might have more sense than Sarah Booth and Tinkie put together," he whispered to the cat plenty loud for me to hear.

"I know you must be exhausted." I felt lightheaded I was so tired. We'd all left the bar with the agreement to meet up at eleven to filter through each detail. I checked my watch. It was three A.M. "Shouldn't you be in bed?"

"I should, but I wanted to give you a heads-up."

Coleman wasn't reactionary. He was talking to me at three in the morning because he was worried.

"Come in," I said. "Would you like some warm milk, coffee, or a drink?"

"Coffee, if you don't mind. I've got a lot of reports to finish."

He followed me to the kitchen and I put on a pot. While it brewed, I sat at the table and signaled him to do the same. Instead of talking, he contemplated the top of my kitchen table.

When the coffee was ready, I poured two cups of black coffee and set one in front of him. He spun his coffee cup, finally leveling a look at me. "Mason and I had a long talk with Bijou, who insists she didn't know anything about the Midnight Templars and their objectives. She also insists you were behind inviting the Foundation Rock Church people to her property."

"Innocent!" I held up a hand. "I swear it. I did not invite them."

"But you know who did?"

I shook my head. "I don't know anything."

"You're a terrible liar and I already know it was Harold."

I checked his expression. He wasn't fishing, he knew. "Big deal."

"You two skated on this, but next time you might not

be so lucky. And just so you know, I'm going to recommend that Wanda Tatum, or Tatiana, be detained in a psychiatric facility. Of all of the people involved in this, I think she's as much a victim as anyone."

Coleman wasn't a softie, but he believed psychological trauma had to be weighed. "Thank you." Still, this was hardly information that warranted a wee-hour visit after days without sleep. "Are you okay?" I had a terrible thought that somehow Coleman was in trouble. His behavior said as much.

"I'm good. Has Scott decided what to do about the club?" Coleman asked.

"When we were leaving Playin' the Bones, he said he'd open up next week. He's not backing down. Jebediah Farley is behind bars, the church's attempts to destroy the club are over. He can realize his dream and bring a lot to the area. The immediate danger is past."

"No, it isn't." Coleman stood and came to me. He held my shoulders. "Gertrude has jumped bail and disappeared."

"But . . ." Words eluded me. "How?"

"Two farmworkers at Bijou's found Frisco Evans. He'd been badly beaten, tied up, and left in the woods near Hemlock Manor. I just left the hospital. Frisco said it was Gertrude. She wanted to take the Mercedes roadster for a test drive. When she turned down that long wooded drive into Bijou's, she hit Frisco in the head with a blackjack. When he was unconscious, she pushed him out of the car, dragged him back in the woods, tied him up, and left him."

"He was there while I was being held prisoner?"

"Yes."

Fear rose like a giant wave, ready to crash over me.

Gertrude had been there too. Had she known I was help-less, she might have killed me. "She has to be in Sunflower County. She has a car just like mine. Just like my mother's. She won't stop until she really hurts me." My voice rose, and I couldn't stop it.

"We'll find her, Sarah Booth."

"No, you won't." Gertrude had taken on the powers of some mythological creature. She was immortal, un-stoppable. She might be mentally unbalanced, but she was very, very smart. "She has plenty of money. Loads of it. Check with Oscar in the morning. I'll bet she took the balance of Yancy's payment for the B&B in cash."

"Which brings up another issue." Coleman had deci-ded to hold nothing back. "The relationship between Yancy Bellow and Gertrude worried me from the start. Something isn't right there, Sarah Booth."

"What are you saying?"

"Oscar gave me the details. Yancy paid Gertrude two hundred thousand more than the B&B was ap-praised at. And Harold was able to trace the offer to buy Playin' the Bones. It came from the same bank in the Cayman Islands that Yancy drew the check to buy The Gardens."

"Yancy was behind the offer to buy Playin' the Bones and all that property and build a blues emporium? But he put up a reward, and he offered to be Scott's partner. You think all that time he was really trying to run Scott out of business?"

"So far, I can't prove it, but I believe that's true. There's nothing illegal about anything he did. At least that I can prove. I just have to question his connection to the Foun-dation Rock Church and the attempt to ruin Scott's club. Farley and the church had been quiet. Suddenly they're putting out flyers and shooting people? Over a club? It doesn't make sense. And the overpayment to Gertrude." He swallowed. "That sets off all kind of alarms. He made her escape possible."

"She won't rest until she exacts her revenge against me. She wants to hurt me for something that never happened."

"If she's smart, she'll get as far from Sunflower County as possible."

"It's not about being smart. She's obsessed." I needed to move, to run, to put my body in motion, but there wasn't anywhere I could go to escape the hard truth Coleman had brought to me.

"I called Lee McBride. She's on the way with a trailer to pick up your horses. She was more than glad to help you. Tinkie and Oscar are waiting at Hilltop for you and the pets. You'll be safe there. Both you and Tinkie."

The idea of leaving Dahlia House empty and abandoned while I hid out from a woman who wanted to harm me was too much. "I'm staying right here. The animals can go—they'll be safer. I won't leave Dahlia House so a psycho can torch it."

"I won't leave you here."

"Then you'll be staying too." The coffeepot hissed and gurgled and I bolted out of my chair. The muscles in my shoulders tightened to the point I thought my bones would snap. "How did Gertrude manage this?" I asked.

"DeWayne and I both were focused on the blues club. With Alton James in town, it never crossed my mind Gertrude would flee. I assumed, with her fancy lawyer, she was going to stand and fight. When I talked to James, though, he admitted he hadn't gotten his retainer yet."

"Gertrude skunked him, too." Under different circumstances, it would be funny. The mighty Alton James taken for a ride by a middle-aged B&B owner turned murderer. "She never intended to pay him."

"James won't take this lying down. His pride's on the line. Gertrude can't stay in the wind forever. If I were her, I'd head for Mexico. I've alerted the feds and law enforcement officials from Florida to Texas. If she tries to flee the country, they'll catch her."

"She's right here." I knew it in my gut. "Gertrude will make a perfect weapon for the Midnight Templars. She's exactly what they need. She can play the role of demure businesswoman and she's capable of anything. You may have stomped out the local group, but Gertrude somehow managed to get to a higher level."

"I'm afraid you're right."

"They'll hide her. They have access to planes and airstrips all over the Delta."

He didn't deny it. "Throw some clothes together and come with me, Sarah Booth."

My stubborn streak demanded that I stay, but I took pity on Coleman. He was running on fumes. "Only for tonight."

"Good enough for right now." He wisely took his victory and avoided another skirmish.

I hurried to my bedroom and threw a few necessities into a bag, pausing for a moment in front of the mirror to stare at the woman with the truly bad haircut who stared back at me. It had been a helluva week. I bounded down the stairs and met Coleman in the foyer. He paused in front of the flowers. "A new admirer?"

"Not exactly." I handed him the note.

He tapped it against his hand. "This is a threat, Sarah Booth."

"Yes, I believe it is."

"Take this with you." He reached into his jacket pocket and brought out my gun. "Mason returned it and your camera, and I believe you should keep it with you."

"Who do you think sent the flowers?" I asked.

"Maybe Alton James, as a method of softening you up, when he thought he was still on the case. Or Bijou. She still has a score to settle with you."

"It's neither of them."

"Maybe Gertrude. That's a Memphis florist. I'll check tomorrow and see if anyone recognized her. You be on your guard." He reached over and ruffled the patches of my pitiful hair, fighting hard to put a note of normalcy into our conversation. "We'll catch Gertrude and life will get back to normal. Beauty salon tomorrow?"

"Tinkie is taking me to her stylist. It was easier to say yes than to argue. Coleman, I'll drive myself to Tinkie's. You have my word I'll go straight there. I want my car with me."

He considered for a long moment, and the same thought ran through both our minds. I saw it clearly on his face. He could stay here with me at Dahlia House. It would be so easy to turn to him to make me feel safe. But I couldn't choose my future out of fear. I refused to do so, nor would Coleman want to begin a relationship that way.

"I'll follow you to Hilltop to make sure you get there safely." He pulled me close.

We stood for a moment, each weighing the future. He opened the front door to reveal headlights coming down the drive. Lee was here to pick up my horses. "Let me give her a hand," he said as he walked out the door.

I almost called him back, but that wasn't the right answer for me. Not right now. Not with Gertrude lurking in the night. Not with my heart still wounded and unsure. As I'd told Jitty, not until I knew myself better.

READ ON FOR AN EXCERPT FROM

Rock-a-Bye Bones

THE NEXT SARAH BOOTH DELANEY MYSTERY
FROM CAROLYN HAINES, AVAILABLE SOON
IN HARDCOVER FROM MINOTAUR BOOKS.

Thanksgiving is no time to leave a desperate woman alone in a haunted house with a knife and a giant squash. Pumpkin spatter covers every horizontal and vertical surface in the spacious kitchen. I heft the five-inch blade and advance on the nine-pound vegetable that defies me. I intend to magically turn the gourd into homemade pumpkin pie, but so far, things are not working out the way I envisioned.

"I'm a lot better with jack-o-lanterns than pies," I say to my red tick hound, Sweetie Pie Delaney, who wisely sleeps under the kitchen table, an area still free of pumpkin guts. She lifts her bloodshot eyes to send a sympathetic stare, and then dozes off. She knows that if I make a mess of the pies, she'll have a treat. Sweetie is not a finicky hound, but it happens that pumpkin pie is one of her favorites. And she doesn't care if it's baked into a flakey homemade crust or tumbled out of a bowl.

A shutter bangs against the side of the house, reminding me to call a repairman to make a few necessary improvements before Old Man Winter comes to Zinnia, Mississippi, for an extended visit. Outside Dahlia House, my family plantation in the heart of Sunflower County, the wind is sweeping across the barren cotton fields. The harvest is in, and winter is coming. But in the warm, cinnamon-smelling kitchen, I am looking forward to a festive Thanksgiving dinner with my best friends in the world. I am playing host—a new role for me.

I turn to the recipe and study it harder. Always the overachiever, I have *two* large pumpkins. Part of one is baking in the oven, but I have another big one on my cutting board. I have been assured by Millie Roberts, owner of Zinnia's most popular café, that pumpkin puree from scratch is far superior to canned. I'm beginning to have second thoughts. What sounded so easy coming from Millie's mouth has turned into an orange orgy in my kitchen.

Putting the knife down, I decide on a break. Cinnamon and maple flavored coffee in hand, I step out on the front porch. Sweetie and my black cat, Pluto, are at my side. White wicker rockers offer a comfortable seat, but I settle on the steps. Here I can look straight down the driveway. The sycamore trees that line the shell drive are leafless. The white skin-like bark, peeling in places, always makes me sad. November, like the gloaming, can be a melancholy time. Endings. I'm not good with endings.

Soon, though, the barren fields that stretch to the horizon will sprout new growth. Spring will return. Another cycle. This year, I have determined to make the holidays joyful.

I've invited all of my Zinnia friends to have Thanksgiving dinner at Dahlia House. Normally I enjoy the holidays at Tinkie's or Harold's—the two designated party givers in the Delta. This year, I want my home to be the party location. November marks the anniversary of my return to Sunflower County. When I'd come home two years ago, tail between my legs, I was destitute. Dahlia House was on the tax assessor's list to be auctioned off for back taxes. Since my return, I'd opened a successful private eye business, Delaney Detective Agency, hooked up with the best partner on the planet, Tinkie Bellcase Richmond, and acquired three horses, a dog, a feline ruler of the universe, and one very bad ass haint named Jitty. All in all, a very busy time.

The first months I'd been home, Dahlia House had felt cold and empty. My parents had died in a car accident when I was only twelve. My aunt Loulane, my father's sister, had raised me until I went to college. Not so long ago, she passed away, too. While I was adjusting to the failure of my acting career in New York, my first breakup with Graf Milieu, and the return home in bitter Broadway theatrical defeat, I'd also found Jitty, my resident ghost.

Jitty is part comforting parent, a big dollop of Hell Hound, and an equal measure of butt-kicker and provoker. She links me to the long history of Dahlia House, the Delaney family, and a system of morals and values instilled in me at an early age. From my father, I learned about justice and fair play. From my mother, I was gifted with a firm resolve to never be a victim, never accept defeat, and never, ever betray a friend.

When my parents were alive, Dahlia House was a holiday destination. My mother loved parties and she loved to dance. She had luncheons, coffees, drink gatherings, formal dinners, game get-togethers—whatever sounded fun.

My favorite memories, though, centered around Thanksgiving and the preparation of the traditional foods that define the holiday. My mother was an exceptional cook, though never a slave to the kitchen. Roasted turkey, dressing, fresh green beans, Brussels sprouts and chestnuts, ambrosia, and pumpkin pies were always on the menu. Even as a little girl, I was allowed to help with the food preparation. I can still remember my mother watching closely as I chopped celery for the dressing.

"Chop it fine, Sarah Booth. No big chunks." And she would lean over me, her hair tickling my face and filled with the scent of Opium, so light and yet enticing. No matter how I try, I'll never be able to duplicate those holidays when I was wrapped so tightly in the protection and love of my parents. This Thanksgiving I want to bring Dahlia House to life the way my mother did.

Only one small problem. My mother was a born chef and party giver. I, on the other hand, am a much better guest at someone else's table. Thinking of tables and guests, I slipped back inside the house. I had to get back in the kitchen and accomplish something other than mayhem. When I returned to the scene of my defeat, I inhaled deeply. At least my kitchen smelled like Thanksgiving.

"Good lard almighty!" A whiff of gardenias came with the outraged voice. Jitty had arrived. I closed my eyes and bit my lip. Though I wouldn't trade her for anything, she is a bane. If she says one word about dying ovaries, I am going to chase her around the kitchen with my knife. Of course she's dead already so it's an empty threat, but it would still give me great satisfaction.

"What have you done to the kitchen?" Jitty asked. She sashayed into the room in the most outrageous outfit I've yet to see her wear—a black and white nun's habit.

"I'm making dessert, and while the kitchen may be a mess, it isn't nearly as bad as that get-up you're wearing. You are officially cut off from any more Whoopi Goldberg movies." My threats were empty and we both knew it. "Get out of the house right this minute. If you draw a lightning strike down on you by pretending to be a nun, I don't want any part of it." I edged away from her. "What order do you belong to, the Holy Tormenters, or maybe Our Lady of the Aggravators? No religious leader in her right mind would let you into a convent."

"I'm not just any nun, I'm Mother Superior, and you'd best be listenin' to my advice, Missy." She pointed at the chunks of pumpkin and the blob of guts and seeds. "That's supposed to turn out to be a pie?"

"Pumpkin pies." I was a bit hesitant to admit that a pie was my goal. What I had was a pan full of rubbery and disgusting baked pumpkin chunks. The slimy guts spilled off the table and half out the garbage can. Add to that the flour dusting the floor and the eggs I meant to whip but accidentally dropped, and I had to admit, I'd made a remarkable mess.

"You did all of this to make a pumpkin pie?" She honestly couldn't take it all in. "Let me know if you ever decide to make cream puffs and I'll take out extra insurance on Dahlia House."

"That's so funny I forgot to laugh." I should be used to Jitty's acerbic commentary, but she can still get me riled, which is great fun for her.

"Have you ever heard of canned pumpkin?" Jitty was appalled. "Seriously, Sarah Booth, this looks like the jolly orange pumpkin exploded in here. How about 911, call Millie's Café and beg her to come to the rescue."

"What's with the nun get-up?" I've learned to keep the focus on Jitty and off me.

"I'm doing my part to get that difficult Delaney womb filled up with an heir to Dahlia House."

"And you intend to accomplish that by dressing as a nun?" Not even I could follow that logic.

"I'm the ultimate mother," she said. "Now listen up. I'm about to lay some wisdom on you."

I had to think fast to avoid another lecture on how my biological clock was ticking and how my ovaries were turning black and shriveling with each passing second, not to mention the Delaney penchant for tilted wombs and bad judgment in the romance department. To Jitty, an heir was the only thing that mattered. Since I'd recently broken off my engagement, she was doubling down on dire fallopian predictions. "It would be a lot more helpful if you would roll out the pie crust. So far, I haven't had a lot of luck with that."

She took a look in the bowl where I'd mixed flour, butter, a little salt, and some cold water—just as the recipe called for. Instead of workable dough that could be rolled thin and placed in the bottom of a pie pan, I'd achieved a glutinous mass of . . . paste. And it kept making noises, as if it were alive, possibly suffering from a bad case of gas.

"Baby girl, that lump of glue is beyond my help. Divine intervention can't save that mess. Fact is, I'd burn it before it turns into a golem. I think it may have a heartbeat." She backed away from it.

"Oh, for heaven's sake!" I picked up the bowl of lumpy,

wet dough and realized, for once, Jitty was not exaggerating. A little bubble of air escaped the goop, followed by a burp. That was enough for me. I used the big wooden spoon and scraped it into the trash. If it came to life, it could do so at the end of the driveway, not in the kitchen.

"Maybe I should call a priest to give it the last rites." Jitty was so pleased with her wit she could hardly contain her glee.

"Do that. It'll be worth watching, since you can't use a phone." My illusions of being the master chef were taking a serious drubbing. Thank God for Millie. She could bake a pie with a snap of her fingers. I could call her if I got desperate.

"Is this is a bad time to discuss what I've come to talk about?" Jitty asked.

"Depends on what you want to discuss." The fact that she *asked* didn't bode well. "If it's about sperm or ovaries, this is definitely not a good time."

"Which man you gone put at the head of that holiday table, Sarah Booth? Being the hostess, seems to me like you've got yourself in a pickle. You'll be at the foot of the table by the kitchen door, but who's gonna sit at the head, which implies a whole lot. The man you put there is the one leading the pack for your affections."

She had a point, and I had a solution. "Harold will sit at the head of the table." I hadn't given it a lot of thought, but this was the perfect seating arrangement. Harold Erkwell had once asked for my hand—and put a four carat diamond on my ring finger. At the time, I didn't know him well, and his tactics seemed a bit ham-fisted. Since I'd been home, though, Harold and I had developed an abiding friendship. And he was, hands down, the best party giver in six states. "Harold is always the host. Coleman and Scott can each sit on a side." I was very pleased with my resolution.

"You can't keep all those men dangling like meat in a processing plant. They keep hanging', there's gonna be an awful stink."

"Jitty! That is a truly awful visual. I may have to scour my brain with Comet to clean it out."

Her soft, low chuckle told me how pleased she was. When I looked at her again, she'd removed the wimple and was shaking out her dark Afro. "That head gear gets hot."

"Not as hot as the pit of hell, which is where you're destined for impersonating a nun."

She only laughed. "Thanksgiving is hot on our heels. You should throw out all that mess you made and order everything from Millie's."

She had a point, but I wasn't defeated yet. "I'll give it one more try. Most girls learn to cook from their mothers, but I never really had that chance."

Jitty instantly softened. "Aunt Loulane tried, Sarah Booth, but you didn't want to learn from her. You missed your mother, and Loulane was wise enough to know she could never fill those shoes."

"Yes, she was very wise, and to this day I remember most of her adages. As she used to say, 'Time heals all wounds and brings wisdom to those who seek.'" Aunt Loulane had a saying for every occasion. While I'd hated hearing them when I was a teenager, now I used them with relish.

"Why don't you give me a hand with the cooking?" I asked Jitty. "Surely during the time when you were alive with great-great-great-grandma Alice you were a good cook."

"I'm drawin' a blank—"

"Jitty, give me some tips on pie crust."

"Can't do it, Sarah Booth. It's time for vespers." And with that she was gone. And I'd learned something new about the ghost who shared my home. She didn't like to cook. She was, for all of her one hundred and fifty years, a thoroughly modern ghost.

My failure with the pie undeniable, I sacked up the sad remains and took them out to the road for trash collection early the next morning. I stamped down the driveway, my breath fogging in the crisp air. Above me, the stars kept the black night company. The acres of land belonging to Dahlia House spread on either side of the long drive, and I stopped when a startled herd of deer broke in front of me and leaped the pasture fence. In a moment they were absorbed by the darkness.

When I'd left the trash, I jogged back toward the house and my warm bed. Before I made a second assault on pie production, I needed a trip to the Pig, as we called the local Piggly Wiggly grocery, to buy more flour and butter and two cans of pumpkin already processed to perfect pie consistency. And perhaps I would call Millie in the morning and see if she could give me some tips.

I washed the dishes, prepared the coffeemaker to turn itself on at six a.m., and went to bed. I had plenty of time to master the art of pie baking. Even if I didn't, my friends would step up. I had many blessings to count, and as I walked through the dining room, I started on my list.

I caught a glimpse of a terrifying specter in the mirror above the sideboard and let out a squawk of fright before I realized it was only me. The new growth of my hair, which gave me the appearance of Woodstock, the bird in the Snoopy cartoons, was standing straight on end and coated in flour. Even though Tinkie had taken me to "her girl" at the most expensive salon in the Delta, my hair was still a terrible mess. I'd caught it on fire in the last case we'd worked, and I was very lucky that it was only hair that burned. It could have been so much worse.

Still chuckling at my fright, I went to my room and promptly keeled over in bed. I'd entered a dreamless state of deep slumber when I heard the doorbell ring. I looked at my phone on the bedside table—three o'clock in the morning. It had to be a dream. Though I heard the chime again, and even Sweetie set up a bark, my attempts at baking had exhausted me. I rolled over, pulled the pillow over my head, and refused to get up.

The creak of a squeaky wheel finally drove me to wake-fulness. When I found out who was interrupting my sleep, I was going to have a hissy fit all over them.

Creak, creak, creak! I opened one eye to catch a glimpse of a woman in a black mini-dress pushing one of the huge old baby prams with the folding leather top.

The only thing I could think was *Rosemary's Baby* and I leaped from the bed to land on the far side of the room. "Get out!" I hissed. I'd watched the movie with my mother and a group of my friends when I was in sixth grade, and the image of that black perambulator sent a primal chill through me. "Get out!"

"It's just a baby." The woman pushed the carriage slowly toward me. "Just an innocent baby."

A shaft of moonlight came through the window and I saw Mia Farrow's shorn head—that looked too much like my own. "You have to get out of here." I gauged the distance to the doorway and wondered if I could leap over the bed and make it to the door before she got me—I had no doubt her intention was to do terrible things to me.

"Remember, Sarah Booth, it's only a baby."

At last the Mia image faded to reveal Jitty. I didn't always like her antics, but she'd never before awakened me in the dead of night while impersonating an actress who played the role of a woman who gave birth to the Antichrist.

"You have taken this one step too far," I said through gritted teeth. "Not only did you wake me out of a dead sleep, you scared me into next year. I've missed Thanksgiving and Christmas and all I have to show for it is my stubbed and bleeding toe." I had smashed my toe on the bed frame, which didn't help my mood.

"Answer the damn doorbell, Sarah Booth. I wouldn't have to resort to extraordinary measures if you didn't sleep like you'd fallen into a forever coma."

"What doorbell?"

"The one that rang about two minutes ago. And rang again. And—"

Before she could finish, the bell rang nine times in rapid succession. "What the hell?" I found a pair of jeans, pulled them on, then trotted barefoot down the stairs to the front door. Before I opened it, I turned on the light and stared into the empty night. There was no one on the porch.

"Screw that," I said, flipping off the light.

"At least open the door," Jitty said. She was suddenly right behind me.

"There's no one—"

"Sarah Booth, please open the door. Right this red-hot minute."

Jitty seldom said please so I opened the door fast. I

was in the process of slamming it closed again when what I'd seen registered on me. A white wicker bassinet had been pushed close against the front door. A pale pink blanket covered the basket, hiding whatever was hidden inside. More ominous was the pool of blood that seeped from the basket and slowly crossed the bitter cold boards of the porch.

Before I could do anything, a vehicle's engine fired and a dark-colored Ford pickup, older model, sped away from Dahlia House at breakneck speed.

"Call 911!" I commanded Jitty as I pushed back the blanket to reveal the still face of an infant. The newborn had been wiped clean, but the blood of birth still smudged its features. I couldn't tell if the child was bleeding, or even if it was breathing. My bare feet seemed to have frozen to the gray porch boards, but I managed to pick up the bassinet and haul it inside. I ran to the kitchen, where the oven I'd heated earlier still warmed the room. Hands shaking, I lifted the blankets and examined the infant, who began to squirm and cry.

"She's okay," I said aloud, as if to reassure myself. "Jitty, she's okay."